I0783219

Brooklyn

Galaxy Traveling Talking Dog

Paul D Escudero

WORKBOOK PRESS LLC
187 E Warm Springs Rd,
Suite B285, Las Vegas, NV 89119, USA

Website: https://workbookpress.com/
Hotline: 1-888-818-4856
Email: admin@workbookpress.com

Ordering Information:
Quantity sales. Special discounts are available on quantity purchases by corporations, associations, and others. For details, contact the publisher at the address above.

Library of Congress Control Number:

ISBN-13:   000-0-00000-000-0 (Paperback Version)

              000-0-00000-000-0 (Digital Version)

REV. DATE: 09/08/2023

Brooklyn Galaxy Traveling Talking Dog

By

Paul D. Escudero
保罗·道格拉斯·埃斯库德罗

Preface

Everyone goes through changes. It's inevitable. When you look into the mirror thirty years from now if you are lucky to still be alive, that person will look different.

We cannot predict how people will change. We get married to a person we think we are in love with. Then later down the road, new discoveries change our agenda, or our spouse, and it may not always work out.

If you have a few good years feel blessed.

The first few years the relationship between Abagail and Chester Toland fit within that mold that seems to be such a repeatable scenario to many couples, it was not unexpected.

In the midst of change, what do we often observe? It seems most people bring a dog into their lives to fill the void a dying relationship manifested. Quite often it starts out with something so innocent and precious, a puppy. Brooklyn arrived as a puppy under such circumstances.

I know many of you who read this book are dog owners or have at one time in the past, had a pet dog or cat. Both animals are relatively smart, and they have emotions. When you're petting your cat and you feel it's purring you are feeling emotion.

How smart are dogs, really?

Nobody really knows for sure, because all dogs are different and have different types of owners who may or may not work on their mental growth. Do your dog's watch TV?

I believe dogs are a lot smarter than we give them credit for, simply because they can't talk or effectively communicate with us.

After you read this Novel, I promise you will look at your dog differently. You will wonder, "Is my dog like Brooklyn?"

Is the notion of putting a chip into a dog's brain to give it speech ability farfetched? Well now, google: "the future of talking dogs." Be ready for a big shocker, it's here already.

If you can give your dog the ability to talk, are you ready for the consequences? How safe is your marriage?

Brooklyn, who began his life on Earth, eventually travels to far off worlds and because of his ability to talk creates scenarios that will give you a glimpse into the future.

The talking dog is now starting, when you go to the next page you will discover the magic of a talking dog and how he changes the timeline for individuals in ways you would never expect. ***

TABLE OF CONTENTS

Chapter One

LIFE CHANGES

It started during the long work at home scenarios for Chester. Abagail in the other hand continued in her life unchanged. Chester suddenly became the house sitter while Abagail, the jetsetter in her prominent business career became more and more successful and the demand for her to take trips increased along with her success and income.

Abagail was a highflyer, and the board of directors loved her as it seemed she was able to cut deals her male counterparts tended to lack achieving. There was some kind of spark in Abagail and hence she booked new business from sources that seemed impenetrable or unlikely.

It was in the background of all this success Abagail's road-warrior days steadily increased and soon it was Chester home alone again and again.

One day Chester was at the shopping mall to pick up a few items and happened to walk past a pet store. Chester had never had a pet since he was a little kid. Abagail expressed she wanted nothing to do with pets and even though she never said no to children, she secretly prevented them. She informed Chester she would start having babies as soon as she felt up to it. Eventually Chester realized those days were never coming.

Chester was waiting for 3:00 P.M. He never drank before 3:00 P.M. as he didn't want it to interfere with his work from home. Chester did such a great job his high-tech employer determined his work at home ethics were so good and successful, they could reduce their real estate footprint and office space because the pandemic proved to them out of necessity, there might be a better way to go about their business model.

The visit to the shopping mall was around noon, when it was expected employees would be off eating lunch or taking care of noncompany activities. As Chester observed the pet shop window, he saw there were several puppies on sale. Half of them looked unhappy as being stuck in a display window all day long simply did not improve their disposition. All those puppies wanted something the rest of the puppies want, to be cherished and nurtured by someone.

Chester had been having a bout of melancholy, and his relationship with Abagail had deteriorated to the point he felt like he was nothing more than a house boy for her. Abagail who used to be the horniest woman on the planet was now subdued and rarely in the mood for some boom-boom. It seemed like love had been let out of their romance tires and Chester had a flat he needed to change.

Chester walked up to the display window and there was one puppy that walked up to the window staring at him. Chester almost felt transfixed by the puppy stare and wondered why that puppy had such an intense interest in him. The puppy didn't budge. It didn't bark or carry on like all the other puppies. It truly was a singularity. It was a good-looking puppy, and the stare continued rather intensely.

The pet store owner walked up to Chester and asked, "Sir is there something you might be interested in?"

"I'm looking at the puppies."

Chester had a funny feeling with that puppy staring at him. The shop owner then said, "I've never seen that puppy stare at anyone before. This is the most unusual sight I've ever seen before."

"How much does that puppy cost?"

"All those puppies are $250.00."

"I'll take this one."

"All right I'll get it ready for you."

"Do you have one of those animal carriers?"

"We certainly do and recommend you put it in one until you get it house broken if you are not actively engaged with the pet."

Abagail would not be coming home for a week. Chester would get to know the puppy before she returned and figure out how he would deal with her negativity when it was likely to begin.

After paying for the puppy, pet carrier, and good size bag of puppy chow, leash and small dog collar, and a few other necessary items, Chester was on his way home with his new best friend.

When they reached home, Chester unloaded the car in the garage and staged everything in his home. Knowing what everyone in the neighborhood did, walk their dogs, Chester took the puppy out of the transporter, snapped on the leash to its dog collar then took it out into the back yard and walked it around hoping it would take care of its business and get a feel for the place, then go back inside where he might soon need to take some business calls and check out required emails.

The puppy seemed unusual. It acted like it knew this place well. It showed happiness and was grateful to be out of that display window and sniffed around the yard as Chester let it walk around and sniff and investigate things. Mindful that at any moment a business call could come in or an email he needed to promptly respond to, in due time after the puppy found a tree to urinate on, Chester picked it up and took the puppy back into the house and into the transporter and sat down in front of his computer.

The puppy didn't make any noise, but it stared at Chester who could not help but notice as he casually looked down. After answering an email and low activity, Chester looked down and picked up the puppy and brought it back to his chair and desk and sat down in front of the computer waiting for a possible conference call that might happen while watching the news feed with the puppy on his lap intermittently petting it. The puppy soon curled up into almost a ball sleeping with the tender strokes of its new best friend. It was a pleasant moment for both until 3:00 P.M.

The lady at the pet store informed Chester, "The puppies had just been fed and will probably not be hungry for several hours. Also, do not feed the dog table scraps. Stick with the puppy chow for about six months then come back in and we'll give you our recommendations as what to switch it to."

Right at 3:00 P.M., Chester stood up and put the puppy back into the carrier, then got out the doggy dishes he bought filling one of them with a half a cup of bottled ward and the amount the pet store owner recommended for a typical meal at least three times a day. Once that was all set up, he got the puppy out of the carrier and took it to the feeding bowls. The puppy probably did not eat a lot in its last meal and acted as if it was hungry. Chester noticed the puppy seemed kind of skinny or under nourished. The puppy ate the puppy chow and drank some of the water.

While the puppy was slowly and casually eating its puppy chow, Chester mixed a dry martini and sat it over at his recliner facing the big screen TV. He then walked back over to where the puppy was eating and drinking water and soon it stopped eating about half the food provided and acted like it wasn't interested in eating any more.

Chester picked the puppy up and walked over to his recliner and sat down putting the puppy on his lap watching the news feed and sipping on his martini. One of the news stories was about Brooklyn, New York. The puppy needed a name, so Chester said to the dog, "Son your name is now Brooklyn."

After watching the news for a while, Chester got up and took Brooklyn over to his pet carrier, then went to the freezer and pulled out a frozen Lasagna dinner and slapped it in the microwave and set the cooking time per instructions on the box. The nice thing about Abagail being gone was that most of the time Chester could eat whatever the hell he wanted. Abagail didn't like 90% of what Chester wanted to eat. So, there was a silver lining in these frequent absences.

While the Lasagna was cooking, Chester decided to take Brooklyn out for another walk, in case he needed to go potty. Soon the two were heading out the back door with the leash attached to the dog collar. They did a lap or two around the yard, Brooklyn managed to take care of business that made Chester happy that he would not have a mess to clean up tonight.

After finishing the Lasagna and another drink, Chester thought the puppy probably had a lot of filth on it from being couped up in the pet shop and took Brooklyn up to the bathroom and proceeded to give him a bath. Chester figured there was dog shampoo he could buy, but for tonight, he would use some of that pleasant smelling shampoo his wife used. Brooklyn was well behaved in the bathtub and acted as if he had complete trust in Chester.

Soon enough Brooklyn was fully lathered up except around his head. Chester took a washcloth and wiped that area with diluted soapy water. He soon drained the tub and wrapped Brooklyn up in a towel and carried him down to his recliner and sat him there while he poured himself another drink and sat it down next to the recliner on a small table with a lamp on it. He then picked up Brooklyn still wrapped up in the towel and sat him on his lap allowing him to dry off more in the towel while he sipped on his drink and channel surfed. In 15 minutes, Brooklyn was out sound to sleep.

About an hour later, nature called, and Chester had to use the bathroom and stood up and gently placed Brooklyn down on the recliner and went to the bathroom and took care of his business.

When Chester returned, there was Brooklyn out of his towel and standing on all four's waiting for his master to return.

Chester picked up Brooklyn, sat down in the recliner and put the towel and the pup on his lap. Brooklyn was just about dry. They watched a little more TV, then Chester knowing what his relatives did with their dogs, picked Brooklyn up and carried him over to the dog carrier and grabbed the leash and clicked it onto the dog collar and took him out to the back yard after turning on the exterior lights.

Chester walked over to the tree where Brooklyn previously made his mark and the dog instinctively carried out his business. It was starting to get a little nippy, so Chester didn't plan on staying outside too long.

Soon they were back in the house and Chester had Brooklyn on his lap while he surfed the internet and looked for emails from his wife. Times had changed. Unlike their earlier years there were no emails tonight from Abigail. That reaffirmed his decision to buy this puppy that would eventually turn into a larger dog.

Now it was nothing more to do than wait for the ticking time bomb to go off when Abigail returned home and discovered her frequent absence had been emotionally repaired by the presence of Brooklyn.

That night, Chester put Brooklyn in the pet carrier and took him with him up to the bedroom and placed the carrier on a chair near the bed, then changed into his sleeping attire and hopped in the bed.

Chester went to sleep feeling restful and halfway through the middle of the night, the dog was whimpering. Chester thought maybe the pup wanted to go outside and take care of nature. So, he took the pup with the dog collar outdoors and the pup stood by his side. Brooklyn didn't look for a tree or budge. After a while Chester was getting cold and picked Brooklyn up and carried him back to the house and put him in the pet carrier and shut the lights off and went back to bed. Within five minutes the pup was whimpering again. Chester figured it out. He moved a chair right next to the bed and put the animal carrier on the chair, so Brooklyn was now only inches away.

The week seemed to pass quite quickly. A couple times Chester took Brooklyn down to Ski Beach Park and walked around. The bird friends feared the puppy but after a couple exposures, the hungry birds approached the two and were awarded treats. For some reason Brooklyn didn't bark at the birds or make any movements towards them. The birds knew Chester quite well and in a matter of time the birds got used to Brooklyn.

A few squirrels often showed up to get their fair share of the bird treats. These squirrels became so tamed over the years that Chester could feed them out of his hand. Just like the birds, the squirrels have facial recognition and approached few other humans at the park, just like the birds.

It took the squirrels twice as long to get used to the puppy, but eventually they discovered the dog was harmless and no threat. The pigeons would come right up to Chester and Brooklyn in the morning especially if they were hungry because Chester had been away, or it had rained, or some other reason kept them away. Every now and then, the rats would come out of the boulders that rimmed the bay and prevented erosion. They too eventually developed no fear of Brooklyn.

The geese and Mallard ducks that often came to the park also had their experiences with Brooklyn.

Brooklyn watched his owner very closely and was eager to please him and follow his instructions. By using his name often. Brooklyn knew his name and seemed to understand statements that Chester said. In due time the ducks and the geese accepted Brooklyn when he was a young pup and watched him steadily grow up. Eventually when Brooklyn was full size the birds had no fear of Brooklyn in particular, but they would fly away if other dogs appeared.

In due time the dynamic dual had a system all worked out getting up at 6:00 A.M., getting the pre-staged bird tweets ready along with the dog's food and water dishes, and a Ziplock bag with puppy chow so that Brooklyn would be eating side by side the pigeons and squirrels.

Brooklyn was always the last one done eating as the birds were generally starving and ate as quickly as possible. Sometimes as many as 100 pigeons arrived, but Chester always had plenty of snacks to give them.

After Brooklyn finished eating, Chester secured his bowls in the car dumping any residual water. The two then set off walking around the park. Since Brooklyn was still kind of small, parts of the trip he was carried the other parts he was put down on the sidewalk and walked. When another person approached with a dog on a leash, Chester took no chances and carried Brooklyn a good distance to have plenty of separation from the other dogs.

During the treks around the park, the dynamic dual would sometimes come up to a couple with two large white dogs and sometimes with their grandkid. The two white dogs were very kind and sweet and took a liking to Brooklyn. The wife of the couple loved Brooklyn and wanted to hold the pup a few times. The two large white dogs who knew Chester quite well were also interested in the pup and had to smell it. If truth be told, those large dogs would love to take Brooklyn home and adopt him. From the first day those large dogs met Brooklyn and every day in the future, they were very gentle and nice to Brooklyn.

Time passed too quickly, and the day of reckoning was around the corner. Abagail most likely would not tolerate the pet carrier in the bedroom. Plus, it would not shock Chester to hear Abagail who was somewhat a cold-hearted woman come right out and say, "get rid of the dog."

It was a shock that day when it happened because Chester's female friends all loved dogs and none of them would ever act like Abagail. In fact, it scored some brownie points with a few of them who ultimately became a fantastic source of information that all dog owners should be aware of.

Abagail had traveled to three cities and made high pressure sales pitches to executives in those cities and influenced their purchasing decisions by laying out charm and influencing their little heads. Abagail was a head turner with movie star quality legs and a rack on her that even impressed women since the geometry was perfect. With a cute face, great smile with perfect ultra-white teeth that almost glowed, she could make most mere mortals almost tremble with idiosyncratic transcendence.

How they married in the first place was not such a big mystery. They were younger then, right out of school and starting their pathway through life. They knew each other in college and had a nice friendship with no expectations. As time passed and their occupations brought their orbits closer together, their socializing increased, and it wasn't Chester's sexual prowess that sealed the deal. It was the lioness Abagail.

Abagail looked at most men with the lens of currency and gainful employment. A few of her lady friends were stuck with losers that had great prospects, but never delivered and it was a growing foregone conclusion they would remain losers and barely keep up. As such some of those marriages did not last because her friends had expectations. In a sense they were high maintenance and spoiled by their parents.

It did not take long for Abagail to evaluate Chester through her financial lenses he was going to be successful and bring home the bacon. Abagail was not necessarily a gold digger; she just didn't want an anchor around her neck like some of her friends who were on the fast bus to nowhere.

Chester's income and bonus' were solid and when they had to start remote work with a large percentage of their workforce due to the pandemic, Chester was one of the star performers and outclassed the few who came into the offices to work in the improved social distancing thanks to thinning out the herd.

There is no way Abagail would tolerate a man who could not please her. Besides the green tinted lenses, she saw the world through, she wanted a man who could do the horizontal tango on a *Theme from Paganini* and knew that a woman's gratification had to be produced or there was no point in performing such acts.

The first time they engaged in a physical embrace it was Abagail cleverly instituting it so she could evaluate Chester. She didn't want a rookie's performance, nor did she desire to be a rookie's coach. She wanted a man poised to perform. Also, it was important how the man was equipped. The man had to have the right tool for the job, or she would not be interested because an *ill-equipped man is no more desirable than a dog humping your leg.*

It was one of those cold wintery nights the two were watching a movie and having pizza with a nice bottle of Cabernet Sauvignon when Abagail swung into action and led Chester to bite the apple in the Garden of Eden. As they got up to the point where intercourse was likely, Chester sadly said, "I'm sorry, I didn't bring any protection. I don't think we can do it tonight."

"That's not a problem, I'm on the pill to regulate my periods and it's unlike I would get pregnant. I have some morning after medications in case I get raped. We can go ahead and do it, don't worry."

"I'm still a little worried I could cause you problems."

"Don't worry Chester, I'm a big girl, well educated, and I know how to protect my reproductive ability. I don't sleep around, and I only picked you because we are great friends and I've grown emotionally attached to you."

"Well, I'm attached to you as well."

Chester was then utterly shocked moments later when Abagail unzipped his trousers and started performing fallatio on him. Once she got him to the point, she knew was a point of no return, she stood up, dropped her panties on the floor and climbed on top of Chester and took his manliness and inserted it inside her. The size was absolutely perfect. It wasn't a shrimp, but it also wasn't a buffalo cock, exactly the way Abagail liked it. Chester was jacked up to the point he was almost ready to explode inside Abagail but her undulating motions which helped her to do clitoris excitement rubbing it against his tool as she performed her magic. Within two minutes Abagail started feeling the orgasmic gratification that was quite intense.

New love always intensifies this sensation, and she would always remember Chester for this moment as she registered his cologne in her memories of him. Abagail had read up on how to please men and studied Egyptian, Israeli, and Korean secrets in this regard. She practiced on wrapped up cucumbers or very large carrots to strengthen her vaginal walls and control the muscles she developed like these other cultures perfected and thus gave it all to Chester who quickly responded with his own psychophysical reaction that resulted in gushing into Abagail.

Sadly, that was the peak of their relationship and it had been on a slow decline ever sense as Abagail's fame and fortune spread as a company rep cutting large deals.

The days of men meeting in bars, smoking cigars together cutting the deals were over. Marketing officials knew when it came to negotiating a deal with the competition as tough as it was, their *modus operandi* shifted, and new techniques were tried and perfected.

It was no longer the good ole boy network of the past. The competition was full of good ole boys, so to engage them with a good ole boy only created stalemates. In the 1980's as Harvard Business School worked hard to level the playing field for women in their curriculum and corporate guidance, they created an entire science of showcasing female sales forces. As a regular executive of a company where the competition for promotions was fierce and quite often unethical, sales is where women could be deployed with the caveat their success was solely based on their efforts and innovation and not subject to the male glass ceiling phenomena.

By the time Abagail entered the workforce in sales, that science was well developed and a chapter out of *Manila Hostitutes* was inserted into her personal curriculum along with guidance by books such as *"You can Negotiate Anything,"* and *"How to Swim with the Sharks Without Being Eaten Alive."*

Abagail had a very high I.Q. and didn't need many of these sources of training because she was inherently fantastic in sales and knew how to affect the little heads of executives that had final authority over procurement.

Abagail just returned from a week of very successful marketing. She booked a couple sales and set up a third one that would eventually be a pushover. Her techniques were highly unethical, she seduced men and would make the author of *Manila Hostitutes* blush.

Abagail wasn't in the mood for romance or sex and upon arrival home was utterly disgusted, there was a dog in the house. Instead of the normal, *"I got a headache,"* routine she played on Chester, the intense *get rid of that dog* routine set the mood for the night.

Chester knew it would not be wise to take Brooklyn up to the bedroom tonight.

After Abagail took a shower and a nice drink heavily laced with Vodka, she took a couple sleeping pills and said, "I had a rough week. I'm going to bed. Try not to wake me up, and if you can't prevent yourself from snoring, sleep on the couch."

Abagail then marched out of the family room and went up to the bedroom, shut the door and turned out the light. All she wanted to do was pass out and get a good night's sleep. She was joyous of her success which no doubt exceeded any good ole boy road-warrior, but she had one nut to crack that would be a huge contract and bonus to her she would have to deal with.

Abagail would also have to deal with a critique of her manager and lay her cards on the table and explain why she thought she was able to get the contracts. The company used feedback from such critiques to fine tune their sales force. Abagail being about twice as smart as her supervisor knew better than to inform him how she manipulates customers little heads. She would do the same thing she always *did, tell the dumb bastard she worked it exactly the way their training manual told them to do it. What a joke!*

The training department loved Abagail as they often quoted her statistics to claim fame to why their processes worked and if all salespeople did what she did they too would have glowing success.

In a few cases when they sent Abagail out to regional offices to work with their training people, some of the sales force believed her line of BS and it's all about mental attitude. They assumed it worked for her so they knew it would work for them and a few of them got lucky without resorting to Abagail's *sekretnyye operatsii* [секретные операции].

Tonight, was going to be a great night for Brooklyn. He wasn't going to have to sleep in the pet carrier. After a few drinks, Chester gave Brooklyn one more walk in the back yard so he could tag his tree, then came back in the house, put a towel down on the sofa in case Brooklyn did something unexpected in the middle of the night.

Chester then took Brooklyn and laid down on the sofa with Brooklyn and turned off the big screen TV that was lighting up the room. Soon Chester and Brooklyn were sound asleep, and Brooklyn loved this way much better than the pet carrier as he felt good lying next to his best and only friend.

Brooklyn was curious as to Abagail and had some intuition that Abagail was angry and didn't like him. As time went by, Brooklyn could not recall a single time Abagail petted him. And the few times Chester had to leave him home with Abagail she put him in the pet carrier and set it outside the home with the thoughts of demanding Chester *get rid of the mut.*

The next morning, just like clockwork, man and his best friend woke up and prepared for their trip to the park as usual. Chester knew Abagail was in a sour mood over the dog, so he didn't wait for her to awaken, which she usually did around 8:00 A.M. and was gone to her office by 9:00 A.M.

Chester had everything he needed in a bag and put Brooklyn in the pet carrier and headed out the door. They were soon on the road to Ski Beach Park and went to an area where they always first met the pigeons in the morning. This was a period when the pigeons and the squirrels were still getting used to Brooklyn and when the blackbirds who always came and watched at a safe distance, they too studied Brooklyn and were probably amazed the puppy no longer scared the pigeons and the squirrels even sometime at out of the same dish with Brooklyn just like they were the best buddies in the world.

Having seen some of the YouTube squirrel videos, Chester knew he could make a pet out of one of them but also knew Abagail would be even more furious if he dared bring home a squirrel. Squirrels are just as good of pets as dogs, and those who have Squirrel pets adore them.

With no less than four blackbirds closely observing the morning animal breakfast, Brooklyn finished up. By then Chester had the other birds treats ready to go in his jacket pockets. It was wintertime in Southern California, so the mornings were cool and required a jacket which was handy to carry bags of treats and a stack of Ritz crackers in the event he spotted his Coot friends.

Coots are black sea birds with a white spot in the middle of their forehead, red eyes, and green alligator feet. They are strange looking birds. But they are also very sweet birds and afraid of humans. They would not get near any other human. One old timer who went to that park fifty-five years in a row informed Chester, he never saw the Coots ever get near a person.

Just like the pigeons the Coots would come right up to Chester, and some would poke at his pant legs to get his attention and treats. Seemingly disciplined at an early age and thanks to being around the pigeons and the squirrels, Brooklyn sat beside Chester's leg and simply observed the coots.

When Chester gave his special bird whistle, he developed for all the birds in the park the Coots came running. They were a little shy with Brooklyn who was still a small pup sitting next to Chester, but they were definitely hungry and loved Ritz crackers.

Thankfully the seagulls were not around and so Chester was able to throw crackers, he broke up three or four feet away and the brave coots went to them and started eating. Coots have a herd mentality; they follow the leader and as soon as the brave ones started eating the rest followed. Within a few minutes there were seventy-five Coots there wanting to get their fair share of broken crackers. Chester systematically threw the crackers closer and the Coots came closer to a foot away from Brooklyn.

Coots are very smart birds, and they were sizing up Brooklyn and by the time they finished all the crackers, they simply started grazing on the grass in that area as Chester eased out and continued his trek around the park meeting up with migratory sea birds that were very beautiful and colorful and not the ugly seagulls you normally see.

Seagulls are very emotional and very smart and territorial. Sometimes when male seagulls start fighting, they will grab on to each other's beak and the one who gets lucky and gets the other seagull's beak in his grip can do a lot of damage. They fight very ferociously until the Alpha gull wins the fight and chases the other away. Sometimes Chester would give the Alpha seagull some treats knowing he would keep the rest away, especially while feeding the pigeons.

The big threat to the pigeons is the redtail hawks that come to the park. The blackbirds and the redtail hawks are enemies. Blackbirds are smart and they will gang up on a redtail hawk. The main reason why Chester fed the blackbirds was to make sure enough of them were around to go after a redtail hawk if they showed up.

There were also Ospreys that showed up at the park. These huge birds of prey were too big for the blackbirds who did not engage them like they did the smaller redtail hawks.

Today was another day Chester met up with the couple that had two large dogs. They were eager to see the pup again. The husband would hold the two dogs most of the time when they were with the grandchild but today, they were by themselves, so the wife had one dog and the husband the other. In a short period of time the dogs were sniffing Brooklyn and enjoying Chester petting them. Also, this led to Chester getting into a conversation about Aliens and some recent news. Time flies when you have those kinds of conversations and over a half hour passed before the couple was ready to finish their walk and drive home.

Chester's favorite grocery store was on the way. He knew six or seven people that worked there. They were wonderful people, and they always found a moment when things were not busy to have a short conversation. It was great because the store was on the way home and Chester did not have to divert or drive out of the way. Hence, he saved a lot of gas money and time.

Today would be one of those days Chester would not start work until 9:00 A.M. He had no expected meetings and his cell phone with him in case his company or a customer needed to reach him. Chester didn't know if he would see Abagail before she left for work and watching the car's dashboard clock was hoping she was gone by the time he reached home.

Today, it all worked out nicely. Abagail was so furious that Chester was gone with the mut she couldn't lay into him, it influenced Abagail to get ready quicker and was out of the house and on the road to the office by 8:45 A.M. By the time Chester got home, including make a stop at the grocery store for dinner, Abagail's BMW was out of the garage and gone and Chester was glad.

This was one more day in the drama of the unhappy household. Brooklyn seemed to have overnight damaged his marriage, but the way things were shaping up he was starting to feel this was nothing more than a bedroom community. Chester was soul searching and wondering what he and Abagail had previously bonded over.

The marriage seemed synthetic and flimsy at best. The good news since no children were yet involved, if they had to separate, there would be no collateral damages and since Abagail was one of those few women that had enormous salaries with all her fabulous bonus' there would be no spousal support or alimony, just a handshake and goodbye. As the marriage decayed further with Abagail's infidelity and lack of appreciation for Chester, the decision was made, *the dog is staying and if necessary, they would leave together.*

As it turned out there was another few nights on the couch as Abagail was in a bitchy mood the entire period while she was home. That was just fine and dandy with Brooklyn as he got to sleep lying next to his "papa" which he really enjoyed.

Chester would talk to Brooklyn as if he were a person. He assumed Brooklyn had no idea what he was saying or what it meant. He was wrong. Brooklyn was a fast learner eager to be with his best friend and experience life together. The two watched a lot of TV together and Chester had no idea how much Brooklyn was being educated.

Even though Chester didn't get any nookie this time while Abagail was home, he was mildly relieved when she left in a couple days on another five-day swing to the other coast making calls on six companies.

A lot of good ole boys had issues getting invites into the companies to lay on the sales pitch, but Abagail metaphorically kicked the door down and walked on in. She had learned how to *not take no for an answer* and in the spirit of *You Can Negotiate Anything* knew as a last-ditch effort she could convince the person she needed to get to and meet her for lunch she would pay for out of her business expenses.

She knew some of these guys were married men and if their wives ever caught them cheating, they would probably *Bobatize* them in the middle of their sleep, so they were safe to lay on the charm. The single guys or a few of the cheaters were problematic because if she wasn't careful, she would end up on her back with a pig on top of her which she sure as hell did not want. However now and then some of these corporate boys were quite charming, well cologned, worked out and were well equipped and knew how to please a woman.

It was a game that backfired on Abagail because after such a rendezvous that was simply gratification for another Casanova, she likely left empty handed with the terrible stigma she was easy. Those Casanova's quickly learned you never get the kitten for free a second time and Abagail's fangs were likely to come out.

A Casanova's worse fear is when a woman like Abagail gets to meet his bride and brag how he has his notch on her belt. Women can be far more vicious than good ole boys imagine.

It was once again peaceful and quiet at Chester's home. This is the way Brooklyn eventually wished it was and regretted every single time Abagail returned home.

Time seemed to pass quickly between Abigail's trips. There were a couple times she came home all lovey and dovey and didn't bring up the dog. The truth of the matter she had sex with Casanova's and had to have sex with Chester in the event she accidently got pregnant, Chester would never know the difference.

Nevertheless, Brooklyn was becoming more analytical every day and studied Abigail every time he was in the same room with her. There was no affection between the two. For Brooklyn that didn't matter, he had Chester his best friend he knew cared for him.

Brooklyn steadily grew and the morning exercise with Chester helped him develop his physical ability especially when Chester attempted to get back up to his ten-mile daily walk after the injuries all healed.

Chester worked up slowly and wasn't going to risk injury again by not over doing it. Instead of peaking quickly he would rise in mileage slowly. Brooklyn was able to keep up as he added the miles and in what seemed like a short time, Brooklyn slowly doubled in size and if one could ever equate politeness and discipline nobody could claim any other dog superior in those manners.

Chester was always studying technology and interested in new designs of new innovations and often read a lot of technical documents nobody else seemed interested in. It was in such reading Chester became aware of a British researcher who had moved to Sorrento Valley by La Jolla California to do his research. This part of San Diego was quickly turning into a Biotech Mecca in part influenced by the Salk Institute.

UCSD campus is across the street from the Salk Institute and a few of the medical equipment manufactures situated there mainly to pick up talent from a declining aerospace business from the end of the cold war. As an example, General Dynamics, which had built missiles and aircraft components in large numbers as well as Teledyne helicopters had shut down all operations. So had Scientific Atlanta which built a lot of the sophisticated black boxes used in the cold war for the military and several government agencies and labs.

The British researcher Dr. Nigel Foster designed and worked on implants to give motor functions back to people with strokes by placing a chip in their brain that replaced the damaged portion. Chester read up on what his status was and why he left England to come to San Diego. It turns out he had to be close to a lot of neuroscientists and researchers and the other two options were the Boston Area or upstate New York and snow was just not all that appealing.

Chester had read about Dr. Nigel Foster ten years prior and to see this article and discover he was now in San Diego doing his research and the article ten years prior had stated that around the year 2023 Dr. Nigel Foster would be ready to start putting chips in dogs' brains. All this research was terribly expensive and there was no way the FDA would let him test it on humans before proving it worked on animals such as primates and other intelligent animals.

What Nigel Foster was going to do to defray the costs coming up when he got approval from the FDA to experiment with humans, by first selling a kit to wealthy dog owners that wanted a talking dog. The literature back ten years prior hinted around a price tag of around $300,000.00 for the cost to a dog owner and highly recommended a younger dog that would have some longevity with the ability.

None of the recent information indicated this chip insertion was in progress, but at least Chester had one thing, the address in Sorento Valley and he would drive there today with his pal Brooklyn and go see how far along Dr. Nigel Foster was in selling his dog kits.

"Brooklyn today is your lucky day. I'm taking you some place to meet an important person," Chester said thinking there was no way Brooklyn understood anything he was saying, but Brooklyn started wagging his tail and appeared happy because when Chester talked to him like that, fun things usually happened.

In a short while they were heading north on I-5 and got off at Genesee Avenue and drove up to Torrey Pines Road and to the research complex where Dr. Nigel Foster's office was located. The sign on the building said: Microneural Therapeutics Research Inc. with bold letters MTR next to it.

When Chester pulled into the parking lot, he got a phone call from his boss asking a few questions and Chester said he was checking in to see a doctor and he would get back to him in a while with the information he needed. Later after his boss got the information and made inquiry about the doctor's visit, Chester said, "No problems, the visit was to the Vet for my pet dog. And he's okay as of now."

The building structure in this research park was no different than many around the area, built with a lot of money from grants out of estates by people hoping they could buy their way into heaven. There was a receptionist at the front of the building lobby with a microphone and a small earphone set.

"May I help you sir?" The woman looked at Chester who was somewhat casually dressed and with the dog and consequently the receptionist exhibited a slight amount of condescension. She wasn't used to having many guests arrive in her ivory palace not wearing a suit or business dress.

"I would like to talk with Dr. Nigel Foster."

"Do you have an appointment."

"No."

"I'm sorry but according to my instructions he only sees people with an appointment."

"That's too bad I was hoping to talk with him about my dog."

Today the planets aligned, Abagail was away on a business trip to not interfere, and Dr. Nigel Foster just happened to walk through an access door to the lobby and the first thing he saw was Brooklyn. He thought it was strange to see a man and a dog in the lobby, so he approached and bent down and petted the nice-looking dog that had now grown halfway from a pup to an adult.

"That's a nice-looking pup you have there."

"Thanks, I like him a lot."

"What brings you here with your dog?"

"I was hoping to meet Doctor Nigel Foster and ask him how far along his research was on the dog chip kit he talked about ten years ago."

"Today's your lucky day. I'm Nigel Foster."

"That's great, Doctor Foster."

"What's your name?"

"I'm Chester and my dog is Brooklyn."

Doctor Foster chuckled and said, "I've heard a lot of names for dogs before, but I must say this is the first time I met a Brooklyn."

"I kind of like the name."

"Say, I was going to drive over to the La Jolla shopping mall and get a Starbucks, would you like to go with me."

"I would love to. Do I need to put Brooklyn in a pet carrier?"

"As long as you don't mind him sitting on your lap, that's not necessary."

"Sure, he loves sitting on my lap."

The Triumphant Trio left the building together with the receptionist all tied up in knots because she couldn't tell that loser to buzz off.

In due time they got their coffee and Brooklyn was wearing a fake service dog jacket, so Starbucks employees didn't hassle them, but they took their coffees out to the courtyard. Chester bought a bottle of water for Brooklyn and the good news; they were near some trees and landscaping in case Brooklyn needed to go tag a tree.

After they were all situated, Doctor Foster started the conversation, "I've not put out much information lately because I've had threats from animal rights groups that claim I'm going to use the dogs like lab rats."

"How far are you along in your research Doctor?"

"I'm actually ready to start selling and installing the dog kits now."

Chester swallowed some coffee hard and now was asking one of the most important questions of his life. "How much have you priced the dog kits Doctor?"

"Once we start doing the routine insertions, they will be about $300,000.00. Are you considering this operation for your dog?"

"I am but $300,000.00 is a little steep and I think my high maintenance wife would divorce me if I spent that kind of money."

"We need to test this implant on at least a dozen dogs before we go into full production, if you were willing to put your dog into MTR's study, I would be willing to install the device at no cost. All you would have to do is let me see a lot of the dog for six months and I would want visits about every three months until we get all the information we need."

"How soon are you going to start these clinical trials?"

"Actually, right now. We are ready to proceed. If you agree we can have you sign the contract that indemnifies us in case something unexpected goes wrong and that you cooperate and make those scheduled visits so we can do the proper protocols for post-surgery and research evaluations."

That shouldn't be a problem.

"One other thing. We will fit a dog collar jacket on the dog similar to what he's wearing. A speaker will be installed on it, but since this is a research dog, you will have an added box next to the speaker which will record telemetry out of the chip and transmit it to us wirelessly. That way we'll be able to remotely monitor the dog and his physiology. Also, this will result in the loss of some of your privacy as we want to record statements the dog makes."

"I'm a decent person I have nothing to hide, and my wife is gone most of the time."

"A lot of dog owners talk to their pets even though they realize the pets most of the time do not know what they are saying. Do you talk to your pup?"

"Yes, all the time. I think he understands me."

"Can you show me an example?"

"Yes, watch this. Brooklyn would you like some water?"

The dog started wagging its tail and moved its body around just like they had done many times before. Chester took the top off the water bottle and cupped his hand and poured some water in it and Chester began drinking until he had enough.

Chester put the top back on the water bottle and sat it back down on the table.

"That's good that you already communicate to the dog. He may be able to start speaking right away after we insert the chip and from experiments, I did in developing this, in due time the speech seems to accelerate their learning."

"How many words will the dog be able to say?"

"About 800 words to begin with. Thanks to the telemetry link if it appears the dog is capable of handling more words, we can download more words into the firmware of the chip."

The men sat the in a casual conversation with Brooklyn back on Chester's lap.

"That dog sure seems to like sitting on your lap."

"During the day, I work at home and while I'm doing emails and reading things on my laptop, Brooklyn likes sitting on my lap."

"Where does Brooklyn sleep at night?"

"If my wife is gone on a trip, he's in the pet carrier on a chair next to my bed so he's a few feet away. When my wife is home, he either sleeps in the pet carrier down near our sofa or with me on the Sofa when my wife is not being friendly."

"Sorry to hear that."

"It's how it is, that's why I got this dog is because she's gone most of the time and I'm home alone doing work at home because my employer is doing social distancing and placing as many people as possible at work at home."

"What's your day like?"

"In the morning we get up at 6:00 because if she's home I'm usually sleeping on the couch with Brooklyn, and we go to the park to walk and feed the birds."

"The birds are not scared of the dog?"

"No when he was a little puppy, they got to know him and have watched him grow up every day and they are his friends."

"Really?"

Chester pulled out his cell phone out of his pocket and said, "Take a look at some of these pictures."

There was Brooklyn in the mix with pigeons and squirrels, and later the Coots and the Mallards, and the Geese.

"This is amazing."

"Birds are smart, they have facial recognition and know me and Brooklyn quite well."

"Maybe I should investigate putting chips in birds too."

"Some bird owners would be quite impressed especially if the bird can speak 800 words."

"Indeed."

Chapter Two

BROOKLYN'S SCHEDULED FOR CHIP INSERTION

Doctor Foster returned Brooklyn and Chester to the parking lot and as they got out of the car, they shook hands after Doctor Foster said, "Be here 08:00 on Thursday. I have three documents for you to sign then we will do the surgery. The dog will be sedated for a couple days. We want you back here when we allow him to wake up because we want him to see you as he's waking up as to feel normal as much as he can under the circumstances."

"Alright."

"I assume you bathe your dog routinely?"

"Yes."

"Okay after the surgery no baths for about a week. What you can do is use damp wash clothes to clean it. After a week you can disconnect the connector on the dog collar device and remove his service dog jacket then bathe him. The power to the chip and speaker wire are a double use connection that sends signals as well as power down the two lines. Once you disconnect the plug there are no live circuits and the computer is in the suspend mode until you hook the power back up."

"That sounds great."

"Yes, we want the production models to be as uncomplicated as possible. The plug to the dog collar device is keyed so polarities cannot be swapped. The dog collar device has rechargeable batteries and when you open the box up to change the batteries you will see there is a switch there. The purpose of that switch is there may be times you do not want the dog to talk for privacy or behavior problems."

"You guys have thought this through."

"Just like you we are always learning."

It wasn't long before time passed, and Chester led Brooklyn back into the facility.

Today the receptionist didn't appear like the high maintenance woman of a few days ago and before Chester announced, "I would like to talk to Doctor Foster."

The receptionist greeted him and asked, "Good morning, are you Chester?"

"Yes."

"Someone will be here in a minute to escort you into the facility."

"Thank you."

A moment later a fine-looking young woman who was classified as a head turner or a woman that could get a married guy elbowed in the ribs for gawking at her, greeted Chester and Brooklyn.

"Good morning, Chester, I'm Felicia, I'm going to take you back to my office to do a preliminary health check on Brooklyn and during those checks an associate will bring in the contracts Doctor Foster mentioned to you."

Felicia turned and walked back towards the door that led from the lobby back into the office spaces and research labs. As she was leading Chester and Brooklyn, Chester could not escape the imagery of her perfect walk that accentuated her hips and thighs in very luxurious designer black silk slacks that made him feel like he wished Abagail was home today to do some Boom-Boom which they had not done in a while.

Inside the room Felicia led them into what seemed like a sterile doctor's office. The examining table was not laid out like an examining table one would see in a doctor's office. This sturdy looking metal table with a wrestling match like top didn't seem like anything Chester saw before.

"Can you please put your dog up on the table and stay beside it until we can establish a gentle awareness of it with me."

Chester put Brooklyn up on the examining table and Felicia started looking it over and petting Brooklyn who seemed very pleasant.

Meanwhile a Microneural Therapeutics Research Inc. Associate walked into the room with a clipboard and documents.

Brooklyn seemed to like Felicia and after petting him a few times he licked her hand in a very sweet and nice manner. Felicia looked at the woman who had a name tag saying Beverly and said,

"Chester, it looks like Brooklyn, and I will get along fine, why don't you sit down and sign the documents, Beverly has for you."

"Sure."

Chester sat down in a chair that had a writing surface like used in schools and started reading the documents that were quite simple with no fine print as Doctor Foster didn't want to overwhelm people with complexities. In the span of twenty minutes Chester read and signed all the documents and handed them to Beverly.

"Thank you, Chester," Beverly said then left the room.

During the time of reading and signing the documents, Felicia looked all over Brooklyn's body and noted he was a very clean and happy dog. Felicia was a smart veterinarian and knew when an owner took great care of their pets. Usually, those pets were also most friendly just like Brooklyn exhibited.

Brooklyn liked Felicia and wished she was with Chester and not the bitch Abagail. Brooklyn had already developed quite a personality in his brief life span. Watching TV all the time hastened his psychological development, and nothing made him happier than to rest on Chester's lap watching TV or watching what he was doing on his laptop computer.

In a few brief moments, Felicia said, "I've finished examining Brooklyn, would you mind carrying him and follow me to the lab where he will undergo his chip insertion."

"Alright."

Chester followed Felicia down the room and into another larger room that had a lot of instruments and several people waiting dressed up just like surgeons.

"Set Chester up on the operating table. We want you to hold him while we sedate him."

"Alright."

Brooklyn was very trustful of Chester who had never hurt him before. Then while Chester held Brooklyn, the dog suddenly felt a sharp pain as the needle was going into his body. Brooklyn looked up at Chester with a look on his face that simply seemed to suggest he was thinking, "Why are you hurting me?"

The sedatives were quick and powerful and whatever Brooklyn was thinking did not last long as he slowly fell unconscious.

Chester noticed there was an observation room slightly elevated behind a glass window to the side and as he predicted, Felicia said to him after Brooklyn was lying unconscious on the table, "Chester, if you would like to watch the procedure, come with me and I'll open the observation room for you. You will have several people join you there shortly. To the back of that observation room is an exit in case you need to visit the men's room during the procedure. We also have a cafeteria you can go and get food and drinks if desired."

"Thank you."

Felicia walked over and keyed in the cypher lock and the door opened. That particular door had cypher locks on both sides and people were not allowed into the operating lab once the procedure began.

Chester took a seat in the middle of the room that had two rows of chairs, one elevated above the other like a small theater. Within a few minutes of seating several other people came in and sat down also observing the procedure, wearing suits and business dresses. They looked distinguished. Chester had no idea who they were or what they did.

The operating team quickly placed Brooklyn into a enclosed device that reminded Chester about the Kowloon Ferry in Hong Kong where certain interesting courses of meals were served.

The device they had Chester inside allowed the head to be outside the box when the two halves were closed the head pointed in such a way the rear of the skull was pointed upwards to allow best access. Just as if this was an elaborate scientific experiment, Brooklyn had all types of cables running into the box where probes were glued onto his body with a fast drying super clue like substance.

Brooklyn had a ventilator hose down his mouth where oxygen was pumped in, and the box had a motor-like function that would move his body providing mechanical CPR if required. The electrodes to zap his heart were also in place in the event he had a heart stopping event.

A clear medical tent was then over the dog's head and one of the research associates took an electric shaver and in a short period of time shaved the area around the back of the skull they would enter to insert the chip that would interface with the non-visual inner brain photoreceptors just like humans have. Theory is one of the purposes of those nonvisual photoreceptors allowed telepathic communication, but it also allowed communication between the two hemispheres of the brain. That's where Doctor Foster's ingenious device worked.

Without elaborate rewiring of the brain it was a neurological "T" where the computer chip installed on the rear of the skull with that transducer cable with the special probes could interface with the brain without a lot of carving. This design was necessary for people with strokes because the side of the brain damaged could not really be used to much of an extent and to attempt interfacing with the damaged tissue was not systematic or reliable.

Doctor Foster was not going to reveal to Chester 95 of the 100 dogs experimented with died. But after redesign and reconfiguration, the prospect was a lot better. The two previous dogs receiving the implant were still viable animals and the speech capability even though only about 400 words was still a huge advancement. If Brooklyn survived the ordeal, thanks to the tweaking of the algorithms, they hoped to expand Brooklyn's lexicon to 800 words.

The theory that with the ability to grow if the dog's I.Q., they created the circumstance for the computer chip to expand the vocabulary. If they discovered a dog had grown the vocabulary because of influences in its environment, they would attempt to expand it with telemetry insertions remotely into the computer chip.

From the observation room, Chester could not see a lot because the doctors were blocking most of the view. However, a video monitor with a camera pointing directly downwards displayed in the upper front area of the room gave all they needed to see. In reality, the glass window didn't offer much to see.

The team of experts doing the work took six hours to insert the chip and wire it up. After they finished the work and sewed up Brooklynn's skull. They started disconnecting items and eventually pulled the respirator hose out of his mouth. When all the external connections were disconnected leaving the dog bare, they opened the box and removed Brooklyn and laid him down on his side and gave him a quick cleaning using special wipes then fitted the dog's vest over him and hooked up the wires that ran a short distance through his skin to a short stem and connector attached to the wires after they were inserted into the box. All the connections were made inside the black box then shut.

Since the black box had wireless no external wires were needed. The computer chip served a second purpose. Besides giving the dog the ability to talk it also could remotely provide a health check on the dog and provide a recording of several factors such as pulse, temperature, blood pressure on a major artery and a few interesting monitors such as hunger and thirst. Hence the dog could be monitored remotely for proper care and per the contract if the owner was neglectful, the contract gave Microneural Therapeutics Research Inc. the legal right to take possession of the dog to ensure its needs were met.

After all the procedures were done and telemetry was flowing that Doctor Foster and his associates were monitoring, Felicia walked into the observation booth and informed everything was finished and she wanted Chester to go to her office with him so she could explain what would happen over the next couple of days.

Lessons learned from the past indicated they needed to allow the dog to wake up in about eight hours and be with his master for a few minutes and given food and water then sedated again. Once sedated the dog would be inside an observation enclosure with 24 hour around the clock personnel available for the dog should it unexpectedly wake up and have issues. Chester was told to go home and rest and come back in eight hours for the next phase of all this.

Eight hours later Chester was in a recovery room with Brooklyn laying on a short table a foot off the floor in case the dog decided to jump off the table, it would not get injured.

Just like Felicia suggested shortly after Chester arrived in the recovery room, Brooklyn was awakened. Water and food for the dog was staged and as soon as Chester was in the room, Brooklyn slowly came too in a drugged haze but slightly coherent.

Then the biggest event of Chester's life manifested. As soon as Brooklyn recognized his master, the magic began.

"Papa," came out of the speaker box.

Felicia and Doctor Foster were there for the event. Part of the programming was to have the dog call his master "papa."

Chester heard the sound but at first did not understand what was going on.

Doctor Foster broke it to Chester. "The sound you just heard came from Brooklyn's speaker box. That sound was meant for you. I want you to now ask Brooklyn if he wants something to eat just like you normally would do at home."

Chester was in a huge emotional state now. His lovely dog was there looking at him and just called him Papa. It took all his willpower to snap out of the emotional spike and respond and say, "Brooklyn do want to eat?"

"Yes Papa." Brooklyn responded.

Chester was now in a huge emotional spike. He couldn't help it, tears were going down the side of his face. Doctor Foster and Felicia saw that and knew something like this could happen and for the sake of getting the job done had to probe Chester a bit to get him to start doing what he needed to do as timing was critical in the learning process.

"Chester, do you need some help with the food and water?" Felicia asked.

"No, I think I can manage." Chester responded after Felicia jolted him back to reality.

Chester put the bowls down on the floor and poured food and water into them and Brooklyn hopped down off the short table and walked over and sniffed the bowls and started eating. The dog food was enhanced with ingredients that would enhance the taste for the dog even better than table scraps owners were directed to avoid at all costs.

While Brooklyn was eating, he was wagging his tail and seemed happy. Of course, he loved being around Chester.

After Brooklyn finished eating and drinking almost a bull full of water, Doctor Foster asked, "How soon after he eats does he need to defecate?"

"Usually in ten to twenty minutes," Chester responded.

"It's still light outside and a warm day, why don't we walk Brooklyn outside so he can find a tree," Doctor Foster said and handed Chester a leash to snap onto the middle of the dog vest as he would not put it on the collar area again.

The dog and the three adults walked out a side door not far from the recovery room and there was lush green grass, some queen palm trees surrounded by a bunch of eucalyptus trees.

Brooklyn was walking around and sniffing things when Doctor Foster said to Chester, "Ask Brooklyn if he needs to poop.

"That's a word we have programmed into the computer."

"Brooklyn do you need to poop?"

"Yes Papa."

Brooklyn walked over to a tree, urinated on it then he squatted and pooped. Felicia had a doggy bag to pick it up and discard it.

"That's amazing, Brooklyn can tell me when he needs to go to the bathroom."

"Let's go for a short walk down the block and back and see how he's doing," Doctor Foster said.

The three adults and Brooklyn were soon walking down the sidewalk that paralleled Torrey Pines drive.

Doctor Foster then abruptly turned to Chester and said, "Ask Brooklyn what he sees."

"Brooklyn, what do you see?"

"Cars."

"Ask Brooklyn if he thinks cars are dangerous."

"Brooklyn are cars dangerous?"

"Yes Papa."

Chester was now utterly astonished.

After about a block, Doctor Foster said, "I think that's all the exercise we want to give Brooklyn now. Us take him back. I want to sedate him and keep him here overnight so we can monitor him."

"Alright."

Soon they were back in the recovery room and Doctor Foster said, "I want you to tell Brooklyn we must give him a shot now. It will hurt a little but it's going to help you."

After stating just that, Brooklyn stood there very calmly while he received the injection. Soon he was sleeping on his side inside the clear protective enclosure on a nice soft cushion.

"Alright Chester, come back in the morning and you can take Brooklyn home. I want you to come back in a week so we can give him a good look over and make sure he's healed from the surgery."

"Sure thing, doctor."

"If he starts acting strange call me right away on the business card. I'll do a reset remotely on his computer and if that doesn't work bring him here right away."

"Understand."

~~~~~~

It was kind of a lonely night. Chester was suddenly confronted with the emotions that a lot of dog owners have when suddenly the dog is taken away for some reason. Chester wondered if the pet cemetery in Sorrento Valley was still there. On his way home tomorrow, he would drive by it.

The Pet Cemetery was located right next to I-805 near the I-5 merge on Sorrento Valley Rd. Chester was surprised some of the pet burials appeared far more expensive and elaborate than cemeteries for humans. *An elderly person with a huge fortune probably spares no expenses since it's right by La Jolla and Delmar.*

No emails or phone calls from Abagail. *The marriage was anything but. It almost seemed like a waste of time. Why bother?*

As the relationship in the marriage slowly decayed, Brooklyn steadily grew more and more important to Chester. *Did I really do the right thing with the chip implant?* Chester thought. *Now it was too late to change his mind, the contract was crystal clear, he was stuck, plus who could remove the chip and the rig without damaging Brooklyn?*

It was a restless night, and a lonely one too. But thanks to a couple glasses of wine and some Melatonin, the night passed quickly,
~~~~~~

and it was morning routine, and a little to eat to hold Chester over. He packed up all he needed for Ski Beach, and then hopped in the car and drove down to Torrey Pines.

Shortly upon arrival Felicia escorted Chester back to the recovery room and there was Brooklyn laying down not looking too cheerful, but he was awake.

"We've not fed Brooklyn this morning so when you take him home you need to feed him right away."

"Not a problem, I planned on it."

About that time Brooklyn was standing up wagging his tail and instead of barking said, "Papa come pick me up."

Chester picked up Brooklyn who then continued talking a few words, "Papa please do not leave me."

"Not to worry Brooklyn we will always be together."

Doctor Foster walked into the room about then and added to the conversation.

"The telemetry coming through the dog collar and jacket device has been working well, no glitches so we were able to get a lot of monitoring of Brooklyn all night long. Every measure is in the green band as we say in our application software results."

"Thank you, Doctor. It appears Brooklyn has recovered quite well."

"You're welcome."

"How soon do you think his hair will grow back out and cover the scar?"

"Dog's hair grows quickly especially at his age. In about a months' time a lot of it will be covered up and from my experience in tests we've done in the past, in about three months you will not know he has a scar."

"Good. What if he gets sick and I need to take him to a veterinarian?"

"If you are out of town on a trip somewhere, you will no doubt have to go see a veterinarian. However, if you are around San Diego, we prefer you bring Brooklyn here. We have our own veterinarians plus they have been involved in this research project so they know the animal as well as the elaborate electronics and the transducer system and how all that works and could play a role into something that might create an issue."

"How long will your support last?"

"We expect this project to continue long past the life expectancy of Brooklyn. His data points are quite important for our research, so we must continue this relationship and collect the data. I know it didn't spell it out too well in the three documents you signed but if you go back and read the copies we gave you, it explicitly states for the life of the dog."

"That's very generous of you."

"Chester, I hope you know that Brooklyn is helping make medical history. Talking dogs is not the focus of our research. They are the means to study it further and produce the funds we need to continue to the point we can achieve our ultimate goal, to put chips in humans that suffered a stroke to give them back their motor functions such as speech and mobility."

"I can see where that would be important to people."

"Especially for a musician, a painter, or an author who would have issues writing manuscripts."

"Alright, over the next few days I will read those documents over again and make sure I didn't miss anything."

Chester, since Brooklyn is currently a very important part of this study, we will keep you informed, and we will email you some analysis of the telemetry we obtain. Because of the uniqueness of this study, we will communicate with you and if we discover something remotely that requires action, we will contact you immediately. As an example, a week from now we want you to bring Brooklyn back in for a checkup. Since this will happen again in the future, we will reach out to you the day before to remind you of appointments we set for you. If for some reason you must go out of town, we want to make plans to keep Brooklyn here especially for the first two years.

"Do you have a contingency if you get called out of town?"

"My wife and I will coordinate it and make sure one of us is here with Brooklyn."

"What about vacations?"

"Lately my wife is too busy for vacations and the last few times I brought it up she said she has bookings out to over a year from now and cannot possibly take time off for a vacation."

"Alright. If for some reason you must travel, let us know and in an emergency, we have the ability to bring in dog setters here at the facility that can take care of Brooklyn in your absence."

"I'm hoping that will not be the case."

"One last thing before we let you take Brooklyn home; this is advice to you for your own good okay?"

"Sure."

"The public may not be ready for a talking dog. We advise you to not broadcast it to the public and if you are going to be at a grocery store or business place where you feel Brooklyn might say something, please turn the switch off before you go inside."

"Not to worry Doctor, in fact I do not even want my wife to know that Brooklyn can talk."

"Smart man."

***

Chapter Three

BROOKLYN STARTS ASKING QUESTIONS

Chester and Brooklyn were soon in the car heading back to Interstate Five which would get him to Sorrento Valley Road quicker so he could drive by the pet graveyard. It was good they didn't have to use it yet.

Chester would drive right past it on Sorrento Valley Road. There was plenty of parking along the road and so Chester parked the car and said, "We are going to get out her just for a minute, they we will go to Ski Beach and feed you."

Chester stepped out of the car and Brooklyn was right behind him as they walked up to the gate that was open and several people were in there visiting graves of their former pets. The extravagance and opulence of some of the graves was quite apparent. The place had filled up quite a bit since the last time Chester just happened to drive by and parked his car by here to walk to a company building, he had to visit for his work.

"What is this papa?"

"It's where they take cats and dogs when they die."

"That's a sad thought," Brooklyn replied.

Chester realized this was not a wise stop, then said, "Us go back to the car."

Soon they were back in the car and back on Interstate Five on their way to Sea World Drive which was much easier to get to Ski Beach than driving through Pacific Beach traffic, especially during tourist season.

In a few minutes after arriving on Sea World Drive, they were pulling into the parking lot of Ski Beach right where the pigeons were waiting.

In short order the food, treats and water were in bowls by the car. The birds had watched Brooklyn drink water from the bowl, and they learned from him, and they politely shared his water. The squirrels came wanting some treats and they had slowly developed the nerve to actually eat out of Brooklyn's bowl with him.

Today a strange event happened. When the squirrel started eating out of Brooklyn's bowl, Brooklyn nonchalantly asked, "What animal is this?"

"That's a squirrel."

"Will you please tell the squirrel to stop eating from my bowl."

Chester started laughing so hard the squirrel got scared and ran away. The pigeons, easy to spook also flew away and circled back and landed and started eating treats again.

Chester kept putting more food in the bowl as it was quite apparent Brooklyn was very hungry and probably wasn't feeling too well from the surgery. One of the reasons for keeping him at Doctor Foster's Microneural Therapeutics Research Inc. facility was to give Brooklyn doses of pain killers and reduce the need for further pain killers once he left with Chester. However, if the dog started having discomfort Chester was given a kit of things for various reasons. One item in the kit was a pain reducer to mix with his food or water, but it was better with food, especially if the dog was hungry.

One added bonus of the chip measuring the dog's brain waves and detecting signals from the brain was, the researchers would get telemetry indicating the dog was having pain and Chester would receive a text or a phone call to inform him of the pain and the course of action recommended. Another possibility might be Brooklyn would tell Chester, "I feel pain." Phrases like that were in the firmware. There were also some adaptive elements as to when the dog learned something the chip could add the word to the lexicon.

Knowing what Brooklyn had gone through, Chester thought it was wise they take it easy for a few days and not do a lot of walking. After taking care of this end of the park, they got back in the car and drove to the other end to meet up with the Coots, Blackbirds, and Migratory Seagulls.

Another surprise happened. Brooklyn asked, "What are these black birds?"

"Those birds are called black birds."

"What are the other black birds?"

"These black birds by my leg are called Coots."

"What are they gray birds with red beaks?"

"Those are Seagulls."

"What are those white birds with yellow feet?"

"Those are migratory Seagulls."

Then the next surprise, "Papa I need to poop."

"Here's a tree right over here waiting for you."

After taking care of business, they were now ready to go home where once again Brooklyn was watching TV.

In a couple days, Chester bought a couple children's books and read them to Brooklyn who didn't seem too enthused. Chester thought it might help develop more I.Q. Then came the biggest shock of Chesters life.

"Papa, us watch TV."

"Want me to read you books?"

"No, watch TV."

"Alright."

From that day onwards, Brooklyn didn't want to read books, he wanted to watch TV. Furthermore, Brooklyn had favorite shows!

"Want to watch this show?"

"No."

"How about this one?" Chester asked as he surfed through the channels.

"No."

The next channel was National Geographic. "How about this one?"

"Yes, watch this one."

A couple days later, Chester received a text message from Doctor Foster, "Based on Telemetry, Brooklyn has learned 25 new words and he now has a vocabulary of 825 words. This is very encouraging. Looking forward to your visit in a couple days."

The routine continued in a similar day to day routine and after a couple days of watching National Geographic unexpectedly Brooklyn asked, "Papa, why do they call female dogs bitches."

"That's the name society gave them."

"Is your wife a bitch?"

"Sometimes I feel that way."

"The bitch is mean to me when you are not home."

"Really?"

"Yes Papa, I do not like your bitch."

"Never talk to Abagail, I do not want her to know you can talk."

"I have no desire to talk to your bitch Abagail."

Chester then said what he was feeling right then. "When I was a kid, people would sometimes say, *what if dogs could talk.*"

"What does that mean Papa?"

"Well Brooklyn, your talking has really opened my eyes. People do not know their dogs know a lot more, but they simply can't talk."

"Papa, why do you call me Brooklyn?"

"When I first received you, I was watching a show on TV discussing Brooklyn, New York. I needed to give you a name, so I picked Brooklyn. Is that name okay or do you want another name."

"Brooklyn is ok can you show me some TV with Brooklyn in it?"

"Sure."

***

A few days later they were in Doctor Foster's examining room looking at Brooklyn.

"Chester, we are rather astonished that Brooklyn's adaptive microcode has sent us telemetry that Brooklyn now has 850 words in his vocabulary."

"He watches a lot of TV."

"Brooklyn, what is your favorite TV show?" Doctor Foster asked.

"National Geographic."

"Any other TV shows you like, Brooklyn?"

"Yes, Japanese SUMO Wrestling."

"Very interesting."

"I hold the remote control for Brooklyn, and he picks the TV channels," Chester said.

"Chester, Brooklyn is amazing to the point I'm willing to offer you one million dollars $$$ for him."

"Brooklyn is not for sale." Brooklyn stated most emphatically.

"That is amazing what he just said," Doctor Foster responded.

"Yea he amazes me every day," Chester added.

"In the future if we get more dogs like Brooklyn with the chip, the public will want this more and more and I can see how this will pay for my research so I can ultimately do what I set out to do in the beginning and that is to help people with strokes."

"I do hope you are successful doctor."

"Thank you."

"Come back and see us two weeks from now. Looking at Brooklyn's scalp it's healed rather nicely, but I'm writing a prescription for you to get a particular type of lotion we like to put on dogs that have surgery to help deal with itching sensations and it has antibiotics in it to help protect the wound while it heals."

"It looks pretty good to me doctor."

"Yes, I realize that, but in the days to come, Brooklyn will complain about itching at the back of his head."

"Alright doctor I'll get it."

"Apply it first thing in the morning then again in the evening approximately an hour before you go to bed."

"Alright."

The dynamic duo of Chester and Brooklyn were soon off to Ski Beach on their way home from Doctor Foster's Microneural Therapeutics Research Inc. office which Brooklyn was looking forward to visiting his squirrel buddies.

As soon as they pulled up to the parking lot next to the edge of the bay and got out of the car, the pigeons were already landing near them in great anticipation. The minute they saw the feeding and water bowl, the pigeons went into a tizzy of delight. They were all super hungry.

Some of the pigeons even pecked in Brooklyn's food bowl which he ignored and a few drank water from his water bowl. One pigeon one time decided it would bathe in the water bowl. Then Chester dumped it and refilled it closer to the food bowl which would stop it from trying it again.

Today was a unique day. Brooklyn allowed two squirrels to share his food bowl because he knew Chester would keep food in it until he had enough.

"I'm a superior animal to you squirrels, because I can talk." Brooklyn said to the two squirrels who then looked at him with a funny face. They knew the sound came from Brooklyn as he was moving his mouth which he did as he talked. People who didn't know would think the sound came out of the dog's mouth even though it came from speakers mounted in the dog collar device located about six inches behind his mouth at the front of the dog collar device.

One of the squirrels stood up on its hind feet and staired at Brooklyn. Chester wished he knew what the squirrel was thinking. But he knew from the number of pet squirrel videos he watched on Instagram, they two had a significant ability to learn.

Brooklyn wasn't looking forward to later in the day because Chester announced that Abagail would be coming home today. She usually took a cab from the Airport home since it was a legitimate business expense.

After they returned home after spending time with all their bird friends, Chester went to work on the internet reading emails and responding while Brooklyn watched the infinite number of National Geographic shows Chester could play for him.

Chester saw Brooklyn's body language showing he wasn't too happy even though he was engrossed in the National Geographic show.

They had a small lunch later and then went back to working and watching TV. Around two P.M. Brooklyn jumped off the couch and ran over to the window and put his front feet up on the windowsill and turned back to Chester and said, "The bitch is back."

"I wish you didn't call her that. Her name is Abagail."

"Alright Papa." Brooklyn said giving those puppy dog eyes to Chester.

Moments later Abagail opened the door and was toting her suitcase behind her and had her leather business satchel strap around her neck. She looked slightly hung-over which people appear if they had been flying all day long after a long night in a night club drinking and socializing.

"How was your flight dear?"

"Terrible, and I have a headache."

Abagail drug her suitcase on wheels through the hallway and then turned down a hallway into the laundry room that had a washer, dryer, sink, and cabinets for supplies.

She left the suitcase there and from past experiences, Chester knew better than to open Abagail's suitcase as she became very irritable if he did. Truth be known she didn't want him to accidentally see some of the snail tracks she left in her panties from a couple of her Casanova friends.

Without saying a word Abagail walked past an area they had staged a lot of bottles of water for themselves or guests who might show up. Abagail grabbed a water bottle and headed up to the bedroom, went inside and locked the door. That was their standard operating posture when she had a headache and didn't want to be disturbed.

Chester knew better than to attempt to enter the bedroom if it was locked. That was her signal she was off limits, either on her period, hung over, or was sick and didn't want to be bothered by the jerk she slowly was wondering why the hell she married him in the first place. *Since he has that stupid dog now that should keep him happy,* Abagail thought.

The day passed uneventfully. No romance, no marriage enjoyment, no realization of marital tranquility. No sex, zip point chit. Another blessed life with the love of his life. Good thing he obtained Brooklyn who seemed to make life more tolerable with what Brooklyn liked to call, the bitch.

Abagail had taken an aspirin and some sleeping pills. By the time she put her head on the pillow just undressing into her bra and panties, it was already past five P.M. but three hours later the time schedule she was on. She tried to nap on the plane, but some goofball kept wanting to talk with her and it irritated her. Then after her connecting flight into San Diego, the nosey woman she sat next was playing that game I got one thousand questions which didn't help her hang over.

The Casanova everyone called "Buster" kept her in that damn bar till closing time because he thought he could lubricate her up well and get some action. He was disappointed because she wasn't in the mood to give out the milk for free.

If Buster wanted the action he was going to have to buy the cow and pay all the divorce attorney fees.

The kind of crap Abagail had to put up with marketing was disgusting, but she read the guide to the successful application of Hostitutes procedures. It was all part of the game. She had to keep the contracts rolling in for a few more years if she was going to get a step up into the corporate executive slot and not have to travel. Would she consider children then? Would it be too late? Her biological clock was running, and she may have run out of time if she wasn't careful. Plus, she wasn't sure she wanted to be continued stuck with that dog lover who was every day starting to be nothing more than a jerk with a dog. If it wasn't for his income, she would have dumped him a long time ago.

Chester could smell a small amount of alcohol Abagail exhaled as she walked past him up to the bedroom and he knew it likely she might have got plastered the night before. Hopefully she didn't compromise herself and suddenly delivered a little bambino with a tan in nine months. There was no point in planning dinner because Chester didn't expect to see Abagail for the rest of the night, so he ordered pizza and delivery. In case she magically woke up hungry there would be plenty left for her to eat as he bought an extra-large split with Hawaiian on one side she liked and pepperoni which he liked on the other side.

Before he started eating the pizza, he put out water and dog food for Brooklyn who was mesmerized by the smell of the pizza and sort of spoiled his desire for the dog food. Chester then poured himself a nice glass of wine and sat down at the table and opened the pizza box up that had packages of grated cheese and crushed red peppers to put on the pizza which he sprinkled on a couple pieces and started eating and drinking. Life was good then suddenly; he was surprised by Brooklyn.

"Papa, can I try eating what you are eating?"

"Brooklyn, the doctor says you are supposed to eat what you are eating."

"Papa, I was watching TV and it said dog food is garbage. I want to try real food like you are eating."

"Brooklyn, actually this pizza is not good for you."

"Papa, if it's not good for me, then it's not good for you as well."

Chester was utterly shocked by Brooklyn's statement. It was something he never ever expected to hear in his lifetime. Nor was he ever thinking one day he would own a talking dog.

When they had pizza, Abagail would eat a couple pieces and throw the rest of it away. There was substantial amounts of ham and pineapple on half the pizza for her.

"I'll tell you what Brooklyn, you eat that dog food and when you are done, I will give you some of this pizza after you eat all your dogfood."

Brooklyn went to work on the dog food in full anticipation of the surreal experience of eating human food instead of the garbage he usually received. After he finished all his dog food, Brooklyn went to his water bowl drank a little bit of water then walked over to Chester and said, "Papa, I finished all the dog food. Can I have some of that human food now?"

Chester took the pile of ham he pulled off the pizza and walked over and put it in the dog food bowl.

Brooklyn started eating the ham and enjoyed every bit of it but noticed

Chester was eating pizza pie crust and said, "Can I have some of that too?"

Chester took a piece of pizza; he pulled the ham off and removed the pineapple and placed it in the bowl. Brooklyn was soon devouring the pizza pie crust.

"Papa what is that food called?"

"Brooklyn, it's called pizza."

"Papa, I prefer pizza over dog food."

The next morning Chester and Brooklyn woke up as usual at 6:00 a.m. and were soon out the door with the tagged dog food and the leftovers in the pizza box.

Abagail never came down during the night so all the Hawaiian portion of the pizza was still available.

The dynamic dual Chester and Brooklyn were soon at Ski Beach and Chester readied Brooklyn's food and water bowls and had all the remaining ham mixed in with the dog food which was a lot more food than normal.

Chester figured the squirrels would love the dog food mixed with the ham so whatever Brooklyn didn't eat would be enjoyed by other animals.

Just like they were buddies, a couple squirrels were helping Brooklyn eat his breakfast until Chester reached down and handed them big chunks of pizza. The squirrels took the pizza and ran over to the nearby rocks and stood on their hind feet and were eating away.

Meanwhile the pigeons were enjoying the left-over pizza and all the animals were happy except the seagulls watching from a distance who knew Chester didn't like them.

A few smaller migratory seagulls showed up and got some tweets. These birds have facial awareness and knew Chester and to some extent Brooklyn.

Based on what Chester experienced with Brooklyn, he knew it was only a matter of time when Doctor Foster would be requested to implant a chip in a bird's brain. Some of the squirrel videos were very interesting and Chester thought they too may one day be included in this study.

Chester didn't know it at the time, but he was being observed.

There was no rhyme or reason for it. The pink skin Drolupric Aliens ship had been parked and cloaked a few days randomly coming back to this spot because a high official had spotted all this strange interaction between the birds, squirrels, the dog Brooklyn, and human and wanted to further observe.

The pink skin Drolupric Aliens were on a combination planetary survey and *Intelligence, Surveillance, & Reconnaissance* (ISR) mission. Earth was under galactic quarantine by the Galactic Federation of Planets. The Drolupric Aliens had to arrive in total secrecy. Their purpose of being here was mainly to monitor the Draco Gray and Tall White Aliens who were interacting with CIA people at Area 51 Sector Four (S-4) in violation of the Galactic Federation of Planets mandate.

What were Draco Gray and Tall White Aliens doing at S-4? What nefarious activities were they engaged in with the American Majestic 12 Group?

Based on the Draco Gray galactic reputation, the Drolupric Aliens knew the Americans were setting themselves up for a disaster if they continued their dealings with the Draco Gray Aliens who normally had no least bit of empathy or interest in other civilizations and races unless there was something specifically that would benefit them.

Tall Gray alien leaders from Orion captured by Galactic Federation of planets forces after a major space battle, were the same group of aliens that had in the 1950s reached an agreement with America's Majestic 12 Group without President Eisenhower's approval and as a result sold out humanity in the process.

Drolupric Aliens would consider a tactical strike on the Draco Gray reptilians, but the fact the Tall Whites were also present at area 51 gave them some hope the Americans might not become a victim of the Draco Gray reptilians who most likely would like to make planet Earth part of their portfolio and move 10 billion Grays here to help reduce congestion on some of their planets.

The Drolupric Aliens could only sporadically get near Area-51 because if their presence was there too long and often, they might be detected by the Draco Gray Reptilians or the Tall Whites who would advise the Americans they were hostile Aliens. Since the Americans have very little knowledge of the Galaxy, they had no idea they had the very worst Aliens among them now.

Until the big showdown occurred which was likely, these Drolupric Alien ISR missions would continue and between the short visits to near Area 51 where they could spy on the activity of the Draco Gray Aliens and the Tall Whites. Between hops to Area-51 they had some leisure time and as part of their mandate surveyed the rest of the planet and provided updates via deep space neutrino transmissions to a mother ship that would then retransmit the information back to the home worlds in the Drolupric Empire.

There was quite a lot of interest suddenly in the Drolupric control room when the chief scientist for the mission informed the captain, "The dog can talk."

"How is that possible? There are no talking dogs anywhere. They do not have the vocal cords to form the words."

"Sir we have now a dozen acoustic records of the dog named Brooklyn talking."

"Let me hear one."

"This is what Brooklyn just said to its owner, he calls Papa:"

"Papa I'm full, let the squirrels have the rest of the food."

"Alright Brooklyn"

The captain sat there stunned and soon the high-ranking diplomat was in the control room being briefed of the revelation.

Soon the control room was hearing the additional audio.

"Brooklyn you ready to walk around the park."

"Yes Papa."

The two headed out on their walk around Ski Beach like they normally did in the morning, encountering routine walkers they knew.

This part of the walk there wasn't much conversation going on between Brooklyn and Chester, but the Drolupric were nonetheless quite animated watching the human bird interactions. This did not happen at other worlds because the birds feared humanoids who would kill them and eat them if they could.

A man and a dog had just turned the opinions and evaluations of the Drolupric science team upside down.

In passing days there were discussions on abducting the two and attempt to figure out how the dog learned to talk and why it seemed far more intelligent than any such animal ever discovered before.

Sometimes during the walks Brooklyn would ask questions about the TV shows he watched. And soon the Drolupric scientists were in great discussions about the analytical ability of Brooklyn. They were completely fascinated, and this led to them returning to the parking spot on Ski Beach that rarely had people walk into the area, for more observations of the dynamic dual.

~~~~~~

That morning, by the time Abagail awakened, the dynamic dual of Chester and Brooklyn were gone and already at Ski Beach doing their morning routine.

Abagail went into the laundry and emptied the clothes out of her suitcase and put in the washing machine things like her under garments she needed to clean and pulled the dry-cleaning items out and put them in a handbag to take to the dry cleaning store on her way to work.

Once the washing machine was working, she went into the kitchen and made a pot of coffee and looked for something to eat. There was not much there unless she cooked something which she didn't desire to do.

Abagail knew that Chester always had snacks in the cupboards and went there and found one of his favorites, a box full of Nature's Bakery Raspberry flavored Fib Bars. These snacks were alright but weren't the kind of food she normally would want in the morning, but since she missed dinner and didn't eat all day yesterday her hunger was strong enough to where they hit the spot with her coffee.

Abagail watched the morning news feed while she was drinking her coffee and munching down on those fig bars that for some reason tasted good this morning. *Am I that hungry*, Abagail wondered.

Soon the Alarm on the washing machine indicated the clothes were washed and ready to put in the dryer which she did then wondering if Chester and the dog would make it home before she left to the office.

The clothes were drying as Abagail took a shower with a cap on because she didn't have enough time to work on her hair. She would brush it and apply some hair spray and that would be enough to get her through the day. She also noted she needed to make an appointment for her hair salon this week while she was home.
~~~~~~

By the time Abagail finished her shower, put on her clothes and took care of her hair and makeup, the clothes were dried and she got them out of the dryer in a basket and took it up to her bedroom where she folded them and put them in her chest of drawers, then took the basket back down to the laundry room carrying her purse with her, ready to go. By now it was almost fifteen minutes before 9:00 A.M. and since Abagail had to stop at the dry cleaner she was not going to wait for Chester and his dog. She grabbed her shopping bag full of dry cleaning and walked to the garage and got into her automobile and opened the garage door with the remote. When the garage door was open, she looked down to see if she needed any gas. Her tank was full. She wondered how that happened.

A lot of times when Abagail was on the road, Chester would take her car to the gas station and fill it up or get the oil changed or do whatever needed to be done including rotating the tires if necessary. The car was spick and span because Chester took it to the Genie car wash that also cleaned the interior up well. Another lackluster day was just about to manifest.

Chester had met a lot of people at Ski Beach over the years and every day just about ran into at least one of them. Today he ran into a man with his dog he got to know. The dog was small and friendly and was more interested in walking than socializing with Brooklyn who had a similar mindset. They would have arrived home sooner, but they got into an interesting conversation and Chester ended up walking a couple extra miles he didn't plan on. Then they went home to the empty house. Abagail had departed for her office turning in contracts she got signed on her business calls.

Abagail was bucking for a promotion as they said in the business. She was the consummate eager beaver, and all those new contracts meant a lot. She was paid less but she outperformed all the male sales reps at the company. She knew that but she didn't care, because she wasn't going to let something like pay disparity get in the way of achieving her goal of getting that promotion and when she got it the pay disparity would be over.

Even though the spark seemed to be gone in their marriage, at least the positive side of Chester was, he never interfered with her plans a single time, never made demands on her, and never took any of her income. She banked it all. She took Chester for granted and never pondered what would happen to her if he was suddenly gone. He was in fact her life support. She never had to concern herself with trivial chores or issues most other women did, especially those with abusive husbands or those with drug, alcohol, and gambling addiction. One of the men she worked with was going through a divorce because his wife was a gambling addict and had slowly worked herself into some outrageous debt.

A while later in the day, about an hour before she was leaving the office to return home, Chester texted Abagail and asked her what she would like for dinner and her response soon afterwards was she would stop and get some takeout on the way home. She never asked Chester if he wanted anything. But Chester expected that.

Chester often purchased groceries on his way home from Ski Beach since it was on the way and didn't take him far out of his way. This morning was no exception. Hence, Chester had some fresh meat, a prepackaged salad and a box of rice pilaf to make. Long before Abagail made it home, Chester did the cooking, fed himself and Brooklyn, put the leftovers in Tupperware and had the dishes all cleaned up and put away. Nobody would know he had cooked and ate a meal as the kitchen, which had a small dining table to eliminate the need to go into the dining room took care of it. This area also had Italian tiles so if he or the dog spilled something it was easy to clean up right away.

This afternoon was another pleasurable time for Brooklyn who received a mixture of unseasoned meat mixed in with his dog food. Chester had ample time to take Brooklyn to his favorite tree in the back yard and had some small plastic bags to pick up anything Brooklyn left behind. The talking ability made things much more convenient for Chester because now instead of guessing what he needed to do with Brooklyn all he had to do was ask, "Brooklyn do you need to go poop?"

If Brooklyn needed he would say, "Yes papa can you please take me outside."

After everything was complete and in order, the dynamic dual was sitting on the sofa watching TV as Abagail arrived home and made her way to the refrigerator knowing one of her favorite beers would be there as Chester was very efficient in keeping two drawers in the refrigerator filled wither favorite light beers.

She sat her food down on the kitchen table, opened her beer, then opened the Styrofoam boxes of her food she purchased at Phil's Barbecue, one of the very successful restaurants in the area and many times had a line waiting to get in. Abagail was smart and phoned her order in and just had to walk up to the counters set up for pickup and get her prepaid food.

Abagail had worked through lunch and was hungry and dove into those ribs and French fries and felt the wonderful feeling of the beer washing it down. She was so hungry she horsed it down, not showing the least bit of table manners but could care less as she was in the privacy of her home.

After she finished Abagail felt bloated and decided she needed to use the bathroom and left all her containers and packaging behind assuming her personal slave would take care of it.

As she walked past Chester and the dog, Chester asked, "Are you all done eating?"

"Yes you can throw what's left over away."

"All right."

Half of Abagail's meal was left. Chester simply took the remaining ribs and fries and put them together in one container and would give them to Brooklyn and the animals at Ski Beach in the morning mixed in with his dog food. He then sat that container in the half empty refrigerator and put the rest of the trash in the trash receptacle on the side of the house, the garbage collections picked up once a week. One container was for trash, the other was for recycling.

Chester never filled his trash containers up at home because most of the time one third of it ended up in trash containers at Ski Beach after he fed the contents to the various animals. It was a win-win for Chester as he got rid of a lot of his trash when he fed the animals.

After Abagail took care of business and soaked in a bubble bath, she put on her pajamas and came back downstairs observing Chester and Brooklyn watching National Geographic again.

"Is there anything else we can watch besides that show?" Abagail asked sitting a few feet away from Chester on the sofa.

Chester handed Abagail the remote control and said, "Here you go deal, pick what you would like to watch."

As Abagail started surfing the TV channels looking for something she wanted to see, Chester got up and walked over to his desk where his computer terminal and Brooklyn followed. Chester sat down, put on earphones so he would not have to hear the TV as he knew Abagail would probably select one of those news journalists shows where biased media spewed out the nonsense for the Koolaid drinkers. Sadly, TV News seemed polarized. All news now was either left- or right-wing nonsense vice common sense.

If Chester was home alone with Brooklyn, he would play classical music on the speakers and tell Brooklyn the composer and the name of the piece. This also had reverberating impact on Microneural Therapeutics Research Inc. when Brooklyn's word lexicon suddenly had a few words like piano concerto and violin. Brooklyn learned the name of a couple composers to music he took a strong liking. By this point Brooklyn's lexicon had 950 words that included the names of the composers Medtner and Bortkiewicz.

Chester knew how much Brooklyn loved classical music, so he purchased an audio splitter that allowed two headphones plugged in at the same time and some small headphones for children that fit Brooklyn perfectly.

Soon Chester and Brooklyn were listening to Yuja Wang perform Chopin piano concerto number two while Chester surfed the internet with Brooklyn sitting on his lap listing to the music.

Abagail watched TV for about an hour and was feeling some jet lag as it's three hours different from where she had just returned and suddenly turned off the TV and said, "I'm tired, I'm going to bed." She then abruptly stood up and went up the stairs and did her normal night routine including taking Melatonin and Vicks sleep enhancer. Again, she locked the door signaling she wasn't interested in romance or Chester.

Once Abagail was gone, Brooklyn asked, "Papa, can we watch TV again?"

"Sure," Chester said after he took the two headphones and placed them on the desktop then put the computer into sleep mode and walked over to the sofa which Brooklyn was now big enough to jump up on. Chester selected the National Geographic channel on and they were showing Ancient Aliens.
By the end of the show, Brooklyn asked, "Papa what are Aliens?"

"Brooklyn do you want to go outside and peepee then I will show you something about aliens."

"Yes, papa I'm ready to go outside."

The two went out to the back yard and it was a clear night sky. When Chester bought the new home, he planted 24 new trees and most of them were queen palms. Sixteen of them were in the large backyard which gave Brooklyn a lot of opportunity to find a new tree every day.

When Chester noticed Brooklyn had finished his business, he walked over towards Chester thinking they were going back into the house. One of the relatives had bought a large outdoor swing that also could be used for an outdoor bed. Chester had laid there before gazing at the stars. He walked over there and sat down and said, "Brooklyn, come over here."

Brooklyn walked over to Chester who grabbed him and lifted him up on the swing and started petting Brooklyn. Then he said, "Look into the sky."

"Alright Papa."

"See all those lights in the sky?"

"Yes papa."

"Those are stars."

"What do they do?"

"In the daytime we have the nice warm sun that warms us in the sky, right?"

"Yes, Papa I know that."

"Each one of those lights is just like our sun but they are a long distance away."

"How far away?"

"They are so far away we can never travel to them."

"There are many in the sky."

"Each one of those stars probably have planets like where we live."

"What's a planet?"

"A planet is a very large round place like the sun in the daytime."

"Alright."

"See the large white object in the sky?"

"Yes papa, what is it?"

"We call that a moon, it's like this planet we live on but it's a lot smaller and nobody lives there."

"Okay."

Each one of those stars in the sky have planets like the moon circling it."

"Just like the moon?"

"Yes."

"Some of those planets are just like here where we live. They have people living there."

"Do they look like you?"

"We do not know."

"What do you call those people that live on those planets papa?"

"We call them Aliens."

From that moment until they went back into the house, Brooklyn stared at the stars and the almost full moon.

Later that night while the dynamic dual Chester and Brooklyn were once again sleeping on the couch, the computer chip inserted into Brooklyn's brain did a download. Health indicators and any new words to the lexicon were transmitted via wireless to Microneural Therapeutics Research Inc.

Eight hours later while Doctor Foster was enjoying his Starbucks coffee, he was reviewing all the telemetry data on the four dogs they now had implanted. There were automated graphs that were a product of artificial intelligence a company up in San Francisco had developed for them. The corresponding timelines had simple moving averages and other graphs showing a graph similar to what stock investors used in analyzing stock prices with convergence and divergence of two different running averages. There was also a graph like Bollinger Bands that showed running averages and running two standard deviations. Finally, there was a final graph similar to a relative strength index showing each dog compared to the other three.

There was no mistake about it. Brooklyn's lexicon was growing faster than the other three dogs combined and he just went over 1000 words. Most humans have a working vocabulary of 800 words because of the way life is. They know other words but practically never use them. Hence those additional words are not considered part of the working vocabulary.

Chinese have 20,000 words but most Chinese have a working vocabulary of 2000 words and a good number of them 4000 words making them substantially more intelligent than Americans. It all gets back to their culture and nurturing process.

The outcome of this morning's review soon led to a meeting with the top six researchers discussing Brooklyn. That dog would now be under a microscope to figure out why his advancement exceeded the other three dogs by such a huge margin. One thing Doctor foster knew was the other three dogs were in a loving family and well-kept since the owners had substantial financial resources. Also, they were not given such an exclusive free ride like Chester received, mainly because they could afford to pay their fair share plus more.

Doctor Foster was now extremely happy he went in the direction he did with Chester because the result was a significant lab animal that would give them spectacular insights into the development of dog speech.

Chester and Brooklyn were due back in for another checkup and visit. Doctor Foster then informed his research associates of his plan.

"I'm going to explain to Chester these remarkable results and I'm going to request he allow me to spend a couple days with him observing exactly what goes on in that home that seemingly influences Brooklyn's lexicon expansion."

"Do you think if we figure out what's influencing Brooklyn that we can inform the other dog owners to copy the activity?" Felicia asked.

"Felicia, as you know each dog has its own personality. The other dogs may not like doing what Brooklyn is doing that has had this impact."

A few days later when Chester and Brooklyn were in Doctor Foster's office seeing a presentation they created and showed on a big screen on the wall.

The presentation was narrated by Felicia who went over the graphs and the pertinent information.

Chester was mildly surprised at what he discovered. He felt Brooklyn was a special dog and now the scientists had just confirmed it.

After the presentation they sat around a conference table, just the four of them. Brooklyn had his own chair and sat next to Chester on the other side of the table observing Doctor Foster and Felicia.

Doctor Foster then pitched Chester his idea then they discussed it.

"I suppose it would be okay for you to visit a couple days, but I would like to wait until my wife goes out of town." "Why is that?" Felicia asked.

"I do not want her to know Brooklyn talks."

"She doesn't know?"

"No. Brooklyn doesn't like my wife and he knows not to talk while she is around."

"How often does she go out of town?"

"Frequently. I expect her to travel again in a few more days."

"When is her next trip?"

"She should be heading out in a couple days and is usually gone for three to five days. I'll text you when Abagail is heading to the airport."

"You don't drive her?"

"No, her company pays for her Taxi, and she has a regular driver with a very clean cab for exclusive clients and has a newspaper and a Starbucks coffee ready for her when she gets into the cab."

"She must tip him well to get all that."

"The company allows her to tip 25% of the cab fare."

"How much is the cab fair?"

"$30 to $40."

"That would barely pay for the Starbucks and Newspaper."

"She tells him to add on $10 on the receipt so that she can give him a bigger tip."

"Her boss hasn't figured it out?"

"He knows she doesn't care about $10. She's more concerned about getting a $50,000 bonus in sales.

"Must be nice."

"She pays the price. She's a road-warrior, must sleep on airplanes and hotels and put up with lecherous customers."

"How does she handle that situation?"

"She tells them the same thing she tells me: I got a headache."

A few days later as expected, Abagail was in the Taxi on the way to the airport sipping her coffee and reading the newspaper which she would take on the plane with her in the event some dude or lady tried talking with her she would read the newspaper.

Abagail always took those 6:30 A.M. flights if she was heading to the East Coast and because of her stature, she was always booked on non-stop flights to her ultimate destination, so she arrived at a decent hour. In some cases, she would meet her business associate later for Happy Hour. She charged the drinks on her company credit card which then became an entertainment tax write-off. Depending on her destination, sometimes she would meet up with Pierre a French man who liked doing boom-boom with her and she liked the way he knocked the rims off her tires. Poor Chester had nowhere near the prowess of Pierre who was one of those guys who liked kissing the wrong end of a woman.

Today there would be no Happy hour or Pierre since Abagail was traveling to a different city to meet the stoic Mr. Bigelow. Mr. Bigelow was almost grandfatherly like person and Mrs. Bigelow wore the pants in the family. The meeting scheduled for 9:00 A.M. the next morning would be all business and professional. Afterwards, at home that following evening, Mr. Bigelow would tell Mrs. Bigelow all about it and how sweet and intelligent Abagail was who knew how to pour on the right type of charm for the right person.

They say you can't judge a book by it's cover. Abagail proved that repeatedly.

The following day after meeting with Mr. Bigelow, Abagail went back to her hotel where she had them store her luggage after she checked out like a lot of high-end clients do who do not plan on spending another night. She then took a taxi to the Airport and went to her next city on the East Coast where she would run into her Casanova and since she hadn't had sex in a while, she was highly vulnerable to his techniques as he made Pierre seem like a Boy Scout.

~~~~~~
~~~~~~

Chapter Four

DOCTOR FOSTER'S VISIT

As soon as Abagail was gone, Chester text messaged Doctor Foster: Abagail had gone out of town on a business trip, and he could come over to the house. Chester would wait for Doctor Foster's arrival then take him to Ski Beach with Brooklyn to show how they started out their day.

Doctor Foster and Felicia were in business attire suit and dress and didn't mind walking around the park dressed as such after Chester said it would be a short walk today just a little over a mile. Chester was recovering from knee pain and was taking it easy for a few days.

An hour after sending the text, the doorbell rang and there was Doctor Foster and Felicia. Chester invited them in and took them into the living room where he had staged all the items, he was taking with him and there was Brooklyn shaking his tail happy they were about to head to the park.

"How are you doing today, Brooklyn?" Doctor Foster asked.

"I'm doing fine sir," Brooklyn responded.

In a few minutes they were all in Chester's SUV heading over to Ski Beach to their usual parking spot. Everyone got out of the car and the two doctors were surprised at the number of pigeons and the fact a bunch of them landed on top of Chester's car.

Chester got the dog bowls out of the car with a sack of dog food and a bottle of water. Shortly after he put the dog food down and the water, the pigeons all approached as Brooklyn started eating. Chester then laid out bird food along the curb and gutter which the pigeons quickly flew too and began an eating frenzy.

"I must keep an eye out for the Park Rangers. They go nuts when they see you feeding the birds."

"You are not afraid they will suddenly appear?"

"No, they work bankers hours and usually do not show up until 11:00 to 12:00, especially on a week day in the winter. During Holidays in the summer, they may show up at 8:30 A.M. to make sure the crowd is behaving and call in the cops if necessary."

Right on cue came three squirrels who made a bee line up to Brooklyn's food bowl. As Doctor Foster was watching, taking it all in he heard Brooklyn say good morning to the squirrels. Chester poured in more dog food which the squirrels liked and did not show any fear at all towards Chester.

At the exact same time, the pink skin Drolupric Aliens in their cloaked ship a short distance away were also observing all this and quite interested in the appearance of the two additional well-dressed people. They also recorded Brooklyn saying good morning to the squirrels.

While Doctor Foster was observing he asked, "Brooklyn, do any of these squirrels have names? Brooklyn stopped eating for a moment and turned his head to Doctor Foster and said, "Yes, the squirrel closest to me is my friend. I gave him the name Dimash."

"What kind of name is Dimash?"

"Dimash is the singer papa loves to hear singing. I also like Dimash singing. Papa says Dimash is the top singer in the world now."

While Brooklyn was talking through the speaker box, he also moved his mouth as if he was sending the sound out his mouth. The Aliens were too far away to know that was the case and were startled as they thought the sound came from Brooklyn's mouth. And they knew Brooklyn's name and his owner was "Papa." The alien scientists started checking out the internet which they had mastered and often pulled huge amounts of information in their study of the planet and to facilitate their ISR operations.

The aliens soon found Dimash on YouTube and started listening to his singing and they were immediately impressed. The fact this dog loved Dimash singing was almost a come to Jesus' moment for the aliens as it now forced them to re-evaluate the entire animal kingdom beliefs. Unwittingly these Earth people had exposed an entire new mindset to the aliens who were culturally shocked and transfixed in their findings.

In due time the feeding was over and with treats for the other birds in his pockets, Chester led the group around the park and was quickly followed by the blackbirds and some seagulls.

Doctor Foster watched Chester put treats up in the trees so the Seagulls could not take them away from the blackbirds. An entire flock of blackbirds followed along, each waiting to get his treat.

Realizing the extraordinary finding of Brooklyn's fascination with the singer Dimash and the fact he had given one of the Squirrels a name, Doctor Foster asked, "Brooklyn, do any of these blackbirds have names?"

"Yes, Papa named one of them Rascal."

"Why did he name him Rascal?"

"If we run into the Mallard ducks you will see Rascal try to get between us and the Mallard ducks to force them away."

More revelations happened on the way. The biggest was that Brooklyn knew the names of the types of birds that had befriended the dynamic dual. As they got near the Gazebo on the North end of the park by the channel that went between Ski Beach and Crown Point, a couple large geese were there. Chester gave his strange bird whistle that had no rhyme or reason, but it was different, and the two geese started approaching. When they got up close ignoring Brooklyn who they knew quite well, Chester handed them treats they ate out of his hands.

Luck was with them today as three Mallards flew up directly to them a short while later and Rascal soon appeared and did his normal technique to try to scare the Mallards away. Chester had learned simply to give Rascal a big snack and he would fly away to a curb and gutter that had standing water to dip his food in while he ate it and as soon as he finished, he was back again threatening the Mallards. The Mallards seemed to really like Chester and Brooklyn and came right up to Brooklyn who said to them, "Good morning, Mallard ducks."

Today Rascal had agitated Brooklyn who then said, "Rascal, why don't you leave the Mallards alone?"

Rascal took that as a clue and flew away. Soon the group left the Mallards behind eating a pile of treats and worked their way back to the car and got in and drove home. The entire conversations had been recorded by the Aliens who were quite versed in the English language. Some of the Alien linguists had a better handle on English than most Americans.

The Aliens knew the man and his dog would be back in the morning like normal, and thus flew away to fly over Russia and China to do reconnaissance. They had picked up their interest in Russia when they discovered a source that told a writer who was penning her story on remote viewing about Russian Air Force Generals talking with Aliens. Apparently, they were having conversations with the Draco Gray Aliens.

After they returned home, Chester informed Doctor Foster and Felicia, "please have a seat and be comfortable. If you get hungry or thirsty, I have soda's, bottled water, beer, and wine in the refrigerator."

Chester turned the TV on and selected the National Geographic channel, then went to his computer terminal and started working, reading emails, and responding.

Doctor Foster pulled out his cell phone, stopped the recording using an app, then started another. Whether he got video or not didn't matter, he wanted the voice recording to go back later and transcribe and put it into Brooklyn's files back in his office to go over later with the research team if he uncovered anything interesting. Today, the experience at the park went beyond interesting. It not only transfixed the aliens secretly observing but it also gave Doctor Foster a lot to think about. One dog, Brooklyn had completely altered his value system. *Would it make him a better researcher?*

Doctor Foster stood up from the sofa he was sitting on which was offset perpendicular to the one Brooklyn sat facing the large screen TV direct and sat down next to Brooklyn.

The National Geographic show discussed ancient Egypt and the Egyptian hieroglyphics. During a TV Ad break Doctor Foster asked, "Brooklyn, what do you think about this show?"

"Sir, I'm most interested in the symbols they show that are about Aliens."

"You see Alien indicators?"

"Yes, some of the people are aliens and if you look carefully you can see their space ships."

"Do you know what any of that means?"

"I think the ancient Egyptians were showing how the Aliens helped build the pyramids."

Doctor Foster sat there stunned. Then he decided he didn't want this moment to be lost because it might reveal substantially more.

"Brooklyn, do you know about Aliens?"

"Yes sir, I see them on TV all the time in shows and when I go outside in the back yard at night with Papa, we look at the stars together and I see where they come from."

This was one of those moments in Doctor Foster's life he never expected to ever experience. A dog who knows about aliens and where they came from. It was quite astonishing to him.

Doctor Foster had not yet looked at the latest telemetry dump on the four dogs this morning and was curious and pulled out his cell phone and clicked on an APP that showed graphics similar to what they had shown Chester.

It was another one of those moments that really hit Doctor Foster in a major way. Brooklyn now had 1400 words in his lexicon. Doctor Foster had the means to drill down into the data with his cell phone APP and went right to the Lexicon and went to the bottom of the page which was the latest and new words and worked backwards from there. He was further almost shocked to see words like Gray Aliens, Spacecraft, Area-51, anti-gravity, light speed, several planet names and a few stars and famous nebulae such as "Horse Head, Cat's Eye," and the James Webb Space telescope. The audio was recorded in the background even though he was using this other APP.

Doctor Foster then asked a few probing questions. "Brooklyn, do you know about the James Webb Space Telescope?"

"Yes sir, I was looking at images it recently provided."

"Brooklyn what did you think about those images?"

"Sir, they were awesome."

Doctor Foster then had an emotional spike like he never felt before.

He knew there were a lot of people on this planet that had no idea the James Webb space telescope existed or the fantastic imagery it was providing NASA and the ESA.

Felicia was taking it in as well. This was an extraordinary moment for her as well.

"Brooklyn how often do you watch TV?"

"Sir, I watch TV while papa is working and with him in the evenings when Papa channel surfs and looks at other shows."

"What about when Abagail is home, what do you watch?"

"All her shows are dumb; I do not watch any of them."

Soon it was lunch time and Chester said, "I'm getting hungry, I'm going to order some pizza, are you guys interested?"

"Sure, I'll have some pizza." Doctor Foster said and smiled.

Felicia added in, "Sounds good."

Now Brooklyn surprised them. "I wish Papa would let me eat the pizza instead of the dog food."

"Pizza is not healthy for dogs," Doctor Foster responded.

"I know, but dog food tastes like garbage in comparison. Papa only lets me have just a little pizza if I eat all my dog food."

Doctor Foster raised his eyebrows and thought *hmmmmmmm.*

A while later they were all enjoying pizza, washing it down with cabernet sauvignon wine while Brooklyn regrettably ate his dog food and hoped papa would reward him. As soon as Brooklyn finished his dog food he said, "Papa, I finished all the dog food, can I have a piece of pizza please?"

Chester pulled off a piece of pizza and put it into Brooklyn's dog food bowl and he immediately ate it, drank some water and walked over and hopped up on the sofa and started watching TV again. After a while the three adults had enough pizza and Chester cleaned off the table but left the bottle of wine in case they wanted more. Chester then went back to his computer terminal and continued working.

Thirty minutes later Brooklyn said, "Papa I need to go outside and poop."

"Alright."

Doctor Foster and Felicia followed Chester and Brooklyn out the back door and into the back yard. Brooklyn went over to an area where the landscaping had crushed rocks and did his business there making it easy for Chester to clean up with the small plastic bag then dump it into the trash container on the side of the house.

The three adults then mingled in the back yard and watched Brooklyn go to the steel bar fence in the back yard where he could look through and see the valley below that was teeming with life. He had done this since he was a young pup and met some of the animals including rabbits and Quail. In the evenings the Quail would walk up to the steel fence and eat some of the bird food laid out for them. They knew Brooklyn all the way from his puppy days and had no fear of him, and soon a rabbit he knew came up to the fence.

Doctor Foster approached Brooklyn who was looking at the rabbit about five feet away eating on some of the vegetation. Doctor Foster asked Brooklyn, "Do you know this rabbit?"

"Yes sir, that's Bulldozer."

"Why did he get the name Bulldozer?"

"See across the canyon those houses?"

"Yes."

"That used to be natural vegetation, then one day people came in with bulldozers and started moving the dirt down into the valley and built those houses down at the bottom. Papa was upset watching all that and when he saw I was friends with the rabbit he told me its name would be Bulldozer."

Between the wine and Brooklyn's statements, Doctor Foster decided he needed to leave and go back to the office where he wanted to write down a bunch of notes based on everything that unfolded and said, "Chester, I think we saw enough for today. I want to go back to the office and do some work. We'll be back in the morning."

"Sure doctor. Let me walk you to your car."

Doctor Foster and Felicia had an interesting conversation on the way back to the office.

"Nigel, you seem kind of detached at the moment."

"Yes, Felicia and I'm glad you are driving because I'm thinking about some things I'm going to write back in the office."

"Do you think we will eventually have other dogs like Brooklyn in our study?"

"Oh yes, and now I'm not sure society is ready for it."

"What do you mean by that?"

"Based on our experience with Brooklyn we now know dogs are a lot smarter than we imagined. Think about all the other dogs watching a lot of TV and learning like Brooklyn. Without the chip implant we would never know."

"Will this affect our operation as we now have it going?"

"We don't have any choice. If we ever want to get to the point of helping stroke victims, we must do this. But we also should know we need to be prepared for consequences."

"Such as?"

We may also have to step up our security because I think there may be groups or individuals out there who will not approve of what we are doing."

"Even though we are doing it so that someday in the future we can help people that suddenly have a horrible life due to their brain injury?"

"Unfortunately, people that have been thoroughly indoctrinated by clerics and certain academia, will feel threatened because we could throw a monkey wrench into their business."

"It's good that Chester is keeping Brooklyn's ability very confidential to the point he will not even inform his wife."

"Tomorrow when we visit Chester, I'm going to convey to him why it's necessary to keep this matter confidential with us because he and Brooklyn could become victims if the public discovers them."

"What about the other three owners?"

"If we start to see a trend in their lexicon like Brooklyn's we'll have to bring them in right away for consultation."

The next day was similar. Aliens observed, all the animals were evident. Brooklyn was approached by the squirrel Dimash. The squirrel Dimash gave a friendly gesture to Brooklyn who turned and licked the squirrel who seemed to enjoy it. As the group left to walk around the park, Doctor Foster watched the Squirrel who stood there on his back legs and watched them leave. This action further elevated Doctor Foster as well as the Aliens who had done facial recognition on him and Felicia and now knew he was part of Microneural Therapeutics Research Inc.

By the end of the day, the Drolupric Aliens researched Microneural Therapeutics Research Inc. and copied all their files which was time consuming, but they got it all and Artificial Intelligence on the spacecraft started analyzing the data and thanks to the fantastic graphics Microneural Therapeutics Research Inc. data scientists had created, the Drolupric Aliens now knew the secrets behind Brooklyn. The dog now provoked even more attention than before. Russia and China suddenly were not as interesting topic as Brooklyn to the aliens. The aliens reduced ISR missions and started total surveillance on Brooklyn, including following them home or wherever they went.

By the end of the second day, Doctor Foster said to Felicia, "I have enough information now to keep me busy for several weeks. We can put off any more visits for a while as I go through all the recordings and make all the notes I want to record."

"What are we going to tell the team?"

"We will have a meeting tomorrow afternoon with the six individuals involved in Brooklyn's chip insertion activities."

The fact the researchers didn't want to visit the next day was fine with Chester because he had a carpenter over to install a dog access for Brooklyn so he could let himself outside whenever he wanted to urinate or simply enjoy the back yard and socialize with his growing numbers of animal friends.

It took all day. The carpenter contacted the home builder who was willing to share certain plans so the carpenter would not have to tear into the side of the house and damage it while looking for a good area to install the access. By supper time it was finished, and the Carpenter had gone with a big smile because Chester told him he would be giving him a substantial tip for finishing it in a day and doing a quality job.

Now with just the two present Chester explained to Brooklyn, "This is how you can go outside in the back yard if you need to go without waking me up or if you want to go out while I'm working." Brooklyn was soon quite versed at operating the access including unlocking it and relocking it when he returned. It was too small for a human to crawl through, but to have it lockable made Chester happy especially if he were gone for a few days.

The modification to the house could not have come at a better time because Chester was notified by his employer, he would have to take a business trip, fly out of town and come back the following evening. It was all on the West Coast, so he didn't have to reset his biological clock like Abigail had too all the time, which seemed to make her irritable and greatly reduced their love life. Unfortunately, Chester didn't know the real root cause, Pierre and another Casanova knocking the rims off Abagail's tires.

Brooklyn wasn't too happy to be left home alone with Abagail. But he realized Chester would only be gone for a short while.

~~~~~~

The following day, Doctor Foster and Felicia had the meeting with the six individuals involved with Brooklyn. They all knew about Brooklyn's lexicon since they observed it every day, and like Doctor Foster they too were astonished.

This was just a verbal discussion, no eye candy, or presentations.

"The main purpose of this meeting is to bring you all up to date on developments and also to discuss security arrangements and precautions we all must take moving forward."

The six researchers were all proud of their contributions to the future of helping stroke victims. But the one thing none of them counted on was these developments and concerns.

Doctor Foster joked, "Up to now the robot factory in Japan that builds all those new humanoid sex robots is the most heavily guarded building on the planet. If we are not careful and we let too much of this information get out, we will surpass them in security measures we'll have to make."

Doctor Foster then discussed a Gorilla a researcher had to take into hiding over death threats because the Gorilla had a vocabulary using sign language of a school age child.
~~~~~~

He also stated, "Concerning the three other dogs, we asked the owners to come in for briefings on enhanced security measures and also lessons learned with Brooklyn if they want to expand the dog's lexicon."

The world just got more complicated for Microneural Therapeutics Research Inc. But none of this could have been predicted.

~~~~~~

Abagail was home for one day before Chester left so he could show here where the dog food was and the black plastic bags to pick up the dog poop in the back yard but also added, "I'm going to be gone just a couple days, I can pick it all up when I get home."

He then showed the dog access he had installed and said, "Brooklyn knows how to go outside, and use take care of business. He's fully house trained. He'll sleep on the couch at night. If you don't want to watch TV, put on National Geographic, he likes that show."

The next day when Chester went out to hop in a cab to go to the airport, Brooklyn's front feet were up on the windowsill watching him go. It was a sad day for Brooklyn but at least they got over to Ski Beach and fed the birds and were back in time for Chester to catch his flight. Chester overfed Brooklyn with left over pizza meat mixed in with his dog food. In case Abagail didn't feed him well, he was stuffed to last him a while. He had the food and water dish placed in the usual location in the kitchen by the dog access door with water in it and informed Abagail, "Only give Brooklyn bottled water. I don't want him to get sick drinking the city trash."

Timing could not be more perfect for Abagail. Mr. Parker at her company was always trying to get in her pants and he could help her get promoted. With Chester gone for a few days, she could invite Parker over, do the horizontal tango and earn a few chips for a promotion.

Abagail also knew something Parker didn't know, if he crossed her, she knew where he lived and would make sure she had pictures of him having sex with her to show his wife.
~~~~~~

She would then send it in email to everyone in the company which means Parker would be fired on the spot for having sex with a subordinate. In the corporate world if you ever dip your pen in company ink be prepared for situations you never planned on.

That evening after work, Parker followed Abagail home and parked in front and went via her garage into the house with her. Abagail had Parker so horned up, it would be easily to call him a dog as he wanted to try a woman with a perfect body, beautiful face and boobs that made his wife look like a dog.

Brooklyn was sitting on the couch watching Ancient Aliens when Abagail brought Parker into the home. They had just come from happy hour at a bar and were pre-lubricated. Abagail took Parker up to her bedroom stripped down and amazed parker who suddenly had an erection like he had not had for years. In due time they were doing the horizontal tango with no protection and Parker was soon giving his multitude of seeds to Abagail then they collapsed.

In about 30 minutes the Weasel Parker got up and put his clothes back on and helped himself to the door like a scared rabbit. The door had been left open and Brooklyn watched every bit of it. He was amused and because Abagail said the phrase, "You fuck so well," Brooklyn was now in search of what meant.

The following day Doctor Foster was shocked when one of the six researchers said the word "fuck" was now in Brooklyn's lexicon.

Brooklyn was a smart dog and had watched Chester punch all the buttons on the remote. After Abigail left for work the next day, Brooklyn went channel surfing and found one that answered questions he knew about, just like google. Brooklyn was quite good at manipulating the TV remote and was soon on that channel discovering the essence of fucking.

In about two hours Brooklyn figured out Abagail had fornicated with Parker and was not a trustworthy wife. That grew the divide between Brooklyn and Abagail that would come to a head soon enough.

A couple words that soon showed up in the telemetry of Brooklyn's lexicon included cheating and infidelity. Now Doctor Foster was really interested.

About 30 minutes before Chester arrived home, Abagail had been cruel to Brooklyn all day long and after a couple stiff drinks actually said, "I don't want a dog here so next time Chester goes on another trip I'm taking you to the dog pound and dropping you off."

Brooklyn had enough of Abagail. He could not stand the "cheater" and against Chester's direction responded.

"Abagail, you are a cheater. I watched Parker fucking you. When Chester gets home I'm going to inform him what you did."

Abagail slightly intoxicated went ballistic and soon went to the Kitchen and grabbed a butcher knife and came after Brooklyn yelling, "I'm going to kill you mut!"

Brooklyn quickly made it out the dog access and the door on the fence to the back yard was wide open because Abagail was so delinquent.

In a few more minutes Abagail was chasing Brooklyn down the blook yelling "I'm going to kill you."

The entire neighborhood saw it, including Chester when the Taxi pulled up.

Abagail was never going to be able to catch Brooklyn, but she tried, nevertheless.

"What are you doing!" Chester yelled at Abagail who suddenly froze in her tracks. She was a mad woman and Chester knew it. And he also knew something transpired between Abagail and Brooklyn.

Abagail also now knew there was more to Chester than she realized and *the fact he had a talking dog was surreal.*

Hand me the knife and us go home and talk about it."

Abagail was worked up more than she had ever been in her lifetime and that talking dog she hated knew she had cheated and could inform Chester. She realized the game was up and handed Chester the knife and they went home with the entire block now talking about it.

Soon they were home and a come to Jesus moment transpired.

Abagail the congenital liar gave the story that Parker had promised her a *promotion over sexual favors.*

"Give me parker's phone number."

"What are you going to do?"

"Call him."

"That will cause me a lot of problems with my company."

"Give me his number now or I'll meet him in the parking lot of your company in the morning and deal with him."

Abagail was so messed up about that time glaring at the dog that had just overturned the apple cart. She gave him the number.

Chester called the number. Parker answered it and was a little alarmed when he saw the caller I.D.

"Can I help you?"

"Yes, put on the speaker phone and call your wife to the phone and if you don't, I will be soon cutting your dick off."

Parker was now super animated, but he knew what he had just done and Abagail's husband had found out and he knew he was in deep shits. His wife was right there looking at him noticing he was sweating and acting strange after coming home late.

Parker thought he could give his wife a bullshit story later and said "Okay, and put on the speaker phone and said, I got it on speaker phone and my wife is here.

"Mrs. Parker are you there?" Chester asked.

"Yes, I'm here what do you want?"

"Are you aware your husband fucked my wife yesterday?"

Mrs. Parker was speechless and could not reply and Chester assumed this would happen and continued even though she did not respond.

"Mrs. Parker you are an innocent victim. Your husband is a creep and I do not appreciate he fucked my wife so she could get a promotion. If he ever gets near my wife again, I will personally cut his dick off, do you understand?"

It was total silence and Abagail was crying because she knew she had just destroyed her marriage and her reputation in the company. All that hard work was now for nothing.

"Parker come back to the phone since your wife is not talking, unless I hear a response from her, I may cut your dick off in the company parking lot in the morning."

Parker was in pure panic and yelled, "Say something!"

"We will discuss this. I'm very sorry." Mrs. Parker than hung up the cell phone.

Abagail turned and went up the the bedroom and locked the door and cried herself to sleep. God help her if Chester ever found out about Pierre or her other Casanovas.

The evening turned into business as usual, the dynamic dual sleeping on the couch with Abagail drugged out and sleeping by herself.

At 6:00 A.M. sharp the dynamic dual was out of the house on their way to Ski Beach.

The aliens had made their decision they were going to abduct the dynamic dual and discover more about Brooklyn.

After feeding the pigeons and the squirrels, Chester and Brooklyn were on their march around the park when it happened. The north end of the park by the Gazebo was empty. Nobody was there. Suddenly a spaceship uncloaked in front of Chester and Brooklyn and Aliens came down and hit both Chester and Brooklyn with a blue ray which incapacitated them. They were hauled aboard the spacecraft. Soon the Aliens were airborne with their precious cargo and by the following day were long away from the solar system as they continued their journey to the Drolupric Empire.

Across from Ski Beach about 200 yards is Crown Point. All along that drive has no homes on one side of the street nearest Ski Beach. People living in those homes have an unobstructed view of Ski Beach and the Gazebo area. Several of those homes have bird watchers who have cameras set up on tripods where they can zoom in on the birds, especially the migratory birds that were here this time of year. One of those people, Barry Flagler, was in the process of photographing a flock of migratory birds and observed the space craft uncloak. It was a come to Jesus' moment for Barry who believed in Aliens and UFO's and knew with his camera he could shut up his neighbor Bill who always gave him crap about his UFO beliefs.

Barry's digital camera had enough memory in it to take 1000 pictures before he had to download them. His camera had been recently downloaded so the memory was mostly empty and had only taken a couple pictures of that area a few minutes ago. Barry was clicking away and saw the men approach Chester and Brooklyn and zap them with the blue rays. Barry captured the attack and the Aliens carrying the dog and the person up in their ship then took off.

Barry knew he had something hot and figured it was unlikely this time in the morning there were a lot of people filming Ski Beach since it was early, and the lighting conditions were not ideal.

Barry took his camera off the tripod, walked over to his desk, hooked up a USB cable to it and started downloading all the pictures to his personal computer. Even though the encounter between the pink skin Drolupric Aliens was very short in time sequence, Barry using a feature on his camera got several hundred images. He didn't quite know what he was going to do with those images, quite frankly nobody would believe him, and he realized many would claim they were CGI technology images or photoshopped.

Barry would expose the pictures to the public when he figured out how he was going to do it. In the meantime, he would hold back and wait and see if someone else captured those images so when he released his images the story would already be out there and people would not be able to criticize him. He also realized there could be some money in those photos if nobody else got lucky and captured those images.

~~~~~~

The first group that discovered something had transpired Doctor Foster at Microneural Therapeutics Research Inc. when the telemetry ended. Doctor Foster sent text messages to Chester that day and got no replies. He then called Chester's cell phone and got no response.

Abagail went to work that morning fearing a hostile environment with Parker knowing that Chester had threatened him and most likely caused damage to his marriage with his conversation. She felt relieved when she discovered Parker did not show up for work and his boss was concerned because it was not like Parker not to show up especially when he had some important work to do with a few of their customers on contracts.

Abagail was quite apprehensive, wondering if she had just arranged for herself to get divorced. Chester was a no-nonsense type of person and now she knew the most bizarre thing. That mut could talk and most likely observed Parker going to town on her. Because of that dog she might end up divorced and her living standards
~~~~~~

would take a dip. Now she also had to worry about Parker going to his boss and have her removed out of the company. She was on shaky ground on many levels. She could not deny she didn't have an affair with Parker now. She was grateful that Chester didn't know about Pierre and the Casanova. If that was ever revealed divorce would be eminent.

~~~~~~

The next day after not being able to contact Chester, Doctor Foster drove to Chester's house to find out why he wasn't answering his phone calls and why the link went down. Did he remove the batteries out of the electronics box on the dog collar device?

Abagail was now worried. Chester had not been around now for almost two days. When she tried calling his cell phone the message was that person was not available. Something weird was going on because he didn't take any clothes or anything and the computer he needed for work sat there in suspended mode.

Then suddenly the doorbell rang. A nice man in a suit was there and Abagail was suddenly sensitive, and she slowly opened the door and asked the gentleman who had a lady behind him, "Can I help you?"

"I'm Doctor Foster and this is my research associate Felicia. We would like to talk with Chester."

"May I ask what's this about?"

"It's about his dog Brooklyn."

"He's not home."

"Do you know when he'll be home? Would it be possible for us to see Brooklyn."

"You mean the talking dog?"
~~~~~~

"You know about that?"

"Yes, that dog may have wrecked my marriage."

"Do you know when Chester will be home, we really need to talk to him."

"I have no idea where Chester and Brooklyn are. I've not seen either one of them in about two days."

"Do you have any idea where they went?"

"No and his cell phone isn't working I tried to call him."

Doctor Foster could see the tears coming down on Abagail and knew something bad might have happened and he was fearful. Their worst nightmare they just had security discussions about may have already struck before they had time to put in place necessary security to protect the dog.

"Do you have any idea where they possibly might have gone?"

"Usually, they leave and go to Ski Beach in the morning. They may have gone there and have come up missing since."

"Have you considered filing a missing person's report with the police?"

"I just had a terrible event in my life. Chester discovered I had an affair with my superior at work and he may have simply left.

I don't know what to do."

"Your name is Abagail, right?"

"Yes."

"If that's the case I think it's even more important you contact the police. The result of your adultery might have led to terrible consequences. We have several million dollars invested in Brooklyn. We need to find out what happened. We can contact the authorities, but it will not carry the weight of your statements would have to the police. May we come in and help you get that process started?"

The tears were now flowing down like a river and Abagail said, "Sure come in."

In thirty minutes, Doctor Foster was talking with a police detective who only took interest in the case because Doctor Foster from Microneural Therapeutics Research Inc. was involved and because of the underlying situation with the infidelity issue, it might be possible Chester committed suicide.

In short order the detective contacted Chester's employer who was also looking for him and his sudden absence was totally out of character.

The detective and several police officers in uniform went to the last place Chester might have gone and had a description of his car and license plate number.

Within five minutes they spotted Chester's car parked at Ski Beach. There were a couple homeless guys parked there who Chester had seen quite often and was polite towards. One of them walked around the park picking up trash and assisted the maintenance crew often. In return for his help, they never called the cops on him and was allowed to sleep in the park which he preferred.

The detective stumbled across that homeless person. He had a recent picture of Chester which Doctor Foster provided from their security camera recordings.

The homeless man was a little apprehensive when he saw the cops but he had been arrested a few times here at Ski Beach and thought the worst they could do is take him down to the city jail, feed him a few decent meals provide him with a shower to clean up and donated clothes members of the community always made available to the police when they dealt with the homeless population.

"Excuse me sir may I ask you a couple questions." The Detective said, then pulled out his badge to show it was an official inquiry.

"Sure, what do you want?"

"Do you know the driver of this vehicle?"

"Yes, I see him every day walking with his dog."

"How long has this car been parked here?"

"It's been there a couple days."

"Do you find that unusual it's been here that long?"

"Yes, he's never left his car here before. He comes here and is always gone in a few hours."

"When was the last time you saw the driver?"

"Probably a couple days now. The same day he left it here."

"Alright, thank you for your assistance."

"No problem."

The homeless guy continued walking towards the restrooms where he was going to take care of business.

The detective directed one of the officers in uniform, "Get a locksmith over here so we can open the car up and look for any clues that may be left behind." The detective felt bad that he might find a suicide note and they were near deep water, the person could have jumped in with weights. They would also bring in divers to look around.

While the detective was thinking about his game plan, he got a phone call from the watch officer back at headquarters and informed him there was a guy over at Crown Point with a story about Aliens abducting a man and his dog. The Police Sargent on the phone chuckled and said something to the effect another crackpot and since the detective was in the neighborhood could he swing by and visit the man who claims he had a lot of pictures of the abduction.

"Text me the address please."

"Sure, no problem."

After the detective hung up on the watch officer he turned to the police officers in uniform and said, "I'm going to go drive over to a residence and speak with a person who may have seen something. You guys wait here for the locksmith. Get the car opened, use gloves so you don't put your fingerprints on any evidence."

The senior police officer who also was a forensics expert said, "It's going to be a while for the locksmith to get here. You might be back by the time he opens up the car."

"Alright see you in a bit."

The detective was soon over at the man's home and showed him the badge and said, "I'm here investigating the situation you reported."

"Sure, come on in I'll show you my pictures on the computer."

"Before you show me the pictures. Is there any chance they might match this person?" The detective showed the man a recent picture of Chester.

"That's him alright," the man stated nonchalantly.

Soon the detective was looking at the pictures with utter fascination. He knew one thing for sure. The man was telling the truth and now he knew what happened to Chester and the dog.

"Can you do me a favor?" the detective asked.

This man has a wife and a family and he's missing. Now we know why. It's going to be a painful episode for his wife because she thinks she may have driven him to suicide by her infidelity. As a human being I'm asking you not to talk about this with the public until our investigation is over. It's going to be heart wrecking as it is already."

"I understand and I will keep this confidential."

"I appreciate your bravery in making this report. A lot of people would receive ridicule for doing that. But your report will help bring closure to the tragedy, especially if the Aliens do not return the man."

"Understand the significance of it. That's why I filed the report."

"Another thing I'm going to warn you about if you have not already figured it out. This is a rather incredible discovery. There probably has never been a recorded Alien abduction before. When I report back to my superior this information, due to internal protocols and agreements we have with the Feds, we have no choice but to call in the FBI. They may soon interview you and possibly confiscate your images. I would guess they will be here in a couple hours. In the event they confiscate this I recommend you make a copy and hide it good so that later if you choose to make a public disclosure you will have your evidence."

"That's a good idea and I appreciate you believing and trusting me."

"It's sad but we are both dealing with the same situation. We are lucky you caught it so there will be no doubt what happened and proves there was no domestic violence or crime associated with his disappearance."

"Glad to help out."

The police detective pulled out his business card and said, "After you make your own personal copies, would you mind sending me pictures of the Aliens zapping him with the blue beam and a few of the pictures of them carrying him and the dog up into the spacecraft?"

"No problem, sir, I will send those images right away."

"Thank you."

The detective drove back over to Ski Beach and the locksmith had just unlocked the car. With rubber gloves on, the detective flipped open the back of the SUV and saw nothing of interest then did a good job of looking for anything that might be of interest to the investigation. Nothing was apparent.

He then turned to one of the uniformed police officers and said, "Have this towed to police impound and schedule a forensics team to give it a good going over."

"Sure boss."

~~~~~~

Doctor Foster and Felicia both decided they would wait with Abagail for a while giving her emotional support and be there to help interface with the police if necessary.

Abagail made about an hours' worth of statements to a police officer who recorded it all with his body camera which sent it live real time to police headquarters. Technicians at the headquarters reported in his ear bud from time to time the video feed was good so he didn't have to re-ask any questions.

About the time the interview was over, the detective was back and informed Doctor Foster, Felicia, and Abagail, "I know what happened to your husband. Do you want me to tell you in private or do you want Doctor Foster to hear it at the same time with you?"
~~~~~~

"Sure, go ahead and tell me. I prefer Doctor Foster and Felicia to be here when you tell me."

"This is going to sound rather bazar, but it's the truth and as I was driving up to the house just now, I received some of the photographs taken that show what happened to your husband. It's all true what I'm going to tell you as you will soon discover looking at these pictures."

In a few minutes, everyone in the room was utterly stunned!

~~~~~~

Just like the police detective predicted, two hours later FBI agents rang the photographer's doorbell and confiscated the removeable hard drive. As they left the house the photographer had that poker face on and made a plea for his images back even though he knew he had made secret recordings and had already passed on some pictures to the police detective.

Abagail was happy because even though they zapped Chester and Brooklyn with the blue beams, they were simply abducted and taken away. *The Aliens were probably interested in the talking dog.*
~~~~~~

Chapter Five

TRAVELING TO THE STARS

The stun gun knocked Chester out for 12 hours and Brooklyn for about 14 hours. By the time they regained consciousness, they were on the mothership heading out of the solar system as the survey and ISR team had determined they obtained sufficient information to return home to their Empire worlds.

The humanoid Aliens looked remarkably like humans on planet Earth except they all had pink skin. They had three types of hair coloring. The predominant one was red hair. The other two types of hair coloring as dark gray and dark blue. Other than that, their bodies were almost identical to humans including larger breasts for females. Their sexual organs were also identical and some of the humans abducted in the past became mates with pink skin Drolupric Aliens. In due time they discovered life was much more pleasant in the Drolupric Worlds and when offered return to Earth, they declined. It was a no brainer to them. Drolupric worlds had no wars, stayed out of other Empires business, had virtually no pollution, more modern and practical architecture with much more advanced transportation methods. Earth people could double or triple their life spans here.

When Chester regained consciousness, he found himself in restraints and a female Drolupric with dark blue hair standing over him and a few more in the large room. Brooklyn was also restrained with a dog muzzle on him preventing any possible bytes.

The female Drolupric as well as most of the away team spoke English fluently. Translators were not required.

"Good morning, Chester. My name is Tasha."

"How do you know my name?" Chester asked.

"Chester, we monitored you for quite a few days. We had plenty of opportunity to record your name, especially when you were with Doctor Nigel Foster and Felicia." Tasha answered looking very analytical.

"You know about them too?" Chester asked.

"We have much more advanced technology. We recorded all their information from their computers and know everything they do," Tasha reported.

"If I may be so bold to ask, why was I abducted?" Chester asked.

"Chester you really do not mean much to us. The only reason why we brought you with us is because we think Brooklyn would be in much better condition if he's with you," Tasha responded.

"You abducted me because of Brooklyn?" Chester asked.

"Yes, Brooklyn revolutionized society on planet Earth with the awareness he gave Doctor Foster and Microneural Therapeutics Research Inc. staff, Brooklyn has also inspired research scientists on this spacecraft."

"How exactly is that?" Chester asked.

"Until we came across Brooklyn, we had no idea the level of intelligence dogs could acquire. Now we know its extraordinary."

"What are you going to do with Brooklyn?"

"We will do some microsurgery and see how the chip is interfaced with the transducer to his none-visual photo receptors in the center of his brain."

"And after that?"

"Your Earth educational systems are obsolete and inferior. It's amazing that Brooklyn was able to learn as quickly as he did simply by watching TV. On your planet you have 8 methods of learning. On Drolupric Empire worlds we have several other methods available."

"Such as?" Chester asked.

Tasha looked at Chester in a way that gave a hint of irritation that he was asking too many questions, but as a researcher she knew she had to answer them to get his cooperation which would help them more quickly develop a rapport with Brooklyn.

"For Brooklyn we will attempt to use our most efficient teaching tool and that utilizes neural sonification's where we target certain parts of his brain and dump large quantities of information in it then wire up that information to more efficiently utilize."

"Is there any danger to Brooklyn?"

"No physical danger, but as he grows wiser and has a much higher I.Q. he will certainly behave differently. His puppy days are long over with."

"Tell me about this microsurgery you indicated a while ago."

"After we get back to our planet and give Brooklyn a chance to run around and get exercise and recalibrate his thoughts to the new reality, he will find himself in, we'll schedule the surgery as we want him in the best possible shape when we do it."

"Alright exactly what will you do to him?"

"First of all, he will be sedated to the point he's almost in a coma. Then we will have Brooklyn X-rayed and look over the images we got from Microneural Therapeutics Research Inc. computer database. We have an ultra-small probe that is about the size of that your hypodermic needs on Earth are used to administer vaccines and therapeutics. We will drill a very small hole in Brooklyn's skull and send this probe down inside it to view the transducer placement so that when we do implants on dogs here, we'll then be able to more precisely know how to achieve what Doctor Foster did with Brooklyn on future dog chip implants."

"And my role is to simply keep Brooklyn happy?"

"Based on our animal psychiatrists' reports, Brooklyn views you as his father so when he calls you Papa, he feels you are his Papa." "I had him since he was a pup, we are close."

"It's our intentions that no harm will come to Brooklyn, but you must understand, he has done what no other animal has ever done before, and he also has changed our opinions on animal intelligence quite an amount by his development."

"As long as you don't hurt Brooklyn in any way, I will go along with you."

"Are you hungry or do you need to use the toilet?"

"Yes, I need to go to the toilet."

"Follow me and I'll show you how to use it. I've saved my bowel movement so that I can teach you. It's all part of living in space on long missions."

"Alright, lead the way."

Tasha went a short distance and a door materialized out of a wall. And she went through, and Chester followed her and the wall closed to a seamless opaque wall that had no real indication anything was there.

"How did you know this is the toilet and that wall would become a door?"

"When we go outside look above the door and you will see a small green light to mark a door entrance. Artificial Intelligence is always watching you so if you have a question simply ask it and if you are by yourself with Brooklyn, Artificial Intelligence will answer you. If you want, you can tell Artificial Intelligence to appear it will and can take on any personality you want."

"Does that include my wife Abagail?"

"Certainly, if that is what you want, but since you will soon be a celebrity with a talking dog, I assure you women far more attractive than Abagail will want to mate with you."

"Do you know how Abagail appears?"

"Yes of course, we had probes monitoring you inside and out of your home. We also know about Abagail's infidelity with Mr. Parker."

"You know about that too?"

"Yes, when Abagail was chasing Brooklyn through the neighborhood with the knife wanting to kill him, we would have intervened before she hurt Brooklyn."

"Why would you do that?"

"We had already determined we were going to take Brooklyn home with us to study."

"How would you have subdued her?"

"Same way we did you with the stun gun."

"Interesting."

"We are not modest like you Earth people are. There is nothing offensive to us about nudity. We only wear clothes to keep warm. On warm days people wear very little, but we do cover up our sexual organs so that we do not accidentally trigger a desire that could lead up to an act and a scandal."

Tasha then unzipped her flight suit and stepped out of it exposing her nudity. She then walked over to the pooper machine that was wrapped around her and then started its movement. It stretched and compacted her body which quicky allowed the green ooze to leave her anus into the collector and when the machine decided she had completed her bowl movement washed her bottom then blow dried it. She then stepped out of the machine revealing her nudity and perfect physical fitness that made Abagail seem like a cow.

She then put her flight suit on and said, "I know you Earth people like your privacy when you defecate. I'm going to leave the room. If you have any questions, artificial intelligence will coach you on how to do what I just did."

"Alright. Thanks."

A couple minutes after Tasha left the toilet, Chester was in the pooping machine getting his body stretched and compacted and soon felt his activity was far more comfortable and successful than what he experienced back at earth where sometimes he sat on the throne for 30 minutes feeling constipation. The pooping machine sent vibrations through his body and the movement with stretching and contraction allowed a more thorough emptying of the bowels. His bottom was soon washed and air dried as the machine's sensors knew Chester had completed his discharge.

Chester's bowel stools were also collected by the pooper machine to be studied by their scientists who had the responsibility to monitor his health.

Chester noticed the small green light above the door entry and walked towards it. As soon as artificial intelligence detected Chester's movement, the door suddenly materialized opening and Chester walked through it. Chester said to himself, "I wonder how that works?"

Chester then walked over to the padded table where Brooklyn laid.

Tasha asked, "Are you hungry, would you like some food?"

"Only slightly, I would like to wait until Brooklyn awakens, then we can eat together."

"All right, I will come back at that time with something for you to eat with Brooklyn."

"Thank you."

"In the meantime, I'm going to show you a holographic presentation as an introduction to Drolupric civilization. In the future if you see something you wish to experience, we can plan your participation."

"Thank you."

Tasha walked towards a wall that turned into a door and exited the room.

A moment later a holographic image appeared, and the announcer said, "Chester, the chair you are sitting on is a conformal chair that reclines and has a leg rest. If you want to recline and have the leg rest rise just lean back and we'll reposition it to the angle, we feel is best for your observation of the holograph."

"Thank you."

Soon Chester was repositioned and felt the vibration in the chair which had a built-in muscle relaxer. The holograph then started showing parts of the Drolupric civilization including its majestic tall buildings that stretched into the clouds, strange transportation devices, and the people and their dress. The narrator stated all the information in native Drolupric language followed by the English version. This was being done for Chester to start hearing the language and become accustomed to it.

Chester knew instinctively he and Brooklyn would always have escorts to translate for them. If he remained for quite a few years, no doubt he would pick up the Drolupric language. Chester was in for a big surprise because not only would Brooklyn receive neuronic sonification's, so would he, to learn the Drolupric language at about one hundred times faster than he would back on Earth.

All the major Drolupric customs were shown and discussed and one item that Chester was wanting to learn was the essence of their religions. If they do not have Christianity, Krsna Science, Buddhist pathway to enlightenment, Muslim, or Jewish law, then what did they have? He soon had his answer.

Drolupric had no formal religion and explained that after hundreds of civil wars and barbaric treatment of citizens by clerics of the past, all religion was banned. The Drolupric government simply said nobody living today knows how the universe was formed or why and past religions led to such tumultuous affairs, the government would spare society and instead teach moral and ethical behavior that allows cohesive coexistence and intellectual transcendence. Later, Chester would learn all the clerics were rounded up and executed and any entity that brought up religion was severely dealt with immediately.

Chester wasn't a bible thumper and quickly realized simply teaching moral and ethical behavior would benefit Earth a lot more than continuing the myths and fairy tells bestowed upon mankind by individuals who did so to control people. Most of the time those central religious figures on Earth had absolutely no belief in what they were teaching. But they knew how effective it was to control people with lesser minds.

In some cases, however, the disciples of those religions were such brainwashed individuals they believed their scriptures were perfectly true.

Chester remembered the time he was having dinner with his friend and the friend's brother, a Catholic priest. The priest got really upset when Chester said the Pope was an idiot, but he wanted to hear Chester's reason for stating that and Chester soon let the machine gun fly by explaining how the Pope was destroying the church by abandoning its Canon laws.

"In what way?" the priest asked.

Chester then sited how the Pope kissed the asses of the great purveyors of abortion. He then further said, *when was the last time the Pope came out with harsh words for the Pro-Abortion people and never spoke about homosexuality even though Leviticus was quite clear on the matter.*

The Catholic priest started cooling off when Chester said he had finished reading the Bhagavad Gita about the soul and abortion destroys an individual that already has a soul.

The Catholic priest then stated the Church's official doctrine is *life starts at conception since the newly conceived has all the DNA of both parents.* He then added Exodus 21:22 Says about Abortion:

This law relates to abortion in that it gives the example of a pregnancy ending prematurely. Basic to the statute is the assumption that the baby delivered prematurely has the same rights and protections under the law as an adult human being. That is, the fetus is a person.

Chester then said to the Catholic priest, "The Pope has never made negative statements about homosexuals and lesbians even though Leviticus 20:13 states: *If a man lies with a man as with a woman, they have both committed an abomination. They must surely be put to death; their blood is upon them. "If a man has sexual relations with a man as one does with a woman, both have done what is detestable.*"

"The fact the Pope never mentions Leviticus 20:13 is confirmation the Pope has inherently damaged the canon laws of the church and should step aside."

The Catholic Priest visiting San Diego for a week spent a lot of time at his brother's house and Chester's friend stated, "When we went home that night my brother sat for two hours writing notes about your conversation because he was unaware of the soul information you pointed out is stated in the Bhagavad Gita."

"Such as?"

"You implied, the Bhagavad Gita reports the soul is smaller than an atom and arrives in the person immediately up on conception. And according to Hindu scholar's that's why all abortions should be considered murder."

Chester's flashback soon ended as the narration of the spectacle unfolded and the imagery of spellbinding Drolupric Empire worlds consumed all his consciousness.

The presentation lasted almost two hours and suddenly some researchers came through the door that suddenly appeared on the wall and approached Brooklyn. Chester looked over and saw Brooklyn stirring and somewhat in a daze. He then looked at Chester and said, "Papa where are we?"

"Brooklyn do you remember we were at Ski Beach and an alien ship suddenly appeared and aliens came out of it and shot us with a blue light?"

"Yes, Papa I remember that."

"We are on their ship now."

"Just like on Ancient Aliens?"

"Yes, just like that."

Chester stood up and walked over to Brooklyn and petted him. One of the Drolupric scientists then asked, "Chester would you like something to eat now?"

"I suppose so."

That Drolupric scientist nodded at his assistant who immediately left then came back with a cart that had what appeared to be an aluminum cover. Two other Drolupric scientists came in carrying a contraption that quickly unfolded to a dinner table. A second chair was brought in for Brooklyn that was elevated and soon it was set. The food appeared like it came from Earth and typical of something that Chester would eat. The dog food looked identical to what Brooklyn normally ate.

Drolupric personnel also brought in a drink for Chester and a bowl of water for Brooklyn. Their surveillance must have been good because the bowl looked like Brooklyn's bowl he left back in the car. In fact, it was Brooklyn's. While Chester and Brooklyn were unconscious during the night, the ship returned to Ski Beach and using Chester's car keys unlocked the doors and pulled the dog food and serving bowels out of the back of the SUV. They had already analyzed the contents of the dog food and could easily make an improved version of it.

Chester's drink an elixir contained pleasurizers. The more he drank the better he felt.

To make Chester feel comfortable on the short trip back to the Drolupric Empire, they simply deposited teams of spies who went into restaurants and ordered takeout. They then returned to the cloaked ship which departed with more than enough food that Chester enjoyed for the short trip.

Scientists analyzed the contents of the food Chester ate and knew they could easily recreate it for him at his new residence.

Messages were sent ahead by the scientists explaining who they abducted and why. By the time the ship headed towards Tymasoara's secure Drolupric ISR base a team was prepared to meet Chester and his talking dog when they arrived a couple days later.

While aboard the ship, sophisticated monitors checked for dangerous pathogens that Chester might have brought along. As an added measure while on the ship, Chester was bathed in solutions that disinfected his exterior and while he was unconscious, blood samples returned negative results for any dangerous pathogens, so he was not required to go through a standard lengthy quarantine period the same results occurred for Brooklyn and with Chester's assistance, Brooklyn also was bathed.

As they approached Tymasoara, the capital city of the Drolupric Empire, just outside the atmosphere, Chester and Brooklyn were transferred to a shuttle as the mother ship was too large and fragile to go to the planet surface unless it was an emergency.

Inside the shuttle, Chester and Brooklyn were strapped into seats where they could observe a surveillance video of where yey were heading. Tymasoara the capital city of the Drolupric Empire was much like Kyoto Japan was, the cultural center of the empire.

Chester was amazed at the tall buildings and the architecture. His immediate thoughts were how almost identical to these buildings were just like the book cover of Isaac Asimov's Novel, "Robots and Empire." *Did Asimov somehow get to see it?*

The shuttle landed at the ISR complex which is a fenced off area next to the Tymasoara Space Port. As Chester was led off the shuttle with Brooklyn attached to a dog leash, they were met by four well-dressed individuals.

"Chester Toland, I'm Doctor Akssiar and these are my research associates. We are here to take you to your new residence where we will try to make life pleasant for you and at the same time gain as much insight into Brooklyn as we can."

Chester decided to lay his cards on the table right there and then with the formal reception committee.

"Doctor Akssiar, I'm pleased to meet you, but one question I have is: will I ever be allowed to return to Earth?"

"Mr. Toland, your final dispensation has not been determined at this time. Plus, as time goes by and you get acclimated with Drolupric society, you yourself may choose to not want to go back to planet Earth."

"Doctor Akssiar, if you were in my shoes, you would want the option to return to the society you grew up with. I'm sure you are aware by now a lot of information about me since you are here as an official receptionist, so you know I have a family left behind on Earth and a spouse who is probably in a mental state right now due to my sudden disappearance."

"Mr. Toland, I was not aware you were coming here until we received deep space neutrino communications a few days ago and reports from Doctor Tasha about the revelations with your dog Brooklyn. Thus, I had no involvement in bringing you here. I also do not have the authority to send you home. Those decisions must come from people far senior to me. The only thing I can do for you is to help make your transition to Drolupric society as seamlessly as possible, do the intended research with Brooklyn because we already know thanks to Brooklyn our ideas about animals are seriously obsolete."

"Who do I get to talk to so that I can plead my case to be returned to Earth?"

"Mr. Toland, I'm sure you are well aware that Drolupric scientists are not able to contain the news that a talking dog has arrived on this planet. There will be huge curiosity and no doubt people in higher places who can make such a determination will likely reach out to you and possibly even befriend you. I really suspect that in due time you will get your audience with the right person who could grant your request."

"Alright, I'm willing to wait for that opportunity, and I will cooperate, but at the same time I want you to know what is in my heart at this time, to one day return to my home, planet Earth."

"That's highly understandable, Mr. Toland. But for now, if you don't mind, we would like to take you to your new residence where we have refreshments and food for you and Brooklyn and we intended to have a question-and-answer session with six of our top scientists."

"Sure, lead the way."

Doctor Akssiar led the dynamic dual over to what appeared to be a Limousine. As soon as they were within ten feet of the car a door rotated upwards exposing half of that section of the passenger compartment.

A small ramp came down from the Limousine and Chester towing Brooklyn with a dog leash followed Doctor Akssiar and the other three researchers into the vehicle that had room for ten or more people. Thanks to the ramp, there were no major steps required as they simply walked into the transportation device that looked sleek and impressive. Everyone instinctively took seats in a U-shaped interior.

Chester found himself sitting directly across from a very beautiful woman wearing a lab coat and a seemingly short dress showing most of her legs and possibly a portion of her crotch. She also smiled as if there was some kind of attraction. As time passed Chester would discover his analysis of her body language conveyed the true reality, she felt attracted to this strange Alien being from a far-off solar system.

Chester had seen Skycars in the holographic briefings he received on the way to the Drolupric Empire but had no reason to believe he was in anything other than a Limousine Land Automobile. After everyone was seated and admonished to have their seat belts engaged by onboard artificial intelligence, the Sky Limousine took to the air.

From Chester's vantage point, he could see out of the Sky Limousine to a great extent and observe the city that shrank in size below them as they gained altitude. The Sky Limousine was soon vectored into a three-dimensional transportation corridor where Skycars, buses, freighters, and other major traffic components flew in perfect alignments of parallel paths and perfect separation.

Underground super computers controlled the Sky Limousine speed, altitude, and direction of and all the other sky traffic. The Drolupric Empire was a wireless society. You would not find any utility lines anywhere on the planet. All electricity was distributed underground from underground nuclear fusion reactors in the event of war or a massive solar flare like experienced on planet Earth during the 1859 Carrington Event.

***

Chapter Six

DUKE TINKTAR

As the Sky Limousine approached the nearby mountain foothills, it slowly curved out of the traffic pattern and was vectored on a private empty airspace and in a few minutes on the side of a mountain went into what appeared to be a well-lighted tunnel while softly contacting the road surface. At the end of the tunnel was an open space and what appeared to be a mansion. This was the home of Duke Tinktar, one of the oversight person's responsible for Drolupric Planetary Security Services. With all the other burdens in his life, he was now also responsible for making sure nothing bad happened to Brooklyn.

Duke Tinktar could be ruthless, but he was smart and fair to individuals as long as they didn't cross him. Dealing with spies and saboteurs required intricate knowledge and ability like Duke Tinktar exhibited to quickly analyze the data and make critical decisions promptly because explosions and loss of critical INTEL happens when someone of authority dilly dallies around.

Ancient Drolupric scholars wrote it was better to let 99 guilty men go free than to kill an innocent person due to a flawed investigation.

Duke Tinktar thought the opposite. He felt it was better to kill 99 innocent men than to let a spy or saboteur escape.
By and large the public thought Duke Tinktar received his power and authority over the Drolupric Planetary Security Services because his uncle was the emperor. The truth was the emperor knew he could

count on his nephew to prevent a coup or assassination. It would not be the first or last time a Drolupric Emperor was killed by one of their own including involvements with military officials who opposed a ruler that went against their better judgment.

Duke Tinktar was gone eighty percent of the time off to Empire planets where he personally had to handle matters. The Drolupric Planetary Security Services didn't want to expose the emperor to any involvement when he had to deal with traitors.

When the group exited the Sky Limousine, Duke Tinktar was there to meet them. He wanted to personally see the talking dog before he left to travel to Zeta Bantor to handle another one of those distasteful tasks that would deal with a traitor who sold out the Empire for pieces of gold that were not even a respectable amount.

The fact the traitor was cheap and easy, gave Duke Tinktar added enthusiasm to dump him alive in a razor teeth hog farm. The traitor was bound cut in several places with blood oozing out to create a feeding frenzy because the razor teeth hogs would smell the blood and they loved raw meat. The farmer was asked not to feed his hogs for several days to make sure they were nice and hungry.

Zeta Bantor was not a homogenous world like Tymasoara, the capital city of the Drolupric Empire where most of society were pink skinned. Zeta Bantor was split into four ethnic groups including plane skin, blue skin, green skin, and pink skinned individuals along with a dichotomy of hybrid mixtures of all those types of individuals. Organized crime on Zeta Bantor had pleasure centers scattered around the planet and the most notorious house of ill-repute was Madam Pang's Parlor. Duke Tinktar looked forward to visiting his friend Madam Pang. Even though Madam Pang was ten or more years older than her working girls, she earned enough credits to obtain the best plastic surgery in the Empire and looked 15 years younger than her real age.

Madam Pang a green skin woman like all those who worked for her liked Duke Tinktar and always looked forward to seeing him and pleasing him. Madam Pang always had a couple of young helpers with who helped prepare her for copulation with the Duke. She knew quite well that Duke Tinktar could close your business down with a simple order. She had to make sure he viewed her favorably.

Duke Tinktar rose to one of the most powerful men in the Drolupric Empire and he put fear in a lot of men's hearts. When he traveled some place like Zeta Bantor, Duke Tinktar always took plenty of firepower along with him including military ships to protect him from space pirates or another Empire who suddenly decided to make a bold move.

Duke Tinktar would spend some time talking to the person abducted from Earth and the talking dog before he prepared to visit the hog farm on Zeta Bantor and deal with a traitor that disgusted him. But he knew at the end of the day that Madam Pang and her assistants would soon help him forget all those things he had to do.

"Your highness, may I please introduce you to the Earth Man Chester Toland," Doctor Akssiar said with the distinguished Doctor Tasha standing by his side.

"Yes please."

"Chester, this is Duke Tinktar, and this is his Villa where you will be staying until further notice."

"Alright," Chester responded then added. "Please to meet you."

Having received some essential etiquette training on the way to Tymasoara, Chester knew to bow and not attempt shaking hands as that was an act that did not exist in the Drolupric civilization. The researchers were very happy with Chester's attitudes and questioned him about it, he simply said, "I was trained early on, when in Rome do as the Romans do."

Chester looked at Duke Tinktar and other than pink skin he could pass for someone from Earth. Duke Tinktar was in superb physical condition. Instead of running miles and working out in a gym like Americans did, wealthy people living in Tymasoara strapped on exotic devices to their arms, limbs, and abdomens and the frequency resonator transponders did to the muscle tissue in fifteen minutes what two-hour workouts in the gym creating a lot of sweat would. If Duke Tinktar took his shirt off then and showed Chester his body and chest, it's likely Chester would say, *you can just about have any woman you want on planet Earth.*

Duke Tinktar was very well educated and after his primary education was further submerged into a vast education in espionage, sabotage, spy catching, and technology required to catch the best spies in the galaxy. It was a daunting challenge, but the emperor was nervous to have a non-family member with such vast authority to see firsthand the secrets of the empire. Since the emperor knew Duke Tinktar from the time he was born and had some influence on his nurturing, he knew everything about him. Duke Tinktar was spied upon all those years by the best intelligence people in the galaxy. There wasn't a single item in Duke Tinktar's life the emperor wasn't aware of or had immediate knowledge if he asked for information.

Inside the emperor's secret archives that only he and his personal librarian had access to, Duke Tinktar's life story existed and was frequently updated as he was engaged in any activity. The one thing the emperor knew quite well, his relative Duke Tinktar was the one person he most trusted. Also, Duke Tinktar solved another serious issue for the emperor.

The route to succession is a serious question the emperor could not take lightly. He didn't want the Drolupric Empire to crumble when his life ended. The people deserved the continuation of enjoying the fruits of their labors and not to wake up one morning and discover a Tyrant had taken over who had no business attempting to run an empire that took finesse, skill, and great ability to resolve issues in such a way the public wasn't penalized because of the lack of skill sets the successor had.

From an early boy, Duke Tinktar was groomed to one day step in the footsteps of the emperor. Only a couple people knew that was the plan and that did not include Duke Tinktar who would only be notified near the end.

The emperor didn't like Duke Tinktar going in harm's way as often as he did and only allowed him to go if he brought along enough firepower the emperor thought was necessary to ensure he would not receive injuries or worse yet a fatality. In some cases, Duke Tinktar didn't like the excessive amount of backup, but if it kept the emperor from preventing him from doing those things, he was willing to accommodate the emperor. He did, however, have one positive feeling about it. He appreciated the emperor cared about his personal safety.

The mansion had a multi-purpose room that could be a dining hall, concert hall, dance hall or provide several uses for his distinguished guests.

They were soon led in and asked to sit at a table Duke Tinktar had set up for refreshments and snacks. He didn't have much time before he had to prepare for his trip to the hog farm but wanted to see the talking dog before he left.

Next to Duke Tinktar was a special chair with cushions for Brooklyn. Another chair was next to Brooklyn's chair for Chester. There were no other chairs, it was quite apparent this was a very private affair, and the distinguished scientists were forced to stand and observe.

"Chester if you don't mind would you please put Brooklyn up on this chair so I can talk to him?" Duke Tinktar asked.

"Sure, no problem," Chester said then bent down to pick up Brooklyn and placed him on the nice soft cushions.

Duke Tinktar then gestured towards the chair for Chester who knew he should sit there.

The moment of truth now manifested as Duke Tinktar looked at Brooklyn and asked, "Brooklyn, how was your trip here?"

"Your excellency, it was fine, and I am glad to be away from the bitch and with my papa."

Duke Tinktar who was versed in English was quite surprised what Brooklyn said and had to ask the obvious, "Brooklyn, who's the bitch?"

"Your excellency its Abagail, Chester's wife."

Duke Tinktar looked at Chester and immediately got a response.

"Your excellency, as you can see Brooklyn is quite intelligent and has a personality and he did not get along well with Abagail."

"That's quite apparent Chester, but it's quite astonishing to see a dog that can convey his feelings about a situation like Brooklyn just did."

"Yes, your excellency, Brooklyn is very intelligent."

"Chester, I'm curious, what do you think led to Brooklyn's learning and ability to analyze people and articulate those impressions as well as Brooklyn just did."

"Your excellency, I think you should ask Brooklyn that question and I believe he can answer you."

Duke Tinktar turned his head slightly focusing on Brooklyn who was sitting on his rear with his upper body resting on his two front legs and asked, "Brooklyn, you seem to be intelligent, where did you get a lot of your knowledge?

"Your excellency, during the day, Chester was home working on his computer dealing with his company and his clients. He turned the Television on for me which I enjoyed watching. I picked up a lot of information watching Television," Brooklyn responded.

"Is that where you picked up words like bitch."

"Yes, and other words that papa doesn't like me using."

"What is one of those words?" "Fuck."

"What does that word mean?"

"One person on Television stated Fuck means Firnification Under the Consent of the King."

"What does fornication mean?"

"Sexual intercourse between people not married to each other."

"Do you know what sexual intercourse is?"

"Yes, I got to watch the bitch bring a guy home while papa was on a trip and the man fucked the bitch in front of me."

Duke Tinktar was utterly shocked. He knew not to continue down that path because he saw the pain on Chester's face.

"What did you enjoy the most watching Television Brooklyn?"

"I like a channel called National Geographic."

"What does National Geographic show?"

"It has videos of people and places all over our world, planet Earth."

Duke Tinktar turned to his Valet and nodded, which was one of their signals to approach closer as the Duke had a new assignment in mind.

"Yes sir, what may I do for you?"

"Go ask my librarian if he has National Geographic videos on any of the information we brought back from Earth."

"I will do that immediately, sir."

"Thank you."

"Brooklyn, is there anything specific on National Geographic you enjoy the most?"

"Yes, your excellency, I like Ancient Aliens."

"What does Ancient Aliens discuss?"

"It shows evidence Aliens visited Earth thousands of years ago."

"Aliens have visited Earth for hundreds of thousands of years. Drolupric Empire ships visited Earth 75,000 years ago," Duke Tinktar stated.

"Do you have any video records of those visits?" Chester asked.

"Yes, we do. I'll have my librarian provide you with some of the video to watch."

"Thank you, I appreciate that."

"You are most welcome."

About that time one of the waiters approached Duke Tinktar and asked, "Your excellency, would you like me to bring food and drinks out now?"

"Yes, please. Also bring in some chairs and place settings for our distinguished scientists so they can relax and enjoy food and drink."

"Right away sir."

In due time the scientists were sitting across from Chester and Brooklyn.

Several waiters walked around the table with bottles of elixirs and pure drinking water filling water glasses with ice water and elixirs of different types. The elixir most of them chose was the purple *Grand Zumbido*.

Chester noticed that was the elixir that Duke Tinktar picked so he selected it as well. He was soon not disappointed as it had immediate effects. There was no delay in the buzz like one experienced with alcohol-based drinks. The chemicals in the purplish *Grand Zumbido* elixir were psychoactive laced with pleasurizers. But unlike alcohol-based drinks the purplish *Grand Zumbido* elixir did not impair individuals that drank it.

As Chester lived in Duke Tinktar's mansion near Tymasoara, he would eventually discover a powder product was sold to men to give to their women, called *Jiān Jiào de Yěxìng,* that would propel her to infinite desire and eagerly seek gratification.

Duke Tinktar looked over at Doctor Akssiar a leading neurological researcher and asked, "Tell me doctor, how do you feel about the talking dog Brooklyn?"

"Your excellency, we know the dog has a chip implanted in his brain that gives it the ability to speak, which is something we could do with our technology, but never thought about doing something like this."

"Quite amazing, isn't it?"

"That's not particularly extraordinary. Nevertheless, Brooklyn has shaken our scientific community as he has demonstrated dogs are capable of learning quite a lot."

"What about this gives the scientific community such a significant interest?"

"Because of his unique ability to talk he's able to elucidate his thoughts very succinctly and communicate his feelings."

"His feelings?"

"Yes, we now know dogs can have extraordinary feelings and personality, which you saw an example of when he conveyed his feelings towards Abagail, Chester's wife."

"Doctor, I can't deny I was extremely surprised about what he said and how he said it."

Chester thought the moment was perfect to bring up his concern.

"Doctor, how long do you plan on studying Brooklyn?"

"Chester, what Brooklyn has done to our scientific community has been rather extraordinary. We never thought we would ever experience something like this. It caught us totally off guard. It deserves great study in our opinion. I know you will not like this answer, but several years."

"This really creates a tragedy for me as my wife Abagail will think I deserted her and worse yet when they find my automobile at Ski Beach someone will assume the worst. By the time I get back to Earth, she may have remarried and possibly even have children by then."

"Chester, we will help you adjust as well as we can, but based on what Brooklyn said earlier about Abagail's infidelity issues, it's unlikely you would have a long-lasting successful marriage."

"Why do you say that Doctor?" Chester asked with a hint of anger in his voice.

"Chester I'm a brain doctor which means I have vast training in psychology. On Earth, which I've studied more than you can imagine, you have a term that says something to the effect *a leopard does not change* its spots. From my behavioral science investigation people do not change unless something compels them to change. Abagail may have a worse behavior than what you realize."

"How can you say that. You don't know that."

"Chester, I'm sad to report to you we spied on you for a while before we abducted you and Brooklyn. We spied on Abagail too. That includes times she traveled out of town for her company, and there were some events you are not aware of nor is Brooklyn, if you want sometime in the future, in a private setting I can show you things that will make you not miss Abagail too much."

Chester looked at the distinguished doctor and could feel the burn. Brooklyn truly felt sorry for Papa because he knew the doctor was spot on, and poor Chester had no idea what that *bitch* was up to. Mr. Parker was the tip of the iceberg.

Chester, feeling publicly humiliated as well as disenfranchised grabbed his elixir and drank it all down at once. It felt good. He turned around to one of the waiters and asked, "Can I have a refill please?"

Duke Tinktar looked at Chester with a feeling of empathy because losing a wife and a world is one thing, but to discover she was unfit as a spouse no doubt now permeated Chester's thoughts. Doctor Akssiar had fully evaluated and understood Chester quite well from all surveillance videos. He knew the abduction would rub Chester raw, but he also knew human emotions and how to truncate some of those feelings Chester had for Abagail. Doctor Akssiar didn't intend on bringing up Abagail in this manner, but the other research associates already knew, and the waiters were sworn to secrecy and if any of them ever blabbed anything about Chester they knew quite well Duke Tinktar would give them a lot of pain on the lines of a trip to the hog farm or worse if they have a family.

Chester was part of the support apparatus for Brooklyn. If they thought Brooklyn could survive and flourish without Chester, there would never have been a reason to bring Chester along, but they planned to use a conservative approach, with all aspects of it planned around accommodating Brooklyn as best as possible.

Brooklyn had been with Chester since he was a small puppy, and their emotional bonds were strong. Brooklyn didn't feel like a dog, he felt like Chester's son. The psychoanalyst in Doctor Akssiar assumed Brooklyn would go through the transition to living on a new world just fine if *Papa* was with him. That assumption proved to be more than true as time passed, and the evaluations and studies continued.

With one elixir down and another one on the way down, Chester was slowly developing a euphoric feeling as the pleasure center of his brain was slowly taking control of his emotions and shielding his grief.

Brooklyn sat there, drank some water in his doggy water bowl in the fixture developed for his special chair. His other bowl had dog food in it and when Drolupric scientists discovered how terrible the dog food tasted, they immediately went to work creating a new taste for Brooklyn who sampled his food and suddenly thought, *the alien dog food is a lot better!*

After talking about irrelevant matters for a while, Duke Tinktar stood up and said, "My dear guests, please continue enjoying food and drink but I must get ready for a trip. I will see you all in a few days from now. Chester and Brooklyn, it is nice meeting you. I'm looking forward to learning more about you when I get back from my trip."

"Thank you," Chester said in a friendly tone knowing Duke Tinktar had nothing to do with his abduction and was trying to help make his transition a more pleasant one.

Shortly after Duke Tinktar was gone, his valet approached Chester and said, "Chester would you like me to escort you to your private suite so you can refresh yourself and relax, change your clothes into something more comfortable?"

"Yes, I'm kind of sleepy because it's been a while since I had a good sleep."

"Alright, would you and Brooklyn please follow me."

Doctor Akssiar interjected, "Chester, I am going with you to your suite as I have something for you."

"Sure."

About one hundred steps from the multi-purpose room was a suite that had been designated for Chester's exclusive use. It was fully ostentatious and had not only a bed and a lot of furniture and fixtures it also had what appeared to be an earth style baby bed with a ramp on it for Brooklyn to sleep in and get in and out of easily. Next to the bed was a doggie potty they developed for Brooklyn he had been trained to use and could in the middle of the night wake up and use if required that included automatic lighting to allow him to see his way there and back. Brooklyn would soon learn the mansion had a wonderful courtyard with plenty of trees to utilize after he marked them.

The valet explained what's available and informed Chester,

"Artificial Intelligence is monitoring the room in case you need anything. All you need to do is say, please send the valet and me or one of the members of the staff will come to you and assist in any manner we can."

"Thank you."

Doctor Akssiar then added, "Chester here is a small bottle of pills. They will help you get a nice restful sleep. There is a doctor and a veterinarian as you earth people call them on staff here to monitor and help you and Brooklyn for all your medical needs. Like the valet said, artificial intelligence is monitoring and if you want a doctor or a veterinarian, just request them verbally and the artificial intelligence will acknowledge your request immediately and send the medical professionals to you immediately. Also, if you ever need to talk to me all you have to state is contact Doctor Akssiar, and Artificial Intelligence will contact me and you will be able to communicate to me via a holograph. May I demonstrate that for you now?"

"Sure."

"Please contact my secretary."

Since the Artificial Intelligence had facial recognition and Doctor Akssiar was on the official guest list, the Artificial Intelligence responded, "Doctor Akssiar, please standby we are contacting your secretary. Would you like to see her holograph image?"

"Yes, please."

A moment later a pretty lady showed up on a life like holograph suspended a short distance off the floor in full size just a few feet away from Doctor Akssiar.

"Hello Doctor Akssiar, how may I help you?"

"Aiaru, I called to demonstrate to Chester how the communications system works in his suite at Duke Tinktar's estate."

"Alright Doctor Akssiar."

"Here is Chester, in case he contacts you to get in touch with me."

"Pleased to meet you Chester," Aiaru said.

"Thank you. Likewise."

"Anything else I can help you with Doctor?"

"No, I just wanted to demonstrate the communications and I will be traveling back to the office in a short while."

"I will be looking forward to your return. You currently have no messages or any concerns to follow up on."

"Thank you."

"You are welcome."

Doctor Akssiar turned to Chester and said, "When you want to terminate the communications, simply say 'off communicator' and the artificial intelligence will secure the holograph and it will disappear like this."

Doctor Akssiar then turned towards the holograph and said, "Off communicator."

The image then disappeared and artificial intelligence in the background stated, "Communications to Aiaru have been terminated as directed by Doctor Akssiar."

"That seemed simple enough," Chester said.

"I'm going to leave you now Chester. One of your maids will be here shortly to help you change or take a bath if you desire and get you water to drink when you take one of those pills. You only need to take one, they are plenty strong enough to help you sleep."

"Thank you doctor."

"It's my pleasure Chester and I promise I will do what I can to help you get adjusted to life on Tymasoara."

"Hopefully one day you can help me return to Earth."

"In a few years the study of Brooklyn will be over, and I imagine Duke Tinktar would help you get back to Earth if you want to go back then."

"I'm sure I will want to go back."

"Chester, you don't know what exists in the Galaxy yet. But as we educate you, there could be a possibility you might not want to go back after you discover the benefits of living here among the Drolupric people."

"Well doctor you all have pink skin; how do I know I will be accepted?"

"Chester, everyone on the planet wants to be friends with Duke Tinktar, who's a very powerful person since he's the emperor's nephew and has a lot of power and authority. Many will want to get to know you as you could be their steppingstone to get in Duke Tinktar's good graces, especially some of the beautiful women you will soon meet. Furthermore, no doubt you will be taken on trips to other planets where there are plain skin people like you, or planets with blue or green skin people that have attributes you will no doubt like if you ever get the opportunity to explore them."

"Alright Doctor, I'll see what happens, but I kind of want to grow old and die on my planet."

"Chester, you are still a young man and with life extending ability we have here, and the benefits to your health we'll improve, by the time you get back to Earth you will be physically younger and in better shape than you are now."

"Alright Doctor, I'm willing to see what happens."

"Give it a chance, I'm sure in a while development will distract you from thinking about Earth."

"Alright."

"I will visit you two tomorrow around lunch time and we'll have a friendly conversation as I give you some idea what our researchers have in mind with Brooklyn."

"See you then."

"Goodbye." Doctor Akssiar said, then left the suite.

Moments later, artificial intelligence in the background said, "Chester your maid is here at the door, do you wish to give her permission to enter?"

"Sure, let her in."

"The well-dressed maid wearing a black dress with a white shirt and black vest came in holding a tray with a silver container and a glass. She walked over to a countertop next to the bed which allowed trays of drinks or snacks to be placed and sit it there and turned towards Chester and said, "Hello Chester, my name is Aizere."

"That's a beautiful name. May I ask you a question?"

"Sure."

"How is it everyone here can speak English to me?"

"Chester, when it was decided you would be abducted with Brooklyn and brought to Duke Tinktar's estate here at Tymasoara, the staff was directed by Duke Tinktar to undergo neurological sonification's to obtain the language skills quickly so that we can communicate with you efficiently."

"Is that a normal function in your society?"

Chester, we have over 500 planets in our Empire with 700 languages and 28,000 dialects. We can't teach people all the languages and we must respond based on circumstances and people need a quick method of learning languages. Neurological Sonification's is how we manage it. Language on demand, just like what we have done to prepare for your visit."

"Would it be possible for me to get Neurological Sonification for the main language and dialect of Tymasoara, since it looks like I will be here for quite some time."

"Chester, it's my responsibility to make sure you are comfortable. I will in a short while contact the coordinator for Neurological Sonification's that provided the Earth English language skills to the staff here and make an appointment for you. If you want a woman for sex, or elixir's or anything that will please you, I will make the arrangements."

"Thank you I appreciate that. It will help me feel more at home if I can communicate to the locals, especially if I'm out traveling around the planet."

"Chester, you might as well know the truth now so that you are not in for a letdown later. You will never leave Duke Tinktar's estate without a bodyguard and a translator. Acquiring Tymasoara is okay if you want to do that to improve your quality of life and discover more about the culture, but it really isn't necessary since a translator will always be with you."

"I figured as much, but when I'm out in society with my

translator and bodyguard and smell the scents and hear the sounds of society, I would feel more at ease knowing what everyone is saying."

"Get some rest, and tomorrow someone will be here to interview and initiate the Neurological Sonification in the near future."

"Thank you I appreciate your help."

"Chester, would you and Brooklyn like to take a bath before you go to sleep?"

"Sure, why not."

"Chester I'm going to have the dog groomer come to the room to handle Brooklyn. He needs to get to know her now as she will be dedicated to his care from now on."

"Please send Rayalna here to assist with Brooklyn." Aizere said knowing Artificial Intelligence would hear it.

In the background Artificial Intelligence voice responded,

"Aizere, you want the dog groomer Rayalna to come to the room to assist with Brooklyn?"

"Yes, that's correct," Aizere replied.

"Rayalna will be notified to report to you at Chester's suite."

"Thank you."

"You are welcome."

"I'm going to start your bath waters, Rayalna will be here momentarily."

Chester noticed Aizere was quite attractive and very well built. But when Rayalna arrived, he was stunned.

Soon Chester was undressing by the bathtub large enough for six people and Aizere took his clothes which were of Drolupric design and fitted on the spacecraft during the journey to Tymasoara. He wouldn't wear them again because he would be fitted with more luxurious clothes that exposed his elevated stature in life. Chester was no longer a commoner from planet Earth. He was now a person of interest to the emperor himself as the emperor was duly informed and quite animated about the story. The emperor would treat Chester quite well because Chester's life took a huge turn to facilitate the Drolupric scientific community which had undergone a metamorphosis and appeared to be having almost geological tremmors from the revelations and implications of what Brooklyn's presence had manifested.

Rayalna knew that Brooklyn was a talking dog and had been fully briefed on the situation. She said to Chester, you have your bath and Brooklyn has his own bath. Before you get in your bath can you assist me with Brooklyn so we can get him into his bath water without any incidents?

"Not a problem, all I need to do is talk to him."

"Brooklyn, I want you to cooperate with Rayalna and get in the bath water she has arranged for you."

"Sure Papa. I kind of like Rayalna."

"See how easy that is?"

Rayalna smiled and said, "I wish all dogs were this easy to deal with."

Brooklyn then surprised Rayalna and said, "Rayalna, I'll let you be my friend if you can sneak me food and not force me to eat dog food."

"Brooklyn, I'll see what I can do, but Doctor Akssiar will be watching your diet very closely. We'll see if we can do something about the taste for you."

"The Dog food I had a while ago was a lot better than on the ship, so that was a nice improvement."

"If you work with us Brooklyn, we'll see what we can do about improving it even more to the point where you will enjoy it."

"Thank you."

"Do you think you need help getting in the water Brooklyn?"

"No, it has a nice ramp, I can get there just fine."

Brooklyn walked up the ramp to his doggie bathtub. He got to water's edge and put his paw in the water and said, "The temperature seems about right."

Brooklyn stepped down into the tub that had a sequence of steps down do deeper water. The mixture in the water of pleasurizers and scent neutralizers quickly made Brooklyn feel great and he commented. "This feels good."

Meanwhile, Chester stepped into his large bathtub that had water temperature around ninety-five degrees. Just about right.

Aizere said, "I'm going to get your sleeping clothes laid out on your bed and take these clothes to send in for cleaning. Then I have a surprise for you.

"Alright." Chester responded.

Aizere left the room for a moment then came back in the bathing room with another very attractive woman wearing a bath robe who took it off and handed it to Aizere.

"My name is Aida; I'm going to shampoo your hair and wash you."

Chester was now super animated. He understood Abagail was a dog in appearance compared to Aida. His sorrow of leaving Abagail behind quickly dissipated. The pleasurizers in his bath water and the psychoactive drugs in the elixir he drank a short while previously was completely adjusting his disposition.

Aida walked into the bath and approached Chester who was sitting on a submerged seat allowing the water to be at his neckline. She soon straddled him, and Chester felt he was getting an *erección*. Aida knew it too because it was right below her love flower, and she felt the rising firmness.

Aida was one of Duke Tinktar's top concubines and was asked by Duke Tinktar himself to please Chester and help him to quickly forget about Earth. Aida, wanting to earn points with Duke Tinktar was more than willing to go the extra mile to facilitate Chester's transcendence to his new life and his new reality created by being Brooklyn's papa.

Brooklyn was being pampered by Rayalna at the same time Aida was exciting Chester who was feeling pressure. Abagail had so many headaches recently, that Chester had not enjoyed any 'Big A' as Abagail liked to call it, in probably a couple months.

Aida had a perfume that was highly stimulating and was shedding pheromones at a much greater rate than anyone in heat wanting sexual gratification.

Aida had a pair of special goggles and said, "put these on while I wash your hair."

Chester put on the goggles that had a suction device that caused it to firmly seal to prevent water or soap to not get in his eyes. As soon as he was situated, Aida took the washing device and drenched Chester's hair, then she took one of the containers sitting on the side of the tub and poured the contents into her hand then spread that on the top of Chester's head. She then messaged it in and was making Chester feel great.

Aizere knew what was going to happen next because she observed Aida doing it to Duke Tinktar several times before. The shampoo was also laced with female pheromones and Chester was getting a storm of those love inducers.

Chester was soon brought into a state of shock enjoying and observing Aida's breasts, but she suddenly grabbed his manliness which was about as hard as it could get and very efficiently put it into her womanhood and slowly rocked back and forth on Chester causing him an incredible sensation. In less than two minutes Chester was feeling tremendous gratification as his body reacted to Aida's magic which propelled him into that splendid euphoria as he released all his stored up essence creating a tidal wave of ensembles of gratification. Chester knew he had exploded inside Aida who was now smiling.

Aida bent down and kissed Chester on his lips like he had never been kissed before and she said, "I will let you fall in love with me if you want."

Chester could not believe the feelings he was having. He thought they were his own brain functions doing it from the arousal, but what he didn't know, he was being manipulated by clever people that wanted to make him feel seduced and quickly forget about the hag Abagail he left behind. They knew how Abagail appeared from their surveillance of her. They also knew that Abagail's self-evaluation was many degrees higher than reality.

Abagail was not in the same league as Aida. The differences were so vast and astonishing. On planet Earth at the time there was no singer or movie star that had the beauty and charisma that Aida flourished with.

Aida was the master manipulator, close to the centers of power of the empire and had expectations of special treatment from Duke Tinktar. Chester didn't know this; he was Aida's ticket to her freedom and a great life.

After a while man and beast were fully groomed.
Brooklyn was led into a dog dryer with glass doors so he could look outside but enjoy the warm dry air dumped into the device. The air that blew onto Brooklyn's fur coat, went through special air driers and it served two purposes. It dried Brooklyn remarkably quickly but kept him warm in the process.

Computer controlled nozzles with optical scanners could pinpoint the dry air onto all the areas needing drying. It was as if Brooklyn was out in a dry desert someplace, the wetness quickly evaporated and was removed by air pumps and sent back through the air dryers in a closed loop system. The Air dryers dumped the water obtained into a drain.

Chester was also led into an air dryer with Aida and the two of them were quickly dried off and given bath robes and sandals. "Would you like me to help you get to sleep by lying beside you?" Aida asked.

"I'm not sure I could sleep if you are lying beside me," Chester responded with all honesty.

"All right. In the night if you get lonely just tell the Artificial Intelligence to have me come back to your suite and I'll be here for you."

"Thank you. I appreciate that."

Aida then left the room to take care of business while Aizere led him over to his bed where his night clothes were laid out.

"Change into these and you will rest better."

"Alright."

In a few minutes Chester was ready for bed and Rayalna escorted Brooklyn over to his doggie bed enclosure with the ramp. It had glass panels so Brooklyn could always observe Chester.

"Brooklyn it's time for bed, climb up into your bed," Rayalna said.

"Alright," Brooklyn responded and climbed up the easy ramp into his bed and figured out how to lay down and keep an eye on Chester.

"Why don't you take one of your pills now," Aizere suggested to Chester, who didn't really have a handle on what time of day it was. He didn't care, he was feeling he wanted to rest.

Chester took the pill and saw the glass of water and took a drink to wash it down. The then crawled in bed and said to Aizere, "I usually sleep with the lights out."

"After I leave the room, the lights will slowly dim into darkness and if you want the lights back on just say 'Turn on the lights.' Artificial Intelligence will then turn your lights on for you."

"Alright, thank you."

"Good night, Chester."

Chester was soon horizontal and resting and wondering about a lot of things. Just like at home he said, "Good night, Brooklyn."

"Good night Papa," Brooklyn responded.

Chester slowly faded into dreamland. In fifteen minutes, he was asleep. Just like the doctor said, the pill would help him sleep really well. He had no idea what time it was, but the medical staff determined he needed several days of good rest to help him get acclimated to the new time and the new world.

During the night Brooklyn needed to urinate and when he stood up in his bed soft lights came on to light up the ramp and the area around hid doggy potty. He then went back to his bed and back to sleep. Twelve hours later, which was the next morning lighting in the room slowly came back on with soft chimes playing in the background.

Artificial intelligence then started the process of awakening Chester.

Brooklyn was bright eyed, and bush tailed as soon as the lights came on.

Chester felt slightly groggy but was slowly regaining full consciousness.

Artificial Intelligence then said, Chester, in a couple minutes, Aizere will be here with your change of clothes to prepare you for morning activities.

"Alright."

Within two minutes Aizere came into the room carrying a special delivery box that had clothes and shoes in it for Chester. Before going to bed the night before, Rayalna had put Brooklyn's special dog collar device back on so he could talk to Chester in the night if necessary. Brooklyn was ready to go wherever.

Chester did not know it at the time, but he was wearing Royal clothes. Only the emperor and the special people he designated were allowed to wear such garments.

Chester thought the clothes looked nice but had no idea of the significance of them. He would slowly figure things out. No Earth person had ever gone where Chester is, all because of a talking dog.

In due time they were led out to a courtyard in the middle of the estate where a table and settings were ready for them. The beautiful flowers and landscaping around made it the perfect place to enjoy a meal.

Soon they were sitting at the table with a waiter standing by to serve them a drink and take orders for what kind of brunch they might like.

Brooklyn was served a drink specifically designed for him to enhance his antibodies and immune system allowing him to transition to this new environment without getting sick. Chester requested a drink like he experienced on the spaceship coming here that seemed to improve his awareness and facilitate better thinking.

Halfway through their drink Doctor Akssiar arrived with Tasha whom Chester met on the spacecraft.

"Hello Chester. I brought Tasha along since she knows you and Brooklyn the best and will go over with you some of our immediate plans."

"Sure."

The waiter asked Doctor Akssiar, "would like something to drink and would you be interested in ordering some food to eat?"

"I'll have a drink, but I'm not hungry."

"How about you Doctor Tasha?"

"I'm find thank you."

In due time a waiter brought food to Chester and Brooklyn. Chester could tell Brooklyn wasn't too happy eating dog food while at the same time Chester was eating some interesting looking food. The conversation continued while the two had their brunch and Tasha explained the key portions of the plan.

"We know about the telemetry the black box put out back on Earth using Earth style cell phone wireless technology. Our engineers reverse engineered the system and have come up with transponders of our own to communicate with that black box. We are not going to tamper with it for a while, but we believe he speaker box and the wireless router take up far too much room, so we are going to miniaturize it so that Brooklyn will be far more comfortable."

"Will he have a dog collar like he has now?"

"No. The new transponder will be inserted inside his body and instead of crude wires running out of his skull to a speaker box arrangement, it will all be wireless."

"How soon do you plan on doing that?" Chester asked knowing there would be no way he could stop them from doing what they desired.

Even though we can have all that hardware ready in six months to install, we are going to hold off and use the existing technology which will work for us to get as much clinical trials done as possible first."

"What exactly are these trials?"

"In a couple days we will be directly accessing Brooklyn's chip through his existing wireless transponder and monitor his current lexicon to establish a baseline of where he's at now. Then we are going to watch him nurture and develop further by means of just normal living and experiencing life. We will watch his progress for a few months and detect any trends that may occur."

"If you an arrange for him to have something like the National Geographic I'm sure he will grow and prosper."

"Yes, we have our own version of your Earth National Geographic, but since we have over 500 planets, we have a lot more he can view."

"Alright then what?"

"Right now, Brooklyn only knows English."

"That's correct."

"We were informed by your maid Aizere, you volunteer to have Neurological Sonification because you want to learn standard Drolupric with a Tymasoara dialect."

"Yes, that's true."

"We have never attempted to perform a Neurological Sonification to a dog before because we had no reason because dogs on this planet similar to what you have on Earth cannot talk."

"What does that have to do with Brooklyn?"

"We want to attempt Neurological Sonification's on Brooklyn and teach him standard Drolupric with a Tymasoara dialect."

"You think that's safe to do?"

"We will first try it on other dogs first to make sure no harm comes."

"Since the other dogs can't talk, how would you know the dog learned anything from the Neurological Sonification's?"

"We can teach them various activities and determine the efficacy of the brain development by their future responses when we communicate to them. We'll video record Brooklyn doing various activities to train the dogs to do the same actions."

"Such as?"

"Take a bath, use the dog potty, walk up to a dog bed like Brooklyn does and other activities."

"I suppose that will tell you the programming of the dog's brain was successful. But how will you determine if Brooklyn is responding as expected."

"That's quite simple, you will be able to talk to him using Drolupric language with a Tymasoara dialect."

"How many Drolupric words will you teach Brooklyn?"

"In our downloads of telemetry data from Brooklyn's black box, we know the current chip allows for a lexicon of 65,565 words and he's currently populated that table with around 1800 words. He has plenty of room for him to learn enough Drolupric language that he will be able to successfully communicate with anyone living in Tymasoara."

"My maid Aizere said she would arrange for an interview with Neurological Sonification's representative to schedule my treatments to learn Drolupric language."

"Consider this that interview."

"How soon will the Neurological Sonification's happen?"

"You have been requested by the emperor who wants a private meeting with you and Brooklyn. He was informed you volunteered to undergo the Neurological Sonification's and is planning on meeting you after the treatments so that you can converse with him in the Drolupric language."

"I see. How soon do we start?"

"After you finish your Brunch, Tasha and I will take you and Brooklyn on a sight-seeing trip to expose some of Tymasoara to you. We want you to relax today to help become more acclimated with life here at Tymasoara. We'll start the first treatment tomorrow late afternoon because we want you to rest afterwards."

"How long does all this take?"

"You will receive five treatments. We like to delay a day between treatments, to give the targeted person time to recover from the Neurological Sonification's because we know it will severely stress you."

"If it stresses people, why do you do it?"

"You will recover just fine. We know that nothing works this quickly. We have the issue with 500 planets and so many languages and dialects, that due to the urgency of need quite often, we do not have the benefit of time to get it done. This technology was developed mainly to keep the empire from fragmenting. Communication is the heart of our survival. This is the only method we've been able to develop that meets all our time urgency."

In due time man and beast were fed and satisfied. The Valet approached and said, "Chester, would you like to go back to your suite to freshen up before you go on the sightseeing tour with Doctor Akssiar?

"That's not a bad idea actually."

In due time Chester was relieved and set to go see the world. Aizere approached him and suggested, "Chester, I think you will blend in better in society if you allow me to bring a hair stylist in to prepare you to be seen in public and not have any curiosity towards you."

"Sure, if you think that's a good idea."

"I do."

Shortly a barber's chair was brought into the room by a couple mansion staffers with the barber in tow.

In less than fifteen minutes the lovely female barber had Chester looking like he was a local. Chester looked in the mirror she provided and he responded, "I do not think I've ever had such a good hair style before."

"We have products that people on Earth do not have that allows me to hair sculpture you this way."

"Thank you. It turned out well."

While the barber and her assistants carrying the portable barber chair out of Chester's suite, the valet entered and said, "Chester, if you are ready let me lead you and Brooklyn to the Skycar you will depart in."

"Thank you."

"This way please."

Standing next to the Skycar was none other than Aida dressed to kill with an evil smile.

"Hello Chester. I was asked to give you a tour of Tymasoara and show you a few sights to help you discover a little about the city."

"Thank you."

Chester noticed inside the Skycar were several men who were mostly part of his security detachment to make sure he and Brooklyn who now was on a leash were not disturbed in any manner.

"Chester, I want you to know this since you are new here and do not yet know about Drolupric society. You are dressed in official Royal clothes. The public we meet will know this and they also know nobody is allowed to wear this type of clothing without the emperor's approval. They will know you have a connection with the emperor, but also, they spot your body guards and know not to approach without you inviting them."

"Alright."

"There will be a lot of curiosity because few Tymasoara's have seen a dog like Brooklyn. Nor do they know he's a talking dog. It will make your sightseeing experience more pleasurable if Brooklyn doesn't talk and you do not approach people. Because if you do, you will quickly create a large crowd following you around with curiosity seekers."

"Understand all. Brooklyn please do not talk on this trip."

"Alright Papa, I will remain quiet."

"Thank you, Brooklyn."

"You are welcome, Papa."

Chapter Seven

A TOUR OF TYMASOARA

Chester, Brooklyn, and Aida were soon in the Skycar which drove on its surface transit wheels over to the long tunnel and slowly sped up. By the time it left the end of the tunnel and was out into air, it was flying in air mode accelerating and rising in altitude on an invisible road in the sky that would soon join into multi-level traffic patterns.

Flying in the direction of the City Center due ahead, Chester could see the magnificent city before his eyes. From a distance the buildings looked rather strange, almost like spires sticking up high into the sky. The first thing Chester thought was, it must be a long elevator ride to the top of the buildings then there was the discovery as they approached by some of the high rise buildings that seemed to be positioned in an intricate pattern.

Chester realized eventually he would discover how tall these buildings were and guessed some of them had to be 400 stories tall. Then he discovered why people didn't have a long elevator ride. After passing a few of these super tall buildings he saw openings suddenly appear on the sides of the buildings and Skycars fly out of them. He also saw another amazing attribute on the sides of these buildings. They were combined buildings with commercial and residential real estate including a few café balconies with glass domes covering them. *Very interesting*, Chester thought.

In a few minutes a large green area opened up before them and the sky car veered down to it and a parking lot. At the parking lot was a couple Skycars waiting for them with more *security* **present.** They were at VIP parking right next to the entrance. After the Skycar landed next to the two others, the doors opened and all the occupants got out except one who ostensibly appeared to be the driver but during the trip, there appeared to be no controls he touched. He did say a few words in standard Drolupric. *Was it all voice activated?* Chester wondered.

Chester was not able to read the sign at the entrance but assumed his tour guide would inform him what this was all about. Once they got inside the complex it all became apparent. This was a combination park and zoo. It was a sprawling complex and there were several individuals waking around enjoying their day. Some were couples in love, others were families with children. In a few cases there were senior citizens out ostensibly for a walk.

As the delegation approached and passed individuals, Chester could see there appeared to be quite a lot of eyes on him and Brooklyn. The public easily recognized Chester was wearing official Royal attire and the bodyguards in suits and the glamorous lady with him easily exposed they were VIP's and someone ultra-important. Tymasoara the capital city of the Drolupric Empire drew in visitors from the five hundred or more planets of the empire plus visitors from other empires from far off distances that often arrived as tourists to take in this grand city thought of as the Pearl of the Galaxy.

Because of the large stretches of property, the animals in the Zoo were not concentrated and there were a few Wild Animal Parks that reminded Chester of the one he used to visit by Escondido California over the years. Soon they came up to a large open area down below them as it appeared they were on a hilltop.

Chester noted a tram like device that reminded him of San Diego California's Wild Animal Park near Escondido. As they walked along and Aida was explaining the park, she caught Chester gazing at the tram and asked, "Would you like to go ride that, Safari Tram?"

"Yes, I think I would."

In a matter of time, Aida let Chester and the entourage to the Safari Tram VIP boarding area entrance.

Chester noticed people going through the public boarding area had a pass like neck device. Those passes were part of the park entrance fee that allowed them to enjoy all the rides and activities. VIPs were not required to have a PASS. Artificial Intelligence identified Aida who had been here before with Duke Tinktar and the stranger wearing official emperor attire and immediately cleared the group to enter to via the VIP boarding area immediately to the next Safari Train that pulled into the little station.

The group including all the bodyguards fit into one of the Safari Train covered gondola cars. The covered gondola with a side entrance reminded Chester of the Gondola Lifts he took up the mountain sides of Swiss Alps mountains back in the days he was swooning his wife Abagail.

Instead of traveling along a track the Safari Tram Covered Gondolas traveled on a wire allowing it to be suspended in the air and have a better look at the wild animals that appeared to flourish below them. They were soon on their way traveling at a comfortable speed designed to enhance the enjoyment of observing all the animals.

Brooklyn quickly found Chester's lap and while they traveled around the park in an "S" pattern pathway, Chester petted Brooklyn who enjoyed every minute of it. Since National Geographic was Brooklyn's favorite Television show back at Chester's home, this was an utter delight being with Papa, getting petted and observing all the strange animals, half of which had no corresponding appearance back on Earth.

"Only twenty percent of the animals are native to this planet the rest were relocated here from outlying planets," Aida explained.

"With over five hundred planets I can imagine there is a lot of animals that live within the empire," Chester responded.

The Safari Tram Covered Gondola came up to an excavated path through a large hill and when they got near, Chester could see glass windows in the hillside and some terrifying looking animals.

Brooklyn was stunned and asked, "What are those, Papa?"

Aida overheard Brooklyn's question and responded, "Those are *Dúshé Dragons.*"

"They look horrible."

"Their venom is some of the most poisonous in the galaxy."

"If they are that dangerous, then why are they kept here."

"In part for two reasons, they are mainly extinct. Secondly some of the poison darts used by our spies use *Dúshé Dragons* poison to coat their darts and knives for a fast kill."

"How do they use such darts?"

"In one of two ways. They have a small blow tube they strap on to the side of their leg when they deploy. The other method is we trained birds to deliver those darts."

"How's their accuracy of hitting the target?"

"Actually, pretty good, but according to Doctor Akssiar thanks to Brooklyn's staggering learning ability, he thinks in the future we'll have animals working in all sorts of scenarios the public will be unaware of."

"Talking birds perhaps?"

"Chester our miniaturization of electronics is thousands of years ahead of Earth. We can build a chip like Brooklyn has with ten times the performance but only one tenth as big."

"I can imagine based on what I'm slowly seeing."

"Doctor Akssiar could easily implant a chip in a bird one tenth the size of Brooklyn's chip and mount a small speak box to give similar ability."

"What's the end game, where is all this research going? Doctor Foster on Earth wants to treat stroke victims."

"Chester, I attended briefings where Doctor Akssiar discussed what this all means. First and foremost, we thought we knew everything about animals. But in reality, we only knew a fraction about them."

"Which means?"

"It means we have to go back and relearn everything about Animals we can."

"What is the big reason?"

"Tremendous implications now exist."

"Such as?"

"Animals that can talk and learn at the rate of Brooklyn can be weaponized. An enemy could be attacked in ways they never dreamed of."

"I suppose so."

"Suppose a dog looks identical to the one the owner has and is substituted. The owner would not catch the switch and we would have the best inserted spy."

"I can see there could be some implications to having a talking dog."

"The biggest if we determine we can use the Neurological Sonification's is we can do training much more efficiently and have better results."

"So, our purpose in being here isn't for the peaceful study of animals to enlighten the public?"

"Chester, every technology including what is on your planet is dual use and you should know it."

"I suppose so."

"Look at the automated flight controls on your passenger aircraft. The displays, inertial navigation systems, satellite navigation systems, communications systems, and other systems are dual purposed and installed in your nuclear bombers."

"How do you know that?"

"We have copies of all the plans to your military equipment as well as your enemies."

"How did you get them?"

"Same way we'll insert dogs into the homes of people who are targets of interest."

"Please explain."

"We have spies on your planet."

"You do?"

"We are not the only Aliens with spies on planet Earth."

"And exactly how do they help get you the information?"

"They recruit your scientists and engineers."

"How do they do that?"

"Classical espionage. Bribes, honeypot schemes, abduction and Neurological Sonification's."

"How are you able to do Neurological Sonification's?"

"Our spies monitor their schedules and when they are due to go on a vacation, we abduct them and by the time they return back to work after their great holiday, they know they work for us."

"I'm surprised you haven't been caught doing that."

"Do you honestly think for one moment your government is looking for Alien spies? They are focused on Russians, Chinese, French, British, German, Japanese, Indian, Iranian, Israeli, and narcotic and human traffickers."

"You seem to know a lot about Earth."

"I was an intelligence operative there running a Drolupric spy ring there for several years."

"Really?"

"Certainly."

"With all that, why did your government abduct Brooklyn and I in the manner you did?"

"By the time that happened our spy ring had been evacuated."

"Found all the information you wanted?"

"No actually there was a lot more we wanted, but we had to evacuate because our Empire was being accused of violating Earth's quarantine."

"What does that mean?"

"It means no Federation Organizations are allowed to tamper with Earth affairs or go there. Your world is off limits."

"How did that come about?"

"Upper-level intelligence officials discovered a possible mole that was informing his government our activities on Earth, and they were going to the Federation to arbitrate this, which meant they would have sent search parties for us."

"So, your team left Earth then."

"We had to bug out, leave immediately and be long gone before the trackers got to earth and discovered any of us."

"But yet your ship came back and abducted us."

"We found the mole and neutralized him. We didn't send a team back, but we have sent ships back routinely to do ISR missions on Russia and China and a few other places to determine if our enemies such as the Draco Grey Aliens are operating there."

They continued their trip around the wild animal park and Chester knew he was in over his head but there wasn't much he could do about it. He wondered if Aida would provide her pleasant affection towards him tonight. Aida was looking extremely seductive, and he got hard just thinking about her. Painfully as he was adjusting to his new reality, he realized what Doctor Akssiar said was a reality check. Abagail could not compete with the likes of Aida. He also knew Aida was more than just a concubine and a servant to Duke Tinktar. There was more to that story as well.

Aida was intriguing to Chester, now knowing she had operated as a spy on planet Earth for a while until they had to bug out. Now the big question to Chester is what brought Aida and Duke Tinktar together. Chester would one day know why vividly as his universe was now rapidly expanding in ways he never contemplated. Sitting in the Safari Tram Covered Gondola next to Aida with his best friend Brooklyn sitting on his lap created a very pleasant moment.

When people radiate happiness, it affects others. Aida was receiving Chester's radiance and was slowly starting to enjoy her new assignment because Chester had a unique appeal to him. Aida could see how much Brooklyn loved his Papa, Chester. Dogs' intuition is usually spot on. Brooklyn's affection towards Chester illustrated a bonding built on continual involvement of a loving relationship.

Aida enjoyed watching that incredible bond and even though one was human and the other an animal, it transfixed her thoughts and increased affection towards Chester. Last night when she toyed with Chester using her awesome power as a seductive spy was all work related. No different than her honeypot schemes of the past. She knew tonight it would be different. It would no longer feel like work. It would be a pleasure and she would add some secret elements to the blissful response she expected out of Chester. After tonight Chester would have a much harder time remembering who Abagail was.

The Safari Tram Covered Gondola continued making those slow S-shaped travel around the park taking in quite a few strange looking animals. When they came upon a group of animals that looked half dragon and half horse, Brooklyn said, "Papa those animals look very scary."

"Yes, they do Brooklyn. I would not want to get near them."

"Those animals are from a non-empire planet and are called *Lóngtóumâ*."

"Do you know what that name *Lóngtóumâ* means?"

"Yes, it means dragon-head horse."

"People back on Earth would be rather shocked to see some of these animals."

"They will be even more shocked if they get involved with the wrong aliens."

"Why do you say that?"

"On Earth the diet of a lot of people is fish and animals. In parts of the galaxy the diet is barbecued humans."

"I suppose that means we taste like Chicken," Chester joked.

"If it were not for the Federation imposing quarantine on Earth, a lot of your population would already have been rounded up and taken away to be butchered as a delicacy."

"I can see where we need to learn more about the Galaxy before we telegraph our presence."

"I think you are a little too late for that."

"How so?"

"Your radio waves have been traveling through space for 120 years. A lot of intelligent life has intercepted those signals. Even though such signals are extremely weak due to attenuation with spreading, modern sensors advanced civilization have can find the buried noise and obtain the information the signals broadcast. In some cases, we know of them restoring TV and FM radio station signals almost 100 light years away."

"Aida, do you know a lot about societies that live within 100 light years of Earth?"

"We have explored that region of space extensively. We know it well. Some of our enemies live there."

"Are they a threat to Earth?"

"They would be if the Federation did not hold them at bay."

The Safari Tram Covered Gondola passed by multiple types of animals that seemed to be fenced in and separated from the others including glass walls in some cases with the more dangerous appearing animals.

Some enclosures had vast numbers of birds with beautiful colors.

There were amphibians and reptiles. One particular reptile that looked kind of strange. Brooklyn said that animal appears to be a cross between a turtle and a crocodile."

"That aquatic animal has a turtles shell for a body and long feet, tail and mouth just like a crocodile," Chester added.

"When they sleep, they pull their arms and legs into their shells," Aida said.

Soon they were back at the loading zone and departed the Safari Tram Covered Gondola and continued walking along the vast park seeing all kinds of sights.

"This in no way looks like the San Diego Zoo where I'm from," Chester said.

"This Zoo and park have undergone numerous changes over the years. The city is lucky a generous man gave the city this large piece of land to put a park on it and had a great legal team to make sure it could never be sold off and parceled out for commercial or residential purposes," Aida responded.

"I can see whereby being the center of the empire, it's important to have a landmark facility like this for all the tourists to visit as part of itinerary when visiting this planet," Chester responded.

They walked around the park for a while and Brooklyn was enjoying the walk and after smelling some of the food being barbecued by visitors at a few locations, the dog said, "Papa, I think I'm getting hungry."

"I'm kind of feeling the same thing," Chester said.

"There is a VIP parking area just ahead. Us walk over there and I'll have the Skycar come pick us up. I have reserved an area of a restaurant with a nice view for lunch."

"Lead the way. We are ready," Chester responded.

"In about fifty yards they came up to a well camouflaged parking area that could simultaneously provide landing zones for a dozen such Skycars. Chester looked up in the air after hearing some noise and a Skycar came down and landed in that parking facility.

"Looks like our ride is here," Brooklyn said very intuitively.

Brooklyn's comment struck Aida in a few ways. She was growing more and more aware of why Doctor Akssiar was so upbeat on his study with Brooklyn. The obvious was now starting to be obvious. Brooklyn was not only a talking dog, but he had significant mental faculties and Aida knew with the right training he could go far in the spy business as a dog, well concealed and the enemy would never suspect a dog involved in espionage.

The group walked to the first Skycar that landed that preceded a second Skycar to pick up the bodyguards. Soon they were on their way to the next stop for lunch.

In less than five minutes the two Skycars approached a very tall building. The height and the architecture truly mesmerized Chester who now understood he was at a very special time and place in his life.

The Skycar continued closer and closer to the ornate golden brown tall building and just when Chester was starting to get nervous, they might crash into it an area on the side of the building suddenly opened. Thanks to the architecture and design, the doors that slid open allowing access to Skycars had nothing to show these were doors since they blended into the side of the building so systematically.

This area of the building located on the floor below a restaurant was a Skycar VIP parking lot. While the Skycar was outside the building computer networks took control of the Skycar and guided it precisely into the building and into a parking spot. The bodyguard Skycar right behind it, was vectored into the adjacent parking spot. As soon as the building computer network deemed it safe to allow passengers to leave their skycars signals were sent to the onboard navigation and management system to open the doors allowing passengers to get out.

Artificial intelligence using sound and holographs directed the group to the elevator that would take them up several floors where their reservations were. Now came a big surprise. Rich people had dogs, but they were not allowed to walk into a restaurant. The way they handled it was the restaurant had doggy transporters. Outside the view of the diners, one of the restaurant employees expecting a dog with the reservation and appraised by artificial intelligence the size of the dog approached the group with the pet carrier.

She opened the door to the doggy transporter and said, "Please put your pet inside the transporter."

The employee was quite surprised when she observed Chester say, "Brooklyn please get inside the transporter."

Brooklyn, knowing Chester did not want him speaking in public walked over to the transporter and hopped into the woman's delight.

"You have a very well-trained dog."

Since the woman didn't speak English, Aida responded in standard Drolupric, "Yes, he's very smart and disciplined."

The doggy transporter was all robotic controlled and electric powered with zinc-manganese oxide and hydrogen pancaked battery like device. The carbon nanotube matrix that separated the hydrogen from the zinc-manganese oxide sliced wafers caused covalent bonding that produced electric currents across the surface areas of each waver slice. Hooked in series the summation of the electricity produced at each wafer slice junction was substantial when all added up. All four wheels were independently controlled and powered with the ability to produce a velocity equal to anyone walking in the restaurant. The doggie transporter could turn very tight corners thanks to four independently controlled wheels.

They were escorted to a glass covered balcony that had a large partition that blocked off their tables from the view of all the restaurant diners. Sophisticated diners of upper class took no time to discover a person wearing clothing with the Royal Seal walking through the restaurant. It seemed like a wave following them as that awareness manifested and then people making quiet conversation discuss this rare sighting.

The emperor's life was heavily guarded, including all members of his family. They simply were not disclosed to the public except on very rare occasions. The immediate speculation now floating around the restaurant seemed to point towards the consensus was this was probably one of the emperor's son's he's never disclosed.

In some past emperor times such relatives were not disclosed until the emperor passed and his heir to the throne was disclosed for the first time in their lives.

The doggy transporter also added to the discussions and that made the people want to discover more about the person and the pet.

Soon the group was on the other side of the large partition diners could not see past and observe the diners.. But no matter how hard they tried to obscure the view, there were always revelations in ways never imagined.

One lucky restaurante client was at a perfect angle to see a reflection off the glass canopy and only in this one spot in the restaurant could someone see what was happening on the other side of the restaurant partition.

Brooklyn was let out by his transporter, and they had a doggie chair set up for him that had bowls of food and water staged for him.

Chester instinctively helped Brooklyn up onto the doggie chair and now that one obscure person in the restaurant saw it. It did not dawn on him to photograph it with his personal communicator until it was too late.

Aida, Chester, and Brooklyn sat alone at a table, while the bodyguards sat at two other tables.

Their food and drinks were ordered ahead of time so moments after arrival the drinks and the first course of the meal were abruptly served.

This upscaled restaurant had dealt with finicky eating dogs in the past who just refused to eat dog food. The restaurant then figured out how to make their own and make it so palatable the dogs had no issues eating their version of dog food.

Chester's purple *Grand Zumbido* elixir hit the spot right away. The only reason why this restaurant had it to serve and instructions to serve it only to this group was the emperor's palace sent it over in advance of their arrival as the entire setting was coordinated from the emperor's mansion since Duke Tinktar traveled to another planet, would normally arrange such matters.

Besides the normal clientele in the restaurant there were additional security people under cover and today the manager was happy because it was quickly becoming a very successful day with a larger than normal lunch crowd along with the VIP's.

Brooklyn grudgingly sampled the dog food and was in for a huge surprise. His food was baked delicacies disguised as dog food. Brooklyn took his time and enjoyed every bit of it.

"Is the food okay Brooklyn?" Chester asked between meal courses.

"Papa these tastes pretty good actually."

The security guys that were in position behind the restaurant dividers with the VIP's knew it was Brooklyn talking. It was a surreal feeling for them, and they were briefed they might hear the dog talking and the fact Brooklyn could talk was considered an extremely confidential matter.

These bodyguards also knew better than to mention the talking dog to anyone because Neurological Sonification could be used to torture them, and Duke Tinktar would polygraph them and use Neurological Sonification to confirm which suspect leaked the information. That person could then easily find themselves being pushed out of an airlock in space to experience hypoxia.

During the twenty course meal, Chester was served small servings to make sure he did not get too full allowing him to eat and sample each type of food being served. One of his thoughts was the garbage Abagail served could not hold a candle to the exquisite taste this restaurant provided.

The balcony edge stuck out twenty feet from the building giving Chester a great view of the area. They were situated in a busy part of the bustling city and from up at the altitude of the restaurant, people, and surface transportation devices he could see below seemed rather tiny. People appeared smaller than ants below.

Chester was facing outward with an unobstructed view. There were a few tall buildings nearby he could observe and now and then saw a Skycar leaving or arriving. He could also see the three-dimensional airway for the Skycars go by slightly above him he guessed 500 feet or so. He knew what an advanced Alien civilization was like. He felt privileged in a way. But at the same token understood Earth was precariously prepared what could be bestowed upon them by an advanced alien race. He would soon learn things about Earth no living Earth person was aware of such as galactic wars that were in the vicinity of the planet and screwed up Mars and Venus making them uninhabitable. What he would also find out about Jupiter and its spin rate would astonish him.

These tall buildings seemed so narrow. *The engineering that went into them must have been rather fantastic.* Chester knew the buildings were segmented in height by functionality. He was at about the same height as some other buildings nearby that exposed residential portions. Some of them had small bubbles and blisters hanging out with glass domes as well. He could see in a few cases people out on those glass covered balconies. *I wonder if they are eating lunch like all of us,* Chester thought.

In a way it was almost hypnotic watching the air traffic flow past. Visual interpolation made Chester think the Skycars and other traffic were flying in straight lines and at precise speeds and distances between each one of them. He had no idea how correct he was in his judgement as they were all a few centimeters per second in speed difference. An advanced society controlled this Skyway with utter precision thanks to the level of computational efficiency gave to society.

All this magnificent view gave Chester an inquisitive person thought in his mind of what the computer power for these aliens must be like. No doubt their miniaturization is significantly greater than Earth.

Chester continued daydreaming and pondering his new world when Aida suddenly snapped him out of his thoughts with a question.

"Chester, are you enjoying the food?"

"Why yes, I am. I assure you Abagail never created any food dishes like any of this. It's rather impressive."

"This is a good restaurant, but its not our finest. We simply stopped here because it's on our way. Some other day I will take you someplace that you will know is better."

"I'm looking forward to that."

Between the food and the purple *Grand Zumbido* elixir and the exquisite appearance of Aida, Chester was feeling rather euphoric. He knew that experiencing life in this advanced world being under the magic spell of the charm Aida created went a long way to modify his personal psychology. The abduction at first was a traumatic experience and at times he felt terrorized. But Aida's blissful nature had quite a calming effect on him. She was so beautiful to look at and her clothing exposed the cleavage of her breasts which he had enjoyed just the day before.

Chester knew there was nothing he could do about the predicament he was in. He would have to let events transpire and cope with the new reality dealt him because he happened to be at Ski Beach with a talking dog when Aliens arrived. The odds of them ever meeting in such a manner were astronomically high. By a sheer accident here he was with Brooklyn in a new world and a new life. But Chester was no fool. He knew that since he was not in position to control his own destiny, the chips would have to fall and he had no say in the matter. Would he one day be allowed to go home to Earth? And like Doctor Akssiar warned him, he may decide he didn't want to go back. One of those reasons was sitting next to him this very moment smiling in a way that evoked ensembles of euphoric resonance.

Aida trained in body language and everything a spy needs to know to keep alive, knew Chester was now thinking with his little head. She had a surprise for him when they got back to his suite at Duke Tinktar's mansion.

The meal was soon over and Chester saw enough of the view and was ready to leave and Aida knew it and also knew she had other places to take him.

"Chester, are you ready to leave?"

"Yes Aida, I'm ready when you are."

Aida nodded to a nearby waiter, and he approached and said, "We will be leaving now, can you get the dog transporter staged?"

"Yes madam, right away."

Soon the dog carrier was next to Brooklyn and Chester asked, "Brooklyn would you like me to help you down?"

"No papa, I can get down, but thank you for offering help."

Brooklyn jumped down from his doggie chair and walked into the dog carrier and laid down. The dog carriers built in microprocessors shut the door to conceal the dog and the group stood up and the restaurant partition slid out of their way so they could comfortably leave.

They were soon approaching the Skycars, and Chester brought up a point:

"Usually after a meal, Brooklyn likes finding a tree or go somewhere he can poop."

"Actually, a dog park was on our list of places to visit today. We'll make it our next stop," Aida said then nodded to the head of her security detail who understood where they were to go next.

Just like his hometown, San Diego, California, Tymasoara had some beaches were identified as dog access authorized. People could take their pets there, enjoy the beach with their dogs.

Unlike Dog Beach in San Diego, next to Ocean Beach where you had to clean up after your dog, this beach had sanitation engineers with pooper scoopers and were immediately on the scene to de-poop that section of the beach.

As soon as they were at the beach, Brooklyn said, "Papa I need to poop, where can I do it?"

"Brooklyn see the sign over there that says in Drolupric "dogs are not required to be on a leash," Aida immediately responded as she pointed to the sign."

"I see that," Brooklyn responded.

"You can poop over there."

"Alright," Brooklyn responded and went over and did his business including marking the sign.

Brooklyn got the attention of a few other dogs who were soon upon him smelling him as he smelled different than any dog they met before.

Brooklyn ignored the dogs and walked back to Papa and said, "What do we do now Papa?"

"Do you want to play in the water?"

"Not really, Papa."

"Alright perhaps we can just stay here for a while and observe."

A couple dogs came up to Brooklyn again and were sniffing him. Brooklyn seemed to ignore them, which caught Chester's attention.

"Brooklyn, what do you think about those dogs?"

"Papa, I really do not care for the bitches, they're not my type."

"Alright Brooklyn if you see one your type, let me know."

The group stood there waiting and watching for 15 minutes. There were a lot of dogs playing with their masters, some going into the water, others chasing after balls and things their master threw.

Chester could see Brooklyn appeared to look bored and asked, "Brooklyn, don't you want to go out there and play with those dogs?"

"Papa, none of that excites me, I would rather go home and watch National Geographic."

Chester was about to ask Aida to return them to Duke mansion or go to the next location when suddenly, a Skycar came down and landed near the Skycars the group came in. It was a wealthy woman in it and soon she got out with her dog that could pass for a poodle back on Earth.

Chester was taking it all in and noticed Brooklyn had swung around and was staring directly at the dog he would say to himself was a poodle. Brooklyn seemed animated and the other dog had an interesting look at Brooklyn. The female owner tried prodding the dog along, but her dog wasn't cooperating and remained transfixed on Brooklyn. Eventually the woman tugged her dog along and got it over where she wanted near the water.

Chester asked Brooklyn, "Do you like that dog?"

"Yea that's a dog alright and I think she likes me."

Aida then jumped in and asked, "Brooklyn would you like to see that dog again?"

"Yes, I would," Brooklyn responded which surprised everyone including Chester. Brooklyn up to this moment had never taken interest in any dogs including the number of them he saw at Ski Beach.

Aida walked over to one of the bodyguards and they had a private conference far enough away where Chester could not hear it. Aida then walked back to Chester and Brooklyn and said, "I think we can arrange for a visit. But for now, we have some other locations to go since Brooklyn has taken care of his business."

"Alright," Chester said.

In a few minutes they were in a Skycar and leaving. Chester could see one of the bodyguards approach the woman. It's highly unusual for a person to be at a dog beach in a suit. The wealthy lady was relatively sophisticated and knew this man was with the other well-dressed men and the woman who just left was with a Gentleman who possibly had on the emperor's logo on his clothes. She knew to take the man very serious and be respectful as he approached.

"Good afternoon, Madam."

"Hello sir, what may I do for you."

"This is a very private matter as you can imagine, but the group that was just here with me had a dog, and they took a fascination in your dog."

"Yes, I saw the dog and so did my dog and I could barely keep her away from it. I think that dog put her in heat."

"If I may say so, that's exactly why I'm talking to you."

"It is?"

"The people that you just saw are actually associated and connected with Emperor Tinktar-II."

The woman felt weak at her knees. But she knew they were going to inform her about something, and she suspected she knew what it was.

"What is it you want from me sir?"

"You may not be aware of it but the dog you saw doesn't have much of a chance to see other dogs. He's very well protected."

"I can imagine if he's connected with Emperor Tinktar-II."

"Here is my business card, that has my contact information on it. I'm the chief in charge of the security detail that is here assigned to provide protection to the people you just saw."

"I suspected as such."

"The reason why I'm giving you this card is it would please the emperor if you would be willing to bring your dog to Duke Tinktar's mansion sometime in the near future so that the dog you just saw can enjoy the company of your dog which we know he likes."

"I suppose I could. Is my lovely princess going to be protected and not molested by the other dog?"

"You can be sure we will also protect your princess unless you agreed to allow them to get involved into some doggy love."

"I'm certainly not going to allow that. No other dog is going to touch my princess."

"What if your princess falls in love with that other dog?"

"I would know and then I would have to decide now, wouldn't I?

"The other dog's owner is a wonderful person. He would not want anything to happen to your princess you wish not happen.

His dog is very intelligent and very well disciplined. After you get to know him, I'm sure you will agree it was a delightful experience getting to know the two."

"I suppose I'm willing to try it and see what happens."

"I can't speak for the emperor but knowing him I'm certain if he discovers that dog likes your dog, you will be given an invitation to visit the emperor at his palace and enjoy festivities with the people you just saw as well as the emperor. I might also add, the emperor loves that dog."

"Alright, I have your card and I will call you in a couple days after my nerves calm down a bit and suggest a time we can go."

"Because of security arrangements and necessities, we will pick you up at your home since we easily know how to find you and bring you to Duke Tinktar's mansion."

"Alright, I'm sure I will be ready."

"In case you do not know it, the man with the dog wearing the emperor's clothing, is single and available. You are a very pretty lady, and I think he will like you."

"Thank you for your compliment's, but I'm not looking for another man. My husband is an intergalactic banker. I really do not need another man in my life."

"Alright madam, I'll be waiting for your call."

"Certainly."

The security man turned around and walked twenty feet and joined the other three who accompanied him to the Skycar. They got inside and took off.

The woman was semi-paralyzed. As the wife of an intergalactic banker who was always gone and boinking women all over the empire, she was sophisticated enough to know, play ball or bad things will happen to you. She was also slightly aggravated her husband had some BS story because he would not be home for a few more weeks as his business on off world planets was extremely busy. She would make that phone call as soon as her nerves calmed down.

Aida took Chester and Brooklyn to a few other places to see and to expose him to the planet and the culture. Overall, it was a joyous experience.

Later when they were back at Duke Tinktar's mansion, the three amigos descended upon Chester's suite where Aida surprised Aizere and asked her to leave for a while, they would contact her when they needed her.

Chester was impressed by the appearance of Aida today. She looked as glamorous as any Earth movie star if not more so. Her perfume was saturated with pheromones. As a very capable spy and well trained in the art of seduction and reading body language, she knew Chester was salivating with his little head. As soon as Aizere was out of the room and Brooklyn was laying up on his doggy bed relaxing, Aida approached Chester. She wanted to confirm her suspicions based on Chester's body language.

Aida walked up to Chester and put her arms around him and kissed him in the most provocative manner and having trained on earth to seduce Generals and Admirals, she slipped her tongue into his mouth that was saturated with pheromones and female amino acids along with a substance called Turnera Diffusa, known as Damiana.

The emperor clothes were designed for easy access for sexual needs. Aida reached into Chester's clothes while she was shocking him with her tongue in his mouth and found his little head and confirmation the dragon was spitting as his underwear had a wet spot and he was almost rock hard. Any less inflation of his manliness was quickly resolved as Aida pulled her tongue out of Chester's mouth and dropped down and started performing fellatio sealing the deal.

Aida knew when to stop because she didn't want Chester to explode yet as she had more plans for him knowing his body would soon respond with the Damiana and Amino acids now in his mouth and throat and slowly being absorbed into his blood stream and on its way to his brain where the pleasure center of his brain would soon start excreting enzymes at a rate that would completely engulf all his emotional and motor functions.

Aida then stood up and knew how to efficiently undress Chester to get him nude and likewise exited her clothing in about 30 seconds and led the startled man over to his bed and got them into position to start copulation.

Just as Chester was reaching a point of no return, Aida said, "You know I spent time on Earth and I seduced a couple admirals and generals and I know what they want to say to women, I want to hear it from you."

Chester was a little confused, so Aida knew she had to help him along and said, "Chester you need to ask me if I want you to fuck me."

Those words drove Chester in a frenzy, and he repeated them followed by Aida saying repeatedly, "Please fuck me and fuck me hard."

In a couple minutes Chester exploded inside Aida in one of the greatest orgasms he ever felt before. His splendid euphoric transcendence was now ensembles of emotional gratification resonance.

If there was any point after the abduction that Abigail's ship was sunk, it just happened. Chester was now seduced to the point that any possible desire to return to Earth to be with Abagail was now extinguished, and the full adventure had not truly started.

Brooklyn watching the horizontal Tango on a theme from Paganini that Papa and Aida were doing caused him to recap his experience today observing the rich lady's poodle dog.

He knew there was a possibility he would see the poodle again and he realized he wanted to hump her. *Would she want him?*

These events along with others were now transpiring elsewhere as Duke Tinktar was just about to administer justice.

~~~~~~
~~~~~~

Chapter Eight

ZETA BANTOR

Prince Tinktar arrived with a small Armada in the solar system that contained the planet, Zeta Bantor. The Armada would orbit other planets so as to not tip off, Zeta Bantor was their ultimate destination to make sure the Traitor was not tipped off authorities were coming to get him.

A lot of good spies live on their laurels. When their detection and eradication occur, they don't see it coming, because counterintelligence is often just as clever as espionage.

The traitor a high-ranking military member had become spoiled and when he discovered how easy it was for him to maintain his lifestyle enjoying the green skin women, fabulous elixirs, and a wonderful chef working directly for him, he let his guard down just a crack, and that crack was just enough to expose him.

Counterintelligence is a lot like traffic analysis when you do not have enough cribs or clues to break the crypto. By detecting the direction of the intercepts as well as the volume, you can start to put together a picture of what is there. You may not know what their intentions are, but thanks to traffic analysis you know where the enemy is operating and how much he has invested in time and effort to achieve the espionage that was going on.

Even the most trivial things can turn into a crib or a clue. After a few cribs and clues, the synergism created eventually begets more cribs and more clues. Add traffic analysis on top of it, then you can start to develop a macro of where abouts the spy is operating, no matter how clever he may think he is.

In many instances spy agencies have watchers. And in some cases, there are issues, and the watchers have watchers. Especially when an area has been identified as a nest of spies.

A watcher is often far more exposed than the spy himself. If you can find the watcher, you can find the spy. But since the enemy involved might have a watcher-watcher, that needed to be determined before you moved in on the Spy because if you arrested the watcher, the watcher-watcher would report back to his superiors and a bugout would be initiated including evacuating the traitor.

Duke Tinktar's main reason for being here besides dealing with the traitor was to make sure some of the counterintelligence personnel didn't get buck fever and arrest the watcher until they nabbed the watcher's-watcher. Then they would round them all up in parallel.

Duke Tinktar didn't want to spend a month waiting for the inevitable, as he was slightly impatient, but he knew it had to be done this way, because none of the rest of his team had the information and briefings he received because of operational security. Because the spy was such a high-level person, they needed to apprehend him before he could destroy the evidence and tip off the enemy the project had been compromised.

The enemy had procedures in place that would determine if the watchers had been turned, and Duke Tinktar knew that, so there was little purpose in thinking they could turn them into a double spy.

The watcher network was all about timing and reports and the overlap was designed so precisely there was little chance they would be detained without the trip wire going off and bugout initiated including immediately evacuating the traitor.

The purpose in evacuating the traitor had no connection between the enemy and their concern for his well-being. The main reason was to deny the enemy the knowledge of just exactly what they lost. The watcher and the watcher-watcher had no knowledge of the INTEL the traitor was providing. That was more operational security for the same reason.

Duke Tinktar knew the possibility of this all unfolding quickly and was utterly delighted to learn his security teams located the watcher's-watcher and had him under long distance surveillance. Now the stage was set for it all to unfold knowing timing was critical. They simply had to get all three at the exact same time.

Forty-eight hours after arriving at Zeta Bantor, the arrests happened in parallel. It required more people at the traitor's home because everyone there including the chef were suspected and had to be arrested and taken away to interrogation.

Neurological Sonification's were always improving. They were slowly turning into great brain washing machines but also when used in conjunction with polygraphs and other techniques, spies had a harder time avoiding the ultimate, the Drolupric INTEL officers and interrogators would get what they wanted out of the spies even if it required them to endure so much pain, they wished they could commit suicide.

Everyone found at the traitor's home received an ample amount of interrogation and torture.

Within seventy-two hours of arrest, the maid, chef, butler, and driver were all broken and in fear for their lives. Their only chance to live was based on cooperation and telling the truth. They got just about all they needed out of the chef who was not fully cooperating. The others all watched his execution and were further warned they too would face a laser firing squad if they did not fully cooperate. After they saw the Chef's body disintegrate into a cloud of debris, they knew the seriousness of it and one of them who had yelled to them to keep their mouths shut was first to see some of the new modes of Neurological Sonification. In due time after watching the traitor scream in severe pain and collapsing a few times the rest of them no longer took his direction to stay shut up. They knew today may be their last day and they all sang like a canary.

They also saw the man after he received special briefings including all their confessions to exactly what they did, that he no longer had the heart to keep silent about the espionage and then he became a canary as well.

The watcher and watcher's-watcher had no idea what the spy was providing, and they also knew by now a trip wire had gone off and the enemy knew the operation was a bust. They were thus separated and sent off to other interrogation centers on other planets where they would disclose procedures and methods or face torture and death. Catching the watchers and the spy at the same time turned out to be a major discovery and an *intelligence bonanza.*

They also nabbed the traitor before he could destroy the evidence, so they now knew some of the INTEL he gave to the enemy. Knowing what got compromised also helps quite a bit because now they have changed their plans and operations, which then makes the previous INTEL simply worthless information. It also makes them susceptible to double agents and disinformation.

After another week it was time to deal with the traitor. He was on his way to the pig farm.

Duke Tinktar was a fair and generous man. The traitor didn't believe anything Duke Tinktar said and since he was going to die anyway, he wasn't going to help him. That was his final statement and Duke Tinktar knew there would be no way to break this man who felt he was a dead man no matter what happened.

But being fair, Duke Tinktar asked the man one more time to cooperate and got a severely negative response about the time they were over the large pig farm in the Vertical Take Off and Landing craft (VTOL).

"This is your last chance, if you do not state you are willing to assist in this investigation, then I have no choice but to gag you and pronounce judgment."

The traitor wasn't going to give Duke Tinktar the satisfaction of responding.

Duke Tinktar didn't like doing it but by the people with him observing this would send a message out to other potential traitors, what happens when you get caught. He nodded at one of his assistants holding a roll of tape who then started rolling it around his face and head, almost mummifying it leaving just a small space at his nose to breath. As soon as the man was taped up and also had his feet and arms bound, Duke Tinktar pulled out his long stiletto style knife and walked over to the man cut him in several place causing the man to bounce around in agony and screaming, but it didn't come out since he was fully gagged.

The pilot announced over the intercom, "We are directly above the pig farm now, ready for the drop. A side door to the VTOL opened up and Duke Tinktar said, throw him out.

At about 500 feet the traitor dropped down in the middle of the sabor tooth hog farm drenched in blood and bleeding badly. The man was seriously wounded in the fall with a broken back and semi paralyzed.

The hogs were at first slightly fearful of the object that landed, but the smell of human blood quickly got their attention and they approached and started smelling it. Some of the hogs licked up his blood, then the feeding frenzy started.

The VTOL craft stayed hovering above the man offset for a while until Duke Tinktar saw the man starting to get torn to threads as the feeding frenzy intensified and the man was surrounded by the hungry hogs that love the taste of human blood and flesh.

The man jerked for a while but soon he laid still as the hogs slowly devoured his body and ripped into his organs including the heart full of blood that drove the hogs into an orgasmic of chewing and devouring the traitor's flesh now in a hyperkinesis state.

"We can leave now, take me back to the safe house."

It was a five-minute flight to the safe house where Duke

Tinktar was deposited and the VTOL went up and out into space to land back in the assault ship now moved into orbit around the planet since there was no longer fear in the spy nest bugging out.

Moments after arrival at the safe house Duke Tinktar's handlers took him in a Skycar to Madam Pang's where he would indulge in her treatments for his nightmarish experience just moments ago. He didn't like doing what he had just done, but unfortunately it was to set an example for others that might want to follow the traitor's career path.

There would be the three personal guards going into Madam Pang's pleasure center. But since this was all planned out in advance there would be another six already there in the event some nefarious activity was to be sprung. That night Madam Pang's pleasure center was the most heavily guarded facility on the planet with additional security outside the building and orbiting overhead in skycars and armored emergency escape craft in case something bad came down. Madam Pang was ready for the grand entrance of her favorite Duke whom she would do her utmost to please tonight with the help of a couple of her best-looking employees whom she would tip lavishly for their divine attention to this exclusive customer.

It was a repeat of many other visits. The nice hot bath and messages to help take his mind off things, then the exclusive elixirs that were highly illegal but overlooked because Duke Tinktar said it was okay.

Duke Tinktar wasn't in the mood for sex. But he didn't mind the distraction and sweetness of the three women. He just wanted to unwind, drink the highly illegal elixirs, and relax and get the images out of his head he had just undergone.

Madam Pang had been with Duke Tinktar before when he was in one of these reflective moods and she explained to the two young ladies that tonight would be soft and pleasing and nothing associated with enticement and recreational sex. They didn't mind this situation and felt uplifted he simply just wanted to unwind and be with the three caring women whom he appreciated beyond words.

There were dozens of hugs and stroking and it all had a calming effect on Duke Tinktar because he knew what he just did. In reality, Duke Tinktar just killed a man in cold blood without a trial, judge, or jury. But in the intergalactic spy business this is how it had to be done, under the radar with no traces back to the source. By morning the traitor's remains would be just more bones out in the middle of the sprawling hog farm. Within weeks, weeds would grow up and cover the remains. All the flesh was now gone. What the sabretooth hogs didn't eat, the smaller varmints did such as brain matter, and anything left in the skull. If the farmer came upon the body now it simply would appear like a skeleton that had been there for a while.

The hog farmer had found a few skeletons before. By then they were weathered and semi brittle. He would crush the remains with a sledgehammer and put them in a barrel and tote the bone and what used to be skull remains to an area he planted feed for the hogs as it made good fertilizer.

While Duke Tinktar was soaking and hugging the three gorgeous women, he was thinking about his predicament about being forced to be the person to carry out such critical operations. It all stemmed from everyone being connected to someone. Then as he thought about it further, he realized in all the empire there was now an individual not connected to anyone with no vested interests. Hence, he wasn't under any sort of patronage.

Duke Tinktar had read all the reports on Chester and Brooklyn. It truly was an extraordinary story. And more so, Chester was a very cooperative soul never making any demands and seemingly just went along with the predicament he landed in from no actions of his own.

He knew the emperor was getting fatigued about his constant involvement in matters like he had just completed. If he had a spare hand he could trust, he could distance himself from a lot of this and he knew that would make the emperor a lot happier.

Right then and there, Duke Tinktar decided the answer to a lot of his problems was to bring in an outsider with no possible connections to nepotism or patronage, and by a strange act and an almost impossible discovery, there was Chester. As soon as he got back to Tymasoara he would go to visit the emperor and talk to him about this and give him his ideas and he felt the emperor would probably go along with it since it meant he would greatly reduce these kinds of trips to the hog farm or out to space to witness a traitor die from asphyxiation as he was shoved tied up out of an airlock.

Suddenly the Duke was full of life again and happy. He would not transcend into copulation or a horizontal Tango on a theme from Paganini, but he would enjoy these three lovely ladies and since they helped him come up with a resolution, he desperately needed by being here for him at the moment of need, he would reward them handsomely tonight.

After a while when he felt reinvigorated to the point of returning to Tymasoara with his new plan he would soon get emperor's approval, he said, "I'm going to get dressed now and leave. This has been a very special evening for me, Madam Pang. You have no idea how much you meant to me tonight. I really appreciate you."

"Your excellency, you were very sweet to us tonight. We enjoyed every moment with you, and I wish you would stay the night."

"I'm sorry my dear, but I must leave now, but I think sometime in the future I will come back and visit you personally. You will not need these two girls; you will be all I need."

"That makes me feel good to hear that from you."

"Come here." Duke Tinktar held out his arms for Madam Pang who approached.

Duke Tinktar hugged Madam Pang like he rarely did, and it felt very good. Madam Pang felt sad she could not make love to him on the spot to show him how much she really liked him. Then to her utter shock and surprise and also to the other two ladies and his bodyguards he reached down and kissed Madam Pang who then felt the shivers go down her back because she knew this was genuine affection. It really was love and he didn't know it but at that very moment he owned her heart. He also didn't know how beneficial that would be for him in the future when you have a woman like this look out for you and protecting your back.

Soon Duke Tinktar was on a shuttle heading out into space and would soon be on his way back to Tymasoara to meet up with Chester and talk to the emperor about his idea he thought emperor Tinktar-II would readily agree to since it's the direction he wanted Duke Tinktar to go in.

Madam Pang also resolved a problem for Duke Tinktar. He felt for her and no longer needed Aida to be his top concubine. When he got back to his mansion, he would find out how far along Aida seduced Chester and he would lead her along just long enough to where Chester could take over as her consummate lover. When he needed romance, he would be back visiting Madam Pang.

~~~~~~~
~~~~~~~

Chapter Nine

LEARNING HOW TO BE A DROLUPRIC

While Duke Tinktar was busy with affairs on Zeta Bantor the next chapter in Chester's life unfolded. The next day, Doctor Akssiar arrived with his technicians to start Chester's Neurological Sonification's.

They all gathered in Chester's suite where there would be plenty of room to conduct the activity. Brooklyn watched it all unfold.

A special reclining chair and a vast instrument array was brought in. Before long, Chester was strapped in the sonification chair, and the wizards began their work.

To Brooklyn it looked like there wasn't much happening as if Chester was simply lying back to take a nap. Anyone watching the procedure would not know the extensive neurological transcendence that was going on. In just one session Chester learned almost two years of Drolupric language training. Afterwards he was sedated and advised to stay in bed until the next morning. The staff would bring him room service and drinks.

In due time Chester passed out and was in a deep dream state. After everyone was gone except Aizere, Aida took off her clothes and climbed in bed with Chester so that he would see her when he woke up and she would be there for him in case he had some mental discomfort, she would then summon the staff doctor to issue him post Neurological Sonification medications which usually involved drugs such as opioid morphine like substances.

It was a long night since part of the time included the evening. Chester had vivid dreams that night as his brain had been diced and rewired and data dumped in. Neurological Sonification sent ensembles of holographs to the brain that was packaged in a way for direct storage. In Chester's dreams he had clouds of words floating above him just like a weather front coming in.

The brain is quite an amazing thing. In the past Chester studied the Chinese Language. He learned thousands of Mandarin Chinese Characters and the complete radical table in his quest to speak Chinese. Along with the Drolupric words floating in word clouds coming at him from the horizon, there was also Mandarin Chinese Characters mixed in. Chinese is one of those things you use, or you lose. But you really do not lose, they simply get buried in the least recently used area of the brain. By relearning the brain simply moves that information into a most recently used area and it appears to a person they relearned it when all they really did was reprioritize where in the brain the information was stored.

Around 3:30 in the morning Chester woke feeling he needed to urinate and discovered Aida was in bed with him. He got up without disturbing her too much and went into the bathroom and took care of the business. Chester then went back to bed and closed his eyes hoping the clouds of words would not come back.

Hoping he had not disturbed Aida he rolled on his side and shut his eyes wondering if he could get back to sleep. Unfortunately, Chester had already slept almost 12 hours and didn't realize it. His brain was not going to let him fall asleep. In some ways he didn't mind because he didn't want to visualize those clouds of words floating by him.

Aida had been with Chester during most of those twelve hours and he woke her up by going to the bathroom. She soon felt the same need to urinate and as she crawled out of bed, artificial intelligence turned on soft light slowly just like it did for Chester so she could find her way to the bathroom without difficulty. Chester saw her nude body and wondered if they had experienced sex the night before, but he couldn't remember as all he had in his mind was clouds of words.

Aida finished her business, then came back into the bedroom and could see Chester's eyes were open. He observed her nudity, and it caused a reaction. Once Aida was back in bed with him, she scooted her body next to his and put her arm over him. She then reached down and found his manliness and confirmed he had an erection and she squeezed it a few times insuring its full hardness. She then rolled his body flat and climbed on top of Chester and started making love to him.

Aida's actions were very pleasing to Chester as it helped eliminate the clouds of words flowing through his thoughts. Aida being the consummate seductress and trained in the fine art of pleasing men to conduct honey pot traps quickly aroused Chester into a strong release of gratification. She felt his release was strong and in abundance which triggered her own surreal gratification and splendid euphoria.

Afterwards the two lay on their sides facing each other with Aida's head resting on Chester's chest. Even though they didn't need the sleep, the post orgasmic activity in the pleasure center of their brains helped induce a sleep and soon they were back in dreamland together. Chester was glad his dream developed without clouds of words.

Chester a few times had some very terrible dreams in the past. Perhaps it was brought on by books or movies, he didn't know. But on one of those events his deep thoughts gave him the notion he could steer his dreams away from discomfortable thoughts and into more pleasant ones. Once he learned he could do that, manipulate his own dreams, he never had serious episodes again until the clouds of words started floating in mind.

Thanks to Aida's presence and her spontaneous love making, Chester now steered his dreams into pleasant thoughts such as riding a train with Aida like he always wanted to do with a lover.

Abagail would never be part of such dreams because it was something she never wanted. But Chester wanted a Contessa for his ride on the Orient Express. And while on the train he wanted to make love to the Contessa. And so, in his current dream Chester had Contessa Aida with him on the Orient Express and they made joyous love. Aida didn't know it quite yet, but she had pushed Chester off the cliff of love.

The combination of Neurological Sonification's and the seduction of a galactic class spy had done more in such a short period of time than any subtle brainwashing could ever accomplish. Chester was now much further along in his assimilation than Doctor Akssiar could ever hope.

The day for Chester and Brooklyn had been planned out in detail, so at 06:30 A.M. as per the plan, artificial intelligence began waking Chester. Soon Aizere was at Chester's bed side urging him to awaken and get up so they could prepare him for today's events.

Aida was simultaneously awakened and got up and put her clothes back on and left the suite. As soon as Chester was ready Aizere helped him out of his bed and took him into the bathroom where he could do his morning affairs and bathe. His bath water would be laced with pleasurizers and subtle medications that would alleviate headaches or mental stress as ordered by the Neurological Sonification Doctor.

Brooklyn received his own bath and care by the illustrious dog groomer Rayalna. After his bath and blow dry while Rayalna was grooming and coming Brooklyn's fur she asked, "How was your day yesterday, Brooklyn?"

"It was quite interesting," Brooklyn responded.

"In what way?" Rayalna asked.

"I was taken to a dog beach and while there I saw a beautiful dog."

"Did you like the dog?"

"Yes, and I know she likes me."

"How do you know that?"

"She was staring at me and didn't want to move, and her owner had to drag her away to get her over near the water."

"Maybe we can get you down to dog beach soon so you can meet this dog."

"I hope so. I think I like her, but I know she can't talk so we will not be able to communicate except for the way dogs normally do."

"And what way is that?"

"A female dog will let a male hump her if she likes him."

"I see." Rayalna said not wanting to take the conversation any further in that direction because Chester was a short distance away and she didn't want to give him any ideas because she knew that if Duke Tinktar thought Chester wanted a crack at Rayalna he would coerce her to accommodate him and she did not want to go there, especially since Aida had already tagged Chester.

After bathing and grooming, Chester and Brooklyn were led into a dining room where they were soon joined by Doctor Akssiar and Tasha who would have breakfast with Chester and Brooklyn.

"Good morning, Chester," Doctor Akssiar said, and Tasha smiled at the same time.

"Good morning, Doctor," Chester replied.

All the surveillance video and arrangements that were being made had been given to Doctor Akssiar to monitor and weigh in on future planning. Things were advancing nicely and today would be a major milestone in the overall execution of the plan.

"Chester, how are you feeling today?" Doctor Akssiar asked.

"I feel okay, but I did have some really weird dreams last night."

"Later today one of my research associates will get with you and discuss the dream to determine if the Neurological Sonification may have had a role in that."

"I already know it did."

"How do you know that?"

Chester then gave the doctor a quick dissertation on how he saw the clouds of words floating by which included the Chinese words.

"That's very interesting Chester, thanks for telling me that."

"You are welcome doctor."

"Later this morning after you finish your meal and freshen up, I want to give you a test," Doctor Akssiar said.

"Why do you want to give me a test?" Chester asked.

"This is to determine the efficacy of the Neurological Sonification you received yesterday."

"Sure, I don't mind taking a test."

"I appreciate your willingness to take the test."

Chester noticed Tasha was looking at him in a strange manner. Tasha's clothing was probably not a good idea this morning because it exposed her stimulation with her breasts because her nipples appeared to harden by arousal for some reason. She too had observed the secret surveillance video and had seen Chester perform the day before and no matter how clinically subjective she tried to be, the woman down deep inside her that wanted to scream and break out of her shell, was now reacting by being just a few feet away from the man that was the subject of her investigation. Tasha felt weak in the presence of Chester.

The morning activities moved along smartly and after Chester and Brooklyn were fed, and taken back to their suite to freshen up, Doctor Akssiar and Tasha were at the door to the suite to escort Chester and Brooklyn to Duke Tinktar's library.

Inside the library was a nice long table so that Duke Tinktar could spread out maps or a series of documents he was studying.

"This library will be available to you when you wish to come here and read. But you can also look at documents in your suite via electronic tablets."

"Alright."

"This test we want you to take will give us some idea how well the Neurological Sonification succeeded in developing your Drolupric language skills," Tasha stated and handed the bound sheets to Chester along with a writing stylus.

Chester took the papers and stylus and sat down at the table and pulled another chair out and asked Brooklyn, "Would you like to sit here next to me?"

"Sure papa."

Chester picked up Brooklyn and sat him on the chair he pulled out, then sat back down and started taking the test written in English as a multiple-choice exam.

All throughout the test were statements in Drolupric. Then a question in English stating "select one of the following that best describes the statement above."

One of the answers always given stated, "I do not know what that means."

It took Chester about thirty minutes to go through the seven-page test. There was only one question he picked: "I do not know what that means."

Tasha critiqued the test with Chester while Doctor Akssiar observed.

"You only chose the wrong answer one time, but that is expected because that question was designed for someone who understands Drolupric culture, so it's designed for you to pick the wrong answer. We did that as part of the quality control process to help make the results less subjective. Also, the question you selected:

"I do not know what that means," contained information you were not taught by Neurological Sonification which also is designed to substantiate the efficacy of your training.

"All right thanks. It looks like I did well in a written multiple-choice test."

"That you did."

"That's great. When do I get my next treatment?"

"That will happen tomorrow afternoon after you have a visitor."

"I have a visitor tomorrow?"

"Yes. Remember when you were at the dog beach yesterday, you saw a lady with a nice-looking dog that Brooklyn seemed to like?"

"Yes, I remember her."

"Her name is Margrét Hansen. She's the wife of an intergalactic banker. After you left the dog beach, one of your bodyguards approached her and asked her if she would like to visit you today because Brooklyn liked her dog and the two of you are kind of lonely."

"Brooklyn has never been involved in another dog. His friends are birds and squirrels."

Based on how Brooklyn responded to Margrét Hansen's poodle and her dog "Princess Tiffany" actions towards Brooklyn, we think the two will like each other and this will help make Brooklyn more satisfied staying here if he has a friend to socialize with.

"Papa, I want to see Princess Tiffany," Brooklyn abruptly stated which surprised Chester.

"Sure, if Margrét Hansen wants to bring Princess Tiffany to visit Brooklyn, then I'm sure it will be okay."

"That's great you feel that way. But for now, there is another test we want to do with you."

"Sure, go ahead."

"This is a verbal test to see if you recognize the sounds of the words."

"Alright, I'm ready let's begin."

Tasha began the aural test with Doctor Akssiar observing and taking notes from the recent conversation and some ideas that popped into his head.

Tasha asked the questions in standard Drolupric saying, "You can answer me in English or Drolupric, which ever you feel comfortable." "Alright."

"How are you feeling today?" Tasha asked in Drolupric.

"I feel fine," Chester answered in Drolupric.

For the next hour there were similar types of conversational questions and answers and checks of Chester's voice recognition.

As the time passed and getting closer to the end of the session the questions became far more comprehensive as well as difficult because Chester had to answer with complete sentences in order to convey his interpretation and translation of the words into his thoughts. After the hour was up, Tasha said, "That will be all for today. You can enjoy the rest of your day and if you want to spend time here in the library reading some Drolupric books, the librarian will be here to assist you in pronouncing the words or translating. He like the rest of the staff here received Neurological Sonification to learn English so that they can communicate with you until you can fully engage everyone in Drolupric."

"What about Brooklyn?"

"I'm glad you brought that up. We are very pleased with how well you responded to Neurological Sonification and the dogs we have done Neurological Sonification, can't talk but they respond to the commands we give them in standard Drolupric. We also have one dog we have given English by Neurological Sonification and so we now are ready to proceed with Brooklyn's first Neurological Sonification. We recommend we do that in your suite so we can lay him in his bed and be sedated after the procedure. You can spend your time in the library learning what is here and read a few things during that procedure."

"Alright."

The group hung out together and Chester got to meet the librarian, a gentleman by the name of Chernega.

"Chernega is a retired Army Regimental Commander."

"Pleased to meet you Chernega," Chester said in perfect Drolupric.

"It is my most pleasure to meet you Chester, and if I may say so, I never dreamed I would see the day of a talking dog," Chernega stated and was well briefed on Duke Tinktar's VIP guests.

"It seems that a librarian job would be significantly less in scope than being an Army Regimental Commander," Chester said.

"Chester, I have two purposes here. One is to maintain the library but also, I have the responsibility of creating and archiving Duke Tinktar's personal and private papers so that in the future, historians who might want to research Duke Tinktar to write a biography, or commentary about him has factual resources that are well cataloged to enable them to understand."

"Is Duke Tinktar a historical figure other than being related to the emperor?"

"Yes, in fact he is. He's had a lot of activities the public is unaware of for his own personal safety as well as safeguarding methods and materials he utilized in conducting various operations. Much of what he's done will not be released until 150 years after his death unless a sitting emperor decides to disclose it earlier."

"I presume the fact he requires a personal librarian to catalog and track his information, he probably had a lot of unique experiences."

"That indeed he did."

After some small talk and the librarian Chernega going over some of the materials that were readily available including permission to take the books or maps to his suite to enjoy, the group was eventually summoned to the duke's dining hall where their lunch had been prepared.

Chernega was expressly invited along by Aida who joined them in the middle of the conversation was seated directly across from Chester so they could continue with their conversations.

Drinks and elixirs were served but for Brooklyn it was water and dog food. Thanks to the chef's ingenuity, Brooklyn's dog food was coated with very tasty flavors which gave him the feeling he was eating the same thing the others were eating. Brooklyn carried on as if he had no concern for the world, though he was starting to get uncomfortable with Papa spending too much time with Aida. Now that Brooklyn was far away from Abagail whom he detested, the last thing in the world he wanted to see was Papa getting hooked by another woman and cause trouble for him.

"Tell me Chernega, what was it like being a regimental commander?" Chester asked.

"Chester the people here at Tymasoara are well isolated from the distant planets of our empire. I'm sure that where you come from there are periods of strife and aggression caused by leaders who have an agenda and miscalculate the response and instigate conflicts."

"That's also been a part of our human experience on my planet Earth over the eons."

"Chester, in the heart of our empire around Tymasoara, there hasn't been much conflict for a few hundred years, but out at the distant planets in our empire, they run into issues not so different than your planet Earth. There we have armed conflicts. Sometimes we have fought over planets that are part of our empire with other civilizations who wanted those planets to be part of their portfolio."

"Did you fight in some of those battles?"

"Yes, in fact my last involvement was at the Battle of Martos."

"What was it like?"

"It started out as an unmitigated disaster because the Drolupric task force commander, General Serbino, a byproduct of patronage was utterly incompetent and led his forces into an elaborate trap. It was a blood bath, and my regiment was sent there to help recover from the disaster."

"Who won the battle?"

"It's one of the classic battles that will be taught at the military academy for many generations because of how we turned it around."

"What was the attributing actions that brought about victory?"

"I might be getting into a sensitive area, but I'm sure Duke Tinktar probably would not mind informing you, but all of you must consider this confidentiality because Duke Tinktar has never permitted me to disclose the information, I'm going to share with you. I'm hoping that sometime soon he will agree to make a public statement about it as its one of those matters, I think the public should know about."

"I do not have anyone to share the information with, so your secret is safe with me," Chester stated.

"When almost all hope was gone Duke Tinktar led a reserve force in to salvage the operation. Martos is one of our planets, belonging to the empire for over 1000 years. Prior to that it was an independent world, but because that part of space became a dangerous place because the despot leaders in nearby empires were in the imperialist mode. Martos sent an envoy to our emperor requesting he consider bringing them into the commonwealth and become a member state of the Drolupric Empire."

Chester looked at Chernega with intense interest knowing this was going to be a very interesting story.

"Nobody knows for sure why the emperor agreed to accept the offer, and historians have written that based on conversations he only did so to protect them and felt for their plight as they were considered low hanging fruit and pushovers almost how your planet Earth is now perceived. I'm sure that had the emperor determined they could protect themselves, he would have turned down their request."

Time passed and after many generations of new emperors, one of the nearby powers, the Malawans decided they had superior forces and their ability to send more reserves to the battle if necessary since they were closer to Martos than the heart of the Drolupric Empire. They subsequently attacked and invaded Martos in a dastardly act of aggression to subjugate the Martos people and steal their wealth and natural resources."

"How long did the battle last?"

"It lasted almost a year. The first six months was the period of the disaster before Duke Tinktar arrived with the reserves."

"You were part of those reserves?"

"Yes. My regiment was used to lure a major force away from Duke Tinktar's landing zone."

"How did that work out?"

"We were very lucky the Malawans left a large escarpment unprotected allowing us to get a sizeable force there and dig in before the Malawans were able to shift a large part of their ground forces to threaten our positions on the escarpment."

"Your men put up a good fight?"

"The Malawans did not attack until the 3rd day after committing many troops. Per our plan the 2nd landing which was the real force to attack their headquarters and communications center launched immediately upon the attack on my forces."

"Sounds like a big battle."

"It was and the reason why the plan worked is because I told my troops they only needed to hold this ground for approximately four days and then we could pull back. We were already getting a lot of casualties, but we had to hold so that the feint would work. When the primary target was hit by Duke Tinktar's assault Force, he relieved the pressure on our original landing force that was on the verge of collapse and quickly running out of weapons. That force was led by General Serbino whom Duke Tinktar relieved and sent home to Tymasoara to make sure he did not usurp him during the continued fighting."

"Sounds like it was vicious fighting." Chester responded.

"The Malawans had been brutal to the civilian population. Duke Tinktar sent radio communications to the Malawans informing their military that if any of them were captured they would be treated as war criminals because of their devastation to the civilian population where indiscriminate bombing of civilian housing and infrastructure was carried out leaving the civilians to live in very primativie conditions with starvation and lack of clean drinking water."

"The Malawans at first didn't react to Duke Tinktar's threats because they knew they could fly in as much spare men and material as needed. They also thought our emperor, the Duke's uncle would not greatly strip our own space defenses in order to put a strike force together to support Duke Tinktar at Martos."

"Some of the space assets that were fighting at Martos were similar in nature to General Serbino and acted timid and overly cautious and spent most of their time protecting themselves instead of assisting Martos forces on the ground."

"I can see where that would be a problem," Chester said.

"The thing the Malawans didn't count on happened. They had received devastating blows and we now had three strong points because the original invasion force received reserve forces along with plenty of weapons and ammunitions. They were suddenly on par with the Malawans forces they faced. The Malawans had to strip that force and others on the planet to put together a task force to hit me and my men on the escarpment. Because the original landing force was on our distant flanks now suddenly refreshed and viable, the Malawans ground forces could not hit us from behind. They only had one way to attack and that was up the escarpment where we were well dug in. The fighting was brutal and actually lasted eight days before that Malawans force slowly ran out of troops, weapons and had a total loss of sprit de corps."

"Based on Duke Tinktar's communications to the emperor, our Drolupric space force commander was relieved the day before the big battle. We did not have a superior space force at the planet, but what we did have was a superior commander who was willing to fly his forces through the jaws of hell and informed his men how crucial it was to save our forces on the planet."

"Finally, the day of the big showdown happened. Probes picked up a major Malawans force heading to the planet Martos with eleven huge troop transports full of reserves to turn the tide of a slowly decaying invasion force. As they approached the planet, long before they were able to get into the atmosphere, our combined space force hit them in a brutal set piece attack. The space force was directed to place the troop transports as the priority targets and ignore the rest for later which is opposite of the paradigm of space warfare that dictates you must take out the offensive space warfare ships before engaging troop and supply ships."

"I can see where that might be a detriment to success," Chester intuitively responded.

"This was a force protection measure steep in tradition and military planning. It was exactly what the Malawans predicted we would do and they formed a battle line with their offensive fighter-bomber craft which our Space Force Commander flew through at high speed and engaged them as they were passing only. At the velocities they were going the enemy only had enough time to get one or two salvos off which destroyed a few of our ships, but in reality it turned out to be almost a one for one loss as they also lost a ship for everyone of ours that blew up into sparkling debris and in some cases created large plasma's from exploding ordinance and antimatter nuclear reactor propulsion plants."

"How did that effect the outcome?" Chester asked as he was visualizing the space battle.

"Due to the incredible misjudgment on the part of the Malawans commanders, our forces hit the troop transports really hard and managed to destroy seven of the eleven sent killing a vast number of enemy ground forces that were not going to make it to the planet and help out in any manner."

"Did it even the odds quite a bit?" Chester asked.

"Everyone one of the cargo ships carrying food, water, and supplies was wiped out by our space force, so the few Malawans who made it to the planet surface had no food, water, weapons, or ammunition. They were only useful to replace dead soldiers that still had viable weapons."

"So, what happened?"

"Our space force commander realizing he had achieved his objective in the destruction of seven out of the eleven large troop transports directed his force to maneuver out of range of the enemy reforming and reassessing the situation."

"It seems to me he should have pressed home the attack then. Did he let an opportunity slip by?"

"There were still substantial Malawans space assets in the vicinity but by reforming out of harm's way, our new Space Commander could then take time to rationally determine his next move."

"What about the enemy? Seems like he inadvertently gave them breathing room in doing so."

"On the contrary, the enemy commander who would soon have to go explain to his emperor why so many of their troops were killed in that space battle had rattled nerves. His plan to get the troop transports down to the planet had failed miserably, and of the four remaining transports, these were truly untested reserves because as it turned out the battle hardened soldiers were all on the transports destroyed. And without supplies that were also destroyed those new recruits were not going to add materially to the outcome of the battle."

"That's rather interesting, what did they end up doing?"

"Part of the next phase of engagement was to take out the surviving four transports that actually made it to the surface at the main enemy stronghold."

"That seems like the logical thing to do."

"With Malawans efficiency they were unloaded, and the cargo was laid out in piles getting assorted by the logistics technicians and were about to be placed on surface transporters to haul to ammo dumps, food kitchens, and ground forces that needed men and materials. All the supplies unloaded in nice, beautiful piles were all intermixed with food, fuel, ammo, weapons such as hand held missiles and laser cannons."

"Beautiful target right?"

"That morning a combined operation from the Drolupric artillery and space fighter-bombers, hit the four troop transports destroying them quickly and after a couple passes over the stockpiles of supplies they too were destroyed and our forces were able to get away because the timid Malawans space force commander was operating too conservatively and had his forces too far away from the planet to offer assistance until it was too late and the supplies and four large troop transports were laying in smoldering debris."

"How long did the battle last after that?"

"Watching all that unfold disheartened the Malawans soldiers who now completely lost their stomach for fighting and a string of desertions began."

"It seems this would be the prefect time to hit them hard, they were obviously off balance."

"You guessed exactly what was in store for the enemy. Duke Tinktar knew he could put the dagger in the heart of the enemy if he could do something to force their space force away from the planet for a few days while he conducted offensive operations."

"How did he manage to do that?"

"After conferring with the emperor, it was decided the best

defense would be an offense and if we attacked the nearest Malawans planet that would create enormous strife and a predictable reaction drawing the space assets away for a few days."

"I would think so too."

"Duke Tinktar was transported up into space after giving his commanders their orders on where and how to strike the enemy in a carefully coordinated attack. Once Duke Tinktar was aboard the command ship, they transited in a circuitous route to get to the Malawans planet Zorbzhang."

"What was so special about Zorbzhang?"

"Zorbzhang was a tourist planet with lots of tropical like paradise areas. It was almost a water world with 75% of the planet's surface water with a vast number of islands and only a couple small continents. It was the last place the Malawans could conceive to be attacked and was currently full of rich clients enjoying their holidays and boundless recreation a sex industry of Malwantutes manifested."

"Did Duke Tinktar attack helpless civilians?"

"There was no need to indiscriminately kill helpless civilians but by creating havoc it would force the Malawans space force to intervene and get them away from Martos long enough for the ground operation to unfold."

"And how did you do that?"

"The plan was to take out all the Zorbzhang power grid. Not all at once but staggered to give them time to call for help and plead for mercy. Since there were few military assets at Zorbzhang since its garrison was stripped down to supply cannon fodder at the battle of Martos. Any air defense that remained was quickly and systematically taken out. Zorbzhang was thus a sitting duck and taking out the power grid in the manner they did not offer any real challenges."

"How did the attack on Zorbzhang achieve results?"

"Panic calls to Malawans central government quickly produced the predictable results. They sent their space force currently supporting Martos combat operations directly to Zorbzhang where a token force was left behind acting as a carrot and a rear guard with instructions to avoid combat and simply lead our forces further away from Martos areas of operations. The rest of the Drolupric space force did an end around and went back to Martos to assist in the ongoing campaign that was quickly rolling up the enemy."

"What was the result of that?"

"On day eight all the Malawans facing my troops were evacuated and sent to their main base of operations because they were being slaughtered. It was a last-ditch effort. Our fighting had achieved the desired results. We forced the enemy to split its forces and we did a good job of damaging the part that came after us, so when they were evacuated, they only had about half the number of warriors they started out with."

"How did you force them out?"

"As Duke Tinktar predicted, the Malawans forces chased after our rear guard to a point "Q" designated where our forces then maneuvered in another direction and eventually rejoined the fleet now systematically taking out all the air defenses the Malawans had making them highly vulnerable from air attack."

"How did they make out?"

"The rear guard actually damaged a dozen Malawans space cruisers and a space battleship with antiquated space mines they were not expecting which forced them to travel in a far more conservative manner allowing our rear guard to high-speed transit back to formations engaged in wrapping up the enemy. By then it was too late. The last stronghold of Malawans at their based called the Iron Triangle were on the verge of starvation and just about out of ammunition and weapons with a lot of desertions during the nights."

"What was the result of all that?"

"Finally, a surrender was offered and by the time the Malawans space force was back to Martos ready to commence ground support operations, it was too late. The ground war was over, and we had over one million Malawans captured and prisoners. Unlike the Malawans our forces now had plenty of supplies pouring in, including air defense systems, space drones, probes, and a variety of sophisticated weapons. Duke Tinktar was advised the planet was now sufficiently supplied with space defense weapons his space fleet was no longer required for planetary defenses or ground support, he could then redeploy the space fleet for complete space operations and start taking out the remainder of the Malawans space force. Which he did."

"It sounds like Duke Tinktar had a significant victory."

"It did not take long for the Malawans space force commander to realize his fleet was in a very perilous posture. The Drolupric supply train was now delivering space assets like drones, probes, neutron torpedoes, space mines, and anti-spaceship missiles and kinetic weapons. His space fleet was systematically being bled to death when all hope of salvaging the ground forces was gone with the surrender, he decided it was time to leave and go back and face his emperor. Normally a space force commander like this would be pondering his execution for disobeying the emperor and leaving the battle with his troops, but after conferring with his top commanders they all knew the obvious, the end game was now confronting them. The operation was a failure and there was no point in squandering the space force over the ego of the emperor, so they simply turned and headed back to the Malawans empire."

"Were they executed for disobeying orders?"

"The Malawans space force commander made sure word traveled ahead of the staggering losses. That would put the emperor in a precarious situation as the population turned on him as word reached home of all the young boys that were squandered because of the emperor's ego and he may have started a gigantic war, because there was good reason now for Drolupric retaliation for the brutality inflicted upon the civilian population of Martos."

"A full-scale insurgency was then ongoing in the Malawans capital. The emperor directed the space force to bomb the insurgency now surrounding him in his holdout in his palace."

Chester looked on as Chernega explained the results that were rather astonishing. Chester was now captivated because he realized space warfare was so far beyond Earth's abilities, it was scary.

"The Space force commander knew that if he saved the emperor, he was still subject to be executed for defying his orders by leaving Martos and returning ending the fighting there. After conferring with his commanders, the decision was they would not harm the civilians now engaged in the insurgency. Three days later the emperor was dead and then the military intervened to restore law and order as they tried to figure out how to piece back their empire and send peace feelers to the Drolupric empire."

"Did you retire shortly after that battle?" Chester asked.

"Duke Tinktar knew my forces had taken a terrible beating and he knew I was not popular for executing his plan as he asked me to perform. I lost half of my men in savage fighting which included hand to hand combat in my own command center once when the enemy troops breached our defenses. In the process I received some terrible wounds, but I knew I had to keep fighting or the whole thing would cave in on us and all the loss of life would have been for nothing."

"You stayed until the fighting ended?"

"As soon as hostilities ended my staff medical doctor insisted, I be a taken to surgical triage immediately and evacuated. An hour later as I was being sedated for surgery Duke Tinktar came to me bedside and visited me and thanked me for what I had achieved. He knew the terrible fighting that had gone on at the escarpment which had been reported to him by the new task force commander. He informed me the fighting was over, the enemy had fully surrendered, and he was going to take me with him on his ship and return to Tymasoara."

"I was soon asleep and transported to his spacecraft which he left in taking me back to Tymasoara. I woke up three days later in a suite here having undergone a few surgeries that saved my life. As soon as Duke Tinktar was informed, I was awake and coherent in my hospital bed in a suite room, he came to visit me and said he was retiring me, he had more important job to do. That's how I became his personal librarian."

Chester suspected there was more to the story that Chernega was not revealing, and he was right. It did not make sense you take your best commander out of the military and make a librarian out of him. The fact the library was also a map room probably means Duke Tinktar used Chernega as a military advisor. But there was far more to the story as Chester would learn when Duke Tinktar brought Chester into his inner circle.

Duke Tinktar was a good judge of character and now the chips were all lining up. Chester didn't know it yet, but he was going to be the person that was going to make the emperor happy to see Duke Tinktar relieved of a lot of responsibility by a low-level intelligence person from planet Earth.

All because he knew Chester had no strings attached to anyone. Through Neurological Sonification's Chester would be brought into a new dimension of ability and understanding. He would also have his talking dog that would facilitate many of his future activities.

The entrees for lunch were delightful and hit the spot for Chester who had gone a while without food.

There was a little additional small talk with such an interesting person the retired Army Regimental Commander turned Librarian, Chernega who Chester developed a lot of immediate respect. At the same time Chernega, who didn't suffer fools could see there was some interesting aspects about Chester.

The fact Chester showed up with a talking dog exposed volumes about him, as nobody before him ever resembled a man such as Chester who was taking this abduction with fascinating calmness. His eagerness to learn standard Drolupric set him apart. Chernega would be observing Chester and when the time comes make appropriate comments to Duke Tinktar.

The meal was soon over and some of them went back to Chester's suite to prepare Brooklyn for his first Neurological Sonification.

When they arrived in the suite there was a special roll around cart that had electronics packages under the main surface padded for Brooklyn's comfort.

The research associates ready to perform the Neurological Sonification's were standing by and asked Chester, "Would you mind picking up Brooklyn and place him on the cart so we can begin?"

"Sure."

Chester picked up Brooklyn and placed him on the padded cart.

"We know that you can communicate with Brooklyn, we want you to get him to lay down on the cushions and relax and we are then going to sedate him to put him to sleep."

"Alright."

Brooklyn was soon resting peacefully on his side and one of the research associates placed a conformal device over his head and very soon the process began.

"This will take a while; I suggest you visit the library and do some reading and research and we will come and get you when it's over or if something happens you need to be aware of."

"Alright."

Aida then spoke up and said, "Chester I will go with you."

"Thanks."

Soon they were back at the Library and the Librarian Chernega was there fully expecting them.

"Hello Chester, is there anything in particular you wish to read or explore?"

"Yes, how about something with a good discussion of the Drolupric Empire? If possible, I would like to see a video.

"We do not have much in the way of video, but we have substantial holographic 3D presentations."

"I'm sure holographic would be fine."

"Alright, let me get one of the data cubes. But I must warn you it will be in Drolupric standard language."

Aida quickly spoke up and said, "I will be happy to interpret for him if he needs an explanation."

"Very well," Chernega stated, and went to a shelve that stored historical cubicles where he knew some of the greatest periods of history.

Soon Chester was enjoying a high-resolution 3D holograph of one of the most tumultuous periods in Drolupric history depicting incredible efforts associated with major events in this area of the galaxy. Chester knew he was being given a privileged view of the Drolupric history recorded and retained in very high fidelity. The narrators were excellent, and Chester was amazed at how many of the words and statements he understood without the need of translation from Aida.

The Neurological Sonification Chester experienced brought him forward in a major way. He was now realizing the enormity of his situation. These advanced aliens were far beyond what people on Earth could imagine. And he was also in for certain surprises as new events in his life unfolded.

After watching holographs for several hours, the researcher Tasha came to the library and approached Chester and said, "We are all done with Brooklyn's Neurological Sonification's procedures. We would like you to come back to your suite and assist us moving Brooklyn in case he wakes up during the movement."

"Sure, no problem," Chester responded.

Chernega then chimed in and said, "Chester I will put this holograph cube on the shelf for you so when you come back here, I will have it ready for you to finish watching."

"Thank you."

Aida accompanied Chester back to his suite. In reality, the only possession Chester had in his life being away on this alien planet far from earth was his best friend Brooklyn.

Aida understood Chester's situation and reflected on it as they took the short walk back and went in the suite and saw Brooklyn. What they didn't see was all the equipment that was here earlier, nor the team of scientists involved in that Neurological Sonification. Brooklyn had gone through a lot in a short period of time. The doctors knew at the peak of the transfer Brooklyn probably came within ninety five percent chance of dying, it was that close a call. Scientists like to push the envelope and they did with Brooklyn. But the good sense of Tasha was to force them to back down and reduce the sonification at the critical moment.

Brooklyn was still sedated but they knew he might be awakened while transfer to his bed from the cart, so it was essential for Chester to be here to intervene in the event he woke up in a crazy fit.

"Is there any reason why Brooklyn can't be moved to my bed?" Chester asked.

The dumbfounded scientists didn't know what to say. It was unheard of people putting their dogs in their beds. Due to their lack of response Aida chimed in and said, "Of course not. We can always change the sheets and blankets."

"Good, us put Brooklyn in my bed so when he wakes up, he'll be by me because if he experienced anything like me, he might be agitated when he wakes up."

The staff stood there motionless not knowing what to do, but Aida and Chester took the matter into their own hands, scooted the car next to the bed and they both jointly picked up Brooklyn and softly moved him over to the bed and gently laid him down on his side.

Afterwards Aida looked at the staff and said, "Chester and I will handle it from here. You all can leave. If we need you, we will contact you."

Everyone left the room except for Aizere. When just the three of them were left in the room with Aida looking funny at Aizere as if she was conveying in her looks, *why are you still here?*

Aizere then spoke and asked, "Would you like to take a bath Chester and put on some sleeping clothes?"

"That wouldn't be a bad idea, but what about Brooklyn?"

"May I make the suggestion of having Rayalna come and stay Brooklyn until you bathe and change." Aizere said

"I could stay with Brooklyn," Aida said.

"Aida, I think your services would be better used taking care of Chester while he bathes."

"Actually, that's a good point," Aida said suddenly feeling dumb.

"I'll initiate your bath and bring Rayalna in to be with Brooklyn until you are ready to go to bed. Why don't you two come into the bathroom now. Brooklyn will only be alone for a minute or so."

The two walked into the bathroom and started undressing while the bath was filling with water and ingredients already planned out. Under microcomputer control the bath would fill to the level required then shut off and keep the temperature around 95 degrees. Aizere walked back into the bedroom and requested Rayalna who showed up promptly. Aizere explained to Rayalna what was happening and she did not react and just nodded her head and moved a chair over next to the bed and sat down monitoring Brooklyn now having shallow breaths.

Brooklyn transcended to his own dog dimension. Just like Chester experiencing Chinese characters floating over his head, Brooklyn was watching Drolupric words flow over his head in his dream state. But for Brooklyn it was an entirely different matter that would shock the researchers who were now able to download the telemetry out of Brooklyn's black box from the chip in his brain.

Brooklyn's chip had a table of 65,535 possible words in its lexicon. Prior to today, Brooklyn's lexicon had filled up to 1,850 words which impressed the researchers. But now the most startling results unfolded. Brooklyn now had almost 40,000 words in his lexicon, approximately half English and the other half Drolupric language words.

Doctor Akssiar sat in his office utterly stunned. The implications were enormous. His secretary Aiaru came into his office and said, "Doctor it's getting late, may I suggest you wrap it up and go home and come back tomorrow and get a fresh start.

In the morning Doctor Akssiar had an appointment to visit Chester and Brooklyn with his associate Tasha where they would attempt to do a test with Brooklyn much like they did with Chester. However, Brooklyn could not use a stylus to indicate numbers so the plan was Tasha would ask Brooklyn which letter to select and she would simply circle it.

Doctor Akssiar was thinking about everything planned for tomorrow and realized he had to answer his secretary Aiaru and said, "I agree, I probably stayed longer than I should have, and I apologize for keeping you here longer than required, so let's call it a day and leave."

"Thank you doctor. I know you are a busy man and I'm happy to help."

"I appreciate that Aiaru."

Doctor Akssiar had a lot to think about and if tomorrow, it appeared Brooklyn could effectively use the 40,000 words in the chip lexicon, that would be a huge game changer. It meant the dog could be programmed for a lot of things, including being a courier of sensitive information. It also meant he could be trained to be a deadly spy. Nobody would even fathom the information a dog could be part of behind enemy lines. Now it was just a question of what to do and how to do it.

Aiaru walked to the front entrance of the building and out to public conveyance. Aiaru only had to take public transportation about six blocks to her luxury high rise apartment. Doctor Akssiar, walked over to the Skycar parking lot and got into his transportation and within moments was airborne flying in the three-dimensional Skycar lane heading home.

Doctor Akssiar's residence was in a remote area that took about ten minutes to travel to. This was a secure area that the general population could not get into. It had one surface entrance with a guard and everyone arriving required an invitation text via the registration list.

The residential computational authority took control of Doctor Akssiar's Skycar and glided it down to his parking spot next to his home.

Doctor Akssiar's arrival alerted his butler and his maid who were there to greet him at his Skycar entrance to the back of his home in a brief few moment of arriving home.

The staff received Doctor Akssiar with the proper level of respect and supportive demure.

"Doctor, your dinner is ready, would you like to freshen up before you eat?"

Doctor Akssiar was already running late and not had eaten in over eight hours and felt he had an appetite and responded, "I think I want to eat now, then I'll freshen up later, go ahead and serve my dinner."

"Doctor please make yourself comfortable in the dining room and I will bring your meal out right away."

"Thank you."

The staff had already had their dinner several hours prior and had learned not to wait on Doctor Akssiar who had at times did not come home from work until the next morning. They knew he was at work because he had a special tracker for his own security, they could monitor his location and if necessary, intervene in a bad scenario perpetrated by a criminal.

Doctor Akssiar's place setting was ready and no sooner than he sat down one of his staff filled his water glass and poured *Chamboreé de Lián* his favorite elixir into his wine glass.

Chamboreé de Lián elixir was fermented rose petals and lotus flowers with a obscure mushrooms that gave it an extraordinary taste and smell. Additional additives gave it a slightly sweet taste. The *Chamboreé de Lián* elixir had mild psychoactive ingredients, so it was best consumed when a person didn't plan on leaving their homes.

Some people drank *Chamboreé de Lián* elixir to enhance sleep and temporarily forget things such as after having a rough day at work. *Chamboreé de Lián* elixir would be consumed more often but was expensive due to the difficulty in obtaining all the ferments and the timely process to create the perfect tasting elixir.

Doctor Akssiar drank half his elixir before his course was served by his chef Brently. Brently only worked four hours per day producing Doctor Akssiar's dinner. During the rest of the day, he worked for restaurants and food companies to produce great flavors in meals. The chef Brently didn't really need the income from Doctor Akssiar, but it slowly helped him to collect wealth and save up for great off world vacations.

The butler Nolak stayed in the home most of the time except for his scheduled days off. Nolak's duties also included protection and safety. The maid had a similar work schedule to the Chef and had four clients she assisted during her twelve-hour long day. Three hours at each client was sufficient time to make the beds, clean the house, and help the chef Brently clean up since Doctor Akssiar was her last client for the day. As part of her benefits, the chef Brently always made enough food to feed Doctor Akssiar and the staff, so the maid Selina had a nourishing diet and because of this nice arrangement seldom had to go grocery shopping which helped her to also save money.

The maid Selina's other clients lived near Doctor Akssiar, so she could simply walk from one home to the other in just a few minutes to the next home she needed to clean. All her clients were by referral only. The maid had a waiting list of 50+ clients that wanted to hire her, but she knew her 4 clients were all she could handle. She saved a lot of money because she was always working and seldom took days off.

The maid Selina saw Doctor Akssiar's wine glass was half empty and she asked, "Doctor, would you like a refill?"

"Yes please."

The maid Selina didn't know why, but she liked Doctor Akssiar, who seemed like a lonely man. He was married a short time and his wife was killed in a space transport plane traveling to visit her sick mother. He never remarried and had been single for quite a while. The maid thought if Doctor Akssiar ever wanted to get frisky with her, she would be ready because he might want to keep her permanently and retire her from her other work.

The maid Selina observed Doctor Akssiar for a while after refilling his wine glass with the *Chamboreé de Lián*. One thing the maid knew was Doctor Akssiar never drank that fast before. *Was something troubling him?*

With almost all the work done, the maid wanted to finish up because it was getting late in the day and she wanted to go home, relax and sip on a drink that was very similar to purple *Grand Zumbido* elixir, that wasn't quite as grand as what Duke Tinktar drank, and much more affordable, but tastes nearly the same and simply had cheaper alcohol and drugs in it to create the same effect.

"I'll be right back Doctor; I have a couple things to do."

"No problem, take your time, if I need something, Brently can take care of it."

"Alright," The maid Selina said then went about her business.

Right after Doctor Akssiar finished his main entrée, he informed the chef Brently he was full and didn't desire desert or anything else. He then picked up his half full glass of *Chamboreé de Lián* and walked into his living room where he had a very comfortable smart reclining chair with a built-in messenger and sat down there and slowly finished his drink as he contemplated Brooklyn and all the implications that dog might have on society.

His first thoughts included they didn't somehow hurt the animal with the Neurotic Sonification. He knew that Rayalna would contact him immediately if there were any prevailing issues with Brooklyn. The *Chamboreé de Lián* was having a nice effect and half of his temporal psyche was easing up a bit to a slight amount of serenity.

The maid Selina helped Brently clean up the dining room then placed the dishes in a mag washer that washed the dish surfaces with a liquid compound rich in magnetic particles and during the draining process electromagnets would collect the magnetic sludge and the rest of the residue would float into recycling pipes that drained into a recycling reservoir where the city would reprocess it and reclaim the water.

After they were all done, the chef Brently, left for the day, saying goodbye to Doctor Akssiar and the maid Selina approached seeing his glass was empty, asked, "Doctor would you like a refill?"

"Yes please."

After refilling the glass, the maid now mildly concerned about the Doctor acting out of character asked, "Doctor, would you like me to stay for a while longer?"

"No that will not be necessary, Selina."

"I'm leaving now Doctor Akssiar, I hope you have a nice evening."

"Thank you, Selina."

After Selina was gone, the house was all nice and quiet and the Butler Nolak was back in his private room where he had a desk, a computational and communications terminal that also provided holographic entertainment, and a bed. He also had a dozen security screens showing parts of the house and the areas outdoors that were constantly archived to their security provider.

Nolak had an emergency button and if he pressed it, high priced security people packing a lot of fierce weapons would descend upon the residence in very short order. Adjacent to the house was an emergency Skycar landing pad programmed into their company craft they would be landing agents within five minutes after Nolak hit the "Chicken Switch."

Since the security people also had electronic keys to the home, they would be coming through the door briskly looking for trouble. Any home invaders would be met with a very capable force. Doctor Akssiar also had artificial intelligence intercom through the house that monitored his statements. If he said, "Nolak, please come to the living room," Nolak would be there within a minute making an inquiry as to what Doctor Akssiar needed. That didn't happen too often, but it did occasionally.

Doctor Akssiar didn't need Nolak, but he felt more comfortable with the added security and realized that if information about a talking dog leaked out, his need for security would grow exponentially.

As he sat in his recliner in silence, Doctor Akssiar `contemplated a lot and realized because of his association with Brooklyn and Duke Tinktar's interest in the matter, he was more or less stuck in this project and had no way out. He knew a lot more about Aida and Duke Tinktar than most people. If they were interested, it put him in the spotlight. With the few scraps of disclosure that came out about Duke Tinktar, the seriousness of this operation was quite compelling. *Would it one day turn into a nightmare?*

Chapter Ten

THE NEW LANGUAGE

Aida did a repeat performance of a couple nights prior in the bathtub with Chester. Chester didn't realize Aida had her own needs to be fulfilled and her only satisfaction came when she felt the results of her stimulus on Chester. When he reached his peak gratification and she felt the results, the cauldron of her psychophysical reactions resonated with ensembles of orgasmic sensations. The covalent and synergistic effects each had on the other multiplied the results leaving Aida quite satisfied. She also knew one important fact. Duke Tinktar never turned her on this much no matter how he or she tried.

There was something about Chester that manifested her psychophysical reactions. And the more time she experienced it the more she liked it and the more often she wanted it. She was slowly less agitated and quite happy Duke Tinktar gave her this assignment which proved to her he had no real emotional bond to her; she was just a piece of meat to him in the past. Chester on the other hand was fully legitimate. He didn't hide his emotions, though he was weary about disclosing them.

In due time they finished their bath, dried off and Aizere delivered their bed clothes to put on in private before they left the bathroom and went back into the bedroom to be with Brooklyn. Brooklyn was sound asleep, and he was breathing more apparent than he was before with shallow breaths.

"I think we are going to bed now," Chester said to give Rayalna the signal she could now leave and attend her business elsewhere.

"Alright, call me if you need any help with Brooklyn."

"We will."

Rayalna left the room somehow knowing what the two lovebirds had just finished up beforehand. She had a slight subtle jealousy towards Aida and wanted to experience a little of what she had. Rayalna was a virgin and was long overdue for some transcendental affection.

Chester and Aida carefully crawled in bed so as not to shake Brooklyn and wake him prematurely. After what he went through today, he needed peace and quiet. Soon they were in bed and cuddling and in due time succumbed to sleep.

Brooklyn slept through the night. His strong medications allowed him to sleep peacefully even though he almost felt drunk with letters flying over his head, just as if they were in Skycar lanes flying through a city.

It was a peaceful night and just before dawn, Brooklyn woke up and saw Chester lying beside him on his back with Aida's head on the side of his chest. Brooklyn crawled next to Chester and put his head on Chesters other side and onto his chest and went back to sleep for another hour and some.

Finally artificial intelligence slowly increased the lighting in the room playing chimes to wake them all up.

Aizere entered the room and continued the process artificial intelligence started with soft words to wake up the three amigos.

Chester slowly came to and soon discovered Aida and Brooklyn were all over him. Brooklyn was awakening and as soon as he realized he was awake said, "Papa I need to use the bathroom."

Aizere standing next to him asked, "Brooklyn would you like me to help you off the bed?"

"Yes, please."

Aizere picked up Brooklyn who was not yet too heavy for her and set him down on the floor. Brooklyn then walked over to his potty and took care of his business.

Aida and Chester slowly got up. Aida put on a bath robe and left the room. Chester had no idea where she went, but the truth is it was very close nearby.

"Would you like to take a bath before you dress, Chester?"

"No that will be not necessary, I'm ready to get dressed."

Chester was surprised he was dressing in Royal Clothes again and asked, "Why am I being dressed up?"

"Chester, Margrét Hansen the wife of an intergalactic banker, is bringing her poodle here to have lunch with you and Brooklyn later after Brooklyn finishes his morning exams."

"If that's the case you better get Brooklyn cleaned up really well."

"We are one step ahead of you, Rayalna will be here in a minute to give Brooklyn his bath."

Not but a few seconds after Aizere finished her statement, Rayalna appeared and said, "Brooklyn I need to give you a bath now to make you presentable to "Princess Tiffany."

"I'm ready to take a bath, I want to look good for "Princess Tiffany."

"Alright let's go to the bathroom."

Soon Brooklyn was enjoying his bath, though he felt hungry, and made a comment, "This bath water smells kind of funny."

"Brooklyn the bath water has some special additives in it to make Princess Tiffany like you more."

"Do you think she will like me enough to let me hump her?"

"Brooklyn, you can't do that unless Margrét Hansen, Princess Tiffany says it's okay."

"What if she says it's not okay?"

"We'll have to figure out a diabolical plan then."

"Papa, I know what diabolical means."

"You do?"

"Yes, I know what diabolical means and how to say it in Drolupric language."

"That's good to know. Do you know a lot of Drolupric words?"

"Papa, I know a lot of Drolupric words now and sometimes it makes my head feel strange."

"In what way?"

"I dreamed I had Drolupric words floating over my head, just like Skycars, we saw yesterday."

"Do you feel okay otherwise?"

"I will feel better when the words stop floating over my head."

"I had that too, but it went away."

In due time Brooklyn was blow dried and to his surprise he had a Royal fabric cover his dog collar device.

"You look spiffy now. I'm sure that when "Princess Tiffany" see's you, she will be more than ready to fall in love with you."

"Papa, I hope she does."

"Me too."

Aida was soon there to escort them to the courtyard where they had breakfast laid out. Chester noticed Aida looked exceptionally beautiful today. Little did Chester know; Aida just had a makeover from a top fashion consultant to make her sizzling hot. It was all part of the conditioning and transcendence for Chester's new life that was just about to get far more complicated.

Halfway through breakfast, Doctor Akssiar and Tasha arrived. They had already had their breakfast but were seated with drinks at the long table so they could socialize with Chester and Brooklyn.

"How do you feel, Brooklyn?" Doctor Akssiar asked.

"Doctor Akssiar, I still feel a little dizzy and see words flying over my head now and then."

"Do you feel like you are slowly getting better, Brooklyn?"

"Doctor, a while ago it was solid words, but now it's just occasional."

"Glad to hear you are slowly feeling better."

Tasha then decided now would be the perfect time to do some checks on Brooklyn and she asked, "Brooklyn would it be okay if I ask you a few questions in standard Drolupric language, and you can answer me in English or Drolupric?"

"Sure, I finished eating."

Tasha started asking the questions in Drolupric and to her surprise Chester answered all the questions in standard Drolupric.

"Chester what was the first thing you thought about when you woke up this morning?"

"I was thinking how nice it was I was with Papa, and he was with Aida lying next to him, and it wasn't the bitch Abagail."

Tasha saw how Aida turned slightly red because Brooklyn just announced to the world Aida was sleeping with Chester which implied sexual intercourse.

Chester smiled knowing how much it probably got under Aida's skin because he knew for a fact, she was a high maintenance woman.

Tasha quickly moved onto other questions asking in Drolupric: "Brooklyn what is your favorite animals?"

"They are birds and squirrels which I got to know back at Ski Beach before we came here."

"Did you talk to the squirrels and birds?"

"Yes, I did, but I do not think they understood me."

"Did you see other dogs at Ski Beach."

"Yes, quite a few of them, but they all seemed to be unfriendly. We just passed by them."

"Did you see a lot of people at Ski Beach?"

"Sometimes yes, but often no because we always went there early in the morning."

"What are you planning on doing today after we give you all your tests?"

"Princess Tiffany is coming for a visit. I hope she decides to become my friend."

"Who is Princess Tiffany?"

"She's a poodle dog that is part of Margrét Hansen's family."

"How do you know about Margrét Hansen?"

"I heard Papa and others discuss her and Princess Tiffany."

"Why are they coming today?"

"Papa promised me I could visit with Princess Tiffany as a reward for going through Neurological Sonification."

Doctor Akssiar was now writing a lot of notes. Brooklyn's responses were genuinely astonishing!

"Brooklyn you seem to be able to talk as well in Drolupric as you do in English."

"I think I know Drolupric as well as English now."

Doctor Akssiar then made the statement to Tasha who had not received the latest status report that would be published in about an hour to the research team:

"Tasha, this morning I reviewed the telemetry data and the Chip that Brooklyn has inserted has a table of 65,535 words in the lexicon space. Currently 40,000 entries are there and half are English and the other half Drolupric."

"Doctor Akssiar, are you are saying Brooklyn in fact now knows 20,000 Drolupric words?"

"That's correct."

"That's more words than most Drolupric speaking people know."

"Yes, I'm quite aware of it."

Tasha sat there utterly astonished. They were waiting for Chester and Aida to finish their breakfast, then they were going to the library to test Brooklyn. Tasha knew her emotions had never reached a spike at this level of before in her life. She was utterly stunned. Now she knew why Doctor Akssiar was acting strange this morning. She had no idea the trouble he had sleeping the night before as he pondered all the future possibilities.

After the meal and freshening up, Aida led Chester and Brooklyn to the Library where Chernega along with Doctor Akssiar and Tasha were waiting for them.

They had Chester put Brooklyn on a chair facing them at the table to his right. Aida sat on the other side of Chester so as to not interfere with Brooklyn.

"Alright Brooklyn, since you can't write at this time, we are going to give you a multiple-choice question test and we'll read out the answers A, B, C, and D. You then tell us which one of those you think best answers the questions by picking one of those letters. Do you understand what we want you to do?" Tasha asked.

"Yes, I understand. I've watched game shows on TV a few times when the bitch Abigail was home because that's all she ever watched. So, I understand multiple choice."

Alright I'm going to ask you the question using standard Drolupric language."

"Alright."

The test was an eight-page test like what Chester was given. The questions were simple if a person understood Drolupric language.

"Brooklyn, what does a space craft do? A. Fly out into Space. B. travel on a road. C. Travel on water. or D. Park in a Skycar parking spot." "The answer is A." Brooklyn chose.

"Next question…."

Tasha went through all eight pages rather promptly while Doctor Akssiar took a lot of notes. He knew it wasn't a difficult test if the test taker had basic knowledge and could speak the Drolupric language. What was totally amazing is Brooklyn didn't make any errors on the multiple-choice test.

The second part of the exam was a conversation to see how well Brooklyn could understand the Drolupric words and respond in an essay like manner. In reality there was no absolute correct answer, but the interchange demonstrated Brooklyn's ability to converse with another person in standard Drolupric.

The overall assessment was rather incredible. Everyone in the room, including Chernega were somewhat enthralled by Brooklyn. Doctor Akssiar understood a very important aspect of Brooklyn. He had a computer chip now full of 40,000 or more words, half in English and the other half in Drolupric. But it took his own brain power to formulate the thoughts. All the chip did was to pick up from the center brain nonvisual photoreceptors via the transducers the verbal coefficients out of the lexicon table.

Hence, Brooklyn's talking process still required him to think about a word to speak which means he also had those words in his brain stored just like a human to think of using it in his awareness in the world. At the end of all the examination which included physical checkups, Brooklyn felt tired as if he wanted to nap.

So, when they went out again to the nice courtyard open area to have lunch, Brooklyn just wanted to lay down and shut his eyes and rest. Chester let him just rest there knowing he was fatigued as they were about ready to serve lunch but were waiting for someone. Brooklyn had a fifteen minute catnap and was further in his slumber when the guests showed up.

In came Margrét Hansen the wife of an intergalactic banker and her poodle "Princess Tiffany." They approached the outdoor dining table, and everyone stood up to greet Margrét and the valet then led her to her reserved seat directly across from Chester. They also had a doggy chair for "Princess Tiffany," they would soon bring bowls for water and special dog food if Margrét Hansen agreed to allow them to serve "Princess Tiffany."

Chester regretted waking up Brooklyn but this visit was all for Brooklyn, so he gently shook Brooklyn and said, "Brooklyn, your friend Princess Tiffany is here."

Brooklyn had just enough of a cat nap to allow him to function again and came back to consciousness and suddenly smelled something unusual.

He popped tall and there she was, the dog of his dreams, none other than Princess Tiffany.

The two dogs stared at each other as if they were in a trance. Margrét Hansen had never seen Princess Tiffany ever focused on another dog like this and totally quiet. Princess Tiffany had been around a lot of other dogs because she and her female friends all had dogs. On many occasions, Margrét Hansen had walked around parks with her friends and their dogs. Princess Tiffany gave them no attention whatsoever to the other dogs as if she didn't even care to be around them.

Margrét Hansen arrived via a Royal Skycar that picked up at her mansion after the royal security manager explained to her why they had to bring her here in this manner due to security protocols. Margrét Hansen had seen pictures of Duke Tinktar's estate and knew this was the real deal, but why wasn't he here and why was the man Chester here wearing Royal attire?

This was all very confusing, but being married to an intergalactic banker Margrét Hansen knew how to play the social role and in fact was somewhat of a social engineer herself.

Aida was planning on being a translator if required, but as it turned out Chester knew enough Drolupric language to fully understand everything Margrét Hansen had to say as well as answer her and converse. Aida, being an accomplished spy, social engineer, and major manipulator did a lot of the talking as to give Chester a much easier experience.

Margrét Hansen thought Chester was simply being polite and responded when he should. Chester's words were also soft and thoughtful.

What Margrét Hansen didn't realize was Chester's Drolupric language was a hybrid function because the two languages English and Drolupric didn't have a 100% overlap. At best it might be near 80%.

Soon after the elixirs were served and the dogs served food and water, the entrées started arriving. Margrét Hansen noticed "Princess Tiffany" didn't touch her food and water until she watched Brooklyn eating and drinking. She then followed his actions. The two dogs slowly and quietly ate their food and drank the water. Then they simply sat there and stared at one another.

Taking it all in, Margrét Hansen saw that Brooklyn was wearing a cloth material over most of his body that had the emperor's design on it. This had never been seen in public before. Never had some animal of any kind been clothed with the emperor's logo. The emperor's design that Brooklyn wore created a surreal experience for Margrét Hansen as she had never experienced anything like this in her lifetime.

After their lunch the group all took a stroll around the courtyard that opened to a private park at the end of the building structures, past a gate. This area was highly landscaped and could be inspirational to anyone. As they walked along simply to help digest their lunch and stretch a bit, Aida walked beside Margrét Hansen discussing some of the vegetation in the park which was rare and utterly fantastic.

Princess Tiffany walked beside her master, Margrét Hansen and Brooklyn positioned himself next to Princess Tiffany. Margrét could tell Brooklyn was very well disciplined and Princess Tiffany gave every indication she was enjoying his company.

Soon they came up upon some park benches and Aida suggested the sit there for a while in the shade and the conversations continued. The two dogs stood out in front of the people and the next big shock happened. Princess Tiffany jumped up on Brooklyn's back and by all accounts it appeared she was hugging Brooklyn who appeared to be quite happy and stood there taking it all in. After a moment while everyone watched, Princess Tiffany slid off Brooklyn's back then walked around and faced him looking deep into his eyes. She then licked the side of his face a few times then positioned herself next to Brooklyn and stayed there like an anchor.

Chester had asked Brooklyn not to talk in front of Margrét Hansen saying it might cause her not to want to bring Princess Tiffany back. Margrét Hansen had no idea Brooklyn was a talking dog.

After some lighthearted talk, it was evident that Margrét Hansen had places to go and people to see and Aida being great at observing body language stood up and said, "We are glad you came to visit, and we are very happy you brought Princess Tiffany. I can tell that Brooklyn really likes her and as you can see, Brooklyn is very well disciplined and gentle."

"Yes, I see that. And also, I've never seen Princess Tiffany attracted to another dog before and she has never jumped up on other dogs back before or licked a face of another dog. I'm quite shocked."

"Margrét, we really like you and Princess Tiffany, and we hope to see a lot more of you," Aida added.

"It's been a pleasant experience for me, and I enjoyed it and I think Princess Tiffany would like to come back for visits."

"I'm sorry for all the security protocol but you can imagine, Duke Tinktar and his close friends have to be protected."

"Yes, I understand, my husband as a banker has worries himself and sometimes has to have ample security."

"We will walk you to the Skycar and we hope we can arrange a future visit real soon."

"I'm sure I can make time as it appears Princess Tiffany enjoys coming here. She usually does not like going to dog beach and your Brooklyn is the first dog ever there she took any kind of interest."

"When they got to the Skycar, with the security men gathered around, Margrét Hansen was in for another huge surprise, Princess Tiffany did not want to leave. She needed help to get the dog into the Skycar and after the door was shut, she put her paws up on the window and stared at Brooklyn.

Margrét Hansen almost wanted to cry taking Princess Tiffany away from her new lover. Never had Margrét Hansen seen any Princess Tiffany behave like this and she suspected Brooklyn threw her into complete heat.

Soon after they were gone, Chester could see Brooklyn looked almost heart broken and he asked, "What do you think Brooklyn did you like Princess Tiffany?"

"Papa, I'm in love with Princess Tiffany."

"You were well behaved and didn't push yourself onto Princess Tiffany."

"She's now in heat and wanted me to hump her, but I knew that there are certain protocols and ways to go about it without creating a spectacle."

"I'm very proud of you Brooklyn."

"Thank you, Papa. When will I get to see Princess Tiffany again?"

Aida listening in on the conversation said, "Brooklyn, don't worry you will have plenty of time with Princess Tiffany in the future and if you want to hump her, we'll try to arrange some privacy for you."

"Thank you I appreciate that."

Now it was time for some more Neurological Sonification. Aida then announced to Chester, "It's your turn to have more Neurological Sonification today. The staff is setting up the equipment in your suite now."

"Alright, let's go do it, I really want to learn more Drolupric language."

Soon they were back in the suite with Brooklyn in his bed watching all the activity in the room and soon Chester was receiving his next dose of Neurological Sonification. This would be just as strong and as intense as he had the last time. When they were done, Chester was helped into his freshly made bed and was given some sleeping drugs he took aurally and was soon fast asleep.

Aida, feeling more and more attached to Chester remained in the room and talked with Brooklyn. After about an hour Brooklyn surprised Aida when he said, "I like you, Aida. You are not like that Bitch Abigail. If she was like you, I would have liked her."

"Thank you, Brooklyn. I like you too."

Aida sat next to Brooklyn for another hour and their entire conversation was in standard more Drolupric language.

Aizere came into the room to check up on Brooklyn and Aida and do a status check on Chester and at that time, Aida said, "Aizere, can you get me some sleeping clothes. I'm going to lay down with Chester."

"Sure, I'll be right back with your change of clothes."

Soon Aida was undressed and into sleeping clothes and lying next to Chester who had shallow breaths just like Brooklyn the night before. Soon the lights were dimming, and Brooklyn laid down in the spot he preferred so he could gaze upon Papa whenever he wanted.

***

Duke Tinktar's command ship went into geostationary orbit above Tymasoara. He then transferred from a shuttle down to the planet's surface and was directed to report to the emperor.

The emperor always had his secret eyes and ears he kept away from Duke Tinktar. That's the way business was done. He already knew exactly what transpired during Duke Tinktar's trip, but he had to require the Duke brief him as if it was new information to keep the facade up that Duke Tinktar was on independent operations and the emperor knew none of what was going on.

This was going to be an interesting meeting because once again the emperor was going to admonish him to reduce his involvement in these clandestine activities because he no longer wanted to take the risk of losing his heir apparent.

The shuttle landed in the emperor's private intergalactic transportation hub. As soon as the door to the shuttle opened and Duke Tinktar stepped out of it, there were four-armed security guards in Palace attire there to escort Duke Tinktar to the emperor.

Moments later they were in the emperor's secret conference room that had around the clock armed guards. The emperor and his special Valet were in the room when Duke Tinktar was escorted in and left for the royal audience.

Duke Tinktar sat down at the conference table next to the Valet across from the emperor.

"I see you made it home safely."

"It was a simple operation; safety wasn't the issue. Capturing the traitor with information he was going to supply our enemies before he could transfer it to them was our chief concern."

"How did it work out?"

"We were able to prevent the unauthorized transfer of military secrets to the enemy and we were able to round up and arrest everyone involved."

"What happened to the traitor?"

"I gave him an opportunity to save his own life, but he obviously didn't believe me when I said I would let him live if he cooperated. He was subsequently executed because those people around him were able to give me what I needed to plug all the holes and send a message to anyone wishing to follow in his footsteps to be aware of what might happen to them.

"At some point in time you are going to have to hand off a lot of your responsibility to someone else because I have more important things for you to do and I can't risk losing you."

"Your excellency, l know we have gone over and over on this in the past and I know I infuriated you by not bowing out of the activity like you requested. I didn't feel I had someone I could trust until now to hand over some of that responsibility."

"You found someone?"

"Yes, I have and I've given it great thought and if you don't mind, I do not wish to divulge who that is in front of your Valet."

"He's my most trusted aid."

"I know he's trustworthy, but until you agree with my plan I don't want anyone else knowing of it."

"That sounds reasonable."

The emperor looked at the Valet and said, "Swìnlàgār, give us some time alone. I'll summon you when we are done with this part of the conversation."

"Yes, your excellency. I will go outside and wait until you ask me to come back in."

"Thank you."

After the Duke was alone with the emperor, the conversation started concerning Chester. The emperor was receiving reports on Chester because he was infatuated with the information on the talking dog Brooklyn. And he had just received information Chester and his Dog Brooklyn had already undergone Neurological Sonification and had learned a quite comprehensive amount of language by the Neurological Sonification processes.

At first the emperor didn't like the idea, but when he realized, his nephew would never have to go into harm's way again, it suddenly felt reasonable.

After two hours right about the time their conversation slowly died down, the Valet asked via intercom, "Your excellency, is everything all right?"

"Swìnlàgār, please come back into the room," the emperor replied.

The stage was set. The emperor started briefing Swìnlàgār.

"The alien Chester who arrived with Brooklyn the talking dog is going to be groomed to help reduce Duke Tinktar's involvement in his Intelligence Oversight activities."

"Your excellency, that's rather astonishing."

"Swìnlàgàr, now you know why Duke Tinktar wanted you to leave the room. It took him two hours to convince me, and his rationale is excellent. I think with our great surveillance apparatus and procedures, Chester can be groomed and brought up up to speed in his new role."

Chester was soon going to become a spook and he would be handled with kids gloves by Duke Tinktar and Swìnlàgàr the Valet who was in charge of the emperor's personal security detail and his chief executive who carried out all his orders.

The emperor only dealt with Duke Tinktar or the Valet Swìnlàgàr for the most serious issues of the empire. Most of the time only these three knew of Duke Tinktar's significant behind-the-scenes activities that needed to be shielded from the public. And in the most secret compartmentalized emperor's directed operations Duke Tinktar and the Valet Swìnlàgàr had no knowledge of what the other person was doing.

Duke Tinktar was keen on operational security and never mentioned any mission or activity to anyone he personally didn't ask for involvement. And those people knew the risk to their own personal lives if they ever revealed any clandestine activity Duke Tinktar was involved in.

The emperor really didn't care how the Valet Swìnlàgàr handled matters, he just wanted his orders carried out without delay or disclosure. All other matters were handled by the bureaucracy and its legions of members.

Duke Tinktar knew he didn't need to stick around to hear the emperor reveal to Swìnlàgàr the change in *modus operandi*.

After paying his respects to the emperor, Duke Tinktar left the palace and was immediately taken to his estate where he would soon meet with Chester and start the conversion process.

Chester, Brooklyn, and Aida were out in the courtyard the following morning having their breakfast and to their big surprise, Duke Tinktar walked up to them. He wasn't hungry because he already had room service, but he sat down at the table and allowed the waiter to get him a drink.

"Good morning, everyone, how's everyone doing?" Duke Tinktar asked in English, already fully briefed on what transpired while he was gone.

"We've actually been kind of busy since you were gone," Aida volunteered the first reply.

Duke Tinktar expected Doctor Akssiar and Tasha at any minute to get direct from them a report on the status of Brooklyn.

"Really, do tell me about it."

"First of all, Chester requested Neurological Sonification to rapidly learn our Drolupric language."

"How's that working out?"

"He had his second treatment yesterday."

Duke Tinktar asked in Drolupric language directly to Chester looking directly at him, "Any side effects or issues from the Neurological Sonification?"

Chester answered in proper Drolupric language, "Your Excellency, In my past I studied Earth's Chinese language and had dreams of Chinese Characters floating over my head. After the Neurological Sonification, I had dreams of those Chinese characters and Drolupric words floating over my head."

"Interesting."

"I still have some of those images this morning, but they are slowly dissipating."

"Your Drolupric language is quite accurate. It appears you have learned a lot."

"I believe I have."

"How many more sessions will you have?"

"Doctor Akssiar said I will only need a total of five and has them spaced out once every 48 hours."

Aida then informed Duke Tinktar, "Brooklyn also has had a Neurological Sonification to learn Drolupric language. He will get his second treatment today."

Duke Tinktar looked at Brooklyn and said in Drolupric language, "Brooklyn, have you learned many Drolupric words?"

Brooklyn looking directly at Duke Tinktar immediately answered in perfect Drolupric through his speaker box, "Your Excellency, yes I've learned about 20,000 Drolupric words."

"Brooklyn, how do you know 20,000 words?"

"Your excellency, that's what Doctor Akssiar informed me."

"He'll be here shortly perhaps he'll have a report for me."

Aida then spoke up again, "Another event happened in your absence. Brooklyn met a female dog."

"Really? I want to hear about that. Brooklyn tell me about it."

Brooklyn then recapped his experience with the lovely "Princess Tiffany."

"Any plans to see Princess Tiffany any time soon?"

"We have the owner Margrét Hansen's contact information to schedule another visit, but Brooklyn will get his second Neurological Sonification this afternoon so I think we should wait a while."

"I have an idea, I will talk to the emperor about it, but first let's get all the Neurological Sonification's completed, then we'll make some arrangements I think all parties will like."

"That sounds wonderful," Aida responded with and eyebrow raised from the word emperor mixed in with Duke Tinktar's statement."

After more small talk, Duke Tinktar noticed everyone appeared to finish eating and he said, "Chester, I would like to talk to you privately. Would you mind coming with me where we can have a conversation."

"Sure, your Excellency."

Duke Tinktar stood up and led Chester to his private office suite that had an administrative aide Daniell, who was the daytime receptionist and appointments coordinator. Nobody got an audience with Duke Tinktar without Daniell's approval, and she was a stickler for schedules.

Daniell, an attractive single female, was a head turner. Her position as Duke Tinktar's administrative aid began out of patronage her family had through several generations with the Royal family. When Duke Tinktar first brought her into his office suites it was out of respect and response to the emperor who requested he employ her.

The emperor was also hoping that Duke Tinktar would one day find sexual interest in Daniell and one day create a relationship with a patronage family so that when it was time for Duke Tinktar to have a family, he would have a nice girl he personally got to know well and would thus have no remorse over selecting her to be the mother of his children.

In a sense, the emperor selecting Daniell to be part of Duke Tinktar's life, was nothing more than ensuring the Royal family blood line remained Royal with the best- and well-connected patrons as a major contributor which the emperor believed ensured longevity of the Monarch.

Daniell had been working for Duke Tinktar over five years and not a single time did he flirt with her or make any suggestive comments that might insinuate he was interested in her more than just professionally.

Daniell secretly revered Duke Tinktar who always treated her with respect and somewhat charming. One would draw the conclusion by observing them together over a period they developed more than a professional relationship, and at the core of it was a real friendship. Duke Tinktar thought about Daniell's well-being but considered her too young and inexperienced to be a successful candidate for his mate.

Daniell had a conniving mother who schooled her on her relationship with Duke Tinktar and made sure she understood he was fair game up until the time he eventually tied the knot with a woman to be his mate and mother of his children. Daniell was a smart woman and knew the implications for her family if she succeeded in achieving that future relationship with Duke Tinktar, thus made sure she never clouded the issue by dating other men. She would one day fall into Duke Tinktar's arms as a virgin.

Daniell was also privy to some of the gossip and rumors that sometimes leak throughout the mansion and knew that Duke Tinktar had an affair with Aida. But she also knew Aida had a history and the emperor would never tolerate her becoming Duke Tinktar's mate. The emperor would arrange for Aida to have an accident long before she captured Duke Tinktar's heart.

In the recent updates to the emperor that the Valet Swìnlàgār provided, including security video of Chester boinking Aida, the emperor was happy that the course of events was such that in a while Aida would no longer be a person of concern. The emperor who knew Aida was a social climber and she would realize the immense power and authority vested in Chester would keep her focused in that direction.

The emperor hoped that one day a relationship would be kindled between Daniell and Duke Tinktar, even if he had to create an arranged marriage.

The emperor knew all about Madam Pang and that she probably owned Duke Tinktar's heart. When the day came, the emperor would explain how emperors handled such matters. You have one woman for the children and the heir to the throne, and you have a concubine to help keep your libido at full strength.

When artificial intelligence observed Duke Tinktar with Chester approach the door to Duke Tinktar's office suite, Daniell was notified they were arriving and solenoid actuators on the door unlocked, and pneumatic powered mechanism slid the two halves of the door sideways to allow Duke Tinktar and Chester walking side by side to enter the office space. As soon as they stepped in the room the door closed behind them and locked.

Inside the room orientated to the left were several desks and chairs where a couple men were sitting. These were Duke Tinktar's agents and assistants doing various tasks for him. They had received special briefings from Swìnlàgār the Valet that Daniell was earmarked the future property of Duke Tinktar, ostensibly his future mate. Even though they worked directly for Duke Tinktar, they also understood they took orders from Swìnlàgār who represented the emperor. One of their collateral functions was to keep all other males away from Daniell to ensure the emperors desires were eventually met. They didn't want a trip to the hog farm, so they knew exactly what they had to do.

Daniell knew something was going on because several possible suitors suddenly shied away and never contacted her again. But she didn't mind if that meant she was the chosen one. She had never been informed of such, but circumstantial evidence seemed to point that way and her sophisticated mother, with good connections to the emperor's court seemed to think she was highly protected from everyone except Duke Tinktar himself. Her mother, the emperor, Swìnlàgār the Valet, and the two men in the room that were protecting Daniell would be highly satisfied if Duke Tinktar made a pass at Daniell to get the process moving along. The sooner Duke Tinktar deflowered Daniell, the sooner they all could breathe a sigh of relief.

Duke Tinktar was his own man and surmised there were some extraneous activities going on surrounding Daniell, but he played along and acted as if he didn't know any of it existed. He certainly wasn't going to commit himself unless the emperor came right out and demanded it.

Duke Tinktar hoped an arranged marriage never happened because he looked up to the emperor as a father figure and wanted that relationship to always remain that way. The emperor also was very astute and intelligent and knew better than to force the issue, but when the time came and the emperor felt for the sake of the Empire it was in his best interest to get Duke Tinktar and Daniell unified, he would then put forth a concerted effort to achieve that purpose.

"Daniell, let me introduce you to Chester," Duke Tinktar said in Drolupric language.

"Pleasure to meet you Chester," Daniell answered in Drolupric but she like everyone in the staff had received Neurological Sonification to be able to speak English to the Alien from Earth. She was fully briefed on Chester and Brooklyn and wondered *why Duke Tinktar was speaking in Drolupric.*

"It's a pleasure to meet you as well, Daniell," Chester responded in Drolupric. A little later when Duke Tinktar was alone with Daniell, he would inform her that Chester requested the Neurological Sonification to be able to speak Drolupric language.

"Daniell, Chester, and I will be in my office for a while talking about a matter. I do not want to be disturbed until we finish," Duke Tinktar said.

"Understand your excellency, I will hold all calls and not receive any visitors."

"Thank you."

"You're welcome."

"This way Chester," Duke Tinktar said as he led Chester into his ornate office that had a lot of display terminals and art objects, a single desk, and several chairs. There was plenty of room so if an important meeting in this private area was required, more chairs and a table could easily be brought through the front double doors his office double doors that now slid shut for their privacy.

"Please have a seat."

Chester sat down not knowing what to expect and listened intently to what Duke Tinktar had to say.

"Chester, the reason why I wanted to have a private conversation with you is to convey a few things."

"Alright."

"I want you to know there are only two people that can get you back to Earth. The emperor and myself."

"Alright."

"I suppose one day you want to return to Earth."

"Yes, I do."

"Are you willing to do something to earn that way home?"

"If it's within my ability, sure."

"Chester when we first brought you here, we didn't really know what to do with you. Your dog Brooklyn is obviously the object of intense study by our scientific community. Brooklyn must stay indefinitely and may not leave here before he grows old and dies."

"I'm not sure Brooklyn is interested in going back to Earth. He clearly dislikes my wife Abagail."

"Chester what is unique about you is you have no ties to anyone in the Drolupric Empire. You have no political or philosophical leanings towards anything that exists here because you just suddenly arrived out of nowhere basically far from here."

"How does that make me fit into things?"

"It means that since you have no connection or affiliation with any group or organization, you do not have any bias and can operate with an open mind and conduct matters strictly based on what is required. Since the emperor is the ultimate adjudicator in all matters, I believe you would be able to carry out his orders or mine if he directs you to do so, to facilitate various activities that will be eventually bestowed upon you."

"Sure, I can help out as much as possible."

"Great, I like that attitude."

"Thank you."

"While you continue your Neurological Sonification's, we will start to insert physical fitness training and other activities in between those treatments. We will also start spacing the Neurological Sonification's treatments out several more days in between so that you do not feel fatigued and can handle training and exercise."

"I'm overdue for some physical fitness. I've not really done any since I left earth."

"Not to worry, I'll make sure you get a good workout and also we will give you supplements so that you will be able to exert more efforts into what we have planned for you."

"How soon does this start?"

I understand that Brooklyn will undergo a Neurological Sonification this afternoon. Obviously, you need to be with him when he wakes up in the morning. So, we'll do your first workout tomorrow afternoon."

"Sounds good to me."

"One other thing, Chester."

"Yes, your excellency?"

"What you will be doing in the future will be very important. The only people that will know what your task is will be the emperor, myself, Swìnlàgār who you have not met, and Chernega. Nobody else is permitted to know what you will be doing. This is for your wellbeing as well as our own. As you get more involved in activities, you will understand why. And you will soon also understand why I picked you. I need someone like you with no ties to anyone."

"If it means one day I can go back to Earth and die there, I will do what you require of me."

"Chester, I know you will. I'm a good judge of character as I deal with a lot of people."

Duke Tinktar then stood up and walked around his desk and said, "I'll walk you back to your suite and visit Brooklyn with you for a few minutes as he's probably close to being sedated for his treatment."

Chapter Eleven

HOW TO BE TRAINED AS A SPY

When Duke Tinktar and Chester walked through the outer office it was as quiet as you could hear a pin drop. They all knew not to ask any questions, but they also knew something big had just happened in that office with the Alien from Earth.

Daniell sat there dutifully and knew Duke Tinktar would tell her something if he needed her to do something, otherwise, she would simply leave work at her designated hour and go home for the evening and try not to let her mother push her around so much.

Duke Tinktar and Chester reached his suite and there was Brooklyn laying in his bed being attended by Rayalna. Nobody else was present. "Hello Brooklyn, how are you doing?" Duke Tinktar asked.

"Your excellency I would be doing better if I could see more National Geographic videos or visit with "Princess Tiffany."

"Brooklyn I will make sure you get enough of both, okay?"

"Thank you."

"I'll leave you now, as I have some arrangements to make. I will see you tomorrow."

"Alright." Brooklyn responded.

Duke Tinktar walked out the door and soon the technicians that would do Brooklyn's next Neurological Sonification came into the room with their padded cart to lay Brooklyn on after they sedated him.

In due time, Brooklyn was unconscious getting his brain filled with Drolupric language. Chester knew from recent experience that Brooklyn would now be sleeping until sometime in the morning. Waiting in his suite was simply a boring waste of time.

Just about the time Chester was wondering what he could do with his time Aida arrived and said, "I'm going to take you to my suite to dress you for some entertainment I'm taking you too, because we do not want to get in the way of these technicians working with Brooklyn."

"Alright."

Aida led Chester about fifty feet down the hallway to the entrance to her private suite. When they entered the room, the staff was already there ready to work Chester over and give him an appearance fitting for the venue they would soon visit.

Chester was informed he had to take a bath so they could apply special hair treatment for his hair design he would get. Aida volunteered to shampoo his hair with the special formula and after given their privacy they disrobed got in the bath and Aida shampooed Chester's hair then gave him a little message and ultimately hopped on top of him and drove him to ecstasy ensembles of gratification. After that was all complete, a satisfied Chester was put in the body dryer and he and Aida were soon in bathrobes going to the other room where a variety of people worked on them. Chester enjoyed a woman cutting his toenails after she did his fingernails while the hair dresser created his new Celestial Wave hair style.

Aida already had her hair styled earlier, but they freshened it up a bit and the makeup artist repaired the damage she did in the bathtub frolicking with Chester.

A fashion designer brought in racks of clothing and slowly picked out what they were to wear that evening.

Aida was dressed in a full-length black sparkling evening gown with small straps but revealing plenty of cleavage.

Chester was fitted with an impressive attire that was a hybrid tuxedo businessman's suit unlike anything he ever saw on Earth. His attire was far more stylish and with his excellent hair style he was indeed attractive and impressed Aida who suddenly had no regrets enjoying his fleshly attributes earlier.

Soon they were escorted to the front entrance where an unmarked Skycar was waiting for them. They were seated in the back seat by themselves, and three hired guns were in the front, two of which were dressed up in equally impressive attire.

The Skycar soon flew out of the big opening on the sheer cliffs of the side of the mountain foothill where Duke Tinktar's estate was situated. In due time they flew to Tymasoara city center and to a very nicely architecture civic center. It was now late afternoon with plenty of sunlight so Chester could see the people converging on the civic center when they got out of the Skycar in front of the venue. Shortly after getting out of the Skycar, it took to the air and left the area. The two well-dressed bodyguards walked in front of Chester and Aida. On the back collars of the two security men were hidden cameras for a rear view.

Artificial Intelligence kept a watch on everything behind them and fed any alerts into the ear buds the security men wore. They walked right up to the front entrance and their reservations were recorded via facial recognition the two security men and their two un-named guests. The civic center employees gestured the four forward and because they were VIP's an escort was waiting to take them directly up to their balcony seats. This balcony section right in the middle of the concert hall normally could contain twenty guests but tonight only four seats would be filled. One on each upper corner by the security men and the two center front seats by Aida and Chester.

Most of the concert hall was already filled with guests. Within five minutes of arrival the lights dimmed, and the conductor walked on stage. There was a large orchestra with a choir in the back and instruments not so different than what Chester experienced on Earth.

In a while the music began. The music provided some of the most incredibly beautiful melodies Chester had experienced in his lifetime and he had listened to a considerable amount of classical music. There were strange sounding instruments that gave Chester pause. From the strings to the percussion, to what appeared to be brass and woodwind instruments, the sounds combined creating a passage of temporal resonance ensembles causing delightful feelings.

Between Aida's physical enticements and a lot of unfolding events, Chester's mind was slowly losing its grip on desires to return to earth. *Was this all part of the plan?*

Actually, this event planned by Aida wanting to please Chester gave him another taste of society and how it existed here in Tymasoara. As a well-trained spy and seductress, Aida understood Chester would be much easier to handle by bestowing upon him incentives like he never experienced before. It already became a foregone conclusion that comparing Aida's sexual prowess to Abigail was like comparing a Volkswagen bug to a Lamborghini. Abagail, who had a fine assessment of herself had no idea the horsepower this alien *Lamborghini* seductress unleashed.

The first music the orchestra performed only lasted fifteen minutes in Chester's estimate. He soon discovered why it was so short. It was just the prelude to the next performance as a Diva walked out onto the stage. This luxuriously beautiful woman with and exquisite body, hair, and face got an ovation before she performed. When she started singing in a few minutes Chester understood why. Her Angelic voice was like some of the singers he heard in concerts recorded in Moscow, Vienna, Paris, London, and Berlin.

The Diva sang with choir backup in portions for almost thirty minutes it seemed. When the music ended there was a rancorous standing ovation with the singer bowing multiple times. Then there was an intermission.

"There is a bathroom in our private balcony directly behind you if you wish to go freshen up," Aida said.

"I don't mind if I do," Chester responded.

Chester stood up and when he appeared to be going to the private restroom, one of the security men opened the door for him and made sure the lights were turned on. After doing his business, Chester walked out of the bathroom back to his seat and there was a waiter standing there holding a tray with four small bottles and a couple glasses.

"Would you like a drink sir?"

"Do you have *Grand Zumbido*?" Chester asked.

"I certainly do," the waiter said, then poured one of the bottles into a glass and handed it to Chester. He then poured Aida her drink she already requested which was a form of a champagne called *Fŏcìn de Oín.*

The waiter had a small folding table he set up to hold the beverage tray. He placed the beverage tray on the table then stepped back several paces and stood in a respectful pose waiting to serve his VIP guests.

"Excuse me one moment Chester, I'm going to use the bathroom now," Aida said, then went in and freshened up.

The *Grand Zumbido* went down too smoothly, Chester gestured to the waiter.

The waiter brought the drink tray over to Chester to refill his glass. "Do you want a refill sir?" The waiter asked in the Drolupric language.

"Yes, I would, thank you," Chester answered in Drolupric with great precision and with the total Tymasoara dialect that placed him in the category of being a snob.

The waiter being quite sophisticated and had worked with the two security men before several times and knew quite well who they were, suggested, "Sir you are with a very luxurious lady tonight and something tells me that she's going to want to be satisfied later this evening. See the bottle with the pink substance?"

"Yes."

"Drink that instead of the *Grand Zumbido* and your sexual prowess will magnify in ways that will make her remember the night."

"May I ask what the name of the drink is."

"This pink liquor is referred to as *Zvèzdnàyà Rōzā.*"

"Let me taste it."

The waiter half-filled Chester's glass. Chester tasted it and felt a strangeness and pleasant taste and drank the entire contents and said, "Yes, go ahead and fill it up."

The waiter complied with a smile.

In a couple minutes Aida came back and sat next to Chester feeling refreshed and ready to enjoy her *Fôcìn de Oín.*

They had enough time to finish their drinks then the lights started dimming and the waiter approached them and took their glasses. With great precision he removed the folding table and took the drink tray away.

Chester didn't know what the hell was in that Zvèzdnàyà Rōzā, but he was already feeling excited. Back on Earth doctors would have advised him he took the equivalent of four doses of Viagra laced with four doses of damiana. The possibility of his erection going down any time soon was out of the question.

Another problem with damiana user is women may appear to be far more attractive than what they really are.

During the intermission, a piano was raised up on the stage from below on a built-in elevator that also conformed into the stage and appeared to be a raised platform standing about a foot above the rest of the stage and the concert hall workers placed stair steps to its approach. Soon an elegant woman came onto stage and stepped up on the stairs and onto the raised platform that had the piano, a chair for the pianist and a conductor's platform and chair in case the conductor needed to sit.

The woman sat there for a few minutes and after signaling the conductor he raised his baton and started the second half of the concert.

One of Chester's favorite music composers back on Earth was the great Prokofiev and most specifically his piano concerto number two. The music sounded very similar to Prokofiev's work.

Drolupric Empire exploration expeditions often brought back music recordings from all over the galaxy. Earth was no exception. The music writers here in Tymasoara had to adapt the music to their instruments without destroying the intent of the composer.

The piano on the stage was a copy of a Steinway brought to Tymasoara by black marketeers who claimed they had never been on the forbidden world planet Earth and stated they picked it up in the Tau Ceti Empire and purchased it to resell to the top musical instrument manufacture in the Drolupric Empire located in Tymasoara. It took the music instrument company almost two years to figure out how to copy it. Their engineers marveled at the incredible ingenuity to build a Steinway piano.

Using optical scanners and sonar equipment to determine mechanical impedances and other factors such as the cast iron bedplate and the treble board and soundboard to accurately recreate the sound of each key. With a vast number of Earth classical music recordings, Tymasoara instrument manufactures spectrographically detailed each and every key and the impact of the foot pedals.

Thanks to Earth's internet broadcast via satellite and microwave, this company was also able to get numerous copies of sheet music to study and thanks to music video's recording hand movements they were able to teach a few people to perform on the piano. Since there were instruments like piano's on Tymasoara robot operated, once they coded the techniques for the robots to accurately perform, they then had a means to integrate the piano music with an orchestra for a concerto or an opera. The woman now performing was one of the early students to learn this instrument when she was a very young lady. She could no doubt perform as well as Yuja Wang, Krystian Zimerman, Martha Argerich, or Khatia Buniatishvili.

The performance wasn't a Prokofiev knockoff, but the techniques were so similar and sound equally about the same, a classical music connoisseur from Earth would think it was Prokofiev perhaps his sixth piano concerto.

Having almost a taste of Earth on hearing this performance created a delightful moment for Chester which now reinforced his desire to do what it took to get back to Earth. He would go to hell and back for Duke Tinktar if that's what it took. Hopefully he could make that trip before Brooklyn expired from old age.

Aida observed Chester during the performance. She could tell he was mesmerized by the piano performance. The earlier performance with the Chorus and the Diva didn't cause a reaction in him like this piano music did. He was transfixed and following every note as if it resonated with him. His body language caused Aida to get more curious and made more observations up until the concerto was almost complete. Then about that time one of the security men walked up to Aida and whispered, "We have a few minutes to leave now to avoid the crowd."

Aida then tapped Chester on his hand and bent over and whispered in his ear, "We are leaving now to avoid the crowd."

Chester nodded and stood up with Aida and the two of them followed the security man out of the balcony into the hallway behind it. Just as they were getting to the front entrance Chester heard the applause of the audience, so he knew it was now over. He then walked out of the civic center with the security men and Aida to a Skycar that pulled up as soon as they reached the end of the sidewalk next to it. They were in the Skycar that was pulling away just as the first concert goers exited through the front entrance.

Chester knew he was getting hungry but was feeling too timid to ask many questions. In the span of five minutes, they flew towards a very tall building that as they got closer appeared to have a rooftop parking for Skycars. On top of that rooftop parking was a decorative structure adding to the architectural mystique about the building. Just like he experienced the other day just before going to the restaurant before Brooklyn met "Princess Tiffany" an access door opened and the Skycar slowly entered through that door to the parking area. As soon as the Skycar was in the parking structure the solid doors closed.

The building security and management system that oversees and controls parking for the exclusive VIP guests had control of the Skycar's navigation system and very efficiently parked it in its designated spot, shut down its propulsion and initiated opening the doors so the passengers could get out.

All five passengers including the driver exited the vehicle and they walked over to the automatic elevator that used facial recognition and immediately confirmed reservations to the restaurant located right under the parking structure. Everyone entered the elevator and very promptly the door shut, and it traveled down one floor and stopped, opened the door automatically and everyone got out.

The reservation indicated a table for two and the other three would socialize at the bar where they knew the bartender quite well from many previous journeys to this restaurant.

This restaurant was by invitation only to those exclusive clients that were well connected to money. There was an orchestra playing soft dinner music and the staff were impeccably dressed. The female waiters had tuxedo cocktail dresses on that showed most of their legs and what appeared to be black hosiery contrasted nicely with their pink skin. This trip to this very expensive restaurant was a game changer for Chester.

This was the capital city for a vast Empire that had over five hundred planets. Within those five hundred planets were thousands of ethnic groups that also had various skin colors from green, blue, pink, plain like Chester, and another which Chester soon discovered, multi-colored. Tonight, was a night that gave Chester the feeling he really was out and into the Universe far from Earth.

As the couple were led to their reserved table next to the large panoramic window that could see a long distance, Chester thought he was seeing forty to fifty miles away and what would normally be way past the horizon. He had no idea how high up he was, but he was almost fourteen thousand feet above sea level. The surface below was only twenty feet above sea level.

The seat that Chester was invited to sit in gave him a view of probably seventy five percent of the patrons in this renowned restaurant. After they were seated and gave the female waitress with a name tag *Trang* obtained their drink requests, Chester started gazing at all the other people present getting a feel for how they appeared. He sensed he was with the upper crust of society and was curious as to their fashions and appearances.

Chester had seen a lot of pink skinned people so that didn't have much of an impact, but the green, blue, and multi-colored people stood out and were a majority of those presently dining and enjoying themselves.

Chester now felt he *was out in space.* If it were not a vast dream, he now was sensing what the universe was like and people back home on planet Earth had no clue. It was mildly astonishing, but at the same token it was no different than looking at the multitudes of strange birds at Ski Beach that came all the time. The blue and green skin women were fabulously beautiful. The only difference between them and Aida by the way they were dressed up, was their skin color. Some of the women especially the green skin women knew plain skin men like Chester lusted for them. So, when one of them caught Chester observing her, she gave a facial expression like, "I know what you want honey."

Chester had not been trained in Drolupric etiquette the way he was going to soon learn. With what Duke Tinktar had in mind for Chester meant he would receive more training and education in a few months than he received in all of his prior education including at the University of California. Neurological Sonifications could provide highly targeted education that allowed rapid advancement in the arts and skills of a variety of capabilities to raise the talent level of someone exponentially.

Those high level Neurological Sonifications were not made available to the public. They were reserved exclusively for the Royal family and people they needed to go perform critical tasks.

Chester now saw the enormity of it all and started to understand why Duke Tinktar singled him out. In an advanced society like the Drolupric Empire it was almost impossible to find someone who didn't have some allegiance to an entity in one form or another. Breaking those allegiances had proven to be almost impossible and the bottom line was not reached until someone was placed in a position they had to choose and often the outcome was unpredictable and a waste of development. By having no allegiances to anyone or entity created the opportunity that Chester now experienced and would soon experience vastly more as he was sitting next to a black widow spy that would eat her lover if required.

Chester and Duke Tinktar both knew one allegiance Chester had. He would do whatever it took to get back to Earth. Chester and Duke Tinktar knew Chester understood there would only be one way to get there. Chester would have to pay the price and work directly for Duke Tinktar and he had no idea what those tasks would be. In some cases, Duke Tinktar didn't know either and would not know until the situation developed.

The waitress named Trang delivered their drinks then gave them menus to look over. She then stepped back to give them space.

Aida was drinking her Fôcìn de Oín champagne while Chester started sipping his purple *Grand Zumbido* elixir.

Chester still felt the effects of Zvèzdnàyà Rōzā. He didn't know that condition would last most of the night. But the *Grand Zumbido* seemed to calm him down a notch or two.

It was like being at a Zoo looking at all the strange people. Chester had watched Star Wars. Now he was living it looking at all these people. But they were not as hideous looking like the Star Wars characters, they were in fact quite lovely. The women present were absolutely gorgeous and dressed in the most expensive gowns in the Galaxy and prepared by the best fashion experts that existed.

Chester had a strange desire to know those women. The green, blue, and multi-colored women have an Aura about them he could not explain but they were magnetic to him. Chester's curiosity grew by the minute and his libido was already prepared. He suspected they were all quite lovely and in fact if made love to any of them, he probably would have regrets to ever go back to Earth.

After enjoying a couple sips of his Grand Zumbido Chester noticed a multi-colored women staring at him. His thoughts were her skin looked like a Leopard except she didn't have fur. It was the colorization and patterns on her skin that made her appear so. It was hard to figure out what her figure was like because she was sitting down, but her shape he could see had perfect geometries and she too was dressed immaculately. What Chester didn't know was that woman named Linap, was one of the richest persons in the Empire and a friend of Duke Tinktar.

Linap, being one of the richest persons in the Empire and a friend of Duke Tinktar also knew who Aida was because she knew Aida had been Duke Tinktar's mistress. And here she was showing total affection to that delightful looking plain skin man.

"What do you want to eat?" Aida asked knowing Chester had no idea what the menu really meant since it didn't explain it in Earth terms.

"Not sure, would you mind ordering for both of us," Chester asked.

"Alright."

Aida turned toward the waiter Trang standing about twenty feet away and nodded at her.

"Are you ready to order now?" Trang asked.

"Yes, I'm going to order the same for both of us," Aida replied.

"What would you like Madam?"

"We would like the baked Placstra."

Aida then handed the menu to the waiter Trang and Chester followed her actions with the same.

"I will get your order for you right away, but I must tell you this entrée takes a little longer time to prepare than most of the other entrée's."

"That's fine, we'll just sip on our drinks and enjoy the music until it's ready."

"Thank you for being understanding," Trang said and smiled.

"Not a problem," Aida responded.

Trang then turned around and walked away to get their order processed. Out of habit Chester's eyes followed Trang as she left. She had a great body with seemingly well-proportioned areas and Chester noted her posterior was second to none. Aida caught Chester's eyeball liberty and smiled and thought, *you are a bad boy after all. I might just have to have fun with you tonight.*

When Chester moved his head forward, he noticed the wicked grin on Aida and wondered, *what's that all about?*

Another thing that caught Chester's attention was the multi-colored woman Linap had glanced at him a few more times. Chester would always remember this moment because he had a premonition one day, he might meet that woman. His wait for that day would not last long.

Chester could not help but think, *I wonder what that woman is like? How does she sound when she talks and what does she experience in her everyday life?*

Multi-colored women like Linap had an advantage over all other women. They looked tantalizing with black gowns on. Tonight, Linap wore a black silk dress. Just like planet Earth this civilization produced high quality silk and other splendid fabrics that luxuriously clothed wealthy like Linap exhibited tonight.

Linap's skin colorization also went well with a variety of other colors, some of which were purposely colorized for the multi-colored well to do women like her.

Linap's lips, cheek bones, forehead, chin, and smile were perfectly proportioned that added to her glamour and illustrious essence. As Chester secretly studied Linap, he knew she had transcendental qualities and most likely would make mere mortals' knees weak, especially if she was bearing herself to make love. The thoughts of how she would please a man did not escape Chester's thoughts. Chester wasn't a pervert, but he wondered how she would appear if that black silk dress suddenly fell down to her ankles and she exposed herself.

As Chester would soon discover, the upper crust of society on Tymasoara knew each other. Linap had frequent business dealings with Margrét Hansen's husband, the intergalactic banker. On one occasion Linap tested the banker to see how loyal he was to his wife. He promptly proved he wasn't very loyal as Linap had a very strong sexual tryst with him so that in the future she would have some leverage if she needed it. The banker wasn't sophisticated enough to know that a lioness like Linap would have the event recorded in great fidelity in sound and holographic video in as great of detail as any porn film director could obtain in Hollywood on Earth.

Linap also took what she wanted when she wanted it. She had a strong ego and had a lot of dealings with Aida in the past who kept her away from devouring Duke Tinktar. And here she was in front of her with a plain skin boy-toy. It crossed Linap's mind that she would have great satisfaction to rip that plain skin man out of Aida's arms and seduce him to the point he would never have second thoughts about Aida ever again.

Linap wasn't vain. But she was inquisitive and demanding. She had her own needs to be pleased and didn't suffer fools for long. Any man she picked would have one shot at her and he didn't produce stellar results upon that first meeting, she would kick him to the curb and move on. Something told her Aida would not be so friendly with this boy toy unless he had prowess she wanted to discover. The fact he was ostensibly banging Duke Tinktar's concubine added a layer of curiosity and the desire to discover exactly what it was with that man that turned on Aida whose body language exposed she was with someone that pleased her.

In due time their entrées were served, and Chester tasted the meat and to his pleasant surprise had a familiar taste to it.

"This tastes like baked pheasant back where I came from," Chester said after he sampled it."

"Do you like pheasant?" Aida asked.

"Absolutely, it's one of the best tasting wild game I've eaten. Is this farm raised or do you think someone hunted it?"

"The menu said it was obtained in the wild. It's not farm raised."

"I imagine they would have to pay someone a lot of money to go hunt this bird."

"They certainly do, and for the price they charge, there is plenty of incentive for hunters to get them."

"Is there a lot of open wilderness areas on this planet?"

"There certainly is. Tymasoara is our second capital city for the Drolupric Empire. The capital of the empire used to be in the domed city of Velaqratantor."

As soon as Chester swallowed his mouthful of baked Placstra he asked, "Is Velaqratantor on this planet?"

"No, it's on a different planet almost halfway across the empire."

"Why was the capital moved here?"

"Partly it was due to safety. Velaqratantor is a lot closer to some of our traditional enemies, but also it was getting very crowded, so Emperor Cornelius decided to rebuild a new Capital here with much more stringent building zoning laws and before construction was started on Tymasoara, many areas were sealed off as natural parks with development strictly prohibited. This was almost a virgin planet when it all started. Most of the structures and infrastructures are less than 500 years old."

"Wow."

"I'll be giving you some sightseeing tours and you will be amazed at how much open areas exist on this planet that will never be developed because that's the emperor's desires."

"How will you handle a growing population?"

"There are twenty or sights slated for future development when Tymasoara reaches its full potential."

"Will the cities appear like Tymasoara?"

"No."

"What will be the difference?"

"Duke Tinktar has shown me some drawings and diagrams of how they will be constructed. They will not be out in the open air like Tymasoara. They will all be domed cities with anti-laser protection as the future laser systems our enemies will possess will make it impossible to have any more open-air cities."

"What will the Dome Cities be like?"

"Half of the city will be under the Dome; the other half of the city will be completely underground with park land on top of it."

"Interesting. Why the underground portions?"

"It's more of a safety and survival plan in case devastating weapons take out the dome portion of the cities, the isolated underground cities will have access via tunnels to the Domes that can be sealed off in emergencies."

What will the shape of these cities be like?

"The Dome cities will be shaped like Velaqratantor Dome. The underground cities can have just about any shape we want. It's simply a build based on how much dirt we want to move."

"I can conceptualize building a dome city. You build a dome and then fill it full of buildings, transportation devices, and people."

"In essence that's the basic concept yes."

"Will you do a lot of tunneling to build the underground part of the cities?"

"Duke Tinktar said the way those will be built is giant earth scrapers will come in and remove all the topsoil and store it at a nearby location. Then by using explosives and modern earth moving techniques we do with devices like the Spatializers, we create a gigantic hole next to the dome city being constructed. Then we install protective cover and a foundation and watertight floors and walls. A certain amount of rock and debris will be placed on the protective convex cover then covered with topsoil and turned into a park for Dome and underground city residents."

"What's a Spatializer?"

"It's a device that uses ultrasonic frequencies to make the rock softer and easier to drill through. It speeds up the drilling process by a factor of one hundred or more."

"When is all this construction going to happen?"

"One of the cities on the other side of the planet is under construction now. Would you like to get a tour?"

"Sure, if you can work it into my schedule."

"I'll see what I can do."

They finished their meal and soon it was time to either stay and enjoy the entertainment for the night or go back and be with Brooklyn. Chester brought it up. "I think I would like to go back and be with Brooklyn in case he wakes up."

"Sure, if that's what you want."

Moments later they were walking out of the restaurant with Linap observing how casual Aida was with the nice-looking gentleman.

Fifteen minutes later Chester and Aida walked into his suite and there was Brooklyn laid out on the procedures table in short breath.

Dog groomer Rayalna was with him observing his medical instrument readouts produced by non-invasive measurement system.

"How's Brooklyn doing? Chester asked.

"All his vital signals are normal."

"Procedure all finished?"

"Yes, the technicians left here about an hour ago."

"Do you think we should move him?" Chester asked.

"No, we would prefer he remained hooked up to the monitors tonight."

"Alright, but could we move the cart closer to my bed in case he wakes up in the middle of the night?"

"Sure, no problem."

After the cart was next to the bed, Chester said, "I'm going to go to bed now. I'll watch Brooklyn now."

"Sure, no problem." Rayalna said.

"Thank you. Chester replied.

"Call me if you have any concerns later." Rayalna said, then turned and walked out the access door.

Aizere then walked in the room carrying sleeping clothes for two people and asked Chester, would you like to take a bath before you change into your sleeping clothes.

"Yes, that's a great idea."

In fifteen minutes, Chester and Aida were in the bath water and Aida asked, "Would you like me to Shampoo your hair?"

"Yes, I want to get all the hairdresser's chemicals out of my hair."

Aida then began the Shampoo and messaging of Chester and when she grabbed his manliness to put inside her, he said, "Wait until we get in bed, I want to please you to show you how much I appreciate everything you have done for me."

"Sure," Aida responded and gave Chester a wicked smile wondering what kind of tricks he had up his sleeve.

In due time they were out of the tub dressed in their sleeping clothes and tucked in bed and the lights slowly dimmed.

Aida was wondering what kind of cerebral stimulation Chester had in mind.

Chester was imaginative, inquisitive, and inductive as he conjured up the agenda for his stimulation of Aida. Chester seemed to be a timid and non-aggressive man. Aida would never have guessed at his skill set and prowess.

A few years ago when Chester was a road warrior for a brief period of time before he met Abagail, he had a very good teacher in the art of pleasing women. This female college professor who liked young talent was more than willing to teach them the secrets of pleasing women and try it out on her first to build up perfection before they applied it to their girlfriends.

Chester was a willing student, but Abagail never gave him a lot of opportunity to explore his talent base and practice his special knowledge on her.

Chester and Aida were soon cuddled and kissing. Chester ran his hand down into the bottom portion of Aida's sleeping clothes and found her womanhood and checked and discovered she was wet with anticipation. After one more kiss, Chester slid under the blanket and pulled off her underwear and sleeping clothes bottom piece. Aida thought at first Chester was going to simply mount her and drive his Scorpio divine stinger into her which would give her a great orgasm. But instead, he started applying the stimulation the way his college professor taught him.

Right then and there is when Aida developed an even stronger attachment to Chester who proceeded to work up stimulation and countless gratification. Chester waited patiently for that special moment he knew would come soon when Aida's body was going to go into neurotic spasms from lingering gratifications, he finally performed for Aida and gave it to her nice and long satisfaction in amazing ensembles of surreal stimulation that took Aida into a different dimension as her endorphins in her brain were exploding in volumes of psychophysical responses..

Aida screamed at the top of her lungs. It was mildly unsettling for people outside the room who thought Chester might be killing Aida, but when they tried to break in to save her, Artificial Intelligence told them to back off, it was nothing more than sound created by surreal manifestation of pleasure. By the time Chester finished with Aida there were 10 security men outside the room ready to dash in and save the woman, but Artificial intelligence kept reminding them, "They are coupling, its none of your business."

When Aida collapsed in splendid euphoria and Chester finished his last act giving Aida such surreal gratification, the room then had complete silence. The security men slowly peeled away, some of them intrigued because nobody had ever gotten Aida to screaming like this having sex ever before.

The night then slowly slipped away into morning in lover's bliss.

In the middle of the night Aida felt uncomfortable knowing she was filled full of Chester's Scorpio venom and went into the bathroom and took a short bath to clean up and then put on her sleeping clothes. The only person naked in the morning was Chester, so when Aizere arrived in the morning to wake them up and help them get ready for the day's events, she accidently saw Chester's nude body and it caused her some mild disturbances because it affected her, and she felt ashamed of herself. She knew that if Chester made a pass at her, she could not resist him and would in fact encourage copulation if the opportunity occurred.

Chester would find out he had three events scheduled after breakfast. First, Duke Tinktar would take him and Brooklyn out to a secure area where they could work out and do physical exercises. Then Aida would fulfill her promise to take him to go visit the new Dome and underground city that was being built in the middle of a tropical rainforest. Chester would then get his third Neurological Sonification treatment.

During breakfast, Duke Tinktar was sitting across from Brooklyn and looked at the dog and asked in standard Drolupric language, "How are you feeling today, Brooklyn?"

Brooklyn who was proving to be very polite to Duke Tinktar and the staff which grew their affection towards him, answered in perfect Drolupric, "Your Excellency, it feels like it did a couple days ago. I have a lot of Drolupric words floating over my head. But its slowly getting less."

"Brooklyn, if there was one thing you could do today with your Papa, what would that be?"

"Your excellency, I miss feeding the birds. I wish papa and I were at the beach feeding birds this morning."

"Brooklyn, I know a place that has a lot of birds. May I suggest after we finish eating, we go there and I'll ask the staff to pack us some things to feed the birds. What do you usually feed the birds?"

"Your excellency, bread and crackers, but for some of the birds they prefer meat, so papa gives them meat."

"Alright, I'll see what I can come up with. When we get there you and Papa can do some exercises. I'll have a coach there for your Papa."

"That sounds really good, Your Excellency."

"Am I going with you?" Aida asked.

"No, just Chester and Brooklyn will come with me."

"Understand," Aida said knowing there was something behind this trip that Duke Tinktar didn't want her to know about."

After breakfast and freshening up and changing into what appeared to be exercise sweatpants and top, Chester with Brooklyn were led out of the front entrance to a couple waiting Skycars. They were ushered into the back seat of the first Skycar that had a driver and Duke Tinktar sitting in the front seat.

The two Skycars soon flew out of the access opening on the side of the steep front hill slope and immediately got into a higher altitude Skycar transit lane. The Skycars flying the upper levels were permitted to go faster and were spread out in much thinner traffic.

Looking out the window, Chester speculated on how fast they were flying, and his best estimate was probably flying three hundred miles per hour.

Chester was not far off the mark, but they were closer to four hundred miles an hour. At that speed they were quickly leaving behind Tymasoara, the capital city of the Drolupric Empire.

Duke Tinktar was taking them to an animal reserve area fully fenced off from the public. Trespassers or wild game hunters were severely punished if they went into this area.

About one hundred miles away from Tymasoara, the Skycars left the intercity sky freeway and veered off into the restricted area. On the other side of a hill that blocked the view from the Skycar freeway, the two Skycars came down and landed at a facility that served multiple purposes. First it had groundskeepers and security force to police the area and keep out intruders. Secondly this was where Duke Tinktar trained his elite forces that had to sometimes perform clandestine activities involving espionage, sabotage, assassinations, abductions, and any serious mission the emperor needed accomplished in a rapid deployment.

This area also had many birds and waterfowl that lived by the lake that existed in the middle of this complex and a few hundred yards from the building complex that housed the full-time staff of park rangers and game wardens there to enforce the quarantined area.

The Skycars landed in Skycar parking slots. There were a lot of empty slots today because there were no teams here training today. But during high mission tempo's the Skycar parking appeared almost filled up.

Everyone got out of the skycars, and a couple men carried a couple bags of treats for the birds.

"There is a spot near here where we lay out bird feed for the multitudes of birds that exist here and often have insufficient food. When our men are feeding them, the bids usually come up close. Us go see how they will react to you."

Duke Tinktar led Chester and Brooklyn over to that bird feeding area selected about 200 yards from the building complex on a gravel walkway with vegetation cleared back making it safe from attack by snakes or other venomous animals.

When they got to the feeding area where there were troughs staged in advance to place the food.

Duke Tinktar gestured the first security man forward and said, "Give your sack to Chester who will feed the birds with Brooklyn."

The man handed Chester the sack. Chester opened the sack and saw there was a lot of feed of some type in it. He had no idea what it was but would soon learn it was a hybrid meal mixture that had taste and smell that would quickly attract birds. Unlike most of the birds on Earth that can't smell, these birds had noses almost as good as dogs for smelling.

Chester walked over to the first trough and dumped some of the content from the bag into it, then he stepped back about 10 feet to see if birds would come.

Brooklyn was standing next to Chester and asked, "Papa when do you think the birds will come?"

"Brooklyn, I hope soon because we have a lot of things to do today."

Hidden in the trees nearby were multitudes of birds who were familiar with humans but had never seen a dog before, but they knew the humans around them in this area were always nice to them and fed them, so they had no real fear of Brooklyn. Suddenly out of nowhere came seven birds who flew down to the trough and started eating the food Chester placed there.

Shortly one or two at a time were arriving quickly filling up the area they could eat, just like Chester experienced at Ski beach.

Chester realized he needed to spread some food into some of the other troughs to give birds space to eat because they were getting aggressive in the tightly packed area, they were now in. Chester walked over to an adjacent trough. The birds paid no real interest in Chester until he started dropping food into the other troughs, then they came in numbers.

In a while Chester guesstimated there were 200 birds now eating. Brooklyn stood beside Chester two feet away from the birds in the last food trough.

"Papa it looks like the birds are not scared of us, just like at Ski Beach."

"Brooklyn, these appear to be very friendly birds. I think we will get to know them better in the future."

"Papa, I hope so. I want to talk to them and be their friend."

"Brooklyn, give it time, it will happen."

The birds were very hungry, some had not really had much to eat in a week and very soon they ate up all the food that had been given. Chester knew there was more bags of food and he asked, "May I have another bag of food please."

One of the security guys walked forward and handed Chester another bag of the birds food.

Chester thinking now would be a good time to test it said, "Brooklyn when I feed the birds again, I want you to act like you are eating the food and us see if the birds will get close to you."

"Alright Papa."

Chester was standing next to the trough with Brooklyn and dropped a large amount of food into it. At first the birds were a little shy with Brooklyn standing right next to the trough. As it is typical, one bird would somehow gain the courage and approached the trough and started eating next to Brooklyn watching him as it ate. A moment another bird came forward and started eating. Then ten more suddenly got courage and came forward. There was plenty of room for them because the other birds were too scared to approach these strangers.

"Us move over to the next one," Chester said and went to it and dumped another large pile of food into the trough. Some of the first group of birds moved to it and started eating. Other birds that were hanging back went to the previous trough, getting into areas where no other birds stood and started eating in earnest.

After a while they walked down the full length of the troughs, and the birds followed him as he dumped more food. As soon as all the bird food was provided and the birds appeared well in hand, Duke Tinktar said, "Lets walk over to the gym and start a workout." Inside the gym some of the best physical trainers in the galaxy anxiously awaited Duke Tinktar and the new trainee. These men trained spies and assassins. No matter how they felt about the looks of Chester, they knew based on Duke Tinktar's instructions to them. This person was one of those they were not allowed to fail. They would get him up to speed in martial arts and physical fitness otherwise their lives could end up in a disaster and a free trip to the Hog Farm.

"Chester you will get one hour of martial arts training today and then they will assist you in your workout," Duke Tinktar stated.

"I will do my best," Chester responded.

Duke Tinktar nodded at the chief instructor who then began the methodic development of Chester.

The instruction seemed simple to Chester for some strange reason, he almost felt like he understood what was all entailed. What Chester didn't know was his Neurological Sonifications he last received had all the martial arts techniques and descriptions of the moves. That reprogramming of his brain was now starting to pay dividends and he learned rapidly to the point the instructor was mildly impressed.

By the end of the hour, the instruction and workout created a lot of fundamental ability Chester now exhibited in his training and workouts.

The efficacy of the Neurological Sonifications was now on display for Duke Tinktar and he knew Chester was learning martial arts about 100 times quicker than he could back at planet Earth. Then it was time to do some running.

"It's more important you run sprints than long distances. You will run the sprints then rest and equalize as you receive more instruction."

"Alright, show me the way."

In due time Brooklyn was having fun chasing after Chester. They were all getting a good workout together.

During the workouts, Chester was given special drinks that would enhance his longevity and sustain high levels of training.

Duke Tinktar had observed a lot of his men over time get similar training and Chester was keeping up with the best in this training.

Duke Tinktar had looked at all the surveillance videos of Chester back at Ski Beach before his abduction. Chester proved to be self-motivated and worked out every single day. Duke Tinktar knew Chester would evolve and slowly become a better Ninja than found on planet Earth over the past four hundred years.

Duke Tinktar knew the real reason behind Chester's dedication to this training and workouts, he wanted to one day be permitted to return to Earth. Unfortunately for Chester that would not happen until the emperor was gone and his replacement was sitting on the throne.

After the workouts were all done, Duke Tinktar took Chester and Brooklyn back to his estate where they were cleaned up and prepared for a trip. They would eat their next meal during the trip.

Today was different. Chester was not dressed in Royal attire. He wore fashionable but traditional Tymasoara apparel.

In due time after they were ready, Chester, Aida, and Brooklyn were all escorted to a waiting transportation device. It wasn't a Skycar and Chester had no idea what it was. Once seated and the seatbelts were all fixed the craft went up into the air and Chester could see by the navigation displays in the control room of this craft, they were indeed heading into space. The craft flew outside the planet's atmosphere and traveled halfway around the planet in 30 minutes and then flew down to the planet surface and landed at what appeared to be a major construction site.

There were several bodyguards with them and they all exited from a single access door and stepped foot onto an area not far from what looked like a big hole residing next to an area that contained a lot of pillars. Adjacent to where they landed was a welcoming committee with electric construction carts used to ferry men around the construction site.

A well-dressed man hopped out of one of the carts that seemed to be empty except for the driver and approached the group. "Hello, my name is Sandstrom I'm going to give you a tour of the new dome city we are building here."

Aida chimed right in and asked, "Sandstrom has the name to the new city been announced yet?

"Yes, it has. News media outlets have been informed this new city has been given the name of New Velaqratantor. It's no longer a big secret."

"Alright thanks," Aida responded.

"Let me introduce you to everyone. This is Chester with his dog Brooklyn, I'm Aida and these other men are our security detail."

"Pleased to meet all of you."

"Thank you, likewise."

"Let's all go over and hop in the carts; we have plenty of room and I'll take you over to the big dig. We have a platform we can walk out on to see more of it."

The electric carts didn't have far to go to get to that platform that was large enough to hold the entire group with a lot of left over room. The carts stopped on the sides of the platform. Soon the group was walking out almost 100 yards onto the platform. Looking around Chester could see three sides and the floor of the structure was completed.

This underground portion of the new city did not have sheer walls. It was terraced and segmented, appearing like an upside-down pyramid with large steps. Chester could also see access ramps for vehicles or Skycars to enter already built and in the bottom of this underground city was a number of construction vehicles.

"Looks like you only have one more side to this huge cavern to build, what's delaying that side?" Chester asked.

"That's where we are going to build the underground transportation corridor that will link other cities such as Tymasoara and future new cities," Sandstrom replied.

"What type of transportation will you utilize in the corridor?" Chester asked.

"First of all, we must maintain the topography of current modes. There will be separate tunnels for each mode such as: intercity trains, surface vehicles, Skycars, pedestrian and intermodal freight."

"That sounds logical, is there extra space to take in account new technologies?"

"Of course, there will be a couple extra tunnels for new technologies that are now being designed that will be ready to implement about the time this city is ready to have people move in."

"What kind of future technology are you considering?" Chester asked.

"We have developed a hyper-velocity gyro stabilized tube carts that will shoot through tubes at high speeds."

"How will the propulsion on such a device work?"

"The car bodies are made of a substance very similar to Teflon, but 100 times smoother. The walls of the hyper-velocity gyro stabilized tube cart, have strips of this same material called Pínghuá Gāng allowing an almost frictionless passage through the tunnel.

Propulsion works off the principle of using air dampers and vacuums and air thrusters. Air vacuums are created in front of the hyper-velocity gyro stabilized tube cart that helps create a frictionless area for it to move into at the same time the air thrusters push the cart from behind. Thanks to the wireless Navigation track at the bottom of the tube, sensors are used to steer the capsule with great accuracy.

"What's the purpose of the air dampers?"

"Once the hyper-velocity gyro stabilized tube cart leaves the terminal, the thruster air is shifted to the tunnel away from the terminal bypassing it, to allow loading the next tube cart with no propulsion air hitting it allowing total stability and coordination of passenger loading without any fear of the cart moving during the loading process. Once the tube cart that left the station reaches the midway point thanks to dampers a vacuum inlet is set up to help pull the next cart out of the station. Another damper further ahead of it allows insertion of propulsion air on the tube cart that just passed. Hence, thanks to the dampers we have two hypervelocity gyro stabilized tube carts traveling in the tunnel at the same time that will not interfere with each other."

"How fast do these hyper-velocity gyro stabilized tube carts travel?"

"For safety reasons during the high-volume portion of the day with a lot of trains running, they are limited to 1200 miles per hour. Early in the morning and after peak hours in the evening, we only run one cart at a time in the tube carts. They are allowed to go 1800 miles per hour."

"That fast? Wow."

"Would you like to drive over to see the dome construction?"

"Sure."

It was quite an eyesight looking down into a huge cavity larger than anything Chester saw in his lifetime. It took a while to drive over to the Dome that was partially finished. It was a lot further away than Chester first imagined.

When they got closer to the dome, the first thought Chester had was, *oh my god!*

Chester now realized he had never seen anything go ginormous in his lifetime. It also sent shivers up his spine when he realized what these aliens could do and how Earth was so primitive in comparison.

The road they traveled on was in fantastic shape and was a supervisory road where engineers, technicians, and supervisors went back and forth over between the dome and the pits. It had to be segregated from the main construction throughways that had huge machines often passing and would make it very unsafe. That's why the road was smoother, but it was also narrower.

There was a partial interior road network inside the dome completed to support the population that would move into there. Construction equipment was forbidden to drive on those roads. Hence, they had to build from one side to the other and Chester could see if he guesstimates it, the dome was probably one third done.

Once they got inside the dome and started looking around, Chester was astonished at the size of the pillars and the area of the dome was larger than anything he could possibly imagine.

"How large will the dome be?" Chester asked.

"The dome has a radius of four miles and will have a circumference of approximately twenty five miles.

"The top of the dome looks pretty high up."

"Yes its 2000 feet from the surface of the planet here, but 3000 feet above the bottom of the dome."

"Why the difference between the surface and bottom?"

"The dome is actually 1000 feet below the surface, its partially submerged so that so much of it does not stick up into the air."

"Why was that done?"

"It was used to reduce the effects of wind and weather conditions."

"No worries about flooding?"

"The bottom of the dome sits in a concrete tub that rises twenty feet above the planet surface that serves two purposes. First it prevents any possible flood waters reaching into the dome, but it also acts as a secondary foundation and part of the multi-sectioned anchoring and stabilization system."

"Interesting."

"There are several concentric rings that are all part of the anchoring system that will give added security during possible earthquakes or seismic tremors we have to plan for even if we don't expect them."

Soon the carts were driving on future city streets that were all complete with no buildings yet next to them. The city streets were all laid out and off to the distance where it appeared the dome was completed there were buildings going up.

"Those buildings appear to be wider than buildings we see back at Tymasoara."

"That's a very astute observation, in fact they are a lot wider."

"Is there a reason for that?"

"Actually, we used a computer artificial intelligence to optimize the size of the buildings based on some of our criteria."

"Such as?"

Since it's a dome city and people on this planet are not used to dome city living, we wanted to deal with their personal psychology and do what we could to enhance their desire to live in a domed city. We built several models and mockups to use while doing a survey of a lot of people and what we discovered, they preferred the designs that incorporated the most park space."

"Sounds logical to me."

Also, since this will have dome living Skycar access, the residents need a place to park their personal Skycar. If you look at the nearest building, you will discover an area in the middle of the building with no windows."

"Why is that?"

"Those are Skycar parking slots inside the buildings next to the residents."

"Do all buildings have these Skycar parking slots?"

"No some buildings only have Skycar parking on their roofs to deliver or pick up passengers or special deliveries."

"How soon will those buildings start filling up?"

"We will not wait until the dome is fully complete before we allow companies and individuals to move in. But for the sake of safety, we have an air corridor plan and none of those buildings will be accessible until the first half of the dome is completed. That will insure they have no overhead potential drops that could hurt someone."

"How soon do you expect that to happen?"

"Right now, it may not look like it, but we'll easily meet that milestone in six months."

"What about the rest of the dome?"

"The entire dome will be complete in approximately 18 months."

"What about the underground portions we saw earlier?"

"All building is going on in parallel. We want the entire complex to be finished at the same time."

"The parks will be installed over the underground cities at that time?"

"Yes, the vegetation and plants and trees will be staged well ahead of transplant dates. Turf will be installed by expert landscapers within two weeks of starting the plantings. You will not know the park was new. The trees that will be transplanted are already twenty to forty feet tall. The plants and shrubs are of substantial size and quantity."

Chester was thinking about the number of new Dome Cities that would be built. If this was an indication of things to come, it truly was amazing.

Aida was feeling a little hungry and noticed Brooklyn wasn't looking so happy either and suddenly asked, "Chester have you seen enough?"

"I suppose so, but I wouldn't mind coming back and looking at it when it's all complete."

"I'll make sure you get a chance to ride in one of the hyper-velocity gyro stabilized tube carts."

"I appreciate that."

Aida looked at one of the security men and said, "Have the transporter come here to pick us up. We do not want to drive back there in the electric carts."

"Right away madam."

Chapter Twelve

MOUNTAIN RESORT

Five minutes later the transport doors were opening, and the group got back in the transporter and headed to the mountain restaurant that was planned as part of the dog and pony show.

It took ten minutes to fly to the mountain top restaurant. This was another one of those upscale places where the wealthy went because it was too hard to get to unless you were in a Transporter or Skycar. That prevented about ninety percent of society getting there as many were stuck on public transportation due to their personal circumstances.

The parking lot was half full which wasn't bad for this time of day, though slightly late for lunch.

As the group went inside the restaurant, they had to put Brooklyn in a dog carrier and like before, the restaurant put up temporary dividers to shield them from the rest of the patrons, which allowed them to get Brooklyn out of the pet carrier and they had a doggie chair set up for him that reminded Chester of baby feeding chairs from his early days and watching friends and relatives put the toddlers into such chairs with their desktop like surface to place food dishes on.

As soon as Brooklyn was situated, he had special dog food and water bowls on his serving tray in front of him and he wasted no time eating because he was hungry. The perfect filtered mountain water had no chemicals or additives. The only thing done to it was boiling it to kill all the possible microorganisms, then bottled in glass bottles for storage.

Aida and Chester were seated at a table for two with Brooklyn to their side and another table near Brooklyn for the security detail, that would be treated to some very lavish food today.

The bodyguard's work was slightly boring as this person was utterly unknown, had no known enemies because he's not from this planet, and the public did not know Brooklyn was a talking dog. They could not see the incredible number of wasted manhours to protect people with no threats. But they also knew better than to ever openly question Duke Tinktar who would not take their comments lightly and probably receive a shitty job on a planet where they would have to live in more austere circumstances. In the end they would rather have all this great food and circumstances than the alternative. Therefore, they remained silent and did what they were told.

The bodyguards knew from the screaming incident recently that the Earth Person was having wild sex with Aida whom they all would love to have a crack at. Aida's appearance exhibited extraordinary beauty and charm. The bodyguards were somewhat perplexed how this male from a backwards planet could so effectively turn Aida on.

Scanning the drink menu, Chester saw an elixir called *Chamboreé de Lián* , and asked Aida, "Do you recommend this *Chamboreé de Lián* elixir?"

"Yes, *Chamboreé de Lián* is a wonderful drink. I have it now and then when I want to feel more reflective or going through tough times."

"I'll have the *Chamboreé de Lián,* Chester said to the waiter.

The waiter looked at Aida who quickly stated before a question, "I'll have the *Fôcìn de Oín.*"

The view from this mountain top restaurant was quite magnificent. Chester had no idea what he was looking at, but he was glad Aida brought him here. Soon the *Chamboreé de Lián* elixir was adding to the ambience that Chester felt.

Chester knew to enjoy Aida and the *Chamboreé de Lián* while he could because later this afternoon, he would undergo another Neurological Sonification session which was becoming annoying, though he knew he brought it onto himself by wanting to learn Drolupric language at a rapid pace. *Be careful what you ask for,* Chester was quickly learning.

After giving the waiter their entrées orders, Aida sitting close to Brooklyn started petting and patting Brooklyn and smiled at him while she did. Brooklyn took it as affection from Aida and was starting to like her more and more. *Too bad that bitch Abagail wasn't like this,* Brooklyn thought.

This was a joyous and happy moment for Chester who was slowly digesting the reality of his future. Aside from being abducted, he wound up associated with the most powerful family and operatives in one of the more powerful empires in the galaxy.

Knowing it was probably a long time before he would see Earth again, he might as well make the most of it and was feeling some muscle pain from his workout earlier today. Chester was also grappling with the thoughts of how he instinctively knew some of those martial arts moves today having never been taught them before. *Are they programming my brain with those Neurological Sonifications?*

Chester also had the desire to learn as much about the universe as possible because people back on Earth didn't know much about the universe, whatsoever. Chester had a good feeling that Chernega the Librarian would help organize his study of the galaxy. Chester also knew he would endure a steep learning curve. Chester didn't realize what Chernega's roles really were and by wanting to learn as much about the galaxy as possible, he was indulging in activity Duke Tinktar wanted him to do as part of his training for what he would soon learn he had to do.

The days of hanging out with Aida and enjoying her body were just about over. Chester would soon discover he had other things he would be doing elsewhere, and it would not be out of the question that he spent some time at Madam Pang's.

Chester was soon tested like never before. His loyalty to Duke Tinktar would go through a variety of tests and ball buster cycles for Chester who would escape death barely by seconds and learn firsthand how violent the galaxy could be at times.

This was a milestone in Brooklyn's life as he slowly evolved to have Papa close to him. Brooklyn knew he woke up in the morning in the same bed as Aida. *That was never possible with the bitch Abagail. Chester also knew Abagail NEVER gave Papa the affection Aida did. He was happy that Papa would have a friend like Aida because he knew back on Earth his life sucked with Abagail who didn't appreciate how great a person Papa was.*

Soon everyone was done eating and it was time to return to Duke Tinktar's estate where Chester was to receive his next Neurological Sonification treatment. The group retraced their steps back to the Transporter and nobody in the restaurant knew they just had a dog in the dining room with them.

The Skycars launched and were soon on their way and after a while there was that unmistakable hilltop with an entrance in the side of it the transporter traveled through the tunnel to unload their distinguished guests.

Chester was led into his suite and shortly after he arrived the technicians were there setting up already for his Neurological Sonification treatment.

While Papa was in his treatment, Aida suggested to Brooklyn, "let's go for a walk, I could use some exercise."

"Alright Madam, I'm ready to go on a walk too."

"Brooklyn don't call me Madam, just call me Aida.

"Alright Aida, if that's what you want."

"Thank you."

"You are most welcome Aida."

Aida walked with Brooklyn first out into the courtyard and then beyond where there were a few walking trails established by Duke Tinktar so his VIP guests could go there to get a little exercise and unwind.

As they walked along there was small talk, and mainly Brooklyn just answering Aida's questions. After walking up one trail for about a quarter of a mile, an animal that appeared to Chester like a squirrel was dead ahead observing the two walking towards him.

Chester stopped and said, "Aida would it be possible to go back and get some food to give to this squirrel?"

"I suppose we could, but some people may not like it."

"It will be our secret; you can tell them I asked for it for me."

"Alright us go back then."

Twenty minutes the two came back. The squirrel-like animal was nowhere to be found. Chester spotted the area the Squirrel was hanging out earlier and said, " Let's go over there and lay the food out. He might come back after we lay the food down and stand back a distance."

Aida followed Brooklyn back to where he thought they should stand and wait. Just as Brooklyn estimated a few minutes later one of the squirrels, like animals approached the food to investigate it. It smelled it then picked up a portion and stood on its back legs and using its front feet hands started eating the food while staring at Brooklyn and Aida.

They made no noise or movement and the animal continued eating, getting braver by the minute. A few minutes later its partner came out and joined it. There was a lot there to eat so they didn't fight over it. Soon a little one emerged and joined the feast, eating and observing Brooklyn now sitting down being quiet and Aida who just stood and watched.

"I think we should now leave and let them enjoy their food, we'll see them tomorrow," Brooklyn stated.

The two turned and walked back to Duke Tinktar's enclave. Brooklyn looked behind and the animals continued eating and watched them leave.

Soon they were back at the compound in the courtyard and Brooklyn asked, "Can we go check up on Papa?"

"Sure, why not."

Soon they went into Chester's suite. His procedure was over, and the technicians had him in his bed sedated and resting with two of the technicians monitoring Chester's vital signatures on various instruments.

"Can I go up and lay beside papa?"

"Brooklyn you have been to a lot of places today and walked all over a lot of areas and probably picked up a lot of dirt and grime. You can lay next to Papa but first you must take a bath."

"Alright, give me the bath."

"Rayalna, can you come here please."

Artificial intelligence signaled Rayalna who then came into the room and asked, "What would you like me to do?"

"Brooklyn needs to take a bath because he was outside in a lot of places today and wants to lay besides Chester up on the bed."

"Brooklyn are you ready to take a bath?"

"Yes Rayalna."

"Alright, let's go do it."

Thirty minutes later Brooklyn was bathed and blown dry and feeling good. When he walked back into the bedroom, he discovered someone had moved his ramp to the bed he could walk up on and lay down next to Papa.

The technicians left the instrument rack in the room as it was monitoring Chester non-invasively. Everyone else left the room except Aida who changed into sleeping clothes and crawled in bed and was next to Brooklyn who slowly progressed into slumber after another big day. Brooklyn was happy for the first time in his life he had a complete family, Papa, and Momma as he viewed Aida. Brooklyn knew Aida liked him, unlike the way Abagail who tried to kill him.

The night slipped into morning slowly and this was going to be a big day for Brooklyn. He was to receive his final Neurological Sonification and not have to endure it again.

***

Doctor Akssiar had been studying telemetry data from Brooklyn's black box and committed to Tasha, "It's amazing and almost hard to believe, but the fact it happened shows Brooklyn could learn a lot more than he has.

"I was surprised the Drolupric words in Brooklyn's lexicon overwrote a lot of the English words," Tasha responded.

"Yea I see Brooklyn now has 55,000 Drolupric words and only 10,000 English words," Doctor Akssiar added.

What are we going to do with him now?

"Brooklyn now has more Drolupric words than we could imagine and based on his lexicon he's smarter than the average Drolupric. I think we need to just go with what he now has learned and observe him and not perform any further Neurological Sonifications for a while."

"I agree."

"We are going over to Duke Tinktar's estate now and check up on Chester and give him the exams you finished writing," Doctor Akssiar stated.

281

"I'm ready, I have my printouts and a few data cubes," Tasha said.

"Alright, let's go," Doctor Akssiar said and stood up and led Tasha out of his office and then outside and got into his official Skycar.

The light in Chester's suite slowly increased with soft chimes playing to help awaken Chester, Aida, and Brooklyn. Aizere came into the room after Artificial Intelligence informed her, Chester and Brooklyn were slowly waking up so that she could help them get ready for morning events.

Aizere walked in the room just as Chester had transitioned to awaken reality. Half of the night he dreamed he had Drolupric and Chinese words flowing past him in the sky just like he experienced when he did strenuous Chinese studies a few years prior.

"Would you like to freshen up then take a bath."

"Yes, that sounds good."

"When you are ready for your bath let Artificial Intelligence know and I'll be right there."

"Alright."

"Brooklyn you want to take a bath?"

"Papa, I took a bath last night, I don't need one now."

"Alright."

Artificial intelligence knew someone needed to tend to Brooklyn since he was not taking a simultaneous bath and requested Rayalna to assist. As soon as Rayalna arrived, Aida volunteered to assist Chester in his bath.

Rayalna was interested in talking to Brooklyn, so she asked him what all he did the day before. Brooklyn had quite a few stories to share and added, "I would like to go visit those squirrels today and see if they will get more friendly."

"I'm not sure we'll have time for that, I've been advised you have to go to several places today with Chester."

"Will we go feed those birds at the park this morning?"

"That's right, I think that's part of the plan."

Soon the bath was filled up and Chester was feeling good after he freshened up and eased into the water. He thought Aida would immediately join him, but she had to take care of her own personal business then she arrived nude and stepped down into the large bath and soon crawled over Chester who was sitting on a submerged surface designed to keep his head out of water.

"How are you feeling Chester?"

"I'm still seeing those images of Drolupric words and Chinese Mandarin Characters floating above me, but they are declining."

"Maybe I can help you forget about those images for a while."

"What do you have in mind."

"Let me show you."

Aida backed off Chester then went underwater and found his manliness and started performing fellatio on him. Chester was quickly feeling elevated and feeling the wonderful sensation. He was also surprised Aida could hold her breath as long as she did."

Eventually Aida came above the water and started breathing and had a wicked smile on her face because she tasted some of the Scorpio venom that leaked out of Chester and left a distinct taste in her mouth. Aida knew she had Chester right to the point where he was ready to explode in her mouth. She then resumed her position on his lap and guided his manliness inside her and she began to exercise her body in a way that emphasized Chester's pleasure to the point he felt an immediate need to release his full deposit. The gratification felt strong and lingered and added greatly to the pleasantness and suddenly all the Drolupric words and Chinese Mandarin Characters floating above him were gone.

Chester knew one thing was happening because of this abduction and now living with the Drolupric people, he was starting to have emotional bonds to Aida. He didn't quite understand where she fit into the overall scheme of things. She was well connected and seemingly directed to please him. *But were the emotions reciprocal?* He was too scared to ask because he knew if it was merely pleasure coordination, it would have a negatively material impact on his emotions.

After the bath, Aida left and went back to her suite to get dressed up and find out about today's events.

Chester was dressed in his exercise clothes and was soon taken to the front entrance with Brooklyn and Aida was not invited along for the ride.

Chester didn't complain but he knew Brooklyn would be hungry. *Did they have bird food with them?*

The two Skycars were soon airborne and headed back to the same secret training facility.

Just like before Duke Tinktar was with them.

Upon arrival Chester discovered the handlers had bird food but they had extra containers that had some other goodies.

"We have food and water for Brooklyn because he used to eat with the birds and squirrels back at ski beach." Duke Tinktar said.

"I'm sure he'll like that," Chester responded.

The assistants set up the food for the birds and Brooklyn. Next, they handed Duke Tinktar and Chester some containers with a screw on lid.

"This is our liquid breakfast. It's going to help us do a lot of hard training," Duke Tinktar said.

Chester watched Duke Tinktar swallow some of the contents of his drink and screwed off the top of his container and sampled it. The substance was very pleasant tasting and had an effect like you feel when you drink an alcoholic beverage.

Chester took a few more sips and could feel the effects it was having. Chester didn't know what he was drinking was extremely expensive. Only emperors and spies could drink this substance because it was that scarce and brought from a planet on the periphery of the empire. Chester would never be told the source of this incredible drink as it was a state secret, and the source guarded the secret very carefully.

Duke Tinktar knew the source of the information but knew that Chester was not emotionally strong enough to deal with how they obtained it and might even disturb him greatly if he knew. This was one of many things it would be better Chester didn't know, nor would it be the last time he was confronted with something like this.

The birds arrived shortly and watched Brooklyn eat and they quickly joined in getting their fair share of the food put out for them. Within twenty minutes birds were eating just a foot away from Brooklyn fully confident in their own personal safety.

In ten minutes, Chester drank the contents of his container and screwed the lid back on and handed it back to the assistant who gave it to him. Duke Tinktar was also finished at that time and said, I think we can start working out now. There will be bodyguards here looking out for Brooklyn."

"Alright," Chester said, then turned towards Brooklyn and said, "I'm going to start working out now, you stay with these gentlemen who are your bodyguards."

"Papa, I will wait here until you come back."

"Thank you."

Duke Tinktar, who also wanted to stay in top shape did the same workout the trainers did with Chester. It was hard and grueling and for some strange reason every time Chester started to feel fatigued, he suddenly felt restored as if he had not done any efforts. The longevity drugs he took for breakfast were working better than adrenaline. After an hour of hard steady running and exercises, Chester now trained in martial arts again.

Chester didn't know why he knew everything they trained him at. His Neurological Sonifications were full of techniques he now demonstrated with utter perfection. His trainers were extremely impressed with Chester and thought Duke Tinktar might be playing games with him by bringing in a well-trained martial artist to check their own abilities. Chester needed to know all this as it may one day save his life. He was kicking and punching like he didn't know he could. His breakfast drink added to the tempo he now demonstrated.

Finally, after three hours of constant workout one of the bodyguards approached Duke Tinktar and said, "Your Excellency, we need to leave and get back to your home so you and Chester can get cleaned up for your next activity."

"Is everything packed up and ready to leave?"

"Yes, it is. All we need to do is get in the Skycars and leave."

"Alright. Thanks everyone for the good workout, and Chester we need to go back and get cleaned up for lunch and a big surprise."

"Alright, your Excellency. Chester followed Duke Tinktar to the Skycars where Brooklyn was waiting when Papa arrived."

Soon they traveled back at Duke Tinktar's estate and Chester was starting to feel some pains when Aizere said, "I'm making a bath for you to clean up for your afternoon activities."

"Thanks, but what I think I really need is a message because my muscles feel really tight."

"I will arrange that for you but please take the bath first and we can put some muscle relaxers in the bath water."

"Thank you I appreciate that."

Soon Chester was enjoying the warm bath and the effects of the ingredients Aizere dumped into them. After soaking about ten minutes Aizere said, "Chester, get out of the bath so we can dry you off and prepare you for your message."

"Alright."

After getting blow dried Chester was given a bathrobe to put on and led into the bedroom where he discovered they brought in a portable message table and there was a scantily dressed attractive female waiting.

"Please take off your bath robe and lay on the table."

"I'm nude," Chester responded.

"Not a problem, I prefer you be that way so I can work on you the best in that manner."

Chester took off his bath robe and handed it to Aizere and hopped up on the table.

"Lay on your stomach I want to work on your back side first."

"Alright."

The masseuse knew what she was doing. The table had built in storage under the message table that held special oils and things the masseuse needed.

The oil had muscle relaxers mixed in it and Chester thought it sure felt and smelled like a product he used on Earth called Bengay analgesic cream. However, he soon discovered what this pink skinned Alien masseuse was putting on him seemed to be a lot stronger. The combination of that oil and her hands were having a great effect on Chester.

The masseuse stretched his arms and legs and messaged him taking him from pure pain to joy repeatedly. Sometimes the pain was so severe Chester almost wanted to pass out and instantly it was gone, and he was feeling utterly fantastic.

The masseuse then turned him on his sides and worked him some more and they were alone except for Brooklyn who had also been bathed again by Rayalna and was sitting on his bed watching intently.

Finally, the masseuse flipped Chester on his back and started working on his front side and when she was working on his legs she bent down and grabbed his manliness and kissed it and gave him a brief amount of fellatio and then messaged it with the oil. About then Chester started thinking about a song he used to listen too: *"I'm Screaming Inside,"* by one of the recent top singing stars from Kazakhstan, a super star named Dimash who changed the world with his singing making opera fashionable.

The effects the message oil had on his little head made him want to scream, it was one of the most intense feelings he had ever felt before and he erupted into uncontrolled exudation that lasted longer than he could imagine as he was *screaming inside.*

The message was soon over, and Chester was glad of it. Next time before he had a message, he would tell the masseuse not to do those extracurricular activity. *I wonder if some of that energy drink I had this morning had some effect on it,* Chester asked himself.

"You need to take a bath again to wash off the chemicals, "The masseuse said.

The masseuse led Chester into the bath again that was already filling via remote control of artificial intelligence who knew the process.

Chester walked into the bath and in his surprise was the masseuse followed him in and had a container and a sponge like device. Chester sat in his normal spot that would keep his neck above the water line and the masseuse poured the contents of the container into the bath water then said, "Turn on the water jets."

Artificial Intelligence always listening complied and soon the water was filling will a lot of bubbles like a bubble bath that smelled good and felt refreshing.

"There are some muscle relaxers in what I put in the water that will work with your message and make you feel fresh when you are done," The masseuse said. She then took the sponge and wiped all over Chester's body, ostensibly getting off all the message oils.

The masseuse now naked gave Chester more but tender messages.

For some reason the masseuse felt a strange attraction to this Alien who brought with him a talking dog. She bent down and kissed Chester in the most provocative manner then said, "The next time I give you a message, I will let you make love to me."

"What is your name?" Chester asked.

"I'm Jazmin."

"Do you know what my name is?"

"Yes, the staff knows who you are Chester."

"Did someone put you up to do this or is this your own emotions and of your personal choice?"

"This is my emotions and my personal choice."

"You realize I'm emotionally vulnerable right now and I could fall in love with you if we do that. Can you handle the consequences if something like that transpired?"

"Chester, I have lust for you, but whatever we do, we need to keep it very private, at least until your presence here is fully understood."

"I agree with you, but even though I know I would love to have sex with you, I must be cautious with my heart. I'm not emotionally ready for love."

"There is something a lot of people here know about you because Aida is very obnoxious in the way she displays herself with you in front of some of the other women who are my friends. I promise you that will not happen with me. My friends will make sure nobody knows about you and me."

"But like I first said, there is always the possibility I could develop some deep emotions for you."

"When that happens, we'll deal with it. But until then just let me please you and in the process, you will please me."

"I'm always willing to be your friend."

"That's the only thing out of you I would expect. Friendship and gratification when you want to give it to me."

Soon they were done bathing and blow dried off and Jasmine had her clothes on and promptly left the suite. Chester was in a bath robe and in his bedroom next to Brooklyn who had enjoyed Rayalna while Chester was bathing.

Suddenly Aizere showed up with people to remove the message table and brought in a barber's chair and clothing designers brought in a cart with clothes hanging from a rack.

"We need to prepare you for a VIP visit."

"Alright. Anyone I know?"

"No, you have not met him, but will in a short while. That's why we must dress you up in Royal attire."

"Aizere Sure. I'll do whatever I need to do."

In a brief period of time the hair stylist gave Chester a Cosmic Swirl hair style, and he was given an elaborate shave, and male makeup put on that gave him a surreal look. Soon he was clothed in Royal designer clothing with the emperor's seal on it, that nobody could wear with the emperor's permission.

Chester and Brooklyn both were starting to feel some hunger pains when it was time to eat and they were escorted out the front of the mansion to the waiting Skycars. They were invited to sit in the back seat and Duke Tinktar sat in front with the driver.

The trailing Skycar was full of bodyguards, and they promptly departed. Chester had no idea where he was going or who he would see. Ever since the conversation between Duke Tinktar and the emperor, every moment of Chester's life was under surveillance. The emperor observed the secret video and audio of him boinking Aida. He also saw the scenario unfold with the masseuse and he liked the way Chester laid out his cards. That secret surveillance alone raised the emperor's appraisal of Chester as he felt his moral and ethical way of life and the way he presented the reality to Jazmine gave the emperor the notion he was dealing with a bona fide altruistic person, someone who would be less likely to betray him.

The emperor also watched the secret workout videos, Brooklyn's interactions with the squirrel and the birds.

At first the emperor didn't like Duke Tinktar's plan and thought it to be farfetched, but since he always had significant surveillance on Duke Tinktar, he was slowly coming to realize Duke Tinktar truly knew how to spot talent and people he could trust.

The emperor counted heavily upon his valet Swìnlàgār to give him affirmative backup to his decisions. In this particular case Swìnlàgār was not willing to commit one way or the other. He wanted to see things develop for a while before he weighed in on it. As the video's poured in Swìnlàgār could no longer stay on the sidelines, and he stated that, "In all appearances, the plan was developing in a positive manner and that perhaps Duke Tinktar had figured it out early on and this would solve a lot of issues when he delegated a lot of authority to Chester to handle some of the matters that required travel to multiple planets."

'Thus, this plan would be safely keeping Duke Tinktar at Tymasoara where he would have significant security and protection and not risk the future of the Royalty."

The emperor responded, "I was growing impatient about ending Duke Tinktar's clandestine activities. If this works out, it will be important to me."

That issue led up to today's events which the emperor initiated. Duke Tinktar and the emperor's mansions were widely separated on the other sides of Tymasoara for one logistical reason. If there was a military coup or one from an unknown source, this distance hopefully allowed them to preserve one of them. Preservation of the monarch was the primary goal.

The Skycars carrying Duke Tinktar, Chester, and Brooklyn merged into Sky-traffic going in the general vicinity of the emperor's palace. Chester noticed the absence of Aida and wondered if something happened to her that she was suddenly not accompanying him everywhere. The main reason is Linap contacted the emperor and made some inquiries into who the man was seen in public with Duke Tinktar's concubine.

The emperor had already decided to invite Chester to meet him and thought it might be a good idea for Chester to meet a powerful woman like Linap, especially with Chester's future role in working with Duke Tinktar.

The emperor also knew of the vitriolic relationship between Linap and Aida that centered around possessive feelings towards Duke Tinktar, who was still single and available for future unification and family. It was best to not have the two of them together at the palace today, which easily could lead to outright hostilities in front of other guests.

Traveling in the fast corridor at the higher altitudes and velocities, it only took the Skycar ten minutes to reach the emperor's palace. The Skycar flying on autopilot was vectored to the reserved Skycar parking spots designated for this visit close to the mansion.

Very few Skycars were ever allowed in this close. Upon landing and as the doors opened so the passengers could get out of the Skycars, a couple contacting rods moved up out of the concrete parking stall and began charging the Skycar's cyclodyne energy storage, allowing it to leave later in the day fully charged with maximum endurance and capability if needed.

The emperor's personal Valet Swìnlàgār stood about twenty feet from the Skycar parking stalls and as soon as the doors opened, he approached Duke Tinktar and a few feet away from him bowed and said, "Your Excellency Duke Tinktar, welcome to the emperor's palace."

"Thank you Swìnlàgār, it's good to be back. Let me introduce you to Chester and his dog Brooklyn."

Swìnlàgār turned towards Chester and bowed and said, "Welcome to the Emperor's palace. The emperor is looking forward to meeting you and Brooklyn."

"Thank you, I feel honored."

The emperor's personal Valet Swìnlàgār knew the security detail was aware Brooklyn could talk and were sworn to secrecy, looked down at Brooklyn and said, "Good morning, Brooklyn, we hope to make you comfortable while you are here today."

"Thank you." Brooklyn promptly responded.

The emperor's personal Valet Swìnlàgār knew he would enjoy talking with a dog like Brooklyn today, since until recently no such ability was assumed possible.

Brooklyn had in a brief period turned the Drolupric scientific community upside down including giving the great researcher

Doctor Akssiar a lot to think about. Swìnlàgār had read all of Doctor Akssiar's reports and analysis on Brooklyn and how he speculated some possible impacts to society and future exploitation of animals for nefarious purposes including clandestine operations.

To some extent Doctor Akssiar now wished they had never brought Brooklyn here, but since too many people knew of his presence, it was too late. Doctor Akssiar also assumed Duke Tinktar himself would utilize any capability available for his projects including weaponizing Brooklyn and placing him in the spy game where he could do surveillance in ways nobody would expect.

They went into the mansion and were led down a long hallway that turned into a large room where one complete wall was the side of an aquarium. Looking through the thick glass window Chester could see it was a very large Aquarium with numerous types of marine life in it. This large room facing the aquarium could easily seat 50 people for elaborate dinners.

To the side Chester could see the staff had set up a couple tables and there were a dozen chairs and places at the two tables. Observing one of the tables it was clear there were two doggy chairs set up like they had seen before with silver bowls for food and water. Nobody else was present. The men stood around looking at the fish in the aquarium. The emperor's personal Valet Swìnlàgār asked, "Brooklyn have you seen fish before?"

"Sir, when I was back at planet Earth, I liked watching a program on cable TV called National Geographic. They had several shows that filmed fish, sharks, whales, and a variety of Marine life."

"Are any of these fish similar to what you observed watching those shows?

"Yes sir, especially the smaller ones are very similar. The larger ones are slightly different."

Duke Tinktar then spoke, "Chester, I would like you to ask Brooklyn not to talk when the other guests arrive. We do not want to disclose to the public Brooklyn is a talking dog."

"Understand, your excellency," Chester said then turned toward Brooklyn and asked, "Brooklyn did you understand Duke Tinktar's request you do not speak when the other guests arrive?"

"Yes, Papa I understand, and I will not talk when other guests arrive."

"Thank you."

"You're welcome, Papa."

The Valet Swìnlàgār said, "Brooklyn you are a very polite dog. I like you."

"Thank you, sir."

"Brooklyn I'm going to go get Emperor Tinktar-II now. He wishes to meet you."

"I'm looking forward to meeting the emperor." Brooklyn replied.

The Valet Swìnlàgār smiled and said, "I will be right back." He then left the room and walked to the emperor's private suite which artificial intelligence notified the emperor he had arrived and knew he had to go with him to meet Chester and Brooklyn.

"Your Excellency are you ready to greet your guests?"

"I am. What did you think of the dog?"

"I'm truly impressed, your excellency."

"That's good to hear because if you are impressed it means something to me."

The two men walked to the aquarium dining room and as soon as they arrived all the bodyguards and everyone except Duke Tinktar, Chester, and Brooklyn lined up in a straight-line showing respect.

The emperor who had seen a lot of surveillance videos already knew Chester and Brooklyn, far more than they could imagine. The emperor approached Chester and Brooklyn and said, "Hello Chester and Brooklyn, thank you for coming here today. I was looking forward to seeing both of you."

Chester responded, "You are most welcome Your Excellency." He then made a long deep bow.

The emperor looked at the dog and said, "Brooklyn, I understand you can talk."

"Your Excellency, I can talk. I've never met and emperor before and view this as a privilege to me."

"Brooklyn, nobody before ever dreamed we would see the day where a talking dog would appear. You truly are amazing and I'm looking forward to being your friend."

"Thank you, Your Excellency. I'm very happy that you would wish to be my friend."

"Brooklyn the fact you said what you just did, really truly amazes me and it shows far more than just the ability to talk. It shows you have empathy and other human like characteristics."

"Thank you, Your Excellency."

"Brooklyn, how do you like living here at Tymasoara the capital city of the Drolupric Empire?"

"Your excellency coming here has changed my life. I no longer have to be around Abagail, and I met a lovely female dog I really like."

"What's the name of the female dog?"

"Princess Tiffany."

"Do you know who "Princess Tiffany" lives with?"

"Actually, I do. I've met her. Her name is Margrét Hansen."

The emperor turned to Swìnlàgār the Valet and asked, "Do we know who Margrét Hansen is?"

"Yes, your excellency."

"Could you please send some agents out to invite her here today and make sure she brings "Princess Tiffany" with her?"

"Your excellency, it will be my pleasure. May I suggest we have the guests eat now because they have gone quite a few hours without food because of all their activities today?"

"Yes, we will have our meal now. Go make the arrangements with Margrét Hansen."

"I'm on my way sir."

"Thank you."

"You are most welcome your excellency."

Swìnlàgār left the room, and the guests were invited to sit at the table where their name placards were set up. A few moments later one of the waiters came to the table and put-up additional placards, one stated "Princess Tiffany" right across from Brooklyn and the other right across from Chester was a placard now that said Margrét Hansen.

Another placard said, " Linap," but the chair was empty.

Right about the time Chester was swallowing his first sip of a purple *Grand Zumbido* elixir, a well-dressed multi-colored woman walked into the room. Chester thought she easily could pass for the woman he recently saw while having dinner with Aida. He had no way of knowing since he had not met her and her hair style had changed like it usually did.

Everyone stood at the table as Linap approached carrying an attitude that evoked a bitchiness to her. And here she was merely feet away from the man she saw with Aida, Duck Tinktar's concubine recently. She thought how amusing it was and smiled.

Linap was escorted over to her chair next to Chester. She held out her hand and said, "My name is Linap, how are you?"

Chester took Linap's hand in a gentle show of respect and then bowed.

Linap saw the dog a couple feet from the dinner table and thought, "*how disgusting*." Her disgust would be compounded sooner than she realized.

Within five minutes, the Valet Swìnlàgār came into the room and whispered something in the emperor's ear then left again. The Kitchen had been told to delay another five minutes, more guests were on the way and would arrive shortly.

Duke Tinktar in his behind-the-scenes manipulations had Margrét Hansen prepared to be here. All the Valet Swìnlàgār men had to do was simply go pick them up.

Brooklyn was getting hungry and wasn't happy with the delay, he didn't know why, and it seemed time went on forever. Nevertheless withing 10 minutes of the emperor sending his Valet Swìnlàgār to make arrangements, Margrét Hansen and "Princess Tiffany" walked into the room and were escorted to their seats.

One look at Princess Tiffany and Brooklyn forgot he was hungry. Princess Tiffany gave Brooklyn that unique look, and Brooklyn gave Princess Tiffany back that look and they were both suddenly very happy.

As soon as Margrét Hansen was seated a waiter had trays of drinks for her to choose from. She picked Fôcìn de Oín and was immediately served.

With the money that Margrét Hansen had, she could afford to get dressed up to look smoking hot, like she was now. Chester was utterly amazed he was in the company of two luxurious women.

Linap had met Margrét Hansen at social gatherings and knew her husband was a philanderer. She knew firsthand because she herself had enjoyed his acquiescence as a sperm donor. She didn't want a relationship with the banker, she just wanted his DNA for her future child. Unfortunately, pregnancy didn't manifest and when checked by her gynecologist discovered he was shooting blanks. The morning after sex tests revealed no sperm in her vagina. She was utterly disgusted and angry and needless to say, Margrét Hansen's husband Waldo, never was allowed to do the *Tour de France* with Linap again. But she was certainly wanting a bona fide donor and maybe perhaps the man sitting next to her might just be the one to accommodate?

Margrét Hansen the banker's wife and social climber with her own spy network, knew who Linap was and also knew she had fooled around with her husband. But Margrét Hansen was cool as a cucumber and knew how to plot and make every move she made. Her marriage with Waldo was long ago destroyed by his unethical behavior.

As Margrét Hansen's personal spy network filled her in with the details, the fact he no longer wanted sex or romance with her was just fine. She didn't want to give it to him anyway. But she played the role of a great actor and he never had a clue. A half dozen banker wives became best friends and co-dependent and helped create their own spy network to track all the dirty things their husbands did.

Most of the bankers thought their wives were just home bodies with no real meaning in life and simply there for status.

Some of that was true, but when the cat is away the mice will play. These banker wives had their own little mafia and they routinely enjoyed special men half their husbands ages that could perform much better in every aspect. When you have enough money getting laid is not a problem, especially if you owned penthouses in resorts.

The main reason for Margrét Hansen to be here at this moment was it added positively to her social climbing agenda. If she could find her way into the inner court of the emperor, then her destiny would be charted the way she wanted. And if the emperor wanted her for sex, she would screw his brains out. In a sense she was no different than the woman across the table from her. They were both smart women, risk takers and were willing to go beyond what most women would if it would elevate them.

Linap proved that concept well as she now was fabulously rich. Her only problem is she wanted a Child and her clock was running out of time.

The first guests to be served were the dogs, food and water and the chefs made them some excellent food.

Then the guests were soon given the most fabulous meal of their lifetime. This was a joyous occasion because the emperor was very happy because, his biggest concern with Duke Tinktar was now slowly being resolved by the appearance of this Alien from planet Earth.

The emperor looked at Chester with great relief and gratitude because Chester would ensure the longevity of his monarch and now the emperor could start to spend his final days on the throne passing down to Duke Tinktar his wisdom and all his secrets. The emperor knew he was no longer a young man and time was running out. If he was still alive in twenty years, he'd feel grateful.

Because the Drolupric lived a lot longer than Earth people, the emperor knew Duke Tinktar could easily be on the throne for over one hundred years. Duke Tinktar knew the strategic plan and understood his responsibilities and did not take them lightly. That is one of the reasons why Aida was not here tonight. She would interfere with Chester's development and two women he wanted him to develop relations with were here tonight.

Because of the location Chester was sitting, he could easily see and communicate more with Margrét Hansen than he could with Linap. As they enjoyed their meal that had music being played by live performers brought in when the food was served, playing softly, everyone developed a happiness. Their drinks were spiked with pleasurizers, and it added to the ambience. There was no malice at the dinner table, and everyone felt happy. It was a joyous occasion, especially for the emperor who loved the way this all unfolded.

Swìnlàgār the Valet stood near the emperor for a few reasons. First, he was his chief protector. Swìnlàgār, an expert in martial arts and always carried a blaster in his clothing had to be near the emperor at all times to protect him. Swìnlàgār had lived through coups and other disgusting events and wanted to make sure none of that happened on his watch. Anyone attempting to do harm to the emperor would have to deal with him.

Swìnlàgār was a very smart man. He knew the emperor was a great leader, which the empire needed, and he also knew if someone harmed the emperor and prevented him from carrying out his authority, the empire would have terrible consequences. Hence keeping the emperor safe was also predominantly important for the safety and wellbeing of the empire and like the emperor knew Swìnlàgār didn't take his job lightly and was always focused on the top twenty issues that confronted the emperor.

In his heart, Swìnlàgār knew his conduct was directly proportional to the safety and well-being of the Empire. He gave it all and the emperor knew it. Behind every great man is a great person like Swìnlàgār.

Swìnlàgār also knew how important it was for Duke Tinktar to be relieved of a lot of responsibility so he could spend more time with the emperor and at the same time prevent him from being injured or killed. Preserving Duke Tinktar's life was now more important than rounding up all the spies and people who wanted to attack this empire.

Swìnlàgār did not like Duke Tinktar's plan at first and as time evolved, he slowly got on board, hence was curious as to every aspect of Chester. By studying Chester and Brooklyn every day, Swìnlàgār came to realize why Duke Tinktar selected Chester to be in the role he was soon to begin. It took a while for Swìnlàgār to come to grips with the notion an Alien would eventually oversee their spy apparatus. But with Brooklyn's help, Chester proved he was worthy of being the chosen one.

Chester had surveillance on him like no person before or after. Swìnlàgār now had a complete assessment of Chester and Duke's concerns about allegiances people had, made this Alien far more necessary.

The group had enjoyable conversations and Margrét Hansen skillfully navigated around all Linap's land mines she put out to make sure Chester never went in that direction.

The guests were all positioned so they could see the Aquarium either to their right or their left sides. All the schools of fish that swam by from time to time gave an air of feeling and in many ways set the psychological transcendence into a pleasurable evening.

The emperor was glad all the guests were well behaved, and no cat fights erupted between Linap and Margrét Hansen. The emperor knew about Margrét Hansen's husband's sexual trysts with Linap since he was under investigation for money laundering and loaning money to the enemy.

To make sure the guests were mildly placid, all their drinks were spiked with pleasurizers and a unique tranquilizer drug that dissolved hostile thoughts for six to eight hours.

Duke Tinktar was a little disappointed in this procedure because he didn't mind cat fights now and then. At least he didn't have Aida here to slug it out with Linap. No doubt that cat fight would have started in five minutes when one of them bitch slapped the other and they soon would turn into hair pulling wrestlers.

The meal went by peacefully with small talk and Margrét Hansen the consummate politician avoided all the land mines that

Linap threw out before her as a master politician and avoided any escalation which seemed to at times infuriate Linap because she didn't fall for any of her traps.

This would not be the first or the last time the emperor had to accommodate his court by improvising and manipulating guests. Having the dining tables set up next to the aquarium worked miracles as the fish had a hypnotic effect on everyone and helped to set the ambience further improved by the background music played by some of the best musicians in the empire.

Chester had no bone in that fight and he and Brooklyn were simply enjoying the company. Brooklyn for the most part was the happiest at the dinner facing across the table at "Princess Tiffany" who stared at him relentlessly through the dinner.

Brooklyn knew those doggy looks. They were facial expressions of desire and attraction. The two dogs causally ate their dog food and drank the pleasant tasting water, but even with the gaps of time were short and sweet and the total focus continued in quiet solitude.

Margrét Hansen knew there was something going on with Princess Tiffany who was never this calm and focused around a bunch of strangers. She also knew the focus was directly on the other dog, Brooklyn. *Perhaps we can give them some doggy time together after dinner for a short walk so they can find a tree?* Margrét thought.

To the emperor's delight the meal ended peacefully, and the group remained relatively happy.

Linap saw all she needed to see. She would soon communicate with Duke Tinktar about setting up a meeting between her and Chester to develop a relationship. She soon excused herself and left the party.

Margrét Hansen feeling for Princess Tiffany who she knew was in total heat suggested after Linap left, "I think it would be a good idea to take Brooklyn and "Princess Tiffany" for a walk so they can take care of their business."

Chester responded, "Great idea, "and the emperor nodded at Swìnlàgār the Valet who took it for action.

Soon Swìnlàgār led Chester and Margrét with the two dogs out to the private park that surrounded much of the mansion. The dogs were on a leash though Brooklyn really didn't need one as he was fully trained and obedient and could think far beyond any dog and quite a few humans.

After they walked for a while, each dog took their turn doing their business. A staff member loosely following them had plastic bags to pick up the dog deposits.

Swìnlàgār was utter amazed Brooklyn had not uttered a single word since the other guests showed up. It was now clear to Swìnlàgār the level of control and discipline that Brooklyn exhibited. Brooklyn appeared to be very happy as he was utterly delighted Princess Tiffany was giving him company. At some point Princess Tiffany hopped on Brooklyn's back signaling something. Margrét knew exactly what it was, her dog was in total heat.

Brooklyn turned and faced Chester. It was a look of pain. Chester knew Brooklyn was moved and if it were not for the fact, he had a role to play and would only accommodate Princess Tiffany in privacy.

Princess Tiffany now started acting playfully and when she put her face up to Brooklyn, he did a movement that could be classified as he wanted to attempt to kiss her. He then rubbed the side of her head and whispered something that none of them could make out, but Chester got a rush out of it because he was afraid that Margrét might figure out Chester could talk.

But the volume was so low that only Chester had an idea what happened. Swìnlàgār had watched a lot of surveillance videos and knew everything about Brooklyn and knew he probably uttered some words and he suspected he knew what Brooklyn had said. He then started pondering the situation and would take his idea to the emperor.

Margrét Hansen being the wife of an intergalactic banker, knew how to keep secrets. Because of the dog situation and Brooklyn's psychological needs, Swìnlàgār could simplify things greatly if the emperor allowed him to brief Margrét Hansen about the talking dog. She would also be briefed this situation had to be kept confidential and it was in her best interests to be in good graces with the emperor. For the sake of Margrét Hansen husband's business activities which the emperor could abruptly shut down and inform the husband it was because Margrét leaked something she wasn't authorized to do so. The empire was all about leverage. That action would not happen today, but the conversation with the emperor would.

The group walked around the park a while longer and it appeared Princess Tiffany slowly settled down quite a bit and was simply following Brooklyn in a calm manner.

After a while Margrét Hansen decided she had enough of the dog business for today and informed the Valet Swìnlàgār, "I would like to go home now."

"Let's walk up to the front entrance and I will have a Skycar take you home immediately."

"Thank you."

As they walked back to the front entrance Margrét Hansen was secretly stewing about Linap knowing that wretched black widow wanted to get her fangs into Chester and add him to her list of trophies. She then thought of an immediate plan to intervene and scuttle that plan of Linap's. Since her husband was going to be away quite a bit with some of his new projects at far off planets, she would get Chester over to her home in the guise of allowing the two dogs to be together. She had her needs too and she surmised that given the opportunity, Chester probably wouldn't mind banging a rich banker's wife, especially since she could get a wonderful makeover and be one hell of a sex kitten.

Chester, in a few more days, I would like you to bring Brooklyn over to my home so he can spend time with Princess Tiffany.

"I'm sure Brooklyn would like that."

"When you have some free time contact me. I will make sure you will be able to reach me with your communicator as I will instruct my communicator to receive your calls."

"Alright."

Within minutes, a Skycar was ready to take Margrét Hansen home. Just like before Margrét Hansen had to force her precious dog Princess Tiffany into the Skycar because she did not want to leave Brooklyn who understood her body language quite well.

No sooner than Margrét Hansen was gone, Duke Tinktar walked out of the front entrance and said, "The emperor is busy now and so we are going to return back to my home."

One minute later two Skycars appeared, and Duke Tinktar walked to the lead Skycar and gestured to Chester and Brooklyn, and said, "Go ahead and get in the back seats."

Moments later they were well on their way back to Duke Tinktar's estate, well fed and feeling special since very few people ever got to meet the emperor.

While Chester and Brooklyn were out walking in the park with Margrét Hansen and Princess Tiffany, the duke talked with the emperor in his private suite about the two and how things were developing.

"Eventually Chester is going to have to do distasteful acts like you have done in the past."

"You mean like visits to the hog farm."

"Exactly."

"I'm sure it's only a matter of time before we have to deal with another traitor."

"I'm sure one will be exposed sometime in the near future; the enemy continues to probe and they have good experience in finding out people's prices."

"We need to find out if Chester has the stomach for all this."

"I'll have my Librarian Chernega show Chester some recordings we have of terrible things the enemy has done to our people. I have some good recordings in my library of the Battle of Martos which to this day still upsets Chernega."

"He has every right to be upset because he lost half of his regiment in heavy fighting, and he knows the horrors the enemy inflicted on our civilian population."

"I'd also say if I didn't have Chernega protecting my flank during the battle, the casualties would have been far severe."

"Do you have good recordings of the civilian carnage?"

"I do and I know it will be rough for Chernega to watch it again, but under the circumstances we have a lot at stake and if Chester is able to deal with these types of situations, it will speed up my change of command."

"Perhaps we should have Doctor Boonkar work with Chester to help with psychological adjustments necessary?"

"Not a bad idea. Doctor Boonkar was instrumental in brain washing and turning some spies into double agents for us."

"I'll have Swìnlàgār contact Doctor Boonkar and invite her to the Palace tomorrow and brief the distinguished doctor on what we hope she can do to help adjust Chester so that he will be able to do some of these despicable acts that are necessary."

"I think I have the most inducement possible."

"What's that?"

"He wants to eventually go back to Earth. I view him as someone working on a temporary assignment. Eventually we'll need to reorganize so that we don't have to place so much reliance on a single person."

"How long do you suppose that will take?"

"Most likely ten to twenty years because it will take a while to test people in their roles and validate, they accomplish what they must do to protect this empire."

"He'll be a much older man when he returns to Earth if that's the case."

"I think he simply wants to grow old and die there."

"In the meantime we can give him all the thrill and excitement he ever wanted."

"I think he's already enjoyed some of that." The emperor smiled because he had seen some of the surveillance recordings. No doubt Chester wasn't getting that kind of excitement at home with his partner Abagail.

The emperor also received a communique from Linap stating she would like to see Chester again and would like him to visit her. The emperor knew Linap quite well and knew she never made those kinds of requests unless she wanted something out of the man. *To deny such a powerful woman would be a terrible shame.*

Chester and Brooklyn soon arrived back at their suite where they were thinking about what they wanted to do. Chester thought now would be an excellent time to talk to Brooklyn privately about today's events.

"Brooklyn, did you have a good time today with "Princess Tiffany"?

"I was glad to see her but she's in full heat and wanted me to mount her."

"Is that why you looked at me funny?"

"Yes."

"You showed very good self-control, and I was very proud of you."

"I know I have a public image, and I must be careful as it appears the people around you do not want the public to know I can talk."

"Yes, just like it was with Abagail."

"Is there anything you want to do now Brooklyn?"

"Papa, there are some squirrels on the walkway around the hill. Can we get some food and go out and feed them?"

"Sure, let's contact Rayalna and see if she can get us some food for the squirrels."

Then Chester said, "Please send Rayalna here."

Artificial Intelligence in the background asked, "Chester do you want Rayalna to come to your suite?"

"Yes, I do."

"Rayalna is being contacted now."

"Thank you."

"You are welcome, Chester."

Moments later Rayalna entered the suit and asked, "Is there something you need me to do?"

"Yes. Brooklyn would like to go feed the squirrels again. Would it be possible for you to get us a small container of food we can give to them?"

"I will see what I can do."

"Thank you."

Rayalna left and fifteen minutes later, Aida arrived carrying a small bag of food she knew the squirrels would like."

"I'm going with you and Brooklyn to feed the squirrels."

"Alright."

Having Aida along was actually good because she knew where she was going, and they got there very promptly.

Soon they were back at the same location and Brooklyn was looking for his squirrel friend who was nowhere in sight.

"Think the squirrels will show Brooklyn?"

"Papa yes, follow me over to their feeding spot."
Brooklyn walked over to precisely they gave the food previously.

"Lay some food on the ground here then step back. The squirrels are watching us and will come down and get it."

Aida poured some food down on the ground and then they all stepped back about 30 feet. They waited about ten minutes and there was no sign of the squirrels so Chester thought they should just leave now.

Brooklyn responded, "They will be here. I've already heard them make some noise."

"Alright we'll wait for a while longer."

Just when Chester was about to say they should go back, the first Squirrel came out of his hiding spot and ran up to the food. He smelled it, looked at the three standing a short distance away, then picked up one of the pieces of food and stood on his hind legs starting to eat it. He finished the first food particle, then reached down and picked up more.

Moments later the second Squirrel showed up and started eating, then a smaller one joined in. Finally, a fourth Squirrel arrived and started eating as quickly as it could.

In a few minutes Brooklyn said, "They are almost done, I think we can leave now."

The three left and went back to Chester's suite. Aida then said, " The librarian Chernega asked me to let you know he has some videos to show you that you might be interested in."

"Oh yea? Do you know what they are about?"

"He said it pertains to the Battle of Martos."

"I do not have much to do now, perhaps it might be interesting to watch the videos. What do you think Brooklyn?"

"Sure, I'll go see it with you."

Aida led them to the library and Chernega was there reading a document and looked up and observed them coming into the room.

"Good afternoon, Chester and Brooklyn."

"Aida said you have some video you wanted to show us concerning the Battle of Martos."

"That's right. Why don't you have a seat and I'll start the presentation."

"Alright."

After the three were seated with Brooklyn sitting in the middle, Chernega said aloud. "Play the Battle of Martos video."

Artificial intelligence said softly in the background, Chernega you want the Battle of Martos video shown."

"Yes, that's correct."

Suddenly the lighting in the room dimmed and a panel slowly lowered from the ceiling not far from the table where they were sitting.

The video started and the narrator spoke in standard Drolupric language since they knew Chester and Brooklyn now understood that language thanks to their Neurological Sonifications. The animation showed in essence the course of the battle giving a high-level discussion on what all occurred and the dates. The fighting lasted a long period of time before the enemy was forced to withdraw licking their wounds on their retreat.

Now the narration started getting into more detail and exposed the savagery the Malawans did to the helpless people on Martos. Nobody saw this coming, and they were ill prepared to fend off an invasion. The Martos people managed to film some of the savagery and transmit it to Tymasoara to the Drolupric Emperor while asking for help. It was a terrible crisis.

For Chester, the video was sickening. It compared with some of the holocausts on Earth. Halfway through the video Chester regretted he agreed to watch it. He wondered; *will I have nightmares after watching this.*

Just before Chester was going to ask to stop the video, it suddenly showed activity around Chernega's regiment. Instead of watching a continued steady stream of horror inflicted on Martos civilians by the Malawans, it was now combat footage.

The second half was much easier to watch, and Chester had feelings of satisfaction watching the Malawans receive some of what they had dished out to the civilian population of Martos. Chester didn't know he was watching specially crafted propaganda designed to influence him. Doctor Boonkar's fingerprints were all over this video.

Chester's facial expressions were recorded throughout the presentation. Using super computers as well as her own intuition, Doctor Boonkar would analyze Chester and his reactions and probably emotional response based on his facial expressions throughout the video presentation. She would know immediately the efficacy of the video which they would build upon and during future Neurological Sonifications, Chester would receive more knowledge about the terrible characters in the Galaxy that had caused a lot of strife.

The presentation with great video and surreal sound lasted over two hours. Chester was glad when it was finally over. It gave him a lot to think about.

"What did you think about the video, Chester?" The Librarian Chernega asked.

"To be honest some of it was tough to watch, but I was glad to see you in action with your troops. I was sorry to see you get wounded during the battle."

"It was all part of my job. If I had it all to do over again, I would."

"Do you ever get in contact with any of your former troops and staff?"

"No, they do not know I'm alive."

"Why is that?"

"Duke Tinktar wanted me to disappear, he said he had important tasks for me to do and if everyone I knew thought I had perished in the fighting they would not come looking for me."

"I can't believe being a librarian would be of such significance that Duke Tinktar would think he needed to hide you."

"Chester, you are near here and do not know the delicate fabric of he empire, though I know in due time you will realize more and more that goes on, and then it will become clear to you why things are the way they are."

"I will say this has been quite a journey for me."

"In what ways?"

"When I was living on Earth, I suspected there were higher intellect beings in the Universe, and we Earth people were simply living in a faraway location where we didn't get exposed to it. And here I am today, having met the emperor of a great and vast Galactic Empire. Just that meeting alone means my life journey has gone beyond anything I ever expected in my lifetime."

"Chester, I assure you in due time there will be more adventures for you and this all may seem trivial to you later on, especially if one day you have your own battle similar to Martos."

"Chernega, if I ever have to go someplace to a battle like Martos, I will want you to go with me."

"I would be most happy to accompany you, especially if it results in me getting my own regiment again."

Aida then intervened in the conversation and said, "Chester, I think Brooklyn is probably getting hungry by now, why don't I take you to back to your suite to freshen up and prepare to meet for dinner."

"Are you hungry Brooklyn?"

"I'm a little hungry Pappa."

"Alright, thank you Chernega for showing the Battle of Martos, it gives me a lot to think about."

"Chester, if you wish to have an in-depth discussion of the battle and my involvement, I would be more than happy to sit down with you and discuss it," Chernega replied.

"Thank you, I appreciate that." After the three left the library, Chernega realized one thing because he had evaluated many men in his time, Chester was quite sincere about him desiring Chernega to accompany him into battle. That scored quite a few points with Chernega because he knew Chester was sincere.

Chester and Brooklyn were both happy to be back in the suite to take care of business. Chester felt about five pounds lighter afterwards.

Chester was still dressed in formal attire from the day's events and Aida asked, "Would you like to change into something more comfortable for dinner?"

"I sure would."

"Aizere, could you please come to the room."

Artificial Intelligence in the background asked, "Do you wish to summon Aizere?"

Chester responded, "Yes please."

A moment later Aizere entered the room and asked, "What can I do for you Chester?"

"I would like a change of clothes into something more casual."

"Alright, I will be back in a few minutes."

Thanks to artificial intelligence that could measure Chester's body quite accurately entering and leaving the bath, his dimensions were recorded for moments like this so that clothing apparel could be provided that fit perfectly. In a few minutes, Aizere arrived back with a change of clothes that had been staged for such an occasion.

Chester changed his clothes and was soon feeling a lot better as they felt much better than the formal attire he had just changed out of.

Aida led them to a dining room set up for just the three of them. As soon as Chester was seated a waiter asked what he would like to drink. He picked his go-to-drink, *Grand Zumbido* elixir. Aida was enjoying a tall glass of the golden Fŏcìn de Oín always available to her because of her relationship with Chester. After dinner the three wound down in Chester's suite that included a bath for both Chester and Brooklyn and then a restful sleep.

Chester would be working out in the morning in full vigor demonstrating martial arts he didn't realize he knew and some weapons training. Thanks to his morning energy drink he was performing at spectacular levels. The emperor was happy to see the way Chester was evolving and after reviewing the surveillance video watching Chester's body language report by Doctor Boonkar, that made Duke Tinktar far more assured the process was working and Chester was slowly but surely developing into an expert who could survive a knife fight with a well-trained galactic spy.

~~~~~~
~~~~~~

Chapter Thirteen

FIRST BLOOD

Chester finished all the Neurological Sonifications planned and progressed daily in martial arts, weapons, and physical fitness training.

Aida knew Chester was getting a lot stronger because his love making was gradually improving and she could feel his strength as his coitus delivered stronger and stronger thrusts. Aida loved her assignment and had never experienced such a great time *working under cover.*

Duke Tinktar was notified he needed to visit the emperor immediately. They needed to have a discussion.

Duke Tinktar had no idea what the emperor had in mind and was curious as to why the sudden request for the meeting occurred. When Duke Tinktar arrived in the emperor's suite, there were two others there, Swìnlàgār the Valet, and one other man he didn't recognize.

"Duke Tinktar, I want to introduce you to Panot Tsimor from the planet Barcejena," the emperor said.

"Pleased to meet you," Duke Tinktar said knowing it was always wise to be polite to any of the emperor's friends or acquaintances.

"I'm honored, Your Excellency," Panot Tsimor replied.

"I might as well get down to what this meeting is about," the emperor said, then he added, "Swìnlàgār, will give you the information about this situation."

"Alright," Duke Tinktar responded.

"Panot Tsimor is one of my informants from operations I conducted in the past while I was part of the Intelligence Bureau. I've not heard from him for many years, especially since my new assignment. He recently contacted me and said he had some serious information and now I want him to tell you what he informed me of and took great risk in coming here."

"Alright, let me hear it," Duke Tinktar responded looking at the emperor's face who appeared to have great concern. No doubt the emperor already knew what Panot Tsimor had to offer.

"Since my last involvement with the Intelligence Bureau I've had to keep a very low profile and avoided all contact with my associates and quite frankly I've been living in fear," Panot Tsimor said.

Duke Tinktar looked at Panot Tsimor and could see a scared person with nerves. Just coming here probably stressed him to the maximum.

"One day about two months ago, a former associate of mine who needed some funds and was getting quite desperate came to me. Normally he would sell the information to the appropriate party, but his need for fast cash drove him to see me, because he knew I was one of the few people he could trust and had the ability to give him money."

"So, this information is based on someone selling information?" Duke Tinktar asked with a jaundiced eye.

"Initially it was, but I realized something this big and this important needed vetted. I paid the associate half the money he requested and informed him he would get the rest of the payment after I determined it was all legitimate information. He then gave me the sources to his information which I've gone on to vet and know its accurate."

"How did you vet the information?"

"A couple of my most trusted friends and I broke into a home one night and took a man and his wife to a secure location where they could be properly interrogated. This man supposedly is involved in the coup."

"You mean a coup against the emperor?"

"Exactly."

"And just how did you get the man to offer up all the details?"

"We had a chain saw and told him if he didn't give us passwords so we could access streams of Coup participants secret communications, we would first cut off one of his wife's legs. Her screaming unglued him. As we started cutting her leg off, he yelled please stop, I'll cooperate."

"Did you cut her leg off?"

"No, but as you know something this big we could not leave behind any witnesses or anyone that could identify us."

"What did you get out of him?"

"I got all the passwords to read everything they were planning and the story of what it entails. I have his personal communicator where you can read it all stored encrypted in files stored on the device."

"Alright, let's hear it."

The Valet Swìnlàgār who had already heard many of the conversations grabbed the communicator sitting on the table in front of him and said, "This is the dead man's communicator, I will play the most important conversation recorded."

"I wonder why he recorded the conversation," Duke Tinktar asked.

"With the risk of getting caught I think the man thought it was his insurance policy against the coup members in case they attempted to silence him," Panot Tsimor explained.

"Go ahead and play it," Duke Tinktar said.

The conversation was full of coup planning details and identified several of the key members who had major tasks to perform as part of the coup. But the most troubling part of the conversation was it identified General Crontyke as one of the chief conspirators. One of the most important pieces of information obtained in the various documents indicated the planned assault was no less than two months away. They were cutting it close.

Duke Tinktar would now learn why the emperor built him such an elaborate estate. The Skycar access through a tunnel could be heavily guarded and sealed off. Because of the large hilltops surrounding the estate, air defenses could easily be set up to foil any airborne attempt. Attempting to send in assassins would be extremely problematic as well.

There was more fact finding and then discussions about General Crontyke's situation, where he was currently located and what he was doing.

Panot Tsimor was then ushered out of the emperor's mansion and taken to a safe house where they could reach out to him in the event, they needed to clarify any information.

After Panot Tsimor was gone on his way to a safe house, the emperor laid out his cards and what he planned on doing about it.

"I can't remain here in the mansion in the event we are not able to foil the coup before they hatch it. This mansion cannot be properly protected against a major assault force. I'm going to move into Duke Tinktar's estate for the time being until all the coup members are rounded up and dealt with. I do not want anyone to know where I went. I'll be staying in Duke Tinktar's Suite. Everyone will be kicked out of the suite and the only people allowed in after today will be Duke Tinktar, Swìnlàgār, and Chernega. Swìnlàgār, and Chernega will be armed with our new laser pistol weapons.

Duke Tinktar will set up a task force to take out the top ten men on the Coup list. I expect once it becomes public knowledge those men were executed, the coup will crumble. I want General Crontyke apprehended and taken to Zeta Bantor where we deal with spies. This will be an excellent opportunity to get a feal for how much we can count on Chester to be ruthless against our enemies."

"Your Excellency, since General Crontyke is involved in his coup, I have no choice but to personally manage this operation."

"Duke Tinktar, I understand and even though I would prefer you to stay here so we can protect you, it's going to be a difficult operation and I realize under the circumstances I'll have to let you go to Barcejena to capture General Crontyke."

"I'm taking Chester with me. I think this will be a good experience for him since his may happen again if we do not weed out all the Coup members."

"What about the dog Brooklyn?"

"Brooklyn's grown accustomed to Aida and Rayalna. I think its best we leave him here so that Doctor Akssiar and his assistant Tasha have access to the dog for their research."

"How soon do you plan on going to Barcejena?"

"I'm not going directly to Barcejena. I'm going to first stop at Zeta Bantor to set up General Crontyke's execution there after we interrogate him."

"Are you sure you are not going there for the sake of visiting Madam Pang?" The emperor asked and Swìnlàgār the Valet, smiled.

"If I happen to have an opportunity to visit Madam Pang, it's strictly coincidental."

"Why don't you just bring Madam Pang here, so you don't have to keep chasing after her?"

"Your Excellency, I would be willing to do that, but something tells me the public would not accept a green empress in the event something happens to you, and I have to fill in your responsibilities."

"I'm glad you put the empire ahead of your own personal interests."

"I would have no problem having Madam Pang as my empress, but too many people know what her business is, and the public is not ready for a green skin empress that would cause too many distractions."

"Do you have a woman in mind?"

"Actually, I do."

"And who is that?"

"My receptionist Daniell."

"Does she know this?"

"No yet. I didn't think it was the appropriate time to convey that too her."

"Maybe we need to arrange to have a secret unification before you leave on the mission in case something happens to you, I will have an heir to the empire."

"I would like to wait until this mission is over. I'm sure I will come back."

"Are you delaying just so you can have another tryst with Madam Pang and not feel guilty about cheating on Daniell."

"Yes, something like that."

"Would you mind if I contact her mother who I know and let her know her daughter should refrain from any relationships since she has been selected as the possible next empress when I retire, and you take over."

"That's not a bad idea. But can you wait until after I depart for the mission?"

"I understand your concern and I will wait until after you leave."

"Thank you."

"Swìnlàgār and Chernega will supervise clearing out your staff from your suite today. I will move in there tomorrow. Where do you intend on staying until you depart for your mission?"

"I think it would be best if I stay at the training camp so I can give my team some last-minute workup and refresher training."

"Great idea."

"Chester and Brooklyn will be visiting the training camp every day until I leave. On the last day, Brooklyn will be brought back to the estate and the rest of us will embark to deep space on our way to go arrest General Crontyke and take out some of his key men."

"I'll see you when you get back. But remember I do not want you to put yourself at risk. If there is a dangerous situation, delegate authority and handle matter out in harm's way."

"I will take appropriate measures for force protection."

"Good luck on your mission."

"Thank you your excellency and I wish you good health and happiness."

"You are most welcome. I wish I could trust others as much as I do you."

"My father was killed when I was a small boy. You raised me and for that I will always be grateful."

"It was my distinct pleasure. I look at you as my son."

"I feel it and I do appreciate it."

Duke Tinktar stood up and gave a very long respectful bow.

Swìnlàgār knew the facts surrounding Duke Tinktar's father's death. A Drolupric Empire true hero that sacrificed his life for the emperor and the emperor's father when he purposely crashed his Frigate in the command ship of the enemy that would otherwise have destroyed Tymasoara with a powerful Armada. With the leadership decapitated there was no central control and the pincer attacks by Drolupric Empire forces were creating enough casualties that caused the leaderless forces to withdraw in a haphazard manner which ultimately undermined the coordinated attack that otherwise would have succeeded in taking down the empire.

These past few words brought back memories and the emperor as well as Swìnlàgār's eyes watered slightly in the unexpected exchange of words that surfaced the dormant emotions.

That exchange did one more thing. It intensified Duke Tinktar's resolve to crush the coup. This unexpected scenario played out in the most auspicious times. The Earth man who had no allegiance or sources of compromise since he had no ties to anyone in the empire or any other empire, would get a full dose of what he would have to do by himself in the future. Once Emperor Tinktar-II stepped down and Duke Tinktar was elevated to emperor, he would no longer be able to go on these escapades and all his actions could only be remote assistance. He truly felt that with the man Chester he got to know and observe, that with remote assistance is all he needed to be able to be successful.

The mission actually began that very minute as Prince Tinktar flew from the emperor's palace to the training center where he remained until they left on the mission. Meanwhile all of Duke Tinktar's staff were removed from his suite and taken to the training center where they would be sequestered until long after his departure.

The following morning Chester and Brooklyn were taken to the training center where Chester continued with his morning regiment. Just when he thought they were finished for the day Duke Tinktar took Chester for a walk far away from hearing distance to have a talk with him.

"Chester, I'm going to be leaving soon on a mission of vital importance to the Empire. When I leave, I'm taking you with me. You will gain vital information and training in this mission. I must inform you that there will be elements of danger and elements of risk involved but you can rest assured that I do not want something bad to happen to myself, and since you will be with me, you will be well protected."

"Alright, what about Brooklyn. We've never been separated before."

"Brooklyn is too valuable to risk on a mission. He will remain behind in the good care of Rayalna. Aida will maintain surveillance on Brooklyn at all times to insure he remains safe and well taken care of. Doctor Akssiar and his assistant Tasha will be in daily contact with Brooklyn to monitor his progress and do some things with him that might improve his disposition while you are gone."

"Alright."

"We will also schedule visits with "Princess Tiffany" for Brooklyn and this evening you will be going to Margrét Hansen's home for dinner. I would not be surprised if you did not come back to the estate by morning."

"What do you mean by that?"

"I had an interesting conversation with Margrét Hansen. Her husband is a philanderer, and she knows it. She has her needs, and tonight, Chester, you will most likely give Margrét Hansen a special elixir she wants to receive."

"Something tells me if Brooklyn gets routine visits from Princess Tiffany, he will not miss me that much."

Duke Tinktar smiled from that remark then said, "You will be briefed on the mission when we are out in space heading to our destinations."

"Alright, I'm happy to help you as much as I can."

"I know you are, and I'm pleased by your cooperation."

"Thank you."

"Let's go back to the group. I'm staying here, you and Brooklyn will go back to the estate with your escorts."

"Alright."

"See you tomorrow, hopefully not too late in the morning."

"I'll try to not make it an all-night affair. I don't want to be exhausted for tomorrow's training."

The men went back and those going back to the estate were soon in the Sky Cars heading back to Duke Tinktar's estate.

Duke Tinktar went to the building surrounded by armed guards that nobody approached without an invitation. Inside he met with several of his reconnaissance people that started providing him with briefings on General Crontyke's where abouts along with his top ten accomplices. They had no reason to suspect they were persons of interest and didn't detect the uptick in surveillance, much of which was through surreptitious manners.

Where you find smoke there is usually fire and once you find the fire, you know where the hot spot is. It didn't take long for galactic capable spies to unmask the ten collaborators and their function in the Coup. To put a dagger in the heart of the coup and make sure new Coups did not grow out of simply dismembering part of a Coup, it was essential to apprehend all eleven men and women exactly at the same time so warnings could not go out allowing members to bug out.

Another aspect of taking down the Coup was to detect foreign intervention. If there was such a thing now in existence, that would have meant even greater seriousness and it meant the prelude to galactic war. All this was terribly unsettling to Duke Tinktar who understood his mission was just as important as any other he ever did.

His assistants that worked in his suite back at his estate were now staged near him at the training center where they continued their work.

While Daniell was spending her last day at Duke Tinktar's estate, her mother received a visit from some of the emperor's spies and informed her presence was desired at the mansion because the emperor had something he wished to discuss with her.

Daniell's mother named Dominika was highly aroused because this was quite unusual for the emperor to reach out to a woman in such a private manner. When she was in the Skycar heading to the palace she was terrified because it could mean many things.

The Skycar landed in front of the mansion's front entrance which was extremely rare and almost unheard of. The emperor himself was standing there waiting for Dominika. The people in the Skycar got out and the emperor's personal spies escorted Dominika twenty feet to the emperor dressed in his official dress looking rather powerful with an honor guard behind him in spit and polish that happened during the greeting of official guests.

"Good morning, Dominika, I'm sorry we had to disturb you this morning but there is a matter I wished to discuss with you privately." Dominika did a bow and raised up and said, "Your Excellency, I will try to be most helpful to you any way I can."

"Thank you, and I know that. So please come with me where we can discuss with you what we need to talk about."

Dominika walked forward and the emperor grabbed her hand like an old friend would and gently walked her to his suite that was soon emptied out with everyone except Swìnlàgār who was soon sitting in a chair next to the emperor facing Dominika.

The emperor could tell by her sweating hand that Dominika was terribly stressed, and he needed to cut to the chase and get it out fast to help her calm down.

"Dominika the reason why I called you here for this meeting is because you are Daniell's mother and have great influence over her. The future of the Monarchy is of primary importance to me. When I retire and hand the throne over to my heir, I want him to be unified with a responsible and well-developed woman who had good moral and ethical values."

Dominika was slowly starting to receive the essence of this conversation and now she was more than nervous. What was now going on in her life was quite extraordinary thanks to her daughter who got the lucky assignment working for Duke Tinktar. She remained quiet listening to every word carefully.

"Duke Tinktar and I both know he needs to soon pick a woman to be his future empress. As you know he can practically choose any woman in the empire. For whatever reason I do not know, he has chosen Daniell."

Dominika's heart was really racing now. She felt like breaking down and crying. This information was overwhelming.

"I promised Duke Tinktar we would not reveal this until after he departed on a mission he's going on. He doesn't want Daniell to know until he's gone and when he returns, he will personally tell her what his desires are."

"If that's the case, why are you telling me this now?" Dominika asked, feeling somewhat astonished that such a strange mannerism was now unfolding.

"As her mother, we want you to advise Daniell she should not get involved with another man anytime in the future because there will soon be a big announcement. Because of Daniell's importance to the Royal family, she will now be treated as any other Royalty with security. She will not go anywhere without surveillance and protection just like any Royal would receive. If necessary, the security apparatus would detain any young men making attempts until all this comes to fruition."

"She currently does not have a boyfriend. She tells me that Duke Tinktar has been extra sweet to her lately and she thinks something is about to happen."

"As soon as Duke Tinktar deploys on his mission, we will bring Daniell here with you and advise her of her status. Duke Tinktar is very sincere in his desires for Daniell and unfortunately, his service to the empire precludes him doing events in his private life now. I'm very close to Duke Tinktar. He's the son I never had. In fact, his courageous father lost his life fighting for my father in a very unselfish act of supreme sacrifice."

"I see."

"I know it's not normal for someone to interfere in the love life of their children and in this case assume I feel like Duke Tinktar's father, but he has done so much for me which I can't divulge to you because of the secrecy of those missions where he put his life on the line just like his father did. I want to do something for him in his life to give back to him any way I can for all that he has done for me. Since he has chosen Daniell to be his future empress, I want to do what I can to make sure that happens."

"What if Daniell decides she doesn't want Duke Tinktar?"

"Duke Tinktar is the type of person who would let her choose her own path in life. If she turns him down, he will find someone else. But I would prefer he and your daughter unify because I like your daughter and what kind of a person she is."

"Alright I will talk to her."

"All of Duke Tinktar's suite is being shut down while he's gone for security reasons. Nobody will be allowed in there until he returns from his mission. Your daughter is being sent home on administrative leave until he returns."

"I'm sure she'll like that she has indicated she would like some time off to do some reading and recreation like she hasn't had in a while."

"I'm not sure how long this mission will last. It could be one or two months. We will not know until Duke Tinktar returns. He will be returning to this mansion, and I want Daniell here to receive him so they can have a private meeting and he can give her his proposal."

"She will need to know about this before then."

"You will be contacted in a few days so that you can have that mother and daughter conversation to prepare her. Also, I will send over experts to dress her before that meeting. She will be treated as a Royal even before the meeting if you contact me and let me know she's agreed to all this. I want her dressed up and beautiful in Royal attire to greet Duke Tinktar so the Empires finest fashion experts will be there to prepare her."

"How soon after they meet do you think the unification will occur?"

"Knowing Duke Tinktar doesn't dilly dally around, I would expect within a couple days after returning we'll have the official unification here in my courtyard next to the aquarium."

"Alright."

"Have you seen the Aquarium before?"

"No, I haven't."

"Do you have time for lunch with me?"

"Since my daughter will be a Royal of course I have time for lunch."

"Good come with me Dominika, we are going to have lunch at the aquarium."

<center>~~~~~~</center>

Chapter Fourteen

DOGGY LOVE ON A THEME FROM PAGANINI

Now sooner than Chester was back at his suite he was being bathed by Aizere and Rayalna gave Brooklyn his bath simultaneously, which he enjoyed.

"How was your workout?" Aizere asked.

"It was great, but I got a lot of pain now," Chester responded.

"Would you like a message?" Aizere asked.

"Sure." Chester said and started thinking he had to have reserve bullets in case Margrét Hansen wanted to do some boom-boom.

Aizere knowing Chester had a challenging workout had put muscle relaxers in the bath water and it was already helping him feel a little better.

Eventually Chester's bath was finished, and he was helped out by Aizere and blow dried then put on a bath robe and walked into the bedroom with Brooklyn joining him now climbing up his dog ramp into his bed where he laid down watching what happened to Chester next.

During the bath, the massage table had been brought in and the masseuse Jazmin was there smiling thinking today may be the day she would get an injection of that special venom out of Chester's Scorpio Stinger.

"Hello Chester, are you feeling pain again?" Jazmin asked.

"You can say that again."

"Get up on the message table and lay on your stomach and I will start.

In a few minutes, Jazmin had the special oil all over Chester's backside and arms and legs and started working on him in a loving fashion. Just like before her messages would take him to extreme pain then to great pleasure as she modulated her techniques and gradually loosened up his hardened muscles. She noticed Chester's body mass exhibited far more muscles than before. His flab was almost all gone. *Whatever they were doing to his body they were making astonishing development*, she thought.

Chester had numerous difficult workouts with his martial arts instructors. One critical element they worked on was his response time and his agility. The idea was to avoid getting hit by a real spy that could be deadly. Even though he was padded up their attacks were painful. But lately the instructors have been finding it more and more difficult to land a punch or kick. Pain has a way of training the brain in response. As the chief instructor said, "You will not become and expert at something until you have done it 10,000 times."

When Chester was back at his suite getting a massage, his martial arts instructors were busy filling out reports, watching surveillance video to comment on it. During four hours of training there was so much activity, it had to be recorded so that instructors could play it back in sequences allowing thoughtful comment. Also, in doing so they would come up with the top 20 recommendations to improve his skill set they would work on the next day.

As expected, when Jazmin rolled Chester over and was messaging his legs and arms and abdomen, she went for his little head to stir him up to entice him to perform the coitus with her. Chester stopped her and said, "I need to save that in case a woman I meet tonight requires my services."

"Got a hot date, do you?"

"I do not know if it's hot or not, but it's always best to be positive and plan for positive results."

"What if it turns out negative?"

"I'll let you take care of that problem tomorrow."

After a while the message was complete, and Chester was back in the bath getting the oil removed and his hair shampooed to prepare him for his new hair style. Jazmin straddling Chester tried one more time to entice him to copulate with her, but he didn't though he did feel her which made her feel good for a few minutes. Then it was time to get dry again and dress for his social event.

As they crafted Chester's hair style another Typhoon style cosmic wave, Brooklyn asked, "Papa where are we going next."

"Brooklyn we are going some place that will make you very happy."

"Where is that Papa?"

"We are going to have dinner with Margrét Hansen, and you will get to see Princess Tiffany."

Chester could see the way that Brooklyn was wagging his tail now he was having a happy reaction.

Chester was soon dressed in a gentleman's attire like what any other Tymasoaran would wear when visiting a female under auspicious occasions. Chester would also be delivered to Margrét Hansen's home in an unmarked Skycar as to not give anyone any indication of who he was and where he came from.

Brooklyn was very happy they were leaving the estate and going to visit Princess Tiffany.

Chester toyed with Brooklyn and asked, "Are you sure you would not rather go feed the squirrels?"

"No Papa, I would rather see "Princess Tiffany.""

In due time the Skycar delivered them to a very prestigious looking home with a long circular driveway located a short distance away from a park that resembled a golf course. As soon as Chester exited the Skycar there was a lady standing at the front entrance. It was Margrét Hansen's maid named Regina.

As Chester and Brooklyn walked up to the front entrance, Regina said, "Good afternoon, Chester and Brooklyn. Please come with me we have a little place set up in the back yard for your entertainment."

"Sure," Chester said and followed Regina through the home to the back yard where Margrét Hansen and Princess Tiffany were waiting. As soon as Princess Tiffany spotted Brooklyn she came running. It was doggy love at its finest.

Regina knew Margrét Hansen quite well and her husband whom she had sex with multiple times until Margrét clued Regina in on how many Bimbos her husband was boinking on far off planets.

Margrét knew of some of the sexual contact her husband had with Regina and played like she didn't know it went on and was pleased to show her some of the surveillance video showing him boinking some green skin women in an orgy. From that day forward Margrét knew she could trust Regina who had a sudden displeasure towards her husband.

Regina figured there was probably going to be some good action (big A) going on tonight between Margrét and her guest by the way she was dressed. She confirmed her suspicions when Margrét said, "Regina, I would like you to take the rest of the evening off. Chester and I would like some privacy because we want to discuss our dogs."

"Thank you very much Margrét I will have an enjoyable evening with an early start."

"See you tomorrow." That was the code word not to come back tonight.

Margrét had a lovely catered spread for Chester and Brooklyn.

"Would you like a drink?" Margrét asked.

"Sure, I'll have what you are drinking," Chester responded. Margrét was drinking the pink elixir which Chester had sampled once before called Zvèzdnàyà Rōzā. As soon as Chester tasted the Zvèzdnàyà Rōzā he knew how it would affect him. His glass was filled full and Margrét was smiling knowing how he would soon react as Chester was being drugged with some heavy sexual inducements. Nothing like getting horny and high at the same time.

Out of the corner of his eye Chester saw "Princess Tiffany" hop on Brooklyn's back a few times. She was in magnificent heat and Brooklyn was being very controlled.

"Would you like something to eat?" Margrét asked.

"Smelling the wonderful food and feeling some slight hunger pains, Chester responded, "Actually I like that idea and Brooklyn has not had food in a while."

Within a few minutes everyone was enjoying the fabulous food catered by one of Tymasoara's best chefs. Chester could not help but think, *so this is how rich people eat?*

The dogs ate and drank to their hearts content and Princess Tiffany would not leave Brooklyn's side for a minute. It seemed she liked his gentleness and calmness. After they all finished eating, Chester found Margrét sitting close to him on a backyard swing next to the pool.

"Would you like to go for a swim?"

"Not today, I already had a good workout."

"You know Chester I kind of like you."

"Thank you."

"You have such fine control you are definitely a gentleman."

"Thank you for the comment, I'm not sure I've earned it."

"The best way to earn it is to please me."

"How can I please you?"

"Come with me dear and I will show you." Margrét then stood up and held out her hand as if she wanted to take Chester to some place.

Chester did not know that Margrét looked twenty years younger now because of her makeover, cosmetics, and drug therapy. She was actually his age plus a few years.

Margrét led Chester to her master bedroom. Then she turned around and started undressing him. And after she got his shirt off, she kissed his chest in a way that turned Chester on more. Then she took off his shoes and dropped his trousers and spotted the erection in his under garment and soon took it and started performing fellatio which sent Chester up into orbit.

Margrét knew her business well and when she knew she had Chester reach that point she stood up and slid out of her clothes and pulled Chester into her bed and on top of her.

Soon Chester was in the perfect coitus with Margrét who didn't know he was now about twice as strong as he was when he left planet earth thanks to all the workouts and substances the trainers fed him to make the workouts much better and build his muscle mass now.

One thing Margrét knew was her husband was no match for Chester who was giving her the workout all women ever dreamed of. Then she was in for her next big surprise as Chester pulled out of her and started his workout on her clitoris using his baseball bat size penis as a battering ram on it driving her into almost convulsions with ensembles of orgasms.

After about 25 orgasms Chester re-entered Margrét then started pile driving his load into her that caused Margrét to achieve that Big-A super orgasm. She thought she had died and gone to heaven and laid back totally satisfied.

Brooklyn had watched some of this activity then ran back outside and Princess Tiffany ran after him. As they reached a very private area, "Princess Tiffany" jumped on Brooklyn's back. Then Brooklyn turned around and jumped on "Princess Tiffany's" back and soon was giving her what she had been wanting for a long time. It was pure love that come to a conclusion. The two dogs were exalted in love, but Brooklyn could explain it like no other dog because he could talk.

Brooklyn's telemetry sent off reports and before the evening was done, Doctor Akssiar and Tasha were studying the telemetry files that were full of all kinds of new reports the Earth Scientists had predicted and since until now Brooklyn had never had such an experience those reports did not go out. Now they flooded the telemetry with data.

All Chester had to do was walk out the front entrance of Margrét Hansen's home and a Skycar would be there to take him back to Duke Tinktar's estate. In a while after a nice nap Chester regained consciousness and realized he had just banged a rich banker's wife and thought it would be prudent to leave soon so as not to fuel rumors.

Chester then stood up and started dressing and Margrét asked, "Where are you going?

"I have a hard workout scheduled for the morning. I need to get back to Duke Tinktar's estate so I can rest and be able to train in the morning."

"What are you training for?"

"Mainly self-defense."

"Why do you need that?"

"As a banker's wife you should know there are things we can't talk about."

Margrét hopped out of bed and quickly put her dress back on because she knew Chester would soon be leaving and "Princess Tiffany" would need a leash on, or she would go running outdoors after Brooklyn.

As they reached the front door, Brooklyn and "Princess Tiffany" were there standing and watching them. Margrét attached the leash to "Princess Tiffany."

"When will I see you again?"

"Probably quite often since our dogs like each other. But I may have to make a trip soon, so maybe gone a while. I'll send word to you when I get back."

"I'm looking forward to it, but next time please stay longer."

"Perhaps I would be more comfortable at a resort or someplace nobody knows who we are."

"I know just the place."

"Do they allow dogs?"

"I take "Princess Tiffany" there all the time."

"When I get back from my trip perhaps, we can meet there." Chester and Brooklyn were soon in the Skycar heading back to Duke Tinktar's estate and into their suite.

Chester wanted a bath to wash off all the sweat and scent he obtained from Margrét Hansen. For some reason Brooklyn wanted a Bath too and they were Both cleaned and pampered then dressed for bed.

Chester had a great sleep and, in the morning, woke up and felt refreshed and ready for morning training. This day would be different, and he didn't know yet this was H-hour. They would soon be deploying.

Chester arrived at the training camp with Brooklyn and after they finished feeding the birds, Duke Tinktar said, "Chester, we are leaving now for the mission. You need to explain it to Brooklyn."

"Alright," Chester replied and then explained to Brooklyn what was going to happen now.

"Papa why can't I go with you?"

"Brooklyn, this is a dangerous mission, and you are very important to the study of dogs with Doctor Akssiar and his assistant Tasha."

"Father I can be of help to you."

"Perhaps on the next one. What I want you to do is cooperate with Doctor Akssiar and his assistant Tasha and Rayalna and Aizere will take good care of you and make sure you get visits with "Princess Tiffany."

"Papa, I like Princess Tiffany but I would rather go with you."

"I'm sorry Brooklyn, you are too valuable to risk on a dangerous mission."

"What about you Papa, you are valuable too."

"Thank you, Brooklyn, but Prince Tinktar needs my assistance."

"Alright Papa, I will do my best and cooperate while you are gone, but the next time I want to go with you."

"Brooklyn if you are really good while I'm gone, I will bring you with me the next time I travel, okay?"

"Okay papa, I promise I will be good and cooperate."

"Thank you, Brooklyn."

Chester went down on the grown with one knee so he could hug Brooklyn. They had never been separated since he was a pup. This would be a trying time for Brooklyn, but he aimed to please Chester and did in fact conduct himself in an exemplary manner.

"We must go now Chester," Duke Tinktar said appearing slightly irritated this goodbye was taking too long.

"Alright let's go. Bye Brooklyn."

"Bye Papa."

Brooklyn stood by a couple of the security men who allowed him to watch "Papa" get on the shuttle craft that soon went airborne and out into space. Brooklyn watched the shuttle as long as he could but after it got above 100,000 feet it slowly disappeared from the naked eye.

One of the security guys said, "Brooklyn, please get into the Skycar."

Brooklyn responded, "Sure no problem, and thank you for letting me see Papa fly away."

The security men were slowly getting to like Brooklyn because of his subtle politeness and great behavior. The fact they could talk to him was one hell of a game changer as well. One thing Brooklyn did to these men was shatter their belief system as they now looked at all animals completely different.

They all knew one thing. Brooklyn had more impact on their psyche than all the propaganda they received in their lifetimes. And now he was to be protected more than almost any living human being shy of the emperor and Duke Tinktar.

In a few minutes Brooklyn was brought back to their suite, and he immediately climbed up the ramp to his bed. Brooklyn would be polite, but he would not be happy until Papa returned.

Chapter Fifteen

RETURN TO ZETA BANTOR

The shuttle craft made its way up to a Cosmic Clipper class of space transport. This was a civilian ship with the best trained crew possible.

The reason why Duke Tinktar selected a Cosmic Clipper space transport is because it was the type of black marketeers usually operated due to speed and agility in case, they had to run from law officials.

Cosmic Clipper space transport used was all part of Duke Tinktar's disguise and his support fleet tailed him at long distance so as to not tip anyone off they were part of a security detail. The fast frigates as part of that group could sprint in quickly in an emergency and extract Duke Tinktar if necessary.

It would take several days to reach Zeta Bantor. The Cosmic Clipper could get there faster, but Duke Tinktar did not want to lose his security detail traveling a safe distance behind.

Aboard the Cosmic Clipper, Chester was briefed on the first part of the operation to contact a group that assisted in the hog farm operation where an enemy of the state would soon meet his end.

This portion of the mission would not take long or be terribly complicated. During the private briefing Duke Tinktar explained some of the tangential purpose of coming here first:

"I want to enjoy Madam Pang one more time in case something happens to me on this mission."

The planet Zeta Bantor they would ultimately visit was explained, and numerous holographic videos played for Chester so he would have a feel for the lay of the land. Zeta Bantor was much earth like, and the people there spoke standard Drolupric language with a dialect very similar to Tymasoara.

Zeta Bantor was a tourist destination, so they produced a lot of video ads showcasing places to visit and attractions to experience. Their ultimate destination was a tourist meca called Zamorane that had a reputation not much different than Las Vegas back on Earth. What happened on Zamorane stayed in Zamorane. It was no wonder to Duke Tinktar why the coup manifested in Zamorane since it would be easily explainable by any official why he or she traveled there for recreation.

As Chester observed all the various tourist ads which were probably the best training materials available for general knowledge of the planet Zeta Bantor and the tourist area Zamorane he was surprised his knowledge of the Drolupric language was so good and understood everything discussed. He also pondered how much he had melted into society in such a short period and thought, *perhaps aliens on Earth right now have experienced the same transformations and they too may be involved with governments.*

The actual mission and those involved would not be disclosed to Chester until they left Zeta Bantor and headed to the Planet Barcejena. Duke Tinktar didn't want to telegraph his intentions in the event the conspirators somehow got ahold of Chester.

Every aspect of Barcejena was spoon fed to Chester over the few days it took to get to Zeta Bantor. Some of the elixirs Duke Tinktar served Chester in their private meals together away from the crew so they could discuss various aspects of the things he needed to know for the mission, had enzymes and psychoactive drugs that enhanced his alertness, acuity, and learning through the process.

The same elixir was given to crew members after great victories for celebration. Duke Tinktar had experienced a few of them. One thing for certain was crew members observing Duke Tinktar on a variety of hazardous missions normally didn't have the feeling of esteem towards a Royal or high placed official unless they demonstrated an element of valor and participation with their own skin in the game. Those crew members who had been with Duke Tinktar on such missions will always think highly favorably of him. On this Cosmic Cutter were some of those former crew members hand-picked for this mission. Duke Tinktar had no doubt in their resolve and dedication. He knew when the chips were down, he could depend on them to follow orders even if it cost them their lives.

Finally, they arrived in orbit around Zeta Bantor and the customs official who approved orbit and access to the planet had been secretly notified by Drolupric Intelligence Bureau to certify the Cosmic Cutter space anchorage and permissions to send shuttles down to the planet. He would personally stamp their entrance documents as they went through customs in sections. He would not be looking at the X-ray machine display of the contents of their cargo because he knew better than know about anything associated with these people that were undercover Drolupric Intelligence Bureau and they were wearing masks and faked identification documents provided by the Drolupric Intelligence Bureau (DIB).

The group of five left the customs area and there was a Skycar out in front of the building to take them to a safe house that would be their base of operations.

They unloaded their equipment for this portion of the operation. Duke Tinktar purposely delayed them all from eating their last meal because he had a special place to take them where they would have a private feast and be enamored with green skin women. Only Duke Tinktar had ever experienced the rarified joy of transcendence one of these beauties could provide.

The safe house was operated by Duke Tinktar's handpicked men prestaged for their arrival. One of Duke Tinktar's men that just arrived would stay with them and work over the game plan. Meanwhile Duke Tinktar, Chester, and the two other spies left in a Skycar headed over to Madam Pang's *pleasure and cerebral epitomes center of excellence.*

The other three men had never felt the exhilaration Madam Pang's associates could offer. Chester was not in much need of much surreal manifestations of exhilarated blissful gratifications. But he too would soon learn people that were not hungry often liked desert.

When the Skycar pulled up in front of Madam Pang's establishment, all the exterior lighting reminded Chester of some of Japanese lit up Pachinko establishments or Love Hotels. Even Las Vegas didn't compare.

The four had shed their masks back in the safehouse. There were no inspections of departures so they didn't need to go through customs or immigration upon leaving the planet incognito so there was no need for the masks any longer. If they needed a new mask the local operatives had mask makers and installers available.

Besides the two security men (spies) with Duke Tinktar there were also staged a few more already inside Madam Pangs and overhead were a couple Skycars fully weaponized and people on the ground to intervene if a terrorist or enemy attempted a hit. Any strangers lingering outside would quickly be apprehended and taken somewhere for Neurological Sonifications designed for torture and mind control that nobody could beat. If the person was part of a plot, he would be shown the hog farm and offered to be dropped there if he didn't rat out his coconspirators.

The Galaxy was no safer than planet Earth with all its dicey activities with the CIA, MI6, MSS (China), FSB (KGB), DSG, AIC, etc.

Madam Pang was in her office talking with a couple of her best associates when the chime that came on when surveillance video picked up clients arriving long before they entered the premises. She instantly recognized Duke Tinktar but didn't know who the other three were. She would soon find out.

"Okay ladies, our guests have arrived, us go out and meet them and take them back to my private playroom where the chef has laid out a great dinner for them."

One of the ladies said, "I feel kind of hungry."

"Today is your lucky day. We will be eating with them to show companionship and talk with them and get to know them."

The beautiful green skin woman suddenly had a big smile because she knew their chef provided excellent food for the special guests. The quality of that food in no way compared with the food in the guest dining hall where they could have dinner and order from a menu.

The women followed Madam Pang out to the reception area, and she immediately approached Duke Tinktar who had a modus operendus with her using an alias (Dmitkron).

"Hello Madam Pang. So nice to see you."

"Dmitkron, it's so nice you could come here tonight. I've set up a private room for your meal and enjoyment."

"I appreciate that," Dmitkron (aka Duke Tinktar) said with a big smile.

"Would you men please follow me," Madam Pang said with her beautiful smile.

The group walked down a hallway and turned down a hallway that branched into a series of special rooms. These were kind of unique in they had folding wall beds behind fake bookshelves patrons could actually read books privately in the room. Once the boom-boom was complete the bed would fold back up into the wall and the two bookshelves would swing on hinges and lock into position hiding the bed behind it.

Madam Pang walked up to the room and tapped a number into the cypher lock and the solenoids clicked allowing them to enter.

Inside the room was a large table with settings for ten people since there would be four men and six women having dinner.

The table had the men's name placards and women's names written on them. It was easy for the men to spot their settings. At one end of the table Duke Tinktar's place setting existed. Next to him was Madam Pang and one of her associates Chūn Fāng, also a green skin beauty. Chūn Fāng appeared to Chester (aka Casaniagra) as a famous Japanese Movie Star he once met on Twitter and had a few exchanges. The only difference was the green skin, red hair, and purple eyes. The combination made Chūn Fāng look quite exotic and highly desirable.

Chester (aka Casaniagra) was seated directly across from Chūn Fāng so they could have a conversation.

The rest of the men were scattered among the pheromone shedding hostesses. Madam Pang provided the very expensive perfumes for her working girls. This perfume was illegal on a lot of planets because it was known to be used by organized crime to set up honey pot schemes.

One ounce of this perfume equaled the monthly salary of these well-paid hostesses. There was no way they could afford it, but since Madam Pang made so much money from their services, she could afford it and provided it. Madam Pang was also the consummate perfume applier. She knew the three most important places to apply it where curious men would fondle her girls. One of the well to do customers had the audacity to touch the third spot of one her girls at the bar. Since he pumped a lot of money into Madam Pang's *pleasure and cerebral epitomes center of excellence,* Madam Pang let him get away with it that time even though he had the nerve to ask the bartender if he wanted to smell his finger.

No sooner than everyone was seated the elixirs started coming. Chester had been advised there might be some sexual fraternization with the hostesses at the party and if such an opportunity arose, he would have privacy and be safe.

Chūn Fāng was giving Chester (aka Casaniagra) the evil eye and since there were name placards at each setting, she knew his name was Casaniagra.

"Casaniagra, where do you come from?" Chūn Fāng asked, then took a sip of her Fŏcìn de Oín champagne.

"I live on Tymasoara the capital city of the Drolupric Empire."

"What kind of work do you do there?"

"I'm a research associate."

"Really. What do you research."

"Currently I'm researching dogs."

"What's your dog research about?"

"I want to prove dogs are a lot smarter than we give them credit."

"Is there anything you discovered that leads you to believe that to be the case?"

"Yes, there is and it's in clinical studies, but I'm sorry I signed a nondisclosure about what we learned about dogs."

"Is there anything you learned about dogs that you can tell me without breaking your oath?"

"I would say dogs in general are a lot smarter than we give them credit. As an example, I know a dog that would watch Television all day long if we let it."

"What's Television?"

"It's an older form of holographic presentations only in two dimensional."

"Two dimensional must be pretty boring."

"Your mind could create three dimensional holographic ensembles by watching a Television series of images. What adds a lot to it is music or sound."

"Do you like music?"

"Absolutely"

"Are there any types of music you prefer?"

"Well, I tend to like classical music."

"Do you go to classical music concerts?"

"Yes, in fact I recently went to a classical music concert at the Tymasoara Civic Center and watched a pianist perform as well as a 200-piece orchestra."

"How did that turn out?"

"It was quite lovely."

"Did you go alone, or did you take someone?"

"I went with a very lovely lady."

"Was she more beautiful than me?"

"I doubt there is any woman more beautiful than you are."

"Are you just saying that flattering remark to make me feel good?"

"Chester (aka Casaniagra) glanced at her name placard then said, "Chūn Fāng, you have exquisite beauty like few others I've ever seen before, and I'm very sincere in those remarks."

"Casaniagra, would you like to be my friend?"

"Of course."

"After we finish dinner perhaps you would like to go with me to my private quarters here and listen to some classical music and talk."

"That sounds great, can we order elixirs there?"

"Absolutely, to make it a more enjoyable event."

Chester (aka Casaniagra) looked at Chūn Fāng and could see the incredible beauty and what she said implied there could be some rather pleasant experiences. Duke Tinktar had warned him this might be a long night and to plan on hanging around a long time and make the most of it. Hanging out with Chūn Fāng seemed like a great thing to do. The waiter came to Chester (aka Casaniagra) and asked, "Sir would you like a refill of your *Chamboreé de Lián?*

Chester asked, "Do you have any *Zvèzdnàyà Rōzā?* The waiter well versed in elixir effects smiled knowing what the customer wanted and responded, "Yes we do sir, please give me a minute and I will get you some."

Chūn Fāng also smiled at Chester knowing that if he started drinking. *Zvèzdnàyà Rōzā* he would be primed for what she had planned for him later.

Chūn Fāng was one of Madam Pang's top hostesses in looks, intelligence, and charm. Madam Pang knew her secret lover Duke Tinktar (aka Dmitkron) would pay handsomely for Casaniagra's (Chester) entertainment. She gave special instructions to Chūn Fāng including a handsome bonus if she pleased him well. Even at the risk of pregnancy.

Soon the Entrees were served and as expected the food as marvelous, and the Hostesses were all happy to be eating such fantastic tasting food with their clients. It was a semi-rare treat to eat this well. But Madam Pang would be paid handsomely and knew in her heart that Duke Tinktar had special feelings for her because when they made love, he kissed her like a real lover would.

Duke Tinktar and Madam Pang were in their own little world now savoring the minutes between long separations. But Madam Pang knew her place in society and understood Duke Tinktar, thus they were making the most out of the brief time they had together.

Madam Pang thought this was just one more of many more visits in the future, but in reality, it was Duke Tinktar's Swan Song final visit. He knew the emperor was probably already working on things back home to make the sojourn with Daniell a reality. He knew the emperor was getting impatient and these trips would soon come to an end.

Chester took his time eating and drinking and it seemed the waiter had an endless supply of *Zvèzdnàyà Rōzā*. In reality, the waiter did as the wine cellar had cases of the elixir, so there was plenty more available.

The other two men were being seduced by other women present. Three for Duke Tinktar and three for the rest. Madam Pang planed on having two women help her please Duke Tinktar.

The gala event went on for a while and soon Chester was full and had no desire to eat anymore. Chūn Fāng was also done eating and decided she wasn't going to waste any more time here at the dinner table and stood up and walked around the end of the table up to Chester and whispered in his ear, "Why don't you come with me to my private room?" Right then Chester looked up at Duke Tinktar who gave him the nod signaling go with her.

Thanks to all the *Zvèzdnàyà Rōzā* Chester drank, his libido was more than ready for what was going to transpire.

Chūn Fāng led Chester out of the room and down the hallway to another room and keyed in a combination on the cypher lock and the door solenoids clicked and she opened the door and took him inside.

The door under control of artificial intelligence shut behind them and locked.

The room was well decorated and luxurious. Only the richest men ever made their way in here. Chūn Fāng rarely gave it up. She would socialize with men, but there was never any physical intercourse unless she liked the person and had established a relationship that appeared better than just friendship. To invite a stranger in was totally out of character, but she had some inside knowledge from Madam Pang. This person Casaniagra (aka Chester) was a friend and well connected to Duke Tinktar. He also had a sweet disposition about him and did not presume to make any assumptions about what would happen next.

True to her word, Chūn Fāng started playing some Classical music produced on Zeta Bantor. It was rather pleasant, and Chester thought how it seemed to sound a lot like Saint Saens compositions. Chūn Fāng then asked Chester if he would like to sit down and gestured towards the nice thick sofa which he sat on.

Soon they were facing each other and having a pleasant conversation. Chester didn't volunteer any subject or information, but Chūn Fāng an animal lover asked questions about dogs, much just generalities that Chester could answer without discussing Brooklyn in particular.

Chūn Fāng realized Chester was not aggressive with women and didn't seem to even want to make the first move, so she had to help matters along or the night would be wasted. She approached Chester closer and kissed him like few women could. She was well trained and prior to dinner took a dose of enzymes that would linger in her mouth and cause significant arousal in men if she kissed them and exchanged body fluids in the process.

Chester was already horned up with *Zvèzdnàyà Rōzā* so the added enzymes in his mouth now threw him over the edge in desire.

Chūn Fāng was a strong and deliberate woman. She worked out two hours every day and was in the best possible physical fitness for moments like this. Before Chester could respond or react, she had his trousers and undergarments down to his knees exposing his manliness. There was absolutely no foreplay. Chūn Fāng straddled Chester's body and grabbed his rock-hard manliness and guided it inside her and began to make love to Chester.

The green skinned women from Zeta Bantor had enzymes in their vagina that had a huge impact on a plane skin male. Within moments as Chester's penis started absorbing some of those enzymes, his libido acted as if it were on some serious steroids. His horniness exploded exponentially, and he transcended to caldrons of gratification and transcendence to splendid euphoria and predictably exploded inside Chūn Fāng that caused her to react and have a series of orgasms and massive gratification. Chūn Fāng knew she had not felt like this in a very long time. There was something special about Chester (aka Casaniagra). Part of it was an Earth person's sperm had enzymes in it that did to Zeta Bantor green skin women the same effect their enzymes had on most males.

When it was all over with, the two readjusted their clothes as if nothing happened and then at Chester's request, they simply laid together in the soft plush sofa enjoying the classical music and soon they both fell asleep.

Madam Pang had the combination to all the rooms. The two were sleeping feeling great satisfaction. Duke Tinktar had requested Madam Pang notify Chester he was ready to leave. Madam Pang saw they were cuddling and sound to sleep so she entered the room and shook Chūn Fāng to arouse her and wake her up. When Chūn Fāng was awake she looked at Madam Pang who had seldom done this before and asked, "Is there something I need to know?"

"Yes, he needs to wake up they are going to leave in a few minutes."

"Alright, he'll be right there, give me a moment alone with him please."

"Sure dear."

As soon as Madam Chang was out of the room and the door closed, Chūn Fāng shook Chester and said, "You need to wake up, your friends are ready to leave."

Chester came to and Chūn Fāng stood up and helped him stand up.

"You really made me feel special tonight, I hope we can meet again," Chūn Fāng said.

"If I get a chance to see you again, I will."

"Thank you Casaniagra that means a lot to me."

"Chūn Fāng, I really like you."

"I like you too."

The two hugged and Chester gave Chūn Fāng a kiss that was unmistakable romantic and emotional. She felt it and she knew it.

Thus, it made Chūn Fāng's heart soft for the moment.

Chūn Fāng walked Chester to the front entrance where he met up with Duke Tinktar and the other two gentlemen and they left the establishment and walked outside where a Skycar suddenly appeared, and they got in and left heading back to the safe house.

The next day Chester went with Duke Tinktar to a planned meeting with some unsavory characters. This was the formal introduction to Chester, whom they would deal with in the future for similar operations. Their task was to take the suspect from the Cosmic Cutter down to the planet surface via a black marketer's typical route, with bribes, payoffs, etc.

Near the hog farm Duke Tinktar and his men would take possession of the prisoner and the operatives would leave and disappear.

Once all the negotiations were complete, they departed company and went back to the safe house to wait for nighttime to leave the planet and meet up with the Cosmic Cutter and continue on to the Planet Barcejena.

In due time they were in space and heading for their ultimate destination. Now the final briefings could go on since there was no possible source of compromise since the only people who knew who the target was were onboard the Cosmic Cutter and nowhere else except with the emperor and his valet.

With all good operational security, the informant was no longer in position to discuss General Crontyke with anyone or be found again. Part of his payoff was a change of identity and relocation to a far-off planet clear on the other side of the empire where he would be basking in the sun, drinking tropical drinks spiked with elixirs and enjoying a couple young girls purchased for him. Once General Crontyke was executed his relevance would quickly diminish and when the money ran out, so would the women.

It took several days to reach Barcejena, but once they arrived, Chester knew his assignment full of danger and intrigue. He kind of wished he had Brooklyn with him who would calm his nerves, but that wasn't possible, so he had to suck it up and go with the flow.

This time they could not afford to go through customs or allow anyone to know of their arrival. Hence, they used black marketeers to get them to the planet surface and provide them with escape shuttles at the conclusion of the snatch and grab plus murder times ten.

Chester's role in all this was to assassinate a couple of the coup members. There was some surveillance on the two men he had to kill, and they needed to be taken out rapidly so that nobody would tip off General Crontyke the coup had been compromised.

Chester with a backpack on was flown via Skycar to a location where he would hook up with the first surveillance operative who would give him the final bearing than shoot.

Chester had to walk a ½ mile through brush in the dark to get to the rendezvous. There was no other way for them to meet up without possible exposure to government forces that would then tip off General Crontyke.

The man doing the surveillance was expecting Chester. He didn't know who he was, but he knew the man most likely had toys in the backpack.

"Tango Six Bravo," Chester said as he approached the surveillance man.

"Whisky Tango Foxtrot," the signals were exchanged, and they both knew the other guy was safe.

"Are we ready for fireworks?"

"The target will be arriving momentarily."

"How do you know that?"

"He spends time at a constabulary with the lovely ladies and he usually comes home about this time."

"How much time do we have?"

"We have a lookout where he just left. Will be here in nine minutes."

"Alright."

Chester took the drone out of the backpack which was in the shipping container then set it on a flat spot in the ground. He turned the drone on, and it went into a preflight check off including an airborne test. Within a few minutes there were green indicators on all the self-checks and the drone was ready to do its work.

Chester asked the surveillance man, "Can you please take this scope and point it to where you think the man will exit his Skycar?". "Sure," the man said who was very familiar with that scope. He would press a button that would lock in the coordinates to where they would hit the target. They needed accurate Identification of the man to make sure they killed the right person. That would only take a very short time and the drone would be overhead ready to attack. Just like the man stated, the Skycar came in and landed and the man got out. The drone now 100 feet above him and offset by 40 or more feet started analyzing and soon confirmed it was the target.

One switch had a safety cover that Chester had to flip and switch it to standby. Then he had to do a similar act with the fire switch. Once he did that the programmed built in firmware did everything automatically. The drone came down and exploded about 6 inches above the man's skull instantly killing him. Chester communicated his milestone was complete and soon a Skycar came to his location and picked him up and took him to his second target.

Within fifteen minutes, Chester performed the next kill. He now knew he was an assassin and had never done things despicable in his early years.

As the night unfolded the traitor list of associated names got others exterminated. Based on information discovered during the investigation two conspirators as well as General Crontyke were subdued and transported by shuttle out to the waiting Cosmic Cutter.

Soon Chester found himself back in a shuttle going up to the Cosmic Cutter and heading back to the hog farm on Zeta Bantor.

During the high-speed transit back to Zeta Bantor, Duke Tinktar had a discussion with Chester.

"We are going to interrogate these Coup members. The day may come when you must do similar acts. I'm going to take you into the interrogation room and I want you to observe what goes on."

"Alright, I'm willing to learn."

"You don't need to say anything or do anything during the interrogations."

"Understand." Chester said now realizing he was in way over his head into galactic affairs nobody on Earth would ever believe went on.

Soon Chester found himself sitting across the table from the first man who would undergo interrogation.

"Are you willing to name everyone you know involved in the coup?" Duke Tinktar asked the man who didn't look so happy.

After a long pause where the man being interrogated never responded, Duke Tinktar said, "I'm willing to give you back your life if you cooperate."

The man remained silent. The conspirators obviously knew if they ratted the others out, they would soon be dead.

Duke Tinktar didn't want to waste a lot of time on this man because he had the other and the General to interrogate so he looked up at the two men subduing the prisoner who was bound and shackled and said, "Go ahead and inject him."

Right on cue the man was injected with a drug cocktail that had a mental inhibitor as well as a drug that would impede his motor functions so that he could not interfere with the Neurological Sonifications that would soon be flooding his brain at high amplitude. The intensity was about the same as a person would hear if he were standing by the exhaust of a rocket engine. Chester could feel some of the vibrations sitting across from the table. The two assistants held the man upright during the first five-minute application. Predictably at about the three-minute mark the man started screaming, but the device covering his head prevented a lot of his scream out into the room. It also had a video monitor and Duke Tinktar could see the man's face on a holographic screen offset to his left in an empty area adjacent to the table.

Looking at the elapsed time indicator on the display screen monitoring the suspect, when it showed five minutes had passed, Duke Tinktar said, "Shut it off and remove the Neurological Sonifier helmet."

Duke Tinktar let the man set there for a few minutes to allow his mental functions to adapt back to current reality, but he was still under the influence of the drugs administered.

"Are you willing to start naming names? I will give your life back to you. The man stared at Duke Tinktar and refused to talk. He was going to be a nut too hard to crack. They had his friends and associates' names so even if he didn't cooperate they could follow the bread crumbs he left behind in some of his communications he arrogantly thought nobody could detect. He didn't realize that when you are part of a conspiracy someone else would implicate you. One of the two men Chester nailed with the drone attacks was a person who implicated this man with poor operational security and easily penetrable encrypted communications.

Duke Tinktar wasn't going to waste any more time with this man. He would use his body to make the next man talk. As such he was carried to the air lock that had video cameras in it to allow the control room to communicate with people there egressing from the spaceship during normal at space transfers. The two bruisers with a head piece on allowing them to breath in a vacuum and pressure suits carried the bound man to the airlock.

Meanwhile the next man was brought in for interrogation. This wasn't Duke Tinktar's first rodeo. He wanted to spend most of his time interrogating General Crontyke, so he streamlined the process.

"If you agree to cooperate, I'll give you your life back. You will go through re-education and become a model citizen again, and all will be forgiven for what you were assisting in planning in the coup against the emperor."

The man didn't know where the other two were and had no idea what the man just interrogated went through and he was not about to rat out the co-conspirators.

"We interrogated one of your conspirators. He wasn't fully cooperative, so we are going to give you the opportunity to see what happens to a person shoved out of an airlock into space."

The man did not respond, but Duke Tinktar being a fair man gave him another chance. "I said before, we will give you your life back if you cooperate. Are you going to help us?"

Again, the prisoner remained silent.

"Alright before we give you the special treatment, we are going to let you see one of your coconspirators shoved out of an airlock."

Duke Tinktar nodded at one of the men standing who then pressed a button on a remote control and the video in the airlock with sound suddenly showed nearby on a hologram. Anyone not aware of holograms would believe they were looking at a real sight superimposed a short distance away.

The men in the airlock could hear Duke Tinktar's voice as he said, "We are now going to depressurize the airlock so you can toss the man out into space. The man looked confused and soon felt the decrease in air pressure and suddenly started panicking and screaming. Even if he now promised to cooperate it was too late, Duke Tinktar wanted the other man to observe all this, so he didn't have to waste a lot of time going through the same drill with this man. Right before their eyes they witnessed the man going into hypoxia and as soon as the pressure was equalized with space a complete vacuum, the men opened the outer door and tossed the conspirator out into space, then shut the airlock outer door. Upon artificial intelligence detecting the interlocks were closed meaning the outer door was shut and sealed, it started pressurizing the airlock to fourteen-point seven (14.7) PSI same as what was inside the ship. They soon exited the airlock and secured the inner door providing double isolation to space.

Duke Tinktar looked at the man who now had panic on his face. This man had a lot of breadcrumbs they could track down to find all his associates, so keeping him alive wasn't necessary.

"Do you want to go out the airlock like what you just saw the other man go?"

The man was now sweating profusely.

"There is nobody that can save you now. In about 10 minutes you will be going out that airlock if you do not start cooperating."

The man wasn't showing any indication of cooperation, but Duke Tinktar could see he was in full panic.

Just before Duke Tinktar was to start the Neurological Sonification, one of his security men came into the room with a tablet device with a lot of information printed on it including the man's wife and children were now detained and a list of all his close friends and relatives tracked down through social media.

"So, you don't want to cooperate?" Tinktar smiled.

The man sat there quiet seemingly nervous and sweating like a pig.

"We have your wife and children detained now. I might have to keep you alive so you can watch me shove them out the airlock just like we did to your friend."

"You rotten bastard," the man yelled out and started crying.

"It's no longer me giving you your live back to you. Now I have something more important to offer you. Would you like me to give your wife and children's life back. Plus we have a list of all your relatives and friends who could get a free ride out into space." Duke Tinktar started naming the list of people and he finally broke the man.

"I'll cooperate."

They didn't need a stenographer since Artificial Intelligence was recording the conversation, and over the next five minutes the man named a lot of names that filled in a lot of blanks. Breaking this one man saved them months and months of painful investigations. When you uncover a coup, you have to get all the leaders or it would only be a matter of time before the next coup developed. To make matters worse the investigation now revealed foreign involvement. This meant it was not only a coup but soon there would be a war because of it.

The prisoner was then escorted to his makeshift holding cell where he would remain cuffed and shackled under constant supervision to prevent him from committing suicide because the interrogations had just begun. Once he was taken back to Tymasoara he would receive a series of Neurological Sonifications to help him remember details about the that investigators wanted to fully gather for future activities.

Armed with all the information there really wasn't much more General Crontyke had to offer but Duke Tinktar interrogated him, nonetheless. During the interrogations it was clear to Duke Tinktar that General Crontyke was an arrogant bastard and it pleased him to no end to haul his fat ass to the Hog farm. Now that the coup was foiled there was no longer the urgency to travel in such incognito, so they simply went down to the planet in a shuttle to a commercial airport where they transferred General Crontyke to a VTOL aircraft. He was gagged cuffed and shackled so he was easily transferred the few feet by the two strong brutes.

Chester didn't quite know yet what was going to happen and was aboard to participate. It took fifteen minutes for the VTOL to fly over to the hog farm. Duke Tinktar pulled the tape off General Crontyke's mouth and asked, "Would you like to repent now and have a second chance in life?" "Fuck you," the General said in Drolupric language.

Duke Tinktar directed one of the big boys, "Tape his mouth shut again."

Soon the general was not capable of putting out a lot of sound. Duke Tinktar pulled out his stiletto knife and handed it to Chester and said, "Cut him good in a few places, but don't kill him, we just want him to bleed really well."

Chester was now super animated watching all this horror unfold and knew he was trapped, he had to go along with the program for his own survival. While the goons held General Crontyke so he couldn't move, Chester cut him deep in a few spots and the General started bleeding really well. The pilot came over the intercom and said, "We are directly over the drop zone."

Duke Tinktar said to the two big monsters, "Throw him out." At 500 feet the General got lucky he landed on his head which knocked him unconscious and snapped his neck so he would not feel the saber tooth hogs tearing his flesh to bits.

Duke Tinktar had the VTOL hover a few minutes so Chester could observe the saber tooth hogs tearing into the former General's flesh. It was soon a feeding frenzy.

"Take us back to the airport," Duke Tinktar said.

Chapter Sixteen

REST AND RELAXATION

Chester was glad to get back to his suite. After experiencing life-changing events like he never dreamed of he needed some down time. Duke Tinktar clearly understood what he had put Chester through and canceled all training for a couple weeks to allow Chester to Rest and Relax and spend some time with Brooklyn.

Chester was psychologically wounded. He had never killed someone before and never believed he would ever do such an act. But he just participated in the assassination and killing of four men, though blowing them up with a drone didn't feel the same as cutting General Crontyke and watching him thrown to the Sabretooth Hogs.

Brooklyn had a calming effect on Chester and the dog was all over Chester so glad to see him again.

"Papa, I'm so glad you are back." Brooklyn said while Chester was hugging him feeling instant relief of stress.

"What did you do while I was gone, Brooklyn?"

"Papa, I got to see Princess Tiffany a few times and Aida took me out to feed the squirrels almost every day and we went for a walk afterwards which I enjoyed getting some exercise."

"Brooklyn did you have a good time?"

"Most of the time, but Doctor Akssiar and Tasha visited a few times and gave me some more tests. They had me watch a couple videos and afterwards asked me about them."

"How did that go?"

"I really didn't like the videos, but they were happy with the answers I gave them about what I said about the videos afterwards."

"What did they say about your comments concerning the video?"

"Doctor Akssiar said I was very intuitive and got more out of the video than what most Tymasoaran do."

"I wonder why he thinks that?"

"Probably because I'm not Tymasoaran I do not have their bias and viewpoints and do not overlook and miss things they do."

"Do you know when they are coming back?"

"They said you would be returning, and their orders were to give you and me plenty of time together to help you unwind before they task me again."

"Sounds reasonable. What do you want to do now?"

"Papa, it's about time to go feed the squirrels again. They are getting used to us and more friendly."

"Alright, let's have Rayalna come here with some food for the squirrels."

Artificial intelligence in the background monitoring the conversation asked, "Chester do you wish Rayalna to come to your suite?"

"Yes please."

"She has been notified."

Moments later Rayalna appeared and she asked, "What can I do for you Chester?"

"Would it be possible to get some food for Brooklyn to feed the squirrels."

"Not a problem and I see its about that time-of-day Brooklyn likes going out there. I'll be right back with a small bag of food."

"Thank you."

"You are welcome."

In a brief period Chester and Brooklyn were besides themselves out in the area where Brooklyn knew he would meet up with the squirrels. Brooklyn led Chester to the exact place he placed the food every day. After laying the food down, Chester said, "I think we need to step back a few feet."

"Papa, it's not necessary, the Squirrels are no longer scared of me."

To Chester's surprise, suddenly a couple squirrels crawled down a nearby tree and came running up to the food. They each picked up food. One of them ran off about ten feet and started eating, the other one simply stood on his back feet and started eating the special dog food. They were eating the same food as Brooklyn got.

"Papa this squirrel likes me the best."

"How do you know which one it is?"

"He smells different than the rest."

"Squirrels smell differently?"

"Yes, they do, and besides his smell I can see his tail and his color on his fur is unique."

Suddenly a couple more squirrels came out of nowhere and made a direct run to the food. One of them grabbed food and ran off, the other took food and stayed there and ate it.

Before the first squirrel picked up more food he walked over to Brooklyn and sniffed him checking him out very carefully, then walked back over and picked up another bit of food to eat.

"Looks like that squirrel knows you."

"Papa, he sniffs me every day."

The two waited until most of the food was gone and Brooklyn said, "We can leave now."

"Want to walk on ahead for some exercise?"

"Sure Papa, I've gone that way a few times with Aida."

"Alright, lead the way."

"The path they walked on circumnavigated the major hill next to Duke Tinktar's estate. It was a good walk and eventually they came up to what amounted to a dead end of sorts. There was a stairway that led up the hillside.

"Did you go up those stairs, Brooklyn?"

"No Papa."

"We might walk up there one of these days, but I think I want to go back to the suite and take a nice long bath, maybe get a message."

"Alright Papa, I think I want a bath too."

The two best friends walked back to the mansion and their suite, where Chester notified Aizere, "Brooklyn and I would like to take baths now. Also, I think I could use a massage."

"I'll make all the arrangements, please undress and go into the bathroom," Aizere responded.

Soon man and beast were enjoying their baths. Brooklyn surprised Rayalna when he said, "I just want to lay in the water for a while like Papa is doing, but you can make it a little warmer."

"Alright tell me when its warm enough."

In a while Brooklyn said, "The temperature now is perfect, leave it at this."

"Alright," Rayalna said then sat on a chair watching everything in the room minding her own business. She was soon in for a few surprises.

Within several minutes after getting into the bath, Aida arrived ready to take charge of Chester and he surprised her by saying, "I just want to relax now. I'm not interested in any boom-boom."

Aida was surprised and decided to give Chester some space, so she got out of the bath dried off, put on a bath towel and walked out of his suite. The security men outside were utterly shocked how fast Chester sent Aida packing. After soaking thirty minutes Chester and Brooklyn got out of their baths and dried off.

Aizere notified by artificial intelligence entered the bathroom and informed Chester, "Your massage masseuse is here to give you a workout."

"Alright, thanks."

Chester walked out of the large bathroom and into his bedroom suite and there was Jazmin, all smiles and ready to commence work.

"Please lay on your stomach, its business as usual."

It was a carbon copy of the last message when Chester did not respond to Jazmin's suggestions of a sexual tryst.

"Is there something wrong with me?" Jasmin asked.

"No nothing at all."

"Then why are you not interested in me? A lot of men give me unification proposals every week just to try to get a chance to make love with me and I turn them down. You are the only man I've offered myself to."

"Listen Jasmin, there is nothing wrong with you. I like you a lot."

"Then why are you turning my offers down?"

"I've just been through a lot lately and I'm not very happy right now. I just want to reflect and think about my life and what I'm doing."

"Perhaps I can help you."

"I'm not in a good psychological condition now. I need time to wind down. Give me a few weeks and I will probably feel better."

Alright Chester, I understand, sometimes people need their distance, and I respect that."

"Thank you I appreciate that."

~~~~~~

While Chester was getting his bath and message, Duke Tinktar was requested to personally brief the emperor on the status of the operation. Chester didn't know this, but he was observed the entire trip including during the drone operations and later witnessing the prisoner interrogation and the trip to the hog farm.

He was subsequently observed upon return. Doctor Boonkar was summoned to meet with the emperor and Duke Tinktar during the debriefing. She was not allowed to know about the two
~~~~~~

assassinations Chester did, the man pushed out of the air lock, or the trip to the hog farm. She did however was allowed to see the video recordings of Chester with the green skin woman Chūn Fāng.

Doctor Boonkar watched all the videos they would allow her to see. Chester was briefed he was not allowed to talk about the four men killed in any manner, it was strict operational security.

After watching the videos and the rejection of a super-hot Aida and later the image and conversation with Jasmin, it was clear that Chester was not psychologically balanced at the moment and probably suffered from post-traumatic stress.

"Maybe he just misses the green skin woman Chūn Fāng," Doctor Boonkar said.

Duke Tinktar knew there were some things Doctor Boonkar needed to know or she would have the wrong conclusions and said, "Your Excellency, without getting into any of the details or who was involved, I would like permission to inform Doctor Boonkar what Chester experienced so she will know it's far more than simply missing a sweetheart."

"Duke Tinktar, I think I can parse the appropriate information and inform her without giving up too much of the information, if I may."

"Absolutely your Excellency that's even better."

"Doctor, Chester just observed four men being killed. He might have had a hand in some of it. I'm sure he feels remorse. We will schedule him to see you, but under no circumstances are you to ask who those men are and how they were killed. This is an ongoing case and it's an empire secret that is closely guarded now."

"Your excellency, thank you for telling me that because I would have made the wrong diagnosis thinking this was merely a personal matter where a relationship impacted his psyche. But if he was involved in the deaths of those four men, then that takes it to an altogether different issue and he may be harder to treat."

"What do you have in mind?"

"He needs to have some down time and recreation. Do not task him to do any more activities along the line he concluded for a while until he comes to terms with it. I've done some experimentation with Neurological Sonifications to avoid psychoactive drug therapy and traditional treatments that take too long and are often only partially successful."

"Do you have any examples of where you exercised this methodology?"

"I do and I've not made it public or sent I out to peer review as there are vested interests in the pharmaceutical industry as well as psychoanalysts that would never want this process to come to fruition because it would be ruinous to their business model."

"You are certain about the efficacy of the treatment?"

"I most certainly am."

"How soon would you recommend we start this treatment?"

"As you can imagine this treatment is also stressful because anyone who undergoes Neurological Sonifications suffers a degree of stress."

"That seems to be a logical conclusion."

"I recommend we let him unwind for a couple weeks, let him find a pathway for temporary coping with his demons, then we bring him in and give him the treatments."

"How many Neurological Sonifications do you expect it will take?"

"I think in four or five treatments we can clear all his demons. But we need to stretch them out and not do them every day. In fact, I would recommend we give three or four days between each treatment. Find him something to do in between those treatments."

"I'm sure we can do that; we have been training him at a special camp to prepare him for these kinds of missions. We do the training in the mornings then give him some recreational activities in the afternoons."

"That sounds like the perfect approach. Keep doing that and we will schedule the Neurological Sonifications in starting two weeks from now."

"Should we inform Doctor Akssiar who supervised his Neurological Sonifications in the past for learning Drolupric language and martial arts."

"I recommend you do not inform Doctor Akssiar who I know for a fact will consider my treatments as immoral and unethical."

"Why is that?"

"He thinks I'm brain washing people."

"Well, are you not doing exactly that?"

"Yes, I am, however I believe for the benefit of the patient, it's more important than the ethical boundaries we cross over to get it done."

"Alright Doctor, two weeks from now we will start your treatments. Any suggestions as to where you want to conduct them?"

"Yes, I have a mountain retreat with no nearby neighbors where we have seclusion and the only way in and out is via Skycar."

"Alright two weeks from now we'll take Chester to your location. How long do you want to keep him there for each treatment?"

"I want him to stay there the entire time."

"He has a dog Brooklyn who will be upset if he's gone that long."

"It might be a good idea to bring Brooklyn along because he will be a source of comfort between treatments."

"Alright doctor, we'll make that happen and thank you for coming to this meeting."

"It's been my pleasure, your excellency."

Everyone stood up and bowed and the Valet Swìnlàgār escorted Doctor Boonkar to the front entrance where Artificial Intelligence brought her Skycar there and opened the door for her. She waved at Swìnlàgār, then got into her Skycar and flew off immediately heading back to her office with a lot to think about. One thing Doctor Boonkar knew for sure now was Chester was some type of assassin doing clandestine work for the emperor and Duke Tinktar. It almost made her feel like her skin wanted to crawl. She was a smart lady and knew vividly, there were some things you really do not want to know about.

After the good Doctor Boonkar was gone and Swìnlàgār was absent, the emperor asked, "Tell me in your overall assessment, how well did Chester work out?"

"He did fantastic. He executed his assignments with perfection and did exactly what I directed him. He's a good asset for the team and the future. My opinion is in a brief amount of time he would most likely spring back to normal, but if Doctor Boonkar can speed that process up with her brain washing, that's good in case he needs to go on another mission soon."

"What do you have in mind?" the emperor asked.

"General Crontyke received collateral help and funding from the Wubars, and we know who in their INTEL community was responsible."

"What do you have in mind?"

"Assassination."

"What will that do for us?"

"They will know very quickly who did the assassination because of what their spy was doing with General Crontyke, they will know this is retaliation and if it happens again, could escalate quickly to an all-out war."

"And what do you hope to achieve by this?"

" I believe it will have an impact on them not wanting to get involved in any more coups with our empire after we demonstrate these kinds of operations can blow back into their own faces."

"Alright, we can plan that in the future but for now we have a more pressing issue."

"What's that?"

"I want to bring Daniell and her mother here so you can tell them both what your plan for Daniell is."

"When do you want to bring them?"

"Today. Afterwards I want to make an official announcement that Daniell is now part of the Royal family."

"How soon for the unification?"

"I think we need to give everyone about a week for planning."

"Alright, let me go home and clean up well and have someone contact me to inform me when I should come back here."

"Can you do me a favor?"

"What would you like me to do Your Excellency."

"When you come back bring Brooklyn and Chester with you.

I want to spend some time with the dog Brooklyn. I kind of miss Brooklyn."

"It will be my pleasure, your excellency. I think it might cheer up Chester watching me get engaged with Daniell."

"I think so too."

"I'm going to invite Linap as well. She has taken interest in Chester."

"Is that safe? Linap will eat Chester alive."

"Yes, and in the process help him take his mind off the mission."

~~~~~~
~~~~~~

Chapter Seventeen

THE BIG ANNOUNCEMENT

Chester had just changed into casual clothes when suddenly Aizere came into his bedroom and said, "I'm sorry Chester but you are going to have to Change clothes again."

"Why?"

"Duke Tinktar has a special event tonight and you have been asked to attend by the emperor himself."

"What about Brooklyn?"

"The emperor requests you bring Brooklyn, he would like to spend some time with Brooklyn too."

"Alright."

"You have to dress up so the hair designer will be arriving in a few minutes."

"No problem."

Brooklyn was laying up on his doggy bed taking it all in watching Chester get dressed up in Royal Clothes and his Cosmic Swirl hair design. One thing Brooklyn recognized was Chester was a different person. Chester had gone through a trauma and no doubt had nobody to confide with.

Brooklyn had watched the Doctor Phil show on TV several times because that was Abagail's favorite show. He wondered how he could help Chester. He knew what he had to do. Dr. Phil was a great teacher. Brooklyn would find ways of studying psychoanalysis and that way he could better help Chester deal with his demons he now seemed to carry. Brooklyn would become the ultimate service dog.

As soon as Chester was ready Aizere walked into the room with a bodyguard and said, "Chester, this man will escort you to the Skycar waiting for you and Brooklyn."

"Sure."

"This way sir, the bodyguard said respectfully."

There was a slight tone in the bodyguard's language. What Chester didn't know was this man was part of Duke Tinktar's inner circle of twenty people that knew about his special missions including the one Chester had just gone on. The spotters who provided Chester with targeting information when he did the two drone attacks had told his colleges Chester was as calm as a cucumber and carried out his assignment as good as anyone.

Duke Tinktar's inner circle also knew had Chester been discovered he would have been a dead man very quickly and thus did those missions in great risk to himself. They now knew Chester was dependable and not a chickenshit spoiled by Duke Tinktar. He was the real deal; a killer just like them. They also knew he was an observer of the interrogations, and he personally was the one who sliced up General Crontyke before they threw him to the razor tooth hogs.

None of them knew what the Emperor and Duke Tinktar had planned for Chester. If they did, they would be utterly astonished. But at the same time these clandestine operatives would understand why they had to pick an outsider with no ties to anyone to do the various tasks Duke Tinktar needed accomplished. To make the emperor happy Duke Tinktar had to delegate his authority so they could concentrate on more pressing issues of state.

As soon as they reached outdoors, there was Duke Tinktar dressed up more immaculately than Chester had ever seen him before wearing a big smile.

"Chester, I think you will enjoy the evening. This is an important day in my life and I'm happy you will be there to share it with me."

"It will be my distinct honor Your Excellency," Chester responded in the most positive manner he could.

Chester was also surprised the Librarian Chernega was there dressed in his Regimental Commander's Dress Uniform and going with them. They had plenty of room in the six-person Skycar and soon they were on their way.

Chester knew something big was going to happen because Chernega acted so jovial on the way to the emperor's palace. While on the way there he was sitting next to Brooklyn and had his arm on him and petting Brooklyn who was enjoying the personal affection. When they arrived at the Mansion the emperor, also dressed for the occasion was standing out in front of the mansion a dozen feet away from where the Skycar landed. The men exited the Skycar and as soon as they were out of it, the doors shut automatically and the Skycar took off and flew over to a designated parking spot out of sight of the mansion.

The emperor greeted them and said, "I would like you all to line up with me to greet our guests that will be arriving momentarily.

The sequencing of the Skycars was all synchronized for cause and effect.

Next beautifully adorned Sky Limo pulled up and the magnificent Linap exited her Sky Limo and shortly after the doors shut it too took off and flew to its designated parking spot out of view of the mansion.

The Valet Swìnlàgār approached Linap and said, "my dear Linap, may I escort you to the emperor who wishes to welcome you."

"Yes, I would thank you."

Swìnlàgār took Linap up to a few feet away from the emperor and said, "Your Excellency, may I present to you the lovely Linap, our wonderful member of your court."

"Thank you Swìnlàgār. Lady Linap, you have always been loyal to me, and I appreciate you that's why I invited you to be here this afternoon for this most auspicious occasion. I would like you to stand by Chester who will be your escort tonight."

Swìnlàgār took the black widow over to Chester and said, "Chester you are hereby designated to be Lady Linap's escort tonight and you will be responsible for her pleasant experience."

Chester knew he had to play the game and responded, "It's my distinct honor. Then he held out his elbow which Lady Linap took with a huge smile because this might just turn out to be an interesting evening, especially if she could get her fangs into that handsome man who wore Royal Clothes every time, she saw him. She wanted to get to the bottom of why this man was receiving such Royal Treatment, but the big surprise for her was yet to unfold.

Moments later the key event for the welcoming ritual now manifested. The emperor's personal Royal Sky Limo pulled up and stopped in front of all of them. There was huge suspense as to who was going to exit the Limo. The doors opened then Daniell and her mother exited the Limo dressed up exceptionally as the designers and makeover experts had turned Daniell into a living princess.

Daniell's appearance hit Duke Tinktar hard right then because he had no idea how beautiful Daniell could make herself look. But when you have the finest designers and makeup artists and hairdressers working directly for the emperor, they were quite capable of applying their magic to transform this lovely woman into something far greater. Even the very fashion conscious Linap knew she could not compete with the splendid beauty Daniell illuminated in the most spectacular manner.

Again, Valet Swìnlàgār approached Daniell's mother. This had been choreographed and the women had been informed this is how the welcoming would sequence.

"Madam may I escort you to the emperor?"

"Yes of course."

By now the emperor had several private meetings with Daniell's mother to discuss this whole affair and now it was simply the fulfillment of the verbal contract.

"Your excellency, may I have the honor of introducing you to Lady Daniell's mother, Madam Dominika"

"Thank you Swìnlàgār."

"Madam Dominika, it's a distinct honour to welcome you to my palace."

"Your Excellency, thank you for your wonderful hospitality."

"My pleasure and would you mind standing beside me to introduce your daughter."

"It's my pleasure, Your excellency."

Swìnlàgār then approached Daniell who was now standing by herself waiting and asked, "Lady Daniell may I please escort you to the emperor."

"Yes, thank you."

Swìnlàgār took Daniell's hand and escorted her a dozen steps to the emperor then bowed and stepped away.

"Your Excellency, may I please introduce you to my daughter, Daniell."

The emperor stepped forward and softly grabbed Daniell's hand then bent down and kissed it and said, "Daniell thank you for coming here today. Duke Tinktar loves you and wants to spend the rest of his life with you. He will be your escort for the rest of the evening. If you agree today, I will make the official proclamation that you are now part of the Royal Family deserving all the courtesy of a Royal."

"I agree," Daniell said with a smile having rehearsed this about 100 times with her mother.

The emperor turned to Duke Tinktar standing next to him and said, "Duke Tinktar, will you please take Daniell's hand and escort her with me into the palace with all our guests."

"It will be my pleasure." Duke Tinktar said as he reached out and softly took Daniell's hand and soon followed the emperor led by Valet Swìnlàgār into the mansion and through a hallway out to a lovely courtyard that was already set up for festivities.

Daniell was having the thrill of her life having this huge surprise from the man she had a crush on for quite a while. Daniell understood the level of security and surveillance that went on in Duke Tinktar's estate. *Maybe he was watching me in his suite to see what I was like?* Daniell asked herself.

Musicians were playing music in the courtyard and a dozen waiters were there to provide refreshments as there was a cocktail hour of meeting and greeting the few guests that were invited.

Brooklyn stayed close to Chester who was at the ready for Lady Linap looking quite exotic in her multicolored skin. Chester saw the beauty in the almost leopard pattern on her skin with colors not too far from the wild animal.

Chester and Linap were almost isolated from the rest of the group in their own little huddle to the side of all the activity going on with the Royals and the rest of their guests.

Daniell's mother was grinning ear to ear as her daughter just won the biggest prize possible in the empire, the future emperor. When she met secretly with the emperor, he conveyed to her he was looking forward to stepping down and letting Duke Tinktar fulfill the responsibility of emperor. The emperor was tired and wanted to step away from it all. He didn't want to die in office like all his predecessors and knew Duke Tinktar would be a good emperor.

Daniell's mother, Madam Dominika was a widow. Her husband was killed on a space transport years ago with no indication of how it happened. The spaceship disintegrated far away from any planets with no call for help.

The general consensus is the spaceship Madam Dominika husband was killed on, got hit by an unlucky fast-moving meteorite possibly of good size that demolished the thin skin spacecraft. Normally they could evade such meteorites, but if one came out of a super nova traveling above light speed there would be no reaction time and if the trajectory was on an intersect point along the spacecraft's track, they wouldn't see it coming before it was too late to avoid.

There were other possibilities such as nefarious activity including sabotage and assassination. A time delayed bomb planted could also do the trick but since they were never able to discover a debris field they could not test for pyro-techniques residue.

Dominika's husband's death would be a mystery Dominika would never solve and she knew it, so there was no point in dwelling upon it. Thanks to her husband's loose association with the emperor resulted in Daniell getting a job as an administrative assistant at an early age to have an income and help her mother as their life savings dwindled with no sources of income.

Daniell was an ideal employee and she always showed up to work dressed professionally and conducted herself in a likewise manner. Duke

Tinktar laid out the law early on with some of his male assistants that Daniell was off limits and to stay the hell away from her. She often wondered why none of the men working there ever hit on her, but out in the travels of her private life she was always receiving flirts and requests for socializing by decent men that she turned down as she was waiting for the right day and the right man to appear. Her mother also taught her on being patient and to be highly selective.

Now it appeared her patience paid off. The very moment Duke Tinktar had any notions he might want to possibly seek Daniell in more than a professional relationship, he immediately had his team put her under surveillance and deal with any possible suitors. They did a good job of scaring most of them off.

Unfortunately, just when he was about to openly pursue Daniel the last mission raised its ugly head and he had to put it on hold. However, because he talked with the emperor, he had help while he was gone to make all this come to fruition.

Duke Tinktar had never dated or taken Daniell to any social events. There was no public record of them together, but they had spent countless hours together in the office and quite often in his personal office dealing with pressing matters and scheduling people, so in reality, she had more face time with Duke Tinktar than any other person.

During some of those lonely evenings when they were wrapping up substantial workloads in Duke Tinktar's office and capped the day off with friendly conversation discussing everything possible about their culture and the events that surrounded them. Hence, they got to know each other probably better than most lovers who start to intimate relations.

Daniell and Duke Tinktar would quickly make up for the lack of dating and social events together because Daniell said magic words on the steps to the emperor's mansion. She had agreed to his announcement she was now a Royal. There will be press briefings put out tonight discussing the pending Royal Unification in the very near future. Date and time were not disclosed for security reasons, and only a few court members would be invited to the celebration.

As Chester and Linap watched all this unfold from the sidelines, they slowly evolved into their own private world and talked.

"Every time I see you, you are dressed in Royal Attire," Linap said.

"That's because you never saw me at other events," Chester responded.

"You realize Chester its unheard of to have a stranger that nobody knows seen as frequently as you in Royal attire."

"That's because I'm an official guest of Duke Tinktar."

"What is that relationship about?"

"I assist Duke Tinktar."

"How do you assist him?"

"I'm sure he would not appreciate me telegraphing my assignments, but if you want to ask him and he decides to inform you, then that will be the quickest way for you to find out."

"You wouldn't tell me?"

"I will tell you whatever Duke Tinktar permits me."

"I notice that dog is always by your side."

"There are times when he's not."

"That's rather interesting. I would think the time he wouldn't be is when you are at the emperor's Palace."

"The emperor likes Brooklyn and Brooklyn likes the emperor."

"I want to invite you to my home. What if I asked you not to bring the dog?"

"If I can't bring Brooklyn with me, then I'm sorry I will not be able to make it."

"Is that so?"

"That's so. I do not like going anywhere without him."

"Why are you so attached to that dog?"

"I've raised him since he was a pup. He's all I got in life now that means anything to me."

"You don't have a woman in your life."

"No."

"Why is that?"

"It's a long story and you wouldn't believe it so there is no point in getting into it."

"Do you know how to please a woman?"

"Yes, I'm quite good at it. If I gave you my Scorpio Stinger just one time you would be addicted."

"What do you mean by Scorpio?"

"Back where I came from people who study the stars created this theory called the zodiac. It's based on different parts of the year based on when you were born. Based on my birthday, I fall under the Sign of Scorpio."

"How does that affect things?"

The theory goes that a Scorpio acts according to certain characteristics and each symbol has an image attached to it. My symbol looks like a Scorpion. On this planet at the national zoo, you have animals called Cracatory Desconsitars. It looks just like a scorpion where I came from."

"Those things have huge stingers full of poisonous venom."

"That's correct just like a Scorpio like me and once I give you an injection of that venom, it's like a narcotic, you are addicted."

"Is that so?"

"Yes, so if you have any intentions of receiving my Scorpio Stinger, I suggest you run away from me and that way you will be safe and never have to worry about becoming addicted."

"Maybe I want to experience the addiction."

"It will be problematic for you because my dog always goes where I go. You will have to learn to like Brooklyn, or it would never be feasible."

"You give me a lot to think about Chester. I have an idea."

"And what's that?"

"When this event is over come home with me and let's explore each other a while."

"You realize Brooklyn would have to come with me?"

"If that's a condition in order for me to get to know you better I suppose I will have to learn to like Brooklyn more."

"If you become friends with Brooklyn, it would definitely improve your relationship with me."

"I've never been around a dog before, but I suppose if your Scorpio Stinger is as addictive as you warned, I will find a way to like Brooklyn."

The conversation lingered for a while until the emperor announced, "Everyone we are now going to celebrate the engagement of Daniell to Duke Tinktar with a meal to help celebrate, please follow me down to the aquarium where we may enjoy the food together."

When they walked down the ramp to the Aquarium area, they quickly discovered a fabulous setting and the musicians relocated there to perform soft dining music.

There were placards set up and Chester found himself sitting directly across from Linap. He was at the opposite end of the table across from the emperor who was sitting next to the Royal couple and Daniell's mother. Brooklyn was placed in a doggy chair next to Chester. Across from Daniell's mother, Madam Dominika, Chernega the Librarian sat wearing his splendid Regimental Commander's uniform with all his medals and ribbons.

The medal that stood out was the emperor's seal of Fidelity for Chernega's heroic actions during the Battle of Martos. Adding to the Emperor's and Chernega's attire, Duke Tinktar's dress uniform with the rank of Major General, and Chester's Royal attire, created and image at the dining table for the other guests to behold.

Official photographers came in and photographed the group while elixirs were being served. The emperor stood up after everyone had their drinks and said, "I would like to toast all of you for being here to help celebrate Duke Tinktar's special day."

"Most of you do not know it but Duke Tinktar's father is a national hero who gave his life in supreme sacrifice in wartime fighting for my father. This occurred when Duke Tinktar was a todlar. Since my empress died during childbirth and the infant also perished, I made Duke Tinktar my son. I love him as much as any father would love his son. Thus, Duke Tinktar spent all his years living with me and I raised him as my own son and view him as my son."

The emperor had everyone's focus and it was evident the emperor was slightly teared up and going through an emotional spike.

"Therefore, I'm very proud that my son Duke Tinktar selected such a beautiful bride. To you Daniell," the emperor raised his glass and took a nice long gulp, giving the future empress great respect and admiration.

Emperor Tinktar-II then turned to Duke Tinktar and said, "My son you have never let me down. You put your life at severe risk many times just like your father did for me and my father. I could never ask more from you. I'm blessed to have you and you will always be my son and the most important person in my lifetime. Thank you."

The emperor raised his glass again and said, "This is to you, my son."

The emperor could not help but notice a tear going down the side of Duke Tinktar's face. He had struck an emotional chord. It was the proudest moment in his life. Nobody in the empire would ever receive such words from the emperor himself.

Just when everyone thought all the declarations were finished, the emperor said, "Duke Tinktar has a few things he would like to say." The emperor then sat down.

Duke Tinktar then stood up and began his speech.

"Thank all of you for being here today and thank you Daniell for accepting my invitation and my proposal. I promise to always treat you with the love from my heart in every passing day."

"The reason why I can take more time off from my heavy duties as the empire security chairman is I have someone to help me to free up a lot of my time in the future. Without him being here and helping me none of this would be possible."

Linap then saw the most amazing thing in her lifetime. Duke Tinktar was looking directly at Chester, and it didn't take her but a moment to figure out Duke Tinktar was talking about Chester and so now the Royal clothes were starting to make sense.

Duke Tinktar continued with his comments and the way he focused on Chester left no doubt in anyone's mind who the person of interest was.

"This man has been thoroughly tested and has participated in special operations alongside me in very dangerous circumstances.

He too put his life at great risk in carrying out very important assignments that had a direct impact on the emperor's safety. He's a relatively unknown person and his beginnings must remain private. He's here tonight with his special dog who also has unique abilities and is part of one of the most important studies our biologists have ever undertaken."

Linap was now starting to get excited wondering if there would be disclosure. She would not be disappointed.

"I'm pleased that my friend who helps me here to witness one of the most important days in my life because without him, we would not be together enjoying the festivities."

Now the moment of truth materialized. Duke Tinktar was animated and in a heightened state.

"Chester, please stand and I wish to give you a medal of valor with the emperors seal that proves you earned the highest honors from our emperor for you participation in one of the most important special operations in a generation. Please come forward."

Chester approached Duke Tinktar who pulled the medal with a neck ribbon out of his pocket, then placed it over Chester's head and unknown to most of the people present he held out to shake Chester's hand in the earth style emblematic congratulatory gesture.

After the handshake they then bowed Drolupric style. Duke Tinktar then nodded at Chester releasing him to go back to his seat. Chester then patted Brooklyn on the head because this astonishing honor would not have come about without Brooklyn the talking dog creating the scenario that now came to fruition. Chester knew his road would be long and hard, but he also knew it guaranteed him a trip back to Earth eventually.

Linap now stared poignantly at Chester the mystery man. *So here he is a cloak and dagger man afterall. I should have spotted that right off,* Linap was thinking. *Now it was all becoming more apparent there was far more to Chester than I could have imagined.*

A cloak and dagger man closely associated with the emperor and the future emperor meant that eventually he would wield a lot of power. Linap would find a way to love Brooklyn because now it would be very advantageous for her to be a confidant of his. And she wanted to experience that addiction to Chester's Scorpio Stinger he warned her about.

Staring at Chester's medal almost had a hypnotic effect on Linap. It intensified Linap's lust for Chester and solidified her aims as she thought further about Chester. *There was no question I will pursue him like a bitch in heat.* She knew how to please men, especial special men who could give her a Scorpio Stinger addiction.

Duke Tinktar, a well-trained spy having probably more training on the subject matter than anyone in the galaxy, had a keen eye to analyze his surroundings and spot things and events that would quite often go unnoticed by neophytes. Duke Tinktar knew Linap quite well, had sex with her a few times and saw the change in her and her focus on Chester. She normally would be focused on Duke Tinktar, outright flirting and making suggestive comments. She was totally ignoring Duke Tinktar with her intense stare at Chester. Duke Tinktar was amused with Linap's emotional development.

Brooklyn was also taking it all in and knew where there is smoke and there is usually fire. Linap was acting suddenly just like "Princess Tiffany" when she was jumping on his back. *Papa might have some romance with Linap*, Brooklyn thought.

Just before the twenty four-course meal was served, the Valet Swìnlàgār approached the emperor and bent over and whispered something into his ear. The emperor smiled and turned and said, "Thank you."

The emperor stood up and said, "Ladies and gentlemen, it's a pleasure for me to announce that my declaration of Daniell is now a Royal member of the family was just released to the media and is now making headlines around the empire."

Daniell and her mother Dominika smiled at each other, and Dominika reached out and hugged Daniell who was such a lucky girl. But the fact was Daniell earned this opportunity by the way she conducted herself and Duke Tinktar knew that better than anyone.

"Here's a toast for the splendid news." The emperor once again raised his glass and consumed a good amount of content of the elixir that was improving his mood even better.

Linap meanwhile was analyzing Chester more and more and looked hard at his features and knew he was very attractive. *If he was as good with his Scorpio Stinger as he looks, I will feel in heaven,* Linap thought.

The evening moved along faster than anyone realized. The music, the twenty four course meal, the special elixirs, everything was quite enjoyable. Duke Tinktar was the happiest person present because he didn't know Daniell who dressed conservatively at work could dress up so fabulously.

Duke Tinktar knew in the future when he became emperor, the public would admire her photographs. In fact at the present time, vast beings in the empire were already observing Daniell as the emperor approved release of pictures with the exception he did not want Brooklyn photographed as it would create too much curiosity and make it harder to hide his special talents.

As the evening wound down people started leaving and Swìnlàgār started escorting them out one at a time. The first was his good friend Librarian Chernega looking sharp in his Army Regimental Commander's uniform sporting all those incredible medals of valor.

As Swìnlàgār and Chernega arrived at the Skycar that would take him and Chester and Brooklyn back to Duke Tinktar's estate, Swìnlàgār mentioned, "I was happy to see you in uniform tonight, and it was an honor."

"Thank you but, I think the real hero here tonight was Chester." Chernega replied.

"I understand he's been kind of down in the dumps since he returned." Swìnlàgār noted.

"No doubt his mission was stressful." Chernega said.

"Since I know all the details, I assure you it was. He earned that medal." Swìnlàgār said.

"I will look out for him. He earned my respect." Chernega said.

"That's good to hear because sometime in the future we may have to send the two of you on a mission together." Swìnlàgār responded.

"Why would I be chosen to go?" Chernega asked.

"We might need your military expertise for a hard target."

"You know you can count on me."

"Certainly. I'll be back in a moment with Chester."

The Valet Swìnlàgār walked back to the Aquarium and approached Chester who was standing by Linap and said, "Chester, let me escort you to the waiting Skycar."

Linap immediately chimed in and said, "Swìnlàgār, I'm going to take Chester and Brooklyn home if you don't mind."

"If that's what you wish to do, let me walk you out front, and inform Chernega that he can leave immediately."

"Thank you."

Chester waved at the people remaining and left with Duke Tinktar smiling seeing him leave with Linap. *She will help him forget a lot of the mission tonight*, Duke Tinktar thought.

Daniell and her mother Dominika would not be leaving the mansion tonight. Daniell just made a one-way trip in her life. By tomorrow it would be impossible for them to remain at their home because of the paparazzi and all the intergalactic news agencies would be hounding them. Plus, it would be far easier to protect them at the emperor's palace.

The emperor had a suite set up for Dominika and Daniell. All the items they wanted to have with them were already shipped to the palace during the day, so they had no need to return home any time soon. They would spend a while longer with Duke Tinktar and the emperor, then Duke Tinktar would return to his estate. The new royal couple would be back together tomorrow as they would be taken to a few landmarks for publicity. The royal couple would not show up preannounced so only the tourists already there would get to see the royals and appreciate their presence. They would then be gone before the crowds showed up.

Right after the Skycar taking the librarian Chernega back to Duke Tinktar's estate, Linap's Sky Limo pulled up in front of the emperor's mansion.

Linap led Chester and Brooklyn into the Sky Limo and moments later it took off heading to Linap's mansion. A short distance behind was Chester's security detachment that would not let him out of their sight.

Ten minutes later the Sky Limo came down in a sparsely populated area to a majestic mansion that few people in the empire could afford.

Linap had everything she wanted out of life except for a special man. *Perhaps Chester might become that man?* Linap wondered.

The Sky Limo landed in the large circular driveway that was nearly as elegant as the emperor's mansion.

Linap's mansion contained everything a woman could possibly ever want from a private gym with staff workout instructor, swimming pool, something like a tennis court, beautiful gardens, a large aviary with over 200 birds, a greenhouse to grow her elaborate flowers, and a conservatory botanical garden connected to the mansion Linap could walk directly in from a door from her mansion and never be exposed to the weather. The conservatory botanical gardens, also enclosed in a green house, had over fifty thousand types of flowers and plants and miniature trees. On her staff of numerous employees, Linap had the best horticulturalist in Tymasoara. Her mansion had lavished décor and the artwork abounded was utterly priceless.

When Chester entered Linap's mansion he thought he had stepped into a fairytale and didn't know what to make of it all. The maid was there to greet them and Linap said, "Brianna, this is Chester and his dog Brooklyn."

Brianna was completely shocked because normally Linap would never allow a pet or animal into the mansion. The fact Brookland was here was interesting.

"Pleased to meet you," Brianna said.

"Your job is to keep Brooklyn occupied and take care of his needs," Linap instructed Brianna.

"My pleasure, I love dogs." Brianna said.

"When he needs to go, he will walk to the door. Just let him outside and he will go find a tree then come back." Chester said.

"Alright." Brianna said.

Linap asked, "Chester would you like to see my aviary? I have a lot of birds."

"Sure, I love birds and so does Brooklyn."

Linap led Chester through the mansion and out a rear door then a walk to another building with a screen for most of the roof. They walked through double doors that prevented birds from escaping and into the vast open area under the screened roof that had a dozen trees and numerous plants. The birds were colorful and amazing. Chester could see several hundred birds and they had plenty of space as to not crowd each other. The combined noise of the birds created a cacophony that could be both pleasant or harsh depending on one's mood.

The birds recognized Linap because they have facial recognition. They were excited by her presence because when she arrived, she often went over to storage locker and got treats out for them. The birds had never seen a dog before, so Brooklyn was a novelty to them they observed.

Just like they expected, Linap walked over to a cabinet mounted against the wall and opened it and grabbed one of the bags full of bird food then walked over to where a series of stands were located that had trays, she poured the bird food into. The Linap then crumpled the sack and dropped it into a small trash container next to the feeding stands where the caretakers would discard later.

Several hundred birds converged on the feeding trays atop the stands all at once. Soon there was no space available, and the birds were vying for position. The birds ate up the food real fast and quickly thinned out. Several minutes only a few birds remained looking and pecking at any possible remaining food.

"Let me show you some more," Linap said.

Linap led Chester and Brooklyn out of the aviary and walked into the conservatory botanical garden green house. There Chester saw the most beautiful flowers and plants.

"Are all these plants native to this planet?"

"No, more than half are imported and had to go through careful agriculture screening and examining. All the dirt on the roots had to be cleaned off and deposited into a recycler that heats it up high enough to kill any bacteria or germs."

"That would seem to me to be very stressful to the plants."

"It is, only 10% of them survive this transplant method."

Linap then showed them around some more of the property, then back into the mansion. She asked Chester, "Would you like something to drink and does Brooklyn need anything?"

Brooklyn was trained to answer questions with simple head movements when they were not alone.

"Brooklyn do you anything to drink?" Chester asked.

Brooklyn shook his head, which caught Linap's attention real fast.

"He understood your question," Linap said with great astonishment.

"Yes, he understands everything I say to him in two languages."

"Do you think he would understand me if I asked him a question?"

"Sure, give it a try."

"Brooklyn, do you like me?"

Brooklyn shook his head up and down and Linap giggled immediately and said, "That's so cute."

She then asked Chester "What would you prefer to drink?"

"Surprise me, give me something you like to drink."

Linap had an evil grin on her face and said, "I'll give you my favorite drink."

She then walked over to a bar on the side of the room and grabbed two clean glasses that were hung just like a regular bar for ease of use, upside down so any moisture from washing would drop down via gravity.

She pulled a container out of a refrigerator unit built into the bar with a pink liquid in it and poured each glass two thirds full and went back to the sofa Chester was sitting down and handed him one of the glasses.

"Cheers!" Linap said smiling, feeling happier by the moment because Chester was more than she could bargain for.

After they took a sip, Linap asked, "What happened to the medal Duke Tinktar gave you that you were wearing?"

"I took it off and put it in my pocket," Didn't think I needed to show it anymore.

They sat there drinking the pink elixir when Chester easily recalled the taste. Linap was serving him Zvèzdnàyà Rōzā which gave away her motives. After having sexual relations with pink and green skin women, Chester was wondering what it would feel like with a multi-colored skin woman who's exterior could match a Cheeta or a Leopard.

With half their drinks finished, Linap said, "Let me refill your glass and then I want to change into something more comfortable."

After refilling the two glasses, Linap left for a few minutes then came back wearing some luxurious lingerie that revealed most of her body. She also was not wearing any undergarments and thus Chester could see most of her attributes without much imagination required. She then sat down on the sofa with her bare feet up on it facing Chester and they continued conversing.

"What does Brooklyn like to do?"

"To be honest he would watch holographic videos all day long if I let him."

"What does he like watching?"

"He likes shows about animal life, travel shows, ocean creatures, nature."

Linap looked at Brooklyn and asked, "Brooklyn would you like to watch some holographic video?"

Brooklyn nodded his head up and down in the affirmative. Linap smiled and said in a normal voice, "Brianna will you come here please."

Artificial Intelligence knew the room where Linap currently was at and interpreted the request and notified Brianna to proceed to the Bar room because Linap requests her presence.

Briana responded, "I'm on my way."

Artificial Intelligence in a nice soft voice said, "Brianna is on the way."

Moments later Briana entered the room and Linap said, "Would you please show Brooklyn to the entertainment room so he can watch some holographic video. He likes nature videos with animals, ocean life, and travel."

"I know just the holographic entertainment that shows those kinds of videos specially for children and young adults."

"Perfect."

Chester said, "Brooklyn follow Briana to the entertainment room so you can watch videos, I will be with you after a while."

Brooklyn shook his head up and down that startled Briana causing her a huge smile and she said, "Okay Brooklyn this way." Briana walked in the direction towards the entertainment room that was not far from the bar room with Brooklyn with his tail wagging showing he was happy he would get to watch some animal videos.

Now that Chester and Linap were alone sipping on the Zvèzdnàyà Rōzā, the combination of Linap's beauty and the elixir was already causing Chester to feel a strangeness develop in his libido.

Linap pulled her gown back a little on purpose and the little that was previously blocking the view to her womanhood was now fully exposed. It was unlike anything Chester had seen in his lifetime. The multi-colored skin also transitioned into multi-colored pubis that had quite a mound on it.

Linap knew Chester was infatuated with her and also knew the combination of the Zvèzdnàyà Rōzā and the image he now saw would start to help create the transcendence to a mental state she wanted Chester to reach. She wanted to ask Chester if he wanted to touch her, but she realized that would be far too direct and she would toy with him a little while longer, then move in on him like a bitch in heat.

Linap was glad that Chester had finished his drink and she knew he was by now jacked up with the psychoactive drugs in the Zvèzdnàyà Rōzā that would make him hornier than a three *peckered* Billy goat. Linap stood up, walked over to Chester and grabbed his empty glass and refilled in and brought it back to him and sat it down on the coffee table in front of the sofa. She then moved closer to Chester and soon straddled him and kissed him most provocatively. "I like you Chester, I think I want you," Linap then said and continued to kiss Chester giving him the phenomenal taste of her mouth that was very pleasing to Chester. Her breath, her perfume, everything smells profoundly delightful.

Chester wasn't naïve and surmised what would happen next. Linap reached down and felt Chester's manliness and knew he was now rock hard thanks to the drugs in his drink. While kissing him she undid his trousers and slid them down a bit then moved her womanhood directly over him and guided his Scorpio Stinger inside her and she started the rhythmic actions that accentuated the strange sensation Chester now felt. Linap had extremely strong vaginal muscles. She could squeeze a man real hard and as she was oscillating on top of Chester, she sent cauldrons of pleasure ensembles to Chester. She was also feeling the gratification coming on as her orgasms were now started to make her even more alive and frisky.

Linap pulled back from the kiss and slid the top of her exquisite lingerie away from her body then positioned one of her nipples on Chester's mouth which he eagerly consumed and began sucking in earnest adding to the orgasmic pleasure that Linap now experienced.

Linap then squeezed and jerked on Chester with great strength as she wanted the venom from his Scorpio Stinger. Chester soon had that gigantic release like he never expected and gushed that Scorpio Venom inside Linap's womanhood. Just like Chester warned her, the feeling of that Scorpio venom was very addictive as it created pleasure like Linap never felt before. The chemical reaction from a different living species inside her vagina was triggering multiple cascades of orgasmic ensembles. It was a sensation that Linap never felt before. *Was she falling in love with Chester? Was love causing this? She had a lot to think about* and then suddenly she started crying.

Linap's physical exertion died down with the crying and Chester was fully gratified and had to ask, "Why are you crying?"

Linap responded in a way that seemed like she was forcing the words out. "I'm crying because I think I felt love."

Linap then threw her arms around Chester and placed her body over his with her face and head on the side of his. Chester held Linap and slowly tapped her on the back as she continued to cry for several minutes then whimpered for a few more. Finally, her composure came back, and she bent back up and said, "Chester I feel a lot of your Scorpio Venom inside me I need to go get cleaned up. Would you like to take a bath with me?"

"Sure."

Linap dismounted Chester and stood up and held a hand out for him. Chester stood up and pulled his trousers back up and dutifully followed Linap to her bathroom and they took off their clothes and entered the bath that started filling as soon as artificial intelligence knew Linap was going to take a bath with her friend.

Linap and Chester were soon in the bath now filling with bubbles because the bath system automatically put the bubble bath in that Linap selected for her preference that made her feel good and smell nicely. Chester sat at the side of the huge bath and Linap guided her body into Chester where her back was against his chest. She grabbed his arms and put them around her and took his hands and placed them on her breasts as she wanted to be fondled.

The bath felt marvelous. The two soaked there for a long time and Linap soon felt clean, but she wanted to keep some of that Scorpio Venom inside her as it made her feel special to have made love with some kind of secret agent or spy who worked directly for Duke Tinktar.

Soon they were out of the tub and in the body, blow drying machine that kept them warm and dried them at the same time with super dry air. The drying cycle was remarkably quick and as soon as they stepped out of the drying machine one of Linap's maids was there handing each a bathrobe and slippers to put on. The clothes Chester had taken off were now hung up in a guest closet after dry cleaning.

Chester didn't know it yet, but he had just made love to the richest woman in the empire. His life was now irrevocably changed as his addictive Scorpio Venom was in fact as addictive as he warned, mainly because of the chemical reaction inside Linap had caused her those unusual physical response flooding her brain as the hypothalamus was producing significant levels of oxytocin and her brain produced dopamine followed by elevated levels of prolactin and then later serotonin after her orgasms.

Linap a very intelligent woman who knows how to make tremendous gains on investments and business deals never thought she would meet her match. In the past couple of years, she felt condescending towards most men whom she felt were inferior. But now Chester walks into her life and flips her world upside down. And the control he has over the dog Brooklyn significantly amazed her.

"Chester, I want you to spend the night with me and hold me in your arms."

"I suppose I could do that, but I want Brooklyn in the room sleeping and to be near me."

"Where would he sleep?"

Chester looked around and saw a sofa and said, "he could sleep on the sofa over there."

"That will probably work," Linap said then she said, "Brianna, please bring Brooklyn to my bedroom."

Moments later Brianna arrived with Brooklyn and Linap explained the situation.

"Chester will be spending the night with me. I want you to put a blanket on the sofa for Brooklyn to sleep on."

"Give me one minute Madam Linap." Brianna said then left the room and came back in a moment with a nice thick blanket and laid it out on the sofa."

"Brooklyn, do you need to use the bathroom?" Chester asked. Brooklyn shook his head no.

"Alright Brooklyn, please get up on the sofa to go to sleep now. We are going to bed. Do you need help getting up there?"

Brooklyn moved his head up and down so Chester walked over to the sofa and Brooklyn followed him. When they got close, Chester picked up Brooklyn and placed him on the blanket on the sofa. Brooklyn then laid down like a well-disciplined dog.

Linap looked at Brianna who was smiling because of these radical changes in Linap. The thought a dog would be sleeping in Linap's bedroom tonight utterly shocked Brianna. *Chester must be one heck of a guy to get Linap to do this, Briana thought.*

"Alright, Brianna, that will be all for now, we are going to sleep."

"Yes madam. Good night."

Brianna left the bedroom and closed the door behind her. Linap took her bathrobe off and laid it on a nearby chair and climbed in bed and said, Chester please come here now."

Chester followed Linap's actions and took off his bathrobe and laid it on the same chair and crawled in the King Size bed.

Artificial Intelligence observing the room evaluated it was time to turn down the lights and slowly dimmed them as Linap's back was how against Chester's chest feeling invigorated and her brain was now flooded with serotonin helping her to promptly fall to sleep.

Chester could not quite sleep. His nightmarish experience back at the Hog Farm still grated on his nerves. He tried to silently meditate to get the demons out of his head, but it was no use. He had elevated levels of serotonin in his brain from his orgasm, but that wasn't overcoming the mental anguish perpetuated by the images of him slicing General Crontyke just before they threw him to the hogs that quickly went on a feeding frenzy. General Crontyke was spared the pain and suffering by landing on his head. Had Chester seen the previous man Duke Tinktar dropped into the hog farm and watched him jerk around as the saber tooth hogs bit into him, his nightmares would be ten times as worse than what they were.

Chester knew the only thing he could do was just to lay there and hope that he would accidentally fall asleep somehow.

Chester had no way of knowing but it was an hour or so later his awakened state slowly drifted into the dream world. Once he arrived at the dream world he was in a better position because he learned he could steer his dreams away from unpleasantness.

Brooklyn watched Papa with the woman and that made him think about "Princess Tiffany." It was those splendid thoughts of Princess Tiffany that allowed Brooklyn to drift into his slumber.

Around midnight a person from Chester's security detachment called Linap's home. Artificial Intelligence received the phone call. The security man said he was on Duke Tinktar's staff, and they wanted to know, "When is Chester going to return to Duke Tinktar's estate tonight?"

Artificial Intelligence received the special seal that only came from the government for inquiries knew this was a legitimate call and a legitimate request. Artificial Intelligence answered the question in the most factually that it could since Madam Linap had not given special instructions responded. "Chester and Brooklyn have been invited to spend the night and are already sleeping."

"In the morning we will bring Chester a change of clothes. We do not want him to leave Madam Linap's home wearing the official Royal Attire."

"I will make sure Chester is duly informed when he wakes up."

"Thank you. Call this number back when he wakes up and we will deliver the clothes at that time. If he wants a hair designer before he leaves Madam Linap's home, let us know."

"I certainly will."

"Thank you."

The communication ended.

Planning for the Royal Unification and the next mission were going on simultaneously. Duke Tinktar would be on his honeymoon with Daniell getting public awareness as they suddenly popped in unexpectedly at places not known to be congested. That would give him plausible deniability in the event the next operation blew up in their faces. Plus being on Tymasoara would give him plausible deniability.

The next mission would be Chester and retired Army Regimental Commander, now ostensibly Librarian, Chernega, sent to deal with a foreign government involved with General Crontyke. Chernega was being sent because it was going to be a paramilitary operation. The military do not take orders from Civilians and if they knew Chester was an alien that would be an even harder pill to swallow. But Chester had to go because he would be the ultimate authority reporting directly to Duke Tinktar.

Chester's Alien origination was now one of the most guarded secrets. Only Duke Tinktar's staff knew about Chester and Brooklyn, and they all knew the consequences of leaking that information. To make sure they knew the consequences previously about leaking long before Chester was a known entity, Duke Tinktar systematically made sure his staff knew what happens at the Hog farm.

Chester woke up in the morning and needed to drain his lizard and in the process woke up Linap. She figured real fast what Chester was doing as he went in the bathroom, and she could hear his fire hose letting it rip.

Linap was very pleased that morning because she had developed feelings for Chester in ways, she never dreamed were possible.

When artificial intelligence saw movement in the room when Linap walked towards the chair to grab her bathrobe, the AI briefed her on Chester's instructions from his security staff and requested, "May I have permission to contact the number to schedule the pickup of the Royal clothes and have them deliver of his change in garments to wear?"

"Yes, and ask Brianna, to come to my bedroom to pick up the clothes and stage them by the entrance to give them to the couriers when they arrive."

"Madam Linap, Brianna has been notified."

By the time Chester came out of the bathroom, his Royal clothes were gone and all he had to wear for the time being was his bathrobe. Linap then went to the bathroom and even though the door was shut she could hear a conversation in the other room.

"Papa, I need to go outside and do my doggy doodle," Brooklyn said as he had been trained to say and thought it was alright to talk since nobody else was in the room."

"Sure, I can take you I at least have this bath robe to wear. Do you need help getting down?"

"No, I can get down by myself."

Chester and Brooklyn left the bedroom and went to the back door of the home opening to the park like yard with lots of trees and landscaping including bushes and flowers and other types of plants.

It was easy for Brooklyn to find a nearby tree and when he smelled it, there were no traces of a dog smell that disappointed him.

Meanwhile, Linap who was the consummate voyeur asked artificial intelligence while she was sitting on the toilet doing her morning business, "Did you record Chester's conversation a few minutes ago."

"Madam Linap, we always record what goes on in your bedroom and bathroom and save it for your view for 24 hours."

"Could you playback the conversation holograph for me?"

"Yes, Madam Linap, one moment while we process the request."

In a few minutes Madam Linap was utterly astonished, Brooklyn was a Talking Dog! In some ways she felt fear and in other ways she felt liberated but intrigued. *How could this dog possibly talk?*

This was such a phenomenally huge event in Linap's time. She knew she was falling in love with Chester, the owner of a talking dog. Now she knew why Chester never left Brooklyn for a minute. Something this precious had to be protected at all costs. She now surmised why the two were living with Duke Tinktar who was protecting them both but at the same time Chester had done some clandestine work for Duke Tinktar. The morning was turning out to be one of the greatest days of Linap's lifetime.

Linap needed to confront Chester and find out why all the secrecy surrounding Brooklyn. Chester could be one of the richest men in the Drolupric Empire simply by doing entertainment with a talking dog. All the venues across the empire would sell out for such an event. And what if Brooklyn could sing? The results would be incredible with *a singing talking dog!*

Linap knew the two were outdoors so that Brooklyn could take care of his business on a tree or in the grass. Ground keepers were in site of the two and were ready to clean up anything

Brooklyn left behind. Brooklyn took care of his business but was enjoying the outdoors and observed the Aviary not far from where they were standing.

"Papa, will we go feed the birds today?"

"I'm not sure, Duke Tinktar is very busy now in preparations for his unification with Daniell."

"Perhaps you can ask someone to take us there?"

"I could use a good workout and help clear my mind a bit. I'll ask."

"Thanks Papa."

"Are you ready to go back inside, I need to change my clothes."

"I'm ready."

Chester walked back to the house and as soon as he stepped inside, Brianna said, "Chester, you had a change of clothes delivered. After you are dressed and ready, your Skycar driver will be here to pick you up."

"Thank you. Where do I change?"

"In the room to the left, your change of clothes, are located in there."

"Thank you. What about the clothes I wore last night?"

"They have already been sent back to Duke Tinktar's estate."

"Alright, thanks."

Chester went into the room which appeared to be a spare bedroom for guests. He found his garments staged on a clothing rack and quickly changed.

Chester then left the room and walked back into the large open main assembly room with enough chairs and sofas to accommodate probably 30 people. In the middle of the room was Linap standing beside Brianna all dressed and looking very pleasant.

"I understand someone will be here soon to pick you up?" Linap asked.

"Yes, that's right."

"I was hoping we could spend some time together this morning perhaps had breakfast together," Linap said.

"We'll plan that and do that soon," Chester responded.

Linap knew she didn't want Chester to leave but when the Royals stated they are going to pick up someone like Chester, she knew better than to get in their way. She probably upset them by keeping Chester and Brooklyn overnight now that she was aware of their little secret. She would not be able to have that discussion today, because of Chester's sudden departure, but she would confront him at a later date. She then looked at the innocent looking Brooklyn and thought, wow, *there is a lot more to you than I realized.*

Artificial Intelligence received a communication that Chester's ride was out front in the circular driveway, and it then relayed the information, "Chester your transportation has arrived and is out front of the building."

"Thanks."

Linap walked up to Chester in the most somber fashion having been emotionally charged over this overnight miracle and put her arms around him and gave him a powerful hug sending the message she had feelings for him. Chester was cognizant of the fact Brianna was standing near them, but he didn't care. He truly liked Linap so as her face was pointing at him he reached over and kissed her on the lips in a gentle and deliberate fashion.

That kiss sent electricity through Linap because she knew it was genuine and it pleased her to know Chester had some real feelings for her. She would like to know how deep those feelings went because she would love to throw caution to the wind and fully envelop her love to this splendid man who seemed to captivate her like no other.

After the kiss she said, "Just one moment please." Then she bent down on one knee next to Brooklyn and said, "I'm very happy you spent the night with me. I really like you."

Brooklyn wanted to respond but he knew he couldn't speak but he did the next best thing and raised his head up and down to signal "yes."

Linap then patted Brooklyn and smiled and said, "I hope I get to see you again soon."

Brooklyn copied his earlier movements and moved his head up and down to signal "yes," again.

Brianna walked over to the door and opened it and stood to the side. As Chester and Brooklyn walked past her, Brianna bowed and held her bow until they were several steps out of the home and headed the short distance to the Skycar. Just as Chester arrived at the Skycar he turned and looked back and waved at Linap standing in the doorway. Linap wasn't familiar with that tradition, but she copied his actions thinking it was part of his culture, and now figured he probably came from outside the empire from a distant planet with the dog.

Chester was Linap's mystery man and lover and she would relish the day knowing she had some of his Scorpio Stinger.

The Skycar took little time to reach Duke Tinktar's estate and they immediately went into their suite waiting to hear what the plans for the day were.

Soon Aizere came in the room and asked, "Would you like to have breakfast now?"

"We would like to go to the workout camp and have breakfast there like we usually do, and I want to work out this morning."

"Alright, let me go get that activity started."

"While Aizere was gone, Brooklyn asked, "Papa do you like Linap?"

"Brooklyn, I like her, I think she and I will become good friends."

"Papa, I like her too. I want to be her friend also."

"Brooklyn, I'm sure she would like that."

Moments later Aizere returned carrying workout clothing and shoes for Chester and said, "It's all planned now to take you to Duke Tinktar's workout area. As soon as you get changed, you will be taken there."

"Thank you," Chester responded.

No sooner than Chester had changed clothes and was ready to depart, artificial intelligence announced, "Chester, Librarian Chernega is here to see you."

"Please invite Chernega in."

Soon Chernega walked into the room wearing workout clothes.

"Chester I will be working out with you this week since Duke Tinktar will be busy."

"Great, looking forward to working out with you Chernega."

"Our ride is out front, shall we go?"

"Sure, lead the way."

Chernega knew the routine having observed all of Chester's training videos and knew there was bird food, dog food, and water staged in the Skycar.

The three walked to the front and got into the Skycar that took off immediately to the training camp. They were soon there doing the morning ritual and the birds were a lot more friendly now and didn't show the least bit of fear and ate their food right beside Brooklyn who was hungry and enjoyed his souped-up dogfood. *If the dog food back on Earth tasted this good I would have been happy to eat it*, Brooklyn thought.

Chester and the Librarian Chernega each had their morning energy drinks spiked with range extenders. The men knew that Chernega was quite a bit older and most of them present had never seen him work out before. What they didn't know is Chernega often ran the trail and up the hill where Brooklyn often fed the squirrels. Chernega was in fact in great physical shape and knew he had a dual role of Librarian and Regimental Commander and if conditions prevailed, he would be sent into battle and therefore made sure he would be physically ready for it should the situation develop.

First thing the two men did after drinking their morning meal and energy formula they started their run along a mile long oval that went around a vast parklike open area. They ran at a good pace and Chernega made sure to run in perfect formation with Chester.

As they ran, Chester and Chernega chatted about a variety of matters. Chernega knew everything about Chester since it was his responsibility to analyze all his videos and make reports directly to Duke Tinktar. Chernega knew there was much more to Chester than the staff or anyone else knew. He knew all about Doctor Boonkar and how after Royal Unification, Chester would deal with her.

Chernega reviewed the secret videos of Chester's activities at the Planet Barcejena and later at the hog farm on Zeta Bantor dealing with the traitor General Crontyke. He knew there was an extraordinary aspect of Chester that only a military mind would truly understand. Chester didn't have a bone in this fight. He had no moral obligation or patriotic connection to this situation at Planet Barcejena.

As a military historian and vastly read on the subject matter, Chester was like a mercenary. A man for hire. Unlike mercenaries who only worked under contract for vast sums of credit. Chester had never asked for anything in return, no salary, no nothing. He had no personal bank accounts or personal funds. He had absolutely no history any researcher could find because it did not exist.

Chester was in fact the perfect spook with no connections to anyone. That made him ideal for what he was doing. But there had to be *a reason behind why Chester was performing in an exemplary manner, even better than the well trained Drolupric Empire Special Forces Personnel. What is it?*

The trainers watched the two men keeping pace with each other do five laps then stopped fully drenched with sweat. Their elapsed time was 26 minutes, better than almost anyone they trained. The trainers were in awe that such an older guy like Chernega could run like that.

The two men now had their second drink. The purpose was to hydrate them and help them recover quickly from the run before they started the stretching exercises and physical training prior to the martial arts proficiency training. The two men knew what would be taught today, they would conduct the movements in high speed against well-padded men to build the muscle memory of the punches, kicks, and blocks.

Without the pads the men involved in the training would receive serious life-threatening blows. Two areas were very well padded, the solar plex and the groin areas. They also wore a helmet with a shield and neck brace to protect them from kicks and punches to the head.

Even with all the padding and protection, some of the kicks, punches and blocks still hurt. But the pain killers would quickly take care of that. The trainers that were targets during the training exercises would have a couple days off and others would take turns to facilitate full speed and strength martial arts training.

Chernega had watched Chester on live video doing what he was doing today, but unless you are physically close to hear the snap of the arms and the legs when they unfurled to majestic attacks you don't appreciate how substantial it is like when you are a few feet away with a closeup view of sound and vision.

This workout was a confidence builder for Chernega who would be going with Chester on the next mission. They would have to depend on each other and the last thing in the world Chernega wanted was to work with a chickenshit, many of which he experienced in the past despite being in a force that was expected to show the esprit de corps.

Duke Tinktar was a brilliant man who figured this all out. He knew by doing this type of training and with Chernega working directly with Chester, he would grow more comfortable with him carrying out whatever it took.

This was going to be one of the most important clandestine missions in a very long time. After the fact they would send word to the enemy if they continued to get involved in Drolupric Empire affairs or participate in Coups to expect more of this and possibly a war. It's also safe to say this ruthless Dictator they attacked would not want a direct war with the Drolupric Empire because even though he could do a lot of damage to the Drolupric, he ran the risk of having a lot of his own cities laid to ruin. A hot war with the Drolupric Empire was in fact mutually assured destruction (MAD).

By lunch time, the two men were on the verge of exhaustion. Training was then terminated because the trainers knew that you would reach a point where there was no value added by continuing as the body needed time to heal.

Chernega, Chester, and Brooklyn were back in the Skycar and soon arrived at Duke Tinktar's estate ready for a bath and in the case of Chester a massage was in order.

Brooklyn got bathed at the same time as Chester soaking his sore muscles in the wonderful bath. Aida was soon there to wash Chester's hair and she appeared not to be very happy. Chester assumed she had her designs on Duke Tinktar and since the Empire now knew Daniell was the chosen one, Aida was finished in that relationship. She would be crying in her beers.

The fact Aida didn't try to initiate sex relieved Chester since he had shot all his bullets the night before. Chester was dried off and soon laying on the massage table with Brooklyn watching setting up on his rear in his bed.

Brooklyn carefully observed the message that Chester received and was learning much about how it was done. Jazmin worked Chester really well and because of their last encounter, Jazmin didn't do any suggestive activity, Chester was glad as all he wanted to do was to chill out.

After the message and a second bath to clean off the message oils, Chester was dressed again in Royal Clothes and asked, "Why am I being dressed up?"

"You have special visitors today," Aizere responded.

"Who are the visitors?"

"One of them is Brooklyn's friend."

That's all Chester needed to hear. It was going to be another day for "Princess Tiffany."

The emperor wanted to spend some time with Brooklyn and came up with the idea to invite them and Margrét Hansen over for lunch.

A nice spread was set up by the aquarium and soon Chester and Brooklyn were there long before the other guests were scheduled to arrive allowing the emperor to spend time talking with Brooklyn. Chester and Brooklyn were led down to the aquarium area and the emperor was standing by the large fish tank observing multiple schools of fish gliding aimlessly in front of the emperor who turned towards the approaching group when he Valet Swìnlàgār announced, "Your excellency, your guests Chester and Brooklyn are here to see you."

"Thank you. Swìnlàgār"

"Hello Chester and Brooklyn."

Chester walked up to a few feet away from the emperor and bowed and said, "Thank you, Your Excellency for inviting us over."

"You are most welcome."

"How are you doing today, Brooklyn?"

"Your Excellency, I'm doing quite well and am delighted to see you and also I was informed I would get to visit with Princess Tiffany today."

"That's correct, your friend will be here in a while. I know how you like to feed squirrels birds."

"Your Excellency, yes I like to feed them."

"Would you like to see the fish be fed?"

"Yes, I would like to watch that."

The emperor nodded at Valet Swìnlàgār who then turned and left the room. Moments later from afar they watched a scuba diver swim up to the thick glass window carrying a weighted bag. The diver had a mouthpiece and an underwater communicator that sent his voice through the water to nearby hydrophone sensors that could pick it up with great fidelity. They also had a sound system in the water where transducers produced nice soft music for the fish that had now started playing. Just like magic a lot of fish approached the diver who now reached into his waited pouch and grabbed some content and held it out. Fish swam up to him and ate the food out of his hand. He then continued repeating those actions until all the food was gone, but it was obvious that only a small amount of the fish got something to eat.

"Brooklyn, would you like to feed the fish?"

"Your excellency, I would like to feed the fish, but I do not know how I could do it."

"Come with me and I will show you how."

The emperor led Chester and Brooklyn around to the side of the large aquarium to a ramp and walked up the ramp and were suddenly on the side of the very large pool. He then walked around the side of the pool to directly above where the diver swam and they could see all the bubbles come to the surface from his breathing. There was a bucket set up full of food for the fish. The diver looked up at the emperor who waved at him and the diver swam away, over to a ladder to get out of the aquarium pool.

The emperor said, "Brooklyn, with this machine you can feed the fish. That black thing down beside the bucket is a foot petal actuator. All you have to do is step on it and the mechanism will dump the food in the water for the fish. Go ahead and put one of your feet on the black foot petal."

Brooklyn followed the instructions and soon the bucket was tilted and dumped into the aquarium tank and the water started swirling as a multitude of fish went after the food.

They watched the incredible movement of the fish below in an eating frenzy, but the emperor knew they needed more and the bucket was going to be refilled for the next feeding in a few minutes. "Let's go back down below and watch the fish eat when the diver dumps another bucket of food in the water for them."

Soon the emperor, Brooklyn, and Chester were standing beside the aquarium and the diver dumped a bucket full of food from almost directly above them to the side of the aquarium and the food quickly started sinking towards the bottom. A flurry of activity now happened as large numbers of fish swam in and grabbed food and swam off. Fish that had been far off in the aquarium and almost out of site were now next to the thick glass window and everyone could see fish they hadn't noticed before.

After several more buckets of fish, the activity slowly died down as feeding was complete.

There was about another fifteen minutes before "Princess Tiffany" was scheduled to arrive, and the emperor engaged Brooklyn in more conversation.

"What all did you do yesterday, Brooklyn?"

"We fed the squirrels, then came here for the party, and afterwards, went to Madam Linap's home."

"What did you do at Madam Linap's home?"

"I mostly watched holographic videos with Brianna."

"What was your Papa doing?"

"He was spending time with Madam Linap."

"Do you like Madam Linap?"

"Yes, she's very nice to me and said she likes me. She's not like, the bitch Abagail who tried to kill me once."

"How did she do that?"

"She chased me with a knife and was going to stab me."

"Why did she do that?"

"She found out I could talk and I was going to tell Papa I saw her getting boinked by a man while Papa was gone on a trip."

The emperor wished he had not asked that question but was relieved to have that conversation interrupted by the Valet Swìnlàgār who announced, Margrét Hansen and Princess Tiffany are arriving, I will escort them here momentarily.

The emperor could see Brooklyn was suddenly wagging his tail. This would be a joyous activity.

Moments later the Valet Swìnlàgār escorted Margrét Hansen and "Princess Tiffany" into the room and said, "Your Excellency, may I present the lovely Margrét Hansen and her precious Princess Tiffany."

The emperor smiled and bowed and said, "Margrét thank you for coming here today, and thank you for bringing Princess Tiffany." "Princess Tiffany was not on a leash and she took off and ran up to Brooklyn, there was some doggy sniffs and exchanges and Margrét Hansen knew Princess Tiffany showed signs of happiness waging her small tail and totally enclosing Brooklyn into her sphere. She surprised her owner Margrét Hansen when she licked the side of Brooklyn's head.

They stood and talked about trivial matters while waiters gave them glasses of elixirs to enjoy and over by the fish tank put two water bowls for the two dogs. The elixir seemed to loosen Margrét Hansen's lips who displayed a happy demure and talked freely and friendly which the emperor enjoyed for a while and then the Valet Swìnlàgār entered the room and announced, would everyone please have a seat so the waiters can serve you. There were two doggy chairs set up for Brooklyn and "Princess Tiffany" with food and water and the two were quickly helped into their chairs by Chester and Valet Swìnlàgār.

The two doggy chairs were next to each other a few feet away from the table and the two dogs seemed to enjoy this situation since they were sitting next to each other.

Since there were no other guests present, Margrét and Chester sat next to the emperor. It was a delightful meal and they engaged in a friendly conversation while they ate, with the emperor quite savvy as to not direct the conversation into any areas that could create any anxiety.

The emperor's intelligence bureau knew all about Margaret's banker husband Gandolph Hansen. They also knew Margrét and Linap did not get along because of Margaret's husband Gandolph Hansen's one-time affair with Linap. The emperor knew that Margrét was probably expecting an invitation to the upcoming Unification with Duke Tinktar and Daniell. He could only invite one of them and he planned to ask Chester which one he preferred and based on reports that Chester spent the night with Linap, it was probably a foregone conclusion Chester would pick Linap to be his companion for the celebration.

It might also be wise not to bring Margrét unless she was with her banker husband as to avoid the appearance of a scandal if she was seen as Chester's companion. But the emperor would grace Margrét this afternoon so she would not feel slighted to not have the invitation.

After the meal the emperor asked if Chester and Margrét would like to go for a walk, they all agreed and the three went out into the park-like surroundings with the two dogs that spent some time running, and chasing each other and having a great time.

The emperor felt good to be with Chester and he knew Chester would soon leave after the Unification with the retired Army Regimental Commander turned Librarian, Chernega on a paramilitary operation that if it went wrong would cost Chester his life. It felt good to be around real heroes and Chester had already proved that several times. The emperor was aware Chester had never asked to be paid or anything, but he knew there was one thing Chester wanted, to eventually go home to Earth. Before he stepped down as emperor, he would ask Duke Tinktar as a special favor to him to return Chester before he grew too old. By then Duke Tinktar could make other arrangements so as to not rely on Chester any further.

However, the Emperor was not naïve and realized based on intel reports and they had a means to hack Linap's security system, the two had become lovers. He also knew that after Chester left Linap's home she confided in Brianna that she felt some emotional ties to Chester. Maybe he might change and just decide to stay with Linap. Afterall she could make his life far more pleasant than what he would experience back on Earth.

~~~~~~

The days continued as typical with the morning workouts and visiting the squirrels in the afternoon. Brooklyn had one more visit with Princess Tiffany before the Grand Unification Ceremony.

Duke Tinktar knew vividly how much Chester's presence resulted in this Unification taking place at this time and when he informed the emperor he wanted Chester with Brooklyn as guests, the emperor did not think that was a bad idea. People would be shocked, but the emperor would put out a cover story it was Duke Tinktar's favorite dog which turned out to be the case.

The gala affair soon happened. Chester was dressed in Royal Attire, and Brooklyn had a royal cover placed over his fancy dog collar apparatus to match what Chester was wearing. Today the two would be shuttled to the mansion in a Royal Skycar.

Linap had her invite and Duke Tinktar asked Chester to be her escort for the festivities and give the appearance that he was there for her. Chester had no problems with that request and surprised Duke Tinktar who didn't know about those developments, "I like Linap."

Shortly after the Royal Sky Limo dropped Chester off who was asked to wait because Linap was arriving momentarily.

Within two minutes Linap's Sky Limo appeared and stopped and she got out looking extremely beautiful. The fact that Chester and Brooklyn would be her escort, she was thrilled and went overboard with dressing for the occasion wearing several hundred million credits worth of fine gems decorating her arms, neck , fingers and the stylish hat she was wearing.
~~~~~~

Chester was immediately struck by her grandeur. She truly was magnificently beautiful, and her multicolored skin added tremendously to her beauty.

"Hello Linap," Chester said as he smiled.

"Chester, it pleased me a lot when Duke Tinktar informed me you specifically requested to be my escort for this Unification. That's the only reason why I came."

"If you came for me that pleases me."

"I wish you were not so busy so we could spend more time with each other."

"When I get done with my next project, I will make time for you. I will give my days to you."

"If you do that you will make me very happy, and I will reward you like no other woman has ever been able to do for you."

"Just being near you is a big enough award for me."

"Chester you can be so charming, did you know that?"

"I'm only this way because you have affected me in a very pleasant manner."

"If I can do that for you, then I'm very pleased."

"Shall we go inside now?"

"Yes, please lead the way."

The cameras were all on this couple. Linap was hard to get to, the media always sought her out with no success. She was very private and seldom was seen. The man with the dog wearing Royal Attire with the richest woman in the Empire was already stirring up tremendous reports in the media. Chester didn't know this he was now one of the most viewed people in the Empire. Everyone wanted to know who this man was and ALL ABOUT THE DOG! The dog going into the Royal Unification was HUGE NEWS!

By the time Chester was inside the mansion and escorted by a Royal Guard to his seat with Linap and Brooklyn, another Royal Sky Limousine pulled up. It had Aida well dressed and Librarian Chernega in his retired Army Regimental Commander's Uniform with all his medals and ribbons looking very distinguished. Chester was asked to wear his medal, which was now a broach on his Royal Attire. That too sparked curiosity to a stranger nobody knew about that had the highest emperor's award proudly worn.

Chernega and Aida were seated to the side of Chester and Brooklyn was seated between Chester and Aida who liked the dog so there was no contention there as Aida liked Brooklyn and the feelings were mutual. Aida petted Brooklyn and at the same time was doing some heavy soul searching. Petting Brooklyn gave her some comfort for the surreal manifestation of jealousy that was just about to explode.

All the guests were soon accounted for, and it was time to proceed. The orchestra played a March that Chester thought sounded familiar. A Section of the *Franz von Suppe Overture of the Light Cavalry* when the trumpets started playing seemed to sound like the music now playing. *Was this a coincidence?* Chester wondered. During the Grand march, the emperor personally escorted Danielle up to the platform raised a few feet so the guests could see her clearly and her mother Dominika walked a short distance behind the two. Once they were up at the platform, the trumpets were again playing the *Overture of the Light Cavalry* and Duke Tinktar with an honor guard went up to the platform and he stood beside Daniell.

The emperor had the legal right to Unify any couple, but he sparingly did that only for close court members. He now took a position in front of the couple and asked them each a couple simple questions about their promise of fidelity and then he said,

"In the power vested in the Emperor of the Drolupric Empire, I now proclaim Duke Tinktar and Daniell Unified."

It was now a done deal they were legally and officially a Royal Couple. They would spend their lives together. Daniell obtained the man of her dreams and Duke Tinktar obtained a very strait and decent woman whom he could trust and love and make the mother of his children. They would now proceed down the Aisle and bowing to all the guests on their way to their marriage suite and Change clothes into a Royal Special Design. And while they were to do that, the staff would be eagerly setting up the remainder of the tables and settings on the other side of the platform where all the guests would soon be seated for a 24-course majestic meal. As they slowly moved down the aisle and just before they got to the row where Chester was sitting next to Brooklyn, Aida suddenly stood up and pointed a blaster at Duke Tinktar and said, "If I can't have you nobody can!"

Brooklyn yelled, "Lookout!" and jumped up and locked his mouth around Aida's arm holding the blaster and because of his wait her blaster was pointing downwards when she was pulling the trigger avoiding hitting Duke Tinktar. Security was quickly all over Aida and she was out of the room five seconds later and taken away.

Chester suddenly felt melancholy because he suspected *Aida would be pushed out of an airlock before the day was done.*

Brooklyn received some minor injuries in the scuffle and he and Chester were soon on their way to a Veterinary where Doctor Akssiar and his assistant Tasha soon showed up with a lot of security people. After Brooklyn was treated for his wounds, the Vet suggested he remain there overnight.

Chester said, "I must remain with him."

Moments later Rayalna was brought in to attend to Chester for the night.

Just when they thought things were calming down the emperor himself showed up after being briefed that Chester intended on staying the night with Brooklyn who was heavily sedated and breathing normally.

"Chester, I want you to come back to the palace with me. Duke Tinktar is taking this event very heavily and I think he will be able to cope better with it if you return with me and help cheer him up."

All eyes were on Chester.

"Chester, Brooklyn will sleep through the night, I will be here with him and if there are any changes I will contact you right away," Rayalna said."

"I suppose you are right. If I can help Duke Tinktar, then I should."

The emperor smiled and said, "Chester come with me now."

"Sure," Chester said and stood up and followed along with the emperor who suddenly put his arm over Chester, and said, "This means a lot for me. Brooklyn saved Duke Tinktar's life.

I'm proud of you two. Few have ever served me with the dedication you have."

"Thank you for your kind words, Your Excellency.

By the time they got back to the mansion, all the chairs previously set out for the Unification had been removed and people were standing around drinking discussing the incredible events. Anyone who had any bad feelings about the dog being present for the Unification didn't dare say a word because they knew the emperor would not be happy with them considering the fact the reason why Duke Tinktar was still alive is because that dog was sitting next to the assailant. The other thing that people were starting to talk about is in all appearances it was the dog that yelled lookout. But that was impossible so who warned Duke Tinktar?

Aida taken to a discrete location was now undergoing intensive interrogations.

Some of the men investigating the case knew Aida had been Duke Tinktar's lover, but they wanted to rule out a coup type assassination.

Finally, when it appeared Neurological Sonifications wasn't working they brought in Doctor Boonkar who took over and realized the efficacy of their interrogations were not going to resolve anything, took a different approach.

Doctor Boonkar knew Aida was a deadly spy and after getting reports from several people that explained how she had been Duke Tinktar's lover, understood immediately what happened. A woman scorned did an irrational act, simple as that. There was nothing more to be gained by torture or Neurological Sonifications. She was not working as an agent as part of a coup or with any enemies. It was simply she could not cope with losing her lover.

Doctor Boonkar had Aida sedated for a couple days so she would have a long and restful sleep, then they would have their talk. Doctor Boonkar already knew what the outcome was, a personal tragedy of a woman who lost the man she loved to another woman.

The emperor was seated at the head of the table. Dominika was on his one side and Daniel was on his other side. Duke Tinktar was sitting next to his bride facing Chester sitting next to Dominika.

Linap was sitting next to Chester who tried by all appearances to put on the best face as he knew now was the time he had to help Duke Tinktar who was going through a lot of emotional trauma. Chester's presence and cheerfulness seemed to help Duke Tinktar's mood.

Duke Tinktar worked hard to get Aida out of his mind, but he knew one fact the emperor would act on. Any time someone tried to kill a Royal they were either executed or banished to a far-off planet. *How hard would he go on Aida?*

Chester stayed around until most of the guests departed after the dinner party and paid their respects.

Linap asked Chester, "Would you like to come to my home tonight to help you get over this?"

"No, I'm going to go back to be with Brooklyn."

"Can I go with you and keep you company while you wait there?"

"I suppose that would be okay."

"Let's go say goodbye to Duke Tinktar, I think this celebration is over." Linap said in a positive manner.

The two approached Duke Tinktar and Daniell who were now standing alone as one of the last couples finished their congratulations.

"Thanks for inviting me to your Unification," Chester stated.

"It's a good thing I invited you, I'm still alive thanks to that invite."

"I hope you and Daniel have great happiness and a wonderful life."

"Thank you very much and thank you and Brooklyn what you have done for me."

"I'm glad it all worked out."

"I'll be talking with you in a few more days from now."

"Sure, any time your excellency."

"Enjoy the rest of your evening, I see you are in good hands."

"I think you are right."

Chester and Linap did a deep bow to the Royal Couple then turned and walked towards the front and were immediately escorted when they got near the edge of the venue out to the front where Linap's Sky Limo pulled up suddenly and they got in."

Chester informed Linap the Veterinary Hospital where Brooklyn was taken, and the Sky Limo quickly made its way there. They went inside and found Rayalna sitting next to Brooklyn who was sleeping and sedated.

"You didn't need to come back tonight; Brooklyn will be sleeping till probably mid-morning before we wake him up and recheck his injuries to see if any further treatments are required."

"How soon do you think it will be before he can walk around?"

"He should be fine in a couple days. The fact they got him here so quickly allowed the treatments to occur to allow quick healing."

"I thought I would come here and be with him."

"Brooklyn will need you to be at full strength when he's released here. It's best you go home now, and we will contact you immediately if there are any developments."

Chester felt kind of guilty leaving Brooklyn, but he also had Linap there encouraging him to leave because he wasn't really helping Brooklyn by spending the night here. He needed to go home and rest.

When Chester walked out of the building with Linap, he felt extremely guilty not staying but he also knew he was being trained for another mission. He probably needed some rest.

Linap said, "Let me take you to my home. I don't want you to be alone tonight."

"I suppose you are right."

In a short time, they were once again at Linap's home. Brianna had seen the network news reports on Brooklyn and while he was at the vet Linap and Brianna communicated, so Brianna knew the story and knew Chester was coming over. When she met them at the front door she said, "Chester I'm very sorry what happened to Brooklyn today and I hope he's going to be alright."

"He's in good hands and has a veterinarian there all night with him who takes care of him at Duke Tinktar's estate, so I think he'll do fine."

"Would you like something to drink?"

"Yes, how about a *Chamboreé de Lián?"*

"Madam Linap, would you like a drink?"

"Give me what Chester's having."

Soon their drinks were served as the transitioned over to a sofa where Linap transitioned into Chester's arms.

The *Chamboreé de Lián* hit the spot; Chester was grateful because it took a lot off his mind. In just a few minutes he consumed the entire drink and Linap saw that and asked, "Would you like a refill."

"Sure, why not."

Linap said, "Brianna, please refill Chester's glass."

Artificial intelligence passed the word to Brianna who soon came into the room with a tray of two drinks and sat it down on the coffee table in case Linap wanted another. She handed Chester a new drink and took his empty glass and left the room.

When Chester was half done with his second drink, Linap thought now would be a good time to bring up the talking dog.

"Chester, I know now might not be a good time to talk about it, but you need to be aware."

"What's that Linap?"

"Chester a lot of people saw Brooklyn talk tonight and there is something I need to tell you. I know Brooklyn can talk."

"He may not have been the one yelling at Duke Tinktar."

"Chester I was there and saw it all plus I need to tell you something you need to know."

"What's that?"

"Everywhere you go, assume there is surveillance, especially after today. My surveillance with my artificial intelligence recorded you talking to Brooklyn, so I know he talks,"

"If you know Brooklyn can talk, it would not be wise for you to repeat that to anyone."

"I understand you work for Duke Tinktar, and he is hiding this for some reason."

"No doubt Brooklyn will probably be rewarded for yelling to Duke Tinktar to look out."

They do not want the public knowing Brooklyn can speak."

"I would never do anything to jeopardize my relationship with you. I will do anything for you."

"Thank you, I wish I could promise you the same thing, but I have requirements I must fulfill, that I have no choice about."

"I understand who you work for. It's rare someone wears Royal Clothes. The fact you sat across from Duke Tinktar and close to the emperor at the dinner celebration shows your elevation in society way above most people. I know you have to do what you have to do, but when you are done with your projects and need to unwind, you come back to me, and I will help you remove the scars and the pain."

"Thank you I appreciate that. The only person that came close to being my friend was Aida, and now she's lost and will be away from me forever."

"What do you think will happen to her ultimately?"

"I do not wish to talk about that, it's going to be ugly."

In the back of Chester's mind, he could not help but think Aida would end up at the hog farm.

Aida was still only half done with her first drink, and she knew Chester was going through some tough times. It would not shock her to learn Aida had been one of Chester's lovers. Linap knew Chester was a sophisticated man and when they were together in the past there were some obvious tendrils she spotted.

Linap took Chester's empty glass and sat it down on the tray and grabbed the full drink and handed it to him and said, "Have this, I know you had a rough day."

"Thanks."

Chester took his time drinking this final drink just holding Linap and thinking about everything and eventually finished it about the time Linap finished her drink.

Linap knew it was time for Chester to get some rest, so she said, "Why don't we go to my bedroom and get some sleep."

"Sure, that sounds good."

Linap led Chester to her bedroom and helped him undress quickly down to his undergarments and said, "Let's go to bed like this."

Soon the two were cuddled with Linap's back to Chester and the lights dimmed and they quickly transcended to the dream world. Chester had the benefits of the elixir which changed the chemicals in his brains in a way that induced sleep better than melatonin due to the quantity he drank in a short while.

Eight hours later Chester needed to get up to drain his lizard and, in the process, woke up Linap.

Soon Artificial Intelligence informed Linap a Skycar would soon be there with a change of clothes for Chester, they needed to take him somewhere.

Linap was sadden she wasn't going to get a chance to gobble up her boy toy this morning, but understood Chester was in some serious business and she missed her chance with gratification from him, but she would wait for him because she felt his love holding her during the night.

Chester was more than she could bargain for, and Brooklyn added a layer of mystery to it that made him even more tantalizing.

Moments after Chester finished his business and was lying in bed, Brianna arrived at the room with the change of clothes and informed Chester. "Officials sent by the emperor are waiting for you in the Skycar. As soon as you get dressed, you are to leave with them. I'm going to take your clothes you wore last night down to them now as they want them."

"Alright." Chester said and started changing into his workout clothes they delivered, and he knew where he was going. *Brooklyn would not be awakened for a few hours so he might as well go get his workout done.*

As soon as Chester was dressed, he turned toward Linap who was now dressed in casual clothes, "I have to go now. I'll try to see you soon."

"I'll be waiting for you Chester; I know you got things to do."

Chester was soon out of the house and walking to the Skycar. As soon as he got in there was none other than Librarian Chernega, the retired Army Regimental Commander also in workout clothing.

There wasn't much to talk about. The mood wasn't pleasant since they each had numerous experiences with Aida. Neither of them knew what was to become of her.

Brooklyn wasn't here today but to keep the birds in a routine, they were fed while Chester and Chernega drank their energy drink breakfast standing right next to the birds that had gotten use to Chester's appearance.

Soon they were off running five miles then stretches to get them ready for exercises and martial arts proficiency training.

Today, perhaps because of the emotional situation caused by yesterday's events, they seemed to run harder and indeed finished the five miles in twenty-four minutes while running in perfect synchronization side by side.

The rest of the morning went by as normal and soon they were done and taken back to Duke Tinktar's estate where Chester got his baths and a nice massage. After Chester was dressed in casual street clothes he was transported to the veterinary hospital where they were in the process of waking Brooklyn and checking his injuries. His left front leg was placed in a brace he would wear for a couple of weeks. Chester was there when he awakened.

The Veterinary Doctor said he didn't want Brooklyn doing too much walking for a few days and arranged to have him put in a pet transporter for the trip home.

In due time they were back at Duke Tinktar's estate. Chester asked Brooklyn, "Are you hungry?"

"Yes papa. Would it be possible to eat my meal with my friends the squirrels?"

"Sure, I see why not."

Rayalna who was in the room with them said, "Brooklyn should not be walking but I can arrange to have one of the carts the grounds keepers haul him up to where those squirrels are."

"That sounds fine."

In a few minutes the pet carrier that was on a cart to facilitate moving it around inside the mansion was taken to the front entrance with Brooklyn laying inside it. Chester and Rayalna lifted the pet carrier up onto the ground keeper's cart that had no handles or anything apparent to guide it or assist in movement.

"How are we going to move this thing, it looks kind of heavy," Chester said.

"This cart is fully robotic and artificial intelligence operates it. All you must do is give it verbal commands."

"Sounds simple enough."

"Alright let's go. Cart follow us up to the walking trail where the Squirrels live."

A speaker mounted on the side of the cart in a protective enclosure asked, "Do you wish me to follow you up the trail to the squirrels' nests?"

"That's correct." Rayalna replied.

Soon they started walking and Chester could hear the minor whine of an electric drive and the healthy tires on the walkway. They traversed the side of the Mansion in a parklike environment with beautiful trees and well landscaped terrain. The walkway they followed continued along the side of the mansion and outcropped buildings and structures and met up with the path that would take them to the Squirrels in a few minutes. They reached their destination and Chester helped Brooklyn out of the pet carrier on cart.

The food water and dishes were in the cart pre-staged. Chester and Rayalna grabbed the food water and bowls out of the cart and positioned them where the squirrels were growing accustomed to eating. After filling the bowls with food and water they stepped back. Within ten seconds the brave squirrel that had adopted them ran forward and sniffed the food and started eating. Brooklyn started eating out of another bowl nearby. The squirrel picked up food in its hands and started chewing on it watching Brooklyn eat. Moments later another squirrel ran up grabbed some food and took off with it in his mouth and ran ten feet back then stood up on its hind feet and took the large chunk of food out of his mouth holding it in its hands and started chewing on the exterior of it.

Brooklyn felt thirsty and stepped over a few feet and started drinking the water, the squirrel watched Brooklyn intently and when Brooklyn walked a foot over to his food bowl and continued eating the squirrel investigated the water bowl and licked the water checking it and proceeded to drink a lot of water.

Today there were eventually five squirrels that joined in, but since some of the squirrels ran off with food its possible, they carried it to their little ones.

At the conclusion of the squirrel feast, they all retraced their steps back to the front entrance of the mansion where two grounds keepers were. One was to take the cart back to storage; the other was there to carry Brooklyn and his dog carrier back into their suite on a pushcart.

Chester and Brooklyn were eventually alone in the suite and Chester asked Brooklyn, "What would you like to do, Brooklyn?"

"Papa, may I watch some holographic videos?"

"Sure."

Brooklyn then said, "I want to watch the *'Other Worlds Animal Review'* program which I saw at Madam Linap's home with Brianna.

Artificial intelligence in the background asked, "Do you wish to watch *'Other Worlds Animal Review'*?

"Yes, that is correct," Brooklyn stated. Artificial intelligence was confused taking orders from a dog, but nevertheless complied since Chester didn't say anything.

Brooklyn, feeling good and well fed was laying down on his bed watching the holographic video for a few minutes when suddenly Rayalna walked in the room and said, "Chester, I was just informed that Chernega would like you to meet him in the library. I was sent here to be with Brooklyn while you are there."

"Sure," Chester said, then stood up and said, "Brooklyn if you need anything let Rayalna know, I'll be back after I talk to Chernega."

"Alright Papa, I'm enjoying this holographic video."

As soon as Chester stepped outside his suite, a security man was there and said, "Chester, I will escort you to the library."

"Thank you."

"You are welcome."

Chester knew his movements were tightly controlled and monitored. He would not walk around the estate without eyes on him. Even if he didn't have an apparent escort, artificial intelligence monitored all his movements to take appropriate actions if required.

Moments later they made the long walk down the hallway. Chester thought it was odd two security men were standing outside guarding the room and one of them opened the door for him and he went in and saw Chernega sitting at the main conference table who gestured him to sit down across from him.

Chester acknowledged with a head nod and sat down. Chernega was wearing casual clothes and said, "We need to talk about your next mission."

"Alright how soon is it going to take place?"

"It will be less than a month from now."

"That doesn't give me much time to prepare for it."

"That's why you will be spending a lot of time with me over the next few weeks."

"Alright, I'll learn as much as I can."

"Before we get into the information and the training, I wanted to explain the nature of the mission."

"Alright."

"We are going to hit a military target with a paramilitary operation."

"Sounds kind of serious."

"It is. That's why I'm going with you."

"I will definitely feel more comfortable with you on my team."

"I need to explain to you the interface to the military members of the team."

"I'm all ears."

First of all, you are not a military person, you have no rank so to speak of. You plainly are nothing more than a spy that is developing to take on bigger challenges in the future. I will always be by your side, and only I will give orders to the military members of the team."

"I don't have any problems with that since I have no idea what I would be ordering them to do."

"I'm glad you understand this arrangement and your attitude will make matters easier to handle."

"May I ask a dumb question?"

"I doubt your question is dumb, go ahead."

"What if a lucky bullet or laser hits you and you are killed?

"My second in command will immediately fill in my position and he as well as you will know all the details of what we need to do and how to accomplish it."

Since it sounds like you and your second in command have all the bases covered, then why do I need to go?

"You are the direct interface to Duke Tinktar. You have the authority to cancel the mission, issue the bugout order, and if conditions change where we must alter the plan in situ, then you can approve that change since Duke Tinktar has given you the authority to do so."

"I will not try to screw that up and will be and sure and make sure you agree that's what we need to do, or I would assume in most cases you would be making the recommendations which based on your experience would most likely be the best course of events."
"I would not make any recommendation I did not feel met the spirit and the requirements of the mission."

"I think you proved that in the Battle of Martos."

"I did what I had to do under the circumstances. It was a tough battle, and the enemy was quite capable, though they were unnecessarily brutal towards the civilian population."

"So this is why we have two security men outside?"

"Yes, nobody is allowed to interrupt us or listen to us on the other side of that door."

"That makes sense."

"Now I'm going to tell you the next thing that you are not going to like."

"And that is?"

"In a few days you will start to spend time with Doctor Boonkar and will get Neurological Sonifications to help prepare you for the mission."

"Those Neurological Sonifications are not a pleasant experience, but if I need it, I suppose it's the price I have to pay to ensure success and make sure I come back alive."

"I do not know any of the details. Only Doctor Boonkar is authorized to discuss what it covers with you."

"Alright, anything else before we start digging into this mission?"

"That just about covers it but I want you to know I want the mission to be successful and bring you back alive. I'm a big proponent of force protection. I don't want my men to get slaughtered over needless activity and just want to go in get it done and get the hell out of there in one piece. I don't want to leave there in the same condition I left the Battle of Martos."

"I can appreciate that. I'm ready to learn."

Over the next few hours, they got into the high-level plan that covered everything from when they left to egressing and coming home after they completed the mission and gave the message Duke Tinktar and the emperor a status report. Hopefully that would end the activity this empire did short of triggering a war. If it resulted in tit for tat, there would soon be other missions.

After several hours, Chernega realized that Chester had enough for the day and said, "We are going to end this for the day. We'll get together again tomorrow afternoon."

The holographic briefing imagery suddenly went away, there was nothing left in the room associated with the mission.

"I'll be ready."

Chernega stood up and walked over to the door and Chester stood up and followed him and they soon stepped out of the room together. Chernega said, "I'll walk you back to your suite, I would like a minute to talk to Brooklyn."

"Sure."

The two had small talk during the walk to Chester's suite. Chester had the impression that Chernega had positive impression of him. Chernega was amazed at Chester's development since his abduction. His transformation seemed like a miracle and in many ways it was.

Chester down deep inside felt bad for Aida. Perhaps had I given her more emotional significance she would not have done what she did. He felt partially responsible for her conduct and *had he just performed maybe one or two more acts of kindness and love it might have distracted her enough to not conduct the attempted assassination?*

The two came upon Chester's suite. There was a security man outside as expected who opened the door for them then closed it after they entered.

Brooklyn was entranced watching all the strange animals from around the empire. This show was about ten times better than National Geographic, mainly because it had so much more areas to cover.

"Brooklyn, our friend Chernega wanted to have a few words with you."

"Alright Papa."

"Brooklyn you did an amazing act of courage and prevented a terrible catastrophe. I wanted to come here and personally thank you."

"You are most welcome Chernega."

"Brooklyn, may I ask you why you grabbed Aida's arm?" Chernega asked.

"Sir, I was afraid she was going to hurt Duke Tinktar."

"How did you know she was going to shoot him?"

"Back on Earth I watched a lot of Television shows, that are like your holographic videos. On many of those shows I saw people shooting and killing people. I was worried Aida might kill Duke Tinktar."

"Do you know about death, Brooklyn?"

"Yes, Chernega I know about death and watched a lot of movies showing it. A person stops living when they die. Their world is ended."

"You seem to know a lot for a dog?"

"I'm always learning. Doctor Akssiar says my vocabulary exceeds 65,000 words."

"Amazing," Chernega said then he added, "Sometime in the future I want to do something special for you."

"Can you arrange for "Princess Tiffany" to spend more time with me?"

"I'll see what I can do."

Thank you."

Chernega smiled and said, "I'm going to leave you guys I got some tasks I need to do. It's been pleasant to talk with you Brooklyn." Chernega left the room.

Moments later Artificial Intelligence said softly in the background, "Chester, Madam Linap wishes to communicate with you. Do you wish to receive her communication?

"Yes, please."

Immediately Linap's holograph popped up and there was the delicious Linap dressed up very elegantly.

"Hello Chester, how is Brooklyn doing?"

"He's in good shape and resting."

"Would it be possible for me to pick you up and take you to a restaurant?"

"Brooklyn really can't walk around too much he needs to stay in his bed most of the time."

"Is there someone there who can look out for Brooklyn so we can spend some time together?"

About that time Brooklyn spoke up and said, "Papa, Rayalna will take care of me, you should visit Linap."

"You have such a smart dog," Linap said after hearing what Brooklyn just said.

Rayalna spoke up and said "I will be here with Brooklyn and give him company and anything he needs. You should go visit Madam Linap."

Linap immediately responded to Rayalna and said, "Thank you for helping out."

"My pleasure," Rayalna responded.

"Okay give me some time to get ready," Chester said.

"Call me when you are ready to go, I will get there promptly," Linap replied.

"Alright, I will."

Linap hung up her communicator on her end and the Holograph disappeared. A moment later, Aizere entered the room and said, I was just notified by artificial intelligence to help you dress for tonight's event."

"Yes, I'm going to a restaurant with Madam Linap."

"Do you wish to take a bath before you go?"

"No, I took one just a few hours ago when I had my message. I'm good to go."

"Would you like a fresh hair style?" Aizere asked.

"I suppose I could use one."

"Alright the hair stylist will be here momentarily."

"Thanks."

"Since you are going out on a private matter, how would you like to dress?" Aizere asked.

"I'm going to a nice restaurant that probably has well-dressed Clientele, so I think it needs to look appropriate for the class of people that Linap will expose me too."

"I'll inform the staff fashion designer who is always here in the evenings to prepare people for activities."

"Thank you."

"You are welcome."

In forty five minutes the hair stylist and the fashion designer had Chester dressed for success and he was ready to depart and contacted Linap and said he was ready.

"I'm leaving for a while Brooklyn."

"Have a good time Papa, Rayalna always takes good care of me."

"I appreciate your help Rayalna."

"Chester you are more than welcome. If Brooklyn wasn't here, Duke Tinktar would probably be dead now. The empire owes you two quite a bit."

"Thank you. All I ask is Brooklyn is well taken care of."

"I will personally see to that."

"Thank you, I appreciate what you do."

"My pleasure."

"See you in a few hours."

Chester left the suite walked out to the front entrance with his security guy.

Moments later, Linap's Sky Limo pulled up in front of the Mansion and the door opened for Chester to walk in upright then sat down in the seat and the roof of the Limo curved back down and shut. The Sky Limo was pilotless. It was all artificial intelligence. Linap had already informed the Sky Limo navigation coordinator application her two destinations, now they flew to their destination. As they got near their destination, Chester thought it looked familiar. In fact, it was the fancy restaurant that Aida brought him. The building navigation system efficiently parked the Sky Limo in a Limo stall. Suddenly there were two men there who were their security escorts that Linap always had pre-staged for her arrival. The parking spot and the two security men for a few hours costs more than most workers earn in a year. But Linap had money to burn, she could care less. The security men escorted them all the way to the Metra d' who had the reservation ready with a great view and no wait time. His usual bribe was significant.

The Metra d' remembered Chester from his visit not too long ago with Aida who he also knew. The fact this man was seen socializing with both women impressed the Metra d'. Who was this guy? Then he started thinking about the press coverage of the attempted assassination on the Royal by Aida, obviously a scorned woman, and he thought oh my god, this is the man setting by Aida with that dog before they cut off the video!

Chills went up the man's spine about then.

He then pulled the waiter aside who was to service their table and one other and informed the man, "Stay with just that one table, they are more than VIP's. I'll have someone else handle the other tables."

"Yes sir."

A moment later he was back at the table and asked, "May I get you something to drink?"

"Linap wanted it bad that night. She was feeling the addiction to Chester's Scorpio Stinger."

Before Chester had a chance to answer, Linap said, "We will both have Zvèzdnàyà Rōzā."

Chester was amused because he knew the pink liquor is referred to as Zvèzdnàyà Rōzā had libido enhancers in it.

Unethical people gave Zvèzdnàyà Rōzā to their dates they wanted to have sex with, and it usually worked well.

Chester recalled when Aida gave him Zvèzdnàyà Rōzā she did so because she was a bitch in heat wanting sex.

They were soon served their drinks and Chester liked the taste of the Zvèzdnàyà Rōzā elixir and he liked how it made his body feel.

The music and the elixir changed the mood, and all the negativity of recent events was slowly escaping Chester's thoughts which he liked.

Chester didn't know this, but he had multiple sets of eyes on him. The intelligence bureau people were there watching him and another VIP.

As soon as Artificial Intelligence determined Linap was going to take Chester to a restaurant, they had her profile and knew exactly where she was likely going. They didn't have to scramble agents there because they were already at the bar observing.

These agents knew Linap well because she was here a few times with Duke Tinktar. The agents had rear view video recorder on their eyeglasses that people still wore even though corrective surgery was available to everyone. Some people just did not like the idea of someone tampering with their eyes and preferred to wear optical devices.

Thanks to advanced psychoacoustics exploitation the conversation would also be recorded in high fidelity at a good distance because part of the eye class frame had miniature acoustic cones built into a very complex structure. The agents could hear the conversation in their ear buds.

Advanced holographic technology tracking eyeball movement and jaw movement they could pick a target and zoom in on that person. The system picked up the sound of their teeth contacting upper to lower. The acoustic cones and transducers in the glasses frames fed the wireless system mounted inside their body armor.

Jaw movements of teeth chatter as the instructors called it were programmed. Certain codes meant things.
If the agent was looking at a target and the holographic eyeball tracker pinpointed the person in high fidelity, three chatters on the teeth would signal lock on. Automatic trackers would then observe that person until the abort was signaled.

Linap looked quite elegant tonight. Her total makeover was beyond a glamorous movie star. Linap's appearance tonight along with the help of the help of the Zvèzdnàyà Rōzā, stirred the juices inside Chester.

Soon their orders were taken, and small talk continued. Linap knew it would be unwise to discuss heavy duty things now with Chester because he was probably already stressed with current events.

Linap would get upset with any other man who was as quiet as Chester, except she knew a lot about what his situation was that nobody else did outside of Duke Tinktar's staff.

The way Chester looked at her and smiled at her reassured her that he was infatuated with her and would likely form a bond with her.

Then without any explanation Chester started his dialogue and said, "I'm slowly becoming more than attracted to you. I want you to know I've developed feelings towards you, and quite frankly it scares me."

"There is nothing to be scared about."

"If I grew attached to you and something happened, I don't know if I could cope."

"It's actually the other way around Chester. I'm not sure I'm brave enough to tell you how you affect me."

"If you are willing to give me time and allow me to take care of matters that I must, I would willingly be close to you for the rest of my life."

"Those are big words you just said. Are you brave enough to live by them?"

"It's the only life I know now. One day I will tell you more."

"I will faithfully wait for that day," Linap said looking very serious.

"I have a heavy schedule tomorrow. I can't stay out too late."

"Honey, it only takes you about two minutes to give me an orgasm, I'll get you home early, I know you want to be back with Brooklyn because of his injuries."

"Yes, I do, and he's taken it pretty well."

After a few more drinks and a great meal, the two departed the posh restaurant and Linap took Chester to her home where Brianna was astonished, they walked directly to the bedroom and shut the door.

Brianna was a smart lady and the home's artificial intelligence that had evolved to almost *free will* befriended her. Artificial Intelligence determined at times Brianna needed to know where Linap was located and what she was doing. Her requests slowly reached a point that Artificial Intelligence provided what she wanted and today it was the surveillance video of Linap's bedroom.

Just like Brianna assumed, Linap was soon in bed performing the perfect coitus with Chester. She was also astonished afterward they got out of bed, took a sprite shower to wash off their love making residue and redressed in their clothes. They soon exited the bedroom where Linap led Chester out to her Sky Limo and passing Brianna said, "I will be right back. I'm giving Chester a ride back to Duke Tinktar's estate."

Linap was gone fifteen minutes and returned home and went to bed wishing she had Chester there to cuddle with.

For the next couple days, it was a repeat. Exercise and workout in the mornings followed by mission planning and training in the afternoons. Brooklyn informed Chester, "I'm feeling good now I think I can walk around."

"Let's see what the Veterinary to let you exercise before we go do it."

That afternoon the Veterinary took some X-rays of Brooklyn and removed the leg brace and said Brooklyn could walk around but to take it easy and not do any strenuous exercises.

Chester also had his first visit by Doctor Boonkar. She knew most of what Chester had experienced and was aware of the messiness that must go on in a huge empire where sometimes it appeared that brutal savagery was conducted.

The reality of the galaxy is there are competing empires who often sent unsavory characters that were a major threat. As such they could not be treated with kid gloves and just like the enemy did to Drolupric Empire spies when captured, the same results occurred. It was a disgusting business, but it was a reality that confronted them they had to deal with.

Spies could not be incarcerated because their presence would foretell something the intelligence bureau did not want disclosed to the public in event there was a leak by a disgruntled employee.

Talking and dealing with Chester was simple and straightforward. Doctor Boonkar evaluated that Chester appeared to have greatly recovered from the appearance of a mental letdown after his last mission. Nevertheless, Chester received Neurological Sonifications not only for his psychological conditioning but also to train his brain on matters pertaining to the next mission that was scheduled to launch real soon. There was not enough time in the schedule to train Chester with standard training techniques. Neurological Sonification treatments reoccurred intermittently up until a few days before the mission began.

Chester had a few more soiree's with Linap and since Brooklyn had healed quite a bit, the two of them spent time with her giving her much joy in her life as she slowly became closer to Brooklyn.

On one occasion while Chester and Linap were in the bedroom celebrating the feast of life with the horizontal tango on a theme from Paganini, Brianna said to Brooklyn. I know you can talk, so when we are alone, please feel free to talk to me.

"How do you know I can talk?" Brooklyn asked.

"I can't reveal my source, I'm sorry."

Brooklyn later reported that to Chester who then arranged for Brianna to get transported to a secret Intelligence Bureau interrogation center where she was promised she would disappear if they ever caught her revealing Brooklyn's special capability to anyone.

Linap was soon advised what transpired and the security people having used Neurological Sonifications on Brianna discovered the source was Linap's Artificial Intelligence that had a strange relationship with Brianna. Computer experts were brought in to patch the software making Artificial Intelligence unable to provide Brianna any further holographs of Brooklyn by special filtering.

Chester could not tell Linap he was going on a mission but said to her, "From time to time I will seem to disappear. It's the nature of my business."

"I understand that completely," Linap responded knowing Chester did not originate from the world or this empire. She also thought, *just like Brooklyn, he must have special capabilities to be placed in such a high office with Duke Tinktar.*

***

Chapter Eighteen

CRYSOLAMOUS

The mission began in a calm like fashion. Chester had Brooklyn with him when they met the reactivated Army Regimental Commander Chernega at the front entrance of Duke Tinktar's estate dressed in regulation camouflaged uniform looking as he was going to war.

"Good morning, Chester."

"Thank you."

"I see you have Brooklyn with you?"

"Yes, he's going with me."

"Does Duke Tinktar know you are taking him?" Chernega asked.

"I think you military training manual says something like it's always better to ask for forgiveness than permissions." Chester said.

"Even if it does not explicitly state that, sometimes battlefield conditions dictate such actions." Chernega responded.

"Where's everyone else that's going?"

"They are already on their way, the shuttle that took them up will be here very soon as it landed at a nearby base to get refueled."

"Alright."

"I might as well inform you now, we have a distasteful task to perform on our way to Crysolamous."

"And what's that?"

"Execution of a prisoner. Shove the person out of an airlock."

"Since we'll be killing a bunch of people real soon, I suppose one more body doesn't make a difference."

About that time the shuttle came down vertically because it was too large to maneuver through the access tunnel and landed a short distance from them.

"Our ride is here."

The two men and Brooklyn walked over to the shuttle as its door rotated up allowing them to walk straight in and found plenty of open seats.

"The prisoner is already up on the Frigate?" Chester asked.

"Yes, all men are accounted for and onboard guarding the prisoner."

Soon the shuttle was airborne and after a while pitched upwards as it accelerated giving Chester the feeling of six G forces as it accelerated briskly on its way out into space. Chester noticed the sky was suddenly dark outside as they left the atmosphere.

The time seemed to pass quickly and eventually looking out the window Chester could see part of the Frigate as they approached. The frigate was underway and heading on its track at moderate speeds. The shuttle flew over the top of the frigate and aligned itself with the shuttle bay matching speeds and in the vacuum of space with the help of retrorockets slowly maneuvered down into the shuttle bay that soon grabbed the shuttle with magnetic grabbers and gently landed it. The shuttle bay hatch closed and the sound of pressurizing it penetrated the shuttle and people aboard could hear the slight increase in noise.

In a short time, Artificial Intelligence of the shuttle said, "Shuttle Bay has been pressurized to 14.7 PSI. It is now safe to leave the shuttle.

The shuttle door opened and the three exited and went into the double airlock then into the bowels of the Frigate class spaceship. Inside the Frigate the captain was waiting for them.

"Greetings Commander Chernega." The Ship's captain said.

"Thank you, Captain, let me introduce you to Chester and his dog Brooklyn."

"This is kind of unprecedented taking a dog on a mission."

"Since Chester is Duke Tinktar's Rep, I think we simply need to be aware he can be here and also the dog is very smart."

"Alright but my men are not going to clean up any mess that dog creates."

"Don't worry about the dog," Chester said, then added, "In preparation for this mission, Brooklyn was trained on how to use a human's toilet. All I need to do is sit a chair next to the toilet and he can handle it."

"Since the dog will be living in your stateroom, we'll leave it up to you on how to deal with him." The captain stated with a look on his face.

Chernega asked, "Where is the prisoner?"

"She's in Chester stateroom under guard. She asked to speak to Chester before we put her out the airlock."

"Take us to her," Chester said.

"This way please as the captain led the two into the control room and while there the Navigator said, "Captain we are ready to transition to high speeds."

"Commence high speed transit."

"Commencing high speed transit, the officer responded and repeated back which was customary to acknowledge orders even though they had the artificial intelligence backup.

The Frigate was mostly automated but there were a few crew members in the control room. Just forward of the control room was the captain's stateroom as well as three others for high-ranking officers or important people like Chester and Chernega. The first stateroom on the left was the captain's, the second was the one assigned to Chester. They opened the door and walked inside the roomy stateroom and there she was, Aida, not looking so happy knowing she would soon be killed. She had on hand cuffs and was shackled. The stateroom had 3 bunks because sometimes they had to transport extra riders such as a space amphibian group or special forces like they were doing today.

There were two guards with Aida and Chester said to Chernega, "I would like to talk to her alone if you don't mind."

Chernega nodded at the two guards who worked for Chernega, and they left the room.

Chernega asked, "Would you like me to step outside?"

"If you don't mind."

When they were alone with Brooklyn, the conversation began.

While we were waiting for you to show up, "I had a nice talk with those two guards."

"Is that so?"

"I made a comment it seems an awful waste just to fly me out into space to be shoved out of an airlock. One of them said they were continuing another mission."

"And?"

"At first, they didn't want to say but when I said, I'm going to be dead in a short time there's no big deal about secrecy. Everyone on this ship knows where you are going. No doubt it's a handpicked all volunteer crew."

"Then they said, you are going to Crysolamous. I responded to them, you got to be joking."

"Then they asked why. I told them I was a military analyst and just a short while ago, I was still doing INTEL work associated with Crysolamous which is a military outpost that has significant defenses. If you go there you will probably get killed because I don't see how the hell you can break in there. You don't have enough fire power."

Chester knew that since he had several days before they arrived to their Q-point near Crysolamous on a nearby moon, there was no pressing issue to do the execution. So, he picked Aida's brain and got some information that either Chernega skipped over or deliberately didn't mention: the *Blue Beam Weapon*.

After more discussion that lasted almost an hour, Chester heard enough to the point he wanted to abort the mission until Aida gave him an idea that would make sure this mission did not end up on a disaster.

Chester said, "I'm going to bring Chernega in here and talk with him and you are together. This is what I will offer you in front of Chernega. If you help me on this mission, I will cancel your execution and reinstate you as a member of the intelligence bureau."

"I will be grateful if you do that, and I will personally promise you I will never do something stupid like pointing a gun at Duke

Tinktar again. After I had my sessions with Doctor Boonkar, she recommended to Duke Tinktar that I be reinstated, and I was cured of all jealously and issues associated with the assassination attempt. He was willing to go along with it, but the emperor demanded my execution because he said they needed to set an example so that others would not attempt to copy me."

"I will plead your case with the emperor when I get back. If you help us complete this mission satisfactory, I think Duke Tinktar and I together can convince the emperor. If he still refuses, I will resign my position and take you with me back to planet Earth immediately. I'm not going to let them kill you."

"I know you would really do that and you don't know how good that makes me feel."

Aida started sobbing and Chester grabbed her and hugged her and patted her on the back that made her feel a lot better.

Okay I want you to get ahold of yourself because I'm going to bring Chernega into the room and have the discussion.

"Alright, I'm ready, I feel much better now thanks to you." Chester went to the door and opened it and Chernega was standing next to the two security men.

"Chernega, could you please come into the room for a moment."

Chernega went in and they had two more hours of conversation and in the end, Chernega said, "Duke Tinktar made it explicit that Chester was his representative and had the ultimate decisions in this mission. Therefore, his orders are acknowledged, and Aida will be part of our team assisting us and when we get back to Tymasoara I will immediately offer my resignation and hopefully you have room for me on the trip to Earth."

"Thank you, Chernega," Aida said with life starting to show on her cheeks again.

Chernega was also upset because mission planners understated the importance of the *blue beam weapon* and how it might affect the outcome of the mission. But he now had to deal with the ship's Captain who he outranked and could relieve him if he so desired.

"I'm going to have the security men take off your restraints, and while they are doing that I'm going to get the Captain and bring him here so we can give him the change in our plans."

Chernega went outside the room to the security people and said, "Will you two please come in here."

Inside Chernega said, "Remove her restraints, I'm going to bring the Captain here so we can tell him about the change of plans."

"Yes sir," the first security man stated and the two started taking off the hand cuffs and leg restraints.

Chernega walked the short distance to the control room where the ship's captain was watching sensor scans and images of Tymasoara slowly shrinking to a small dot in the display.

"Captain, I need you for a few minutes in Chester's stateroom."

The captain's eyebrows raised and responded, "Yes sir."

Soon the captain was in the stateroom talking with Chester, Chernega, and Aida.

Chernega said the obvious after the mission high level plan was discussed, "If we don't take out the *blue beam weapon,* this ship may not make it to the pickup point to withdraw the forces deployed to the planet surface. Therefore, we are changing the plan. Aida and Chester will take out the *blue beam weapon* while me and my Space Amphibians destroy their ammo bunkers and their leadership."

"I will make a ship wide broadcast that Aida's sentence has been commuted and agreed to assist us on this mission and is free to walk around the ship. I will also arrange for her some camouflaged battle fatigues, socks, and boots to wear."

"Thank you, Captain," Aida said.

The next few days they did all the replanning. Chester would no longer go to the planet with Chernega and his paramilitary force made up of space amphibians and special forces guys. He Aida and Brooklyn would travel separately to a different target and destroy the *blue beam weapon*. This was a well-guarded hard target. They would carry explosives with a timer to give them a chance to get away from it when the bombs went off. This had to be a heavily coordinated attack and the timers on Chester's bombs had to precisely match the bombs Chernega's forces planted. The timers were started on the shuttles while they were inbound. The Frigate turned around and headed back to the dark side of the moon until it was time to sprint in and land the shuttles. Each shuttle had their own landing bay, so they could all arrive in parallel and speed up extraction then transit flank speed out into deep space heading towards friendly forces that were being sent to force back planetary defenders who would be trying to capture or destroy.

At H-hour, Chester's shuttle left first, they needed more time to work their way into their hardened target. Asked why he was taking Brooklyn along he said, "Brooklyn is well train and will be our scout.

As it turns out Brooklyn was the SECRET WEAPON. With his nose he had a one hundred to one range advantage over the enemy.

As soon as they landed in a forested area and put on the back packs full of explosives with the timer already set, they started out heading towards the *blue beam weapon* that protected this hemisphere of the planet. The *blue beam weapon* on the other hemisphere would not be of concern since they would not be in the line of sight of it.

Using a portable electronic map darkened in night mode they sat out and had a visual reference on the maps that were fastened on their arms like a brace just above the wrist.

Brooklyn was told to move about one hundred feet ahead of them and always keep visual sighting of Chester. They had on their infrared night vision devices and could see Brooklyn and his limbs thanks to his body heat. If Brooklyn spotted an enemy guard, he would raise one of his paws up and down a couple of times then come back close to Chester in a low profile get back to Chester and report what he saw. Chester and Aida would then take cover until Brooklyn gave the details.

The three moved along smartly with no sign of roving guards until they got within a thousand yards of the complex when Brooklyn spotted the first roving sentry. Like most worlds this planet had dogs and people had pets. Chester came up with the idea he would use Brooklyn as a decoy walking up near the solder being friendly and Chester would move in for the silent kill. Aida would hold back in a good defensive position as a rear guard and assist extraction in case they had to bug out.

Moving silently towards the guard each time he faced away Chester made a good time and got into position an signaled Brooklyn to start walking down the road like a lost dog with an easy to see dog collar. The roving patrol saw the dog walking towards him with enough light illuminating the area to see it was a lost pet and the person in some language they didn't know was calling for the dog and Brooklyn walked up to him and bent over and started petting Brooklyn when he suddenly felt a terrible pain as the sharp knife went through his back and into his heart disabling him and killing him within moments. Chester dragged the body next to some shrubs where he would be hard to be seen.

The three slowly worked their way to the facility with Brooklyn leading the way. When Chester looked at the *blue beam weapon*, they were going to blow up his first thought was it was like the picture of the three hundred-foot cannon Canadian inventor, Gerald Bull was building for Sadam Hussein but instead of shooting projectiles the size of automobiles to destroy Israel like Gerald Bull's cannon would, this shot the blue beam that could destroy any ship approaching this hemisphere of Crysolamous.

The final enemy they had to get past was in a guard shack in it, then they could simply walk in, plant their charges, then skedaddle.

There was a ditch along the road Chester could traverse to get near the guard shack. This would be Brooklyn's moment of bravery.

Aida crawled to a spot where she could snipe the guy if she had too, but they wanted to get in silently as soon as the guard in the guard shack was taken down, she would run into the gate and join Chester and plant the bombs.

It all unfolded as they planned, the guard was taken down silently and the three went into the facility and Chester assumed correctly if they placed the charges under the barrel of the blue beam weapon it would most likely severely damage it making it worthless junk.

About the time they were planting the bombs which had several minutes before detonation the enemy security supervisor was concerned, he had not received any reports from his roving patrols or the man at the guard house so he grabbed one other guy who would be relieving the watch in about an hour to go out and investigate. In due time they saw the dead guard laying on the ground and spotted Chester and Aida about the same time they saw them as well.

Fearing sabotage, the supervisor and his assistant start shooting, and Aida and Chester didn't have a lot of cover and the weapons firing was intense. Aida was hit and she knew she was mortally wounded and said, "Chester, I'm hit bad. I'm not going to make it I will cover for you and make sure these bombs go off. When I start shooting, you and Brooklyn make a run for it."

"I can't leave you here."

"Chester I'm badly wounded. Take Brooklyn and leave I love you guys I want you to have a chance to live."

"Alright," Chester said in an emotional state, but he saw the blood and knew Aida was hit badly. He also knew she wasn't going to make it. Aida looked in the backpack and said, "You got two minutes before this blows up. On the count of three start running."

As soon as the count hit three, Chester took off running like a scared jack rabbit. The two enemy were suddenly diving for cover as Aida started laying in the rounds continuously firing and exposing herself. They were paying attention to Aida who was laying out the rounds and not Chester, who had a laser pistol with him and as they were shooting back at Aida, Chester killed one of them with his laser pistol and got by so fast the supervisor had to get behind cover because Aida was going through her clip. By the time Aida finished her 300-round clip, Chester and Brooklyn were 50 yards away and moving into a slightly forested area that was quickly giving them cover. Chester knew he had a chance to survive and dodged behind a tree to assess the situation.

The enemy supervisor thought the saboteur had run out of bullets because the firing suddenly stopped, and Aida crouched down where it was hard to see her. He also saw the backpacks and knew they had to have bombs in them, so he rushed Aida continuously firing waking up the rest of the camp and the other security guards came running out of the block house like ants when you pour water down an ant hill. Aida could hear the shots approaching and ricochets all over the place.

Aida hurt bad now, she had nothing to lose she was dead anyway and only needed to delay a few more seconds.

Using the last bit of her strength Aida lifted her weapon up in the air and started shooting in the direction of the shots which forced the man to dive for cover then there were shots ringing out as others were approaching. She now knew it was probably within ten seconds of detonating so she stood up where she could get a good field of fire and let the rounds fly knowing the gun would be empty in about 10 seconds when it would no longer matter.

Chester had tears going down the sides of his cheeks watching all this and just as Aida's last shots ended when her spare clip ran out of Ammo there was a huge explosion as those two backpacks ripped into that 300-foot blue beam weapon monster raising it into the air and breaking it in half like a ship sunk by a torpedo. The chemical tanks providing the lethal mixtures that created the blue beam that flew at light speed and walloped enemy ships like a sledgehammer were highly volatile and they ignited in the inferno that killed anyone left in the facility.

"Okay Brooklyn we need to get going they will send a force here soon to investigate this big explosion."

The two took off running and Chester was suddenly happy he put in all those training hours because running five miles for him was easy.

Brooklyn just about could not make it but he didn't want to slow down and risk Chester getting shot put forth the last ounce of energy keeping up and they made it to the shuttle with explosions still going of at the facility.

The two got in the shuttle and immediately launched and headed for point Q where the Frigate could safely be thanks to the demise of the blue ray weapon.

Chernega and his men knew it was time to attack and even thought Chester and Aida were far away, they could see and hear the explosions they were that huge thanks to the chemicals blowing up.

The Crysolamous defenders were garrison troops stationed out on a faraway planet where drunkenness and fraternization was ramped and very little discipline existed. These neophytes were in no condition to defend themselves from a paramilitary organization with a supreme leader like Chernega who easily took down the defenders and placed explosives on all their weapons magazines. They also managed to capture a senior officer and his codebook.

Chernega and his force were soon aboard their shuttles heading back out into space and were clear of the area when the magazines started blowing up destroying all the space defense weapons and any assault weapons they had on the planet. This explosion was considerably larger than what Chester and Aida caused.

Chester was aboard the Frigate in the control room when Chernega's group arrived and once the last shuttle was aboard and hatches shut, they transition to high-speed transit.

As expected, the enemy came after them with Space Force assets but being a provincial area, it was a small token force. More than enough to deal with a high-speed frigate who sprinted towards the approaching Drolupric Force that would safely escort them home. Before the Crysolamous Space assets could get within weapons range of the Frigate, their sensors started showing a large formation approaching at high speed. The chase was over, and those space craft reversed course knowing apprehension of the ship of interest was now out of the question.

~~~~~~
~~~~~~

Chapter Nineteen

COMING TO TERMS

All the participants had body cameras on them. The videos were transmitted to their shuttles and relayed to the Frigate after docking. This extraordinary mission was recorded including numerous films of Aida participating.

The emperor and Duke Tinktar were able to review a lot of the video before Chernega and Chester were shuttled down to the planet.

Chester and Chernega were in camouflaged battle fatigues when they arrived at the emperor's palace. Duke Tinktar was there and did not seem very happy or cordial. He led them to the emperor's suite where they were offered to sit down in two chairs at a table facing the emperor and Duke Tinktar.

The emperor asked for a verbal account of the mission. Since Chester was the overall commander, he gave an account of most of it but said, since I was not with Commander Chernega's forces, I would prefer he give you the details of the ammo bunkers and capturing the high-ranking officer.

Chernega went into detail discussing his activities because his force did a lion share of the activity on the planet and in reality, Chester and Aida were a side show but important.

At the conclusion of that, things got a little testy as Duke Tinktar asked, "Why wasn't the prisoner executed as directed."

Chester out foxed Duke Tinktar by answering his question with a question. "Why didn't we know about the *Blue Beam Weapon*. We were flying into a death trap. Without Aida's help none of us would have survived and this mission would have failed.

The emperor suddenly spoke and said, "I've been giving some thought to that *Blue Beam Weapon*, and it troubles me that Aida knew about them but Chernega and Chester were flying into a trap because we had an intelligence failure. I want all of Aida's files checked and I want to know who she reported this to and why it wasn't put into mission planning."

"Yes sir, Your Excellency," Duke Tinktar quickly responded.

"For what it's worth Chester, I know a lot about you and Aida, and I know you were boinking her a few times and there were some feelings she had for you and that's why she informed you about the *Blue Beam Weapons*. I think in the heat of the battle when new information is made available you must then come up with a new conclusion or possibly change your plans such as you guys did."

"The fact Aida gave her life to save you and the mission goes a long way to rehabilitating her image. According to Doctor Boonkar, Aida should have been pardoned but because of my stubbornness when Duke Tinktar pressed for the pardon, I declined, and I have my own reasons for it. Now I wished I had listened to Duke Tinktar."

"Your Excellency you did what you had to do, and I think we should lay that to rest," Duke Tinktar said.

"I suppose you two fine gentlemen thought I was going to scold you for not carrying out my directive on the execution. Like you told Chernega when you decided to take Brooklyn with you, sometimes it's better to ask for forgiveness than permission. As it turns out Brooklyn was a major part of the success story and without him, I seriously doubt you could have taken down that blue beam weapon. So now I owe Brooklyn twice. Once for saving the life of Duke Tinktar, and the other for help saving this operation because had we not taken down the Blue Beam Weapon none of you would have made it back alive."

"On another matter. I have too much work for Duke Tinktar, and he does not have time to head up the investigation of why planning didn't know about the blue beam weapon. Chester, you will head up that investigation with my full authority. Chernega will be assigned as your assistant to help guide you through the bureaucracy to discover where the information flow link was severed so we can prevent this from happening again."

"Since the empire doesn't know who the attempted assassin is, we will give that credit to someone that doesn't exist. We will also have a state memorial service for our agent Aida who was killed in the line of duty sparing the lives of others involved in a complicated mission on a far-off world."

"Thank you, sir," Chester said.

"If you feel up to it, I would like to invite you and Brooklyn here tomorrow for a little celebration. I've never pinned a medal on a dog before, but I would like to do that tomorrow."

"Thank you, sir, I'm sure Brooklyn would like that."

"Alright see you guys tomorrow."

Duke Tinktar said, "Let me walk you out to the Skycar."

As they were walking down the hallway, Duke Tinktar said, "I know you were close to Aida and I'm sorry what happened."

"So am I. She was severely wounded and going to die and wanted to make sure I lived. I would not be alive today without her. I owe her."

"I tried to get the emperor to pardon her, but like you heard from him I was unsuccessful."

"It's kind of ironic, had the emperor not scheduled her for execution, she would not have been in position to save us."

"She's now a hero instead of a hidden felon, I think she always wanted to go in a way like this in a mission."

"I can tell you that on the ship when I decided to attempt to save Aida, she was very appreciative. I think after the mission I could have convinced the emperor to spare her but unfortunately, she turned out to be a casualty and her luck ran out. I got behind a tree and she kept firing until she ran out of ammunition about the time the bombs detonated. I know she was spared pain and was bleeding to death. It took all her remaining energy to keep firing and to save my life. I will always be in debt to her."

"Chester, you really have had some extraordinary experiences since you arrived."

"I have and I look forward to visiting here tomorrow."

"Chester, I'm looking forward to seeing you as well. I'm very proud of you."

"Thank you, but remember I needed Chernega's help in all this. Without him I seriously doubt we could have pulled it off."

"I picked him for his special role for good reason. He's never let me down."

"Nor will I," Chernega abruptly stated and smiled.

About that time the men climbed into the Skycar that already had Brooklyn inside to take them to Duke Tinktar's estate.

Soon Chester and Brooklyn were in their baths removing the scars of war. After they were dried off, Chester put on some casual clothes and asked Brooklyn, "What would you like to do?"

"I miss the squirrels, could we go up and feed them?"

"Are you hungry too?"

"Yes Papa."

Chester arranged it and soon he, Brooklyn and Rayalna were being followed by a grounds keeper's cart up to the Squirrel hangout with food for the dog and squirrels and snacks for Chester and Rayalna using the cart as an improvised picnic table.

Right away Brooklyn's buddy ran out to greet his friend and the two were soon eating their meal together and enjoying clean water. The other squirrels were slowly taking to Brooklyn and not acting as scared as before.

The baked snacks sent for Chester and Rayalna hit the spot and the elixir added to the pleasure.

After about an hour being with the Squirrels, they slowly drifted away full and went back to their squirrel's nest or as called back on earth sometimes a Drey.

"I think it's time to go back."

"I think so to Papa."

~~~~~~

Chester and Brooklyn were soon back at their suite relaxing. "Papa, may I watch holographic videos?"

"Sure, Brooklyn."

Soon Brooklyn was watching *'Other Worlds Animal Review'* and appeared totally focused on the show.

Meanwhile, Chester spent time thinking about the investigation he was going to do.

There wasn't much of a gap between Aida and Swìnlàgār the Valet, or between Aida and Chernega.

Aida wasn't the type of person to be negligent. She had to have told someone whose responsibility was to ensure that report made it into mission planning. The first thought Chester came up with is: even if we had a mole, this mission wasn't planned until relatively recently, that mole would not have known it was on the radar screen. So why would they want to hide the information on the blue beam weapon?
~~~~~~

For several hours while Brooklyn watched all the strange creatures on *'Other Worlds Animal Review'*, Chester thought about his dilemma and how to go about it without tipping off a possible mole. *Tomorrow Chernega and I will check all Aida's files and communications records. Hopefully we can find a bread crumb trail.*

Chester was laid back on the sofa and after a while entered a slumber. His sleep deprivation was catching up on him. In due time Artificial Intelligence reported to Aizere that Chester was sleeping on the sofa, she came into the room and saw Chester was asleep and decided he would be better off if he changed into sleeping clothes and went to bed so reluctantly, she woke him after she got his sleeping clothes laid out.

After about the fourth or fifth time Aizere called Chester's name he slowly came to and saw Aizere standing there.

When Aizere saw it appeared Chester was awake she said, "Chester, why don't you change into your sleeping clothes and go to bed?

"Alright thanks, I will."

Aizere thought Brooklyn was looking sleepy as well and said, "Brooklyn, I think you should go to bed and rest, big day ahead for us tomorrow."

Brooklyn said, "Okay, good idea." He then hopped off the sofa and walked up the ramp to his bed and laid down. Artificial Intelligence determined that based on the conversation now would be an appropriate time to shut off the holographic video and it suddenly vanished.

Two minutes later Chester was in bed and the lights slowly dimmed and it was dark in the room and Chester quickly entered the dream world.

Chester started having a bad dream watching Aida get killed and he knew he could steer his dreams and then he steered them towards Linap where he quickly found happiness. One thing Chester realized was Linap had given him emotional support when he needed it the most and had Chernega not gone alone with him on giving Aida a second chance, he realized he would become emotionally damaged and bitter. The fact she got killed in the way she did was sad but at least it wasn't him doing the killing. Had it been the other way around and he received the wounds he would have covered for Aida and sent her to safety. Sadly, a lucky bullet changed her destiny. The night passed too quickly, and Chester suddenly woke up from a pleasant dream about Linap. As he got out of bed artificial intelligence that had infrared scanners in the room slowly turned up the lighting so Chester could see where he was walking. And as he walked past Brooklyn, he received his morning greet.

"Good morning, Papa."

"Are you awake already Brooklyn?"

"I've been awake for a little while."

"Alright."

After Chester finished his morning business, Aizere walked into the room carrying workout clothes and handed them to Chester to change into. Chester responded, I'm not going to morning workout, I want to meet with Chernega this morning in the library after a little breakfast.

"Would you like to have a bath?"

"Actually, I would thank you."

"How about you Brooklyn?"

"If Papa is having a bath, then I want to have a bath also."
A few minutes later the two were in their baths with Rayalna giving Brooklyn a bath.

After the bath, the two were dressed in Royal attire which amused Chester until he remembered he would be visiting the emperor later in the day.

Chester had a simple breakfast. He requested the energy drink he normally took during workouts as he felt it helped him think clearer.

Brooklyn had his dog food and water and soon they were satisfied and went back to the suite.

"Brooklyn, I need to go to the library for a while do you want to stay here and watch holograph videos?"

Yes Papa, I like watching *'Other Worlds Animal Review'*.

"Rayalna can you please come here."

Momentarily Rayalna arrived and asked, "How may I help, Chester."

"I need to go to the library for a while. Brooklyn is going to stay here and watch holograph videos."

"Not a problem, I'll watch Brooklyn until you finish at the library."

"Thanks."

Chester walked out of the suite and his security man was there advised to where Chester was going and escorted him to the library. Chernega must have guess at what Chester planned on doing and had two security men posted outside the library. One of them opened the door for Chester and closed it behind him after he entered.

Chernega was waiting for him with another man.

"Good morning, Chester, let me introduce you to Raul Bebca."

"Pleased to meet you," Chester said, then sat down at the table.

"The reason why Raul is here is to unlock Aida's files with his special device."

"Aida's files are secured for investigative reasons and archive for future inquiries. Nobody is allowed the passwords to her logins for security reasons. If there is a legitimate inquiry like the emperor assigned you, then I must unlock them for you and relock them after you close the document."

"After you open the documents, I'm going to have to have you step outside because I do not want to discuss this in front of anyone except Chernega."

"That's understandable, may I take a chair with me outside to sit while I'm waiting?"

Chernega stood up and said, "Give me a minute."

He then walked over to the door and opened it and said, "Could one of you come in here and move a chair out into the Hallway for Raul Bebca. In a few minutes he will be waiting there while we work on files."

One of the security men walked into the library and picked up a padded chair and took it out to the hallway and set it down on the opposite side of the hallway where people could not hear library conversations.

After the door was shut Raul Bebca unlocked Aida's main communication server file system listing the file names showing attributes such as dates to help narrow the search results.

Raul Bebca handed Chester a search wand that allowed him to control the screen like a computer mouse back on Earth.

Chester moved the search window to the dates Aida indicated when she first discovered blue beam weapons technology on Crysolamous. There was nothing stating Blue Beam Weapons After exhaustive searching for fifteen minutes without a clue or anything concerning Blue Beam Weapons, suddenly a file called Crysolamous appeared.

"Go ahead and unlock this for us."

Soon they had a 78-page document.

"Raul, could you please step outside until we call you."

After Raul was outside the room, Chester started scrolling down the document on the holographic display. It was a Memorandum from Aida to a Messrs. Sirun.

In the document Chester discovered pictures of the *blue beam weapon* tests. Aida had surreptitiously obtained blue beam weapon photographs. The image of the *blue beam weapon* firing looked terrifying. The best way to describe it was a straight lightening seen in nature but was totally straight.

"Looks like we got our first clue, Messrs. Sirun."

Throughout the morning more documents were unlocked as the two blood hounds, Chester and Chernega slowly gathered the information and developed a road map for Duke Tinktar to deal with these men. Eventually they found where the information flow was truncated. A gentleman who worked directly for Swìnlàgār the Valet appeared to be the bottleneck, a man by the name of Norman von Sweringen.

In a while Raul Bebca curiosity started growing as he was ordered to unlock 1500 Norman von Sweringen documents to view. By lunch time Chester and Chernega had discovered several hundred critical intel reports filtered out he was tasked to inform Swìnlàgār the Valet. He didn't send these vital reports including items pertaining to General Crontyke. He was also in communications with five of the men that were captured on the Planet Barcejena.

Raul Bebca was not allowed to see what were in the files that were copied and placed in the growing criminal record now opened. Chernega was greatly distressed because Norman von Sweringen was the likely replacement for Swìnlàgār the Valet when he retired.

They now had enough information to have a reason to shove Norman von Sweringen out of an airlock in space or dump him off at the hog farm.

Chernega and Chester then debated the course of action to take. Chernega thought it was best to *inform Duke Tinktar then proceed to have the man executed since he was a major threat and close to Duke Tinktar.*

"Back on my planet Earth when our CIA was lucky to catch a well-placed mole, they immediately turned him/her into a double spy."

"Doesn't that result in the loss of valuable intelligence?" Chernega asked playing the devil's advocate.

According to books and sources I've read in the past when I lived there, the CIA claimed the damage they did to the enemy was twenty times more valuable than the damage lost to compromise of information and they limited the loss by cherry picking information they assumed the enemy already had awareness of.

"How will we spoon feed him disinformation?"

"First thing we need to do will take a while; we need to slowly vet the persons who fed him information. We need to also check their communications to see if they lead somewhere. And we need to find anyone who has any sort of connection to Norman von Sweringen because he no doubt has accomplices."

"Do we inform Swìnlàgār?"

"I recommend we do not because we want him to act natural as if nothing has changed."

"How will we inform Duke Tinktar?"

"That's easy, I'm sure he's about satisfied now with his marital bliss and needs a break away from Daniell who's probably working hard to get pregnant. I'll communicate to him after this meeting

I would like him to work out with me tomorrow. And in case the conversation is being monitored by people close to Norman von Sweringen, if he asks me if there is something I wished to discuss with him, I will say, yes, Aida."

"Great idea."

"I think we need to take a break from all this now because we soon need to get ready to visit the emperor."

"Alright. Shut down the holograph."

Artificial intelligence softly in the background asked, "Chernega do you wish to shut down the holograph?"

"Yes, I do."

"Do you wish to save this holograph for future use?"

"Yes, save it and put an encrypted bookmark on it."

"File is saved with your personal encryption."

"Thank you." Chernega said.

"You are welcome," The Artificial Intelligence replied.

Chester left the room and walked up to Raul Bebca the computer security manager and said, "That will be all for today. I would like you to come back tomorrow in case we need you, after lunch." "Understand, I'll be back tomorrow after lunch."

~~~~~~

Chester was soon back in his suite and Aizere asked, "Would you like a hair stylist work on your hair design before you go to visit the emperor?"

"Since I have no idea who the emperor invited, I might as well look my best. Sure, please request a hair stylist.
~~~~~~

In due time Chester was looking great with a combination of his cosmic swirl hair design and male makeup applied by a talented makeup artist. The makeup gave impressive results that made the skin look healthier and slightly more youthful. Just like the magic of a three-dimensional painter, the makeup artists created an image that advanced Chester's appearance way beyond his normal amount of handsomeness.

When the hair stylist and makeup artists were complete and had Chester look in the mirror he commented, "You guys did a fantastic job."

"Thank you," the hair stylist said.

"I think I look ten years younger."

"You definitely have a more youthful appearance," the makeup artist responded.

Chester and Brooklyn were then ushered out to the front bay a security guard and the Royal Sky Limo was there with Chernega standing waiting for them.

"Looks like I'm riding over to the emperor's palace with you guys."

"We are honored to be in your company," Chester responded.

"How are you doing today, Brooklyn?"

"I would be doing a lot better if Princess Tiffany was with me."

"I hope you get to see her soon."

The three stepped into the Royal Sky Limo and the doors rotated down sealing the compartment then the driverless Sky Limo headed for the Tunnel entrance slightly airborne and soon flew into city air traffic and headed for the emperor's palace.

Duke Tinktar was alone at the entrance to greet Chester, Brooklyn and Chernega.

"Thank you for attending, I'm glad you are here and later during our dinner, I'm going to ask you to make a few comments about Aida. Do you feel emotionally able to do so?

"Yes, I think I can handle it, but if I end up with a few tears, don't worry about it."

"I certainly will not. You earned the right to have those tears."

"Your Excellency, would it be possible for you to be at my workout in the morning and do some workout with me. I would like to talk privately with you about Aida."

"Actually, I would like that. I think I need some time away from Daniell, she's such a demanding woman."

"She couldn't be worse than my wife Abagail."

"If you say so," Duke Tinktar responded and smiled.

Most of the guests had already arrived and were escorted to the aquarium area where dinner tables were set up for the feast and remembrance of Aida. Aida's picture on an elaborate wallboard display at the edge of the aquarium, framed in a decorative vine and bouquets of flowers. The picture showed Aida as a slightly younger woman at the peak of her beauty.

The guest list was short so there were not a lot of people attending. What surprised Chester when Duke Tinktar escorted him to the Aquarium, was Margrét Hansen was present with her intergalactic banker husband. Her poodle "Princess Tiffany" was also there on a leash held by Margrét. There were two doggy chairs set up offset from the tables where the two dogs could eat and enjoy each others presence.

When Princess Tiffany spotted Chester, she struggled to get away and make a bee line to Chester. Margrét Hansen struggled to restrain Princess Tiffany, but Chester walked right up to Princess Tiffany which seemed to have a calming effect on the dog.

"Chester, this is my Husband, Gandolph," Margrét Hansen said.

"Pleased to meet you," Chester said with a poker face.

"Thank you," Gandolph replied eyeballing this very handsome man who was the owner of the dog that became Princess Tiffany's dear friend.

Gandolph wondered if Chester had been banging his wife during the doggy visits. He knew that if such a handsome man was alone with his wife starved for attention, he probably boinked her a few times. *I might have to investigate this matter,* Gandolph thought.

Just when Gandolph was starting to speculate on Chester's possible peccadillo, none other than Madam Linap walked in and approached Chester and threw her arms around him like two long lost lovers returning to each other.

Linap suspected Chester had been to hell and back especially since she was invited to this dinner in honor of Aida who met an untimely death. Since Chester was missing during the time Aida got whacked, Linap suspected they had been together during those awful moments, and she suspected during this dinner Chester would do something to give a clue that was the case.

The embrace was long enough to make everyone there speculate something had gone on between Linap and Chester. Gandolph was no longer concerned because if Chester went after Margrét, after this emotional display of Linap, it would be like taking a hamburger to a steak dinner. The emotional display of Linap was quite convincing.

Nevertheless, Margrét was seething with anger *because if he boinked that bitch, it's like stabbing me in the back!* Margrét thought.

But Margrét was quite shrewd and knew not to have any reactions that might tip off Gandolph that *while the Cats are away the mice will play.*

The waiters were giving guests elixirs to drink. Because this was a memorial for Aida, the emperor wanted to make sure they served his very best elixirs. Naturally all the drinks were what they requested but of a much better quality than most had experienced.

When Chester sipped on his glass of *Chamboreé de Lián* he thought it tasted a lot better than he remembered and it gave him quite a kick. Linap was having the same thing Chester was drinking and noticed a slight improvement from what she remembered.

The crowd went through small talk as Duke Tinktar and Danielle walked among them and socialized and spread good feeling tendrils that everyone felt. Halfway through the socializing the emperor and his Valet Swìnlàgār arrived and walked through the crowd. They first talked with Chernega then worked their way systematically addressing each guest and just like Duke Tinktar also spread affection and wellbeing giving everyone present good vibes.

After another ten minutes of socializing the emperor said, "My dear friends will you all please join me at the table and dine and enjoy the food and drink."

There were name placards in at each place setting next to the water glasses. Duke Tinktar and Daniell sat on one side of the emperor at the end of the table and Chester and Linap sat directly across from them.   Margrét and Gandolph Hansen sat next to Duke Tinktar who was on the right side of Daniell.

The Valet Swìnlàgār who was dismissed from his official duties to be a guest at this dinner sat next to Chester who sat on the left side of Linap who sat next to the emperor. Chernega sat on the left side of Swìnlàgār. There were a couple other couples present that were the elite in the emperor's court whom Chester did not know.

The food and the drinks kept coming and the levity was wonderful. The emperor enjoyed himself immensely and Duke Tinktar was enjoying his time but was extremely curious as to why Chester wanted to talk to him about Aida outside of the palace or anywhere near a potential eaves drop machine.

Right after desert the emperor said, ladies and gentlemen, Duke Tinktar has something he wants to say to all of you.

Duke Tinktar stood up and walked beside Aida's picture. It had been magnified and was about twice as big as her real size so that the crowd was able to see her image well. He then began speaking in a solemn manner.

"As you all know you were invited here for Aida's memorial. Sadly, Aida had no living relatives to invite (a bald face lie for part of the coverup). Aida was a great member of teams that dealt with our enemies for several years. She had been sent on numerous missions across vast distances to trouble spots in the galaxy that effect the wellbeing of our empire. She selflessly gave everything and asked very little in return. She was a brilliant woman and quite often gave strategic inputs to help plan our actions in many operations that required critical thinking in planning and execution. Aida died giving her life in a supreme sacrifice for the empire and to save the lives of people present when she perished. I can't get into the details of what went on because it's still an ongoing concern. But I will say Aida conducted herself with esprit de corps until the very last moments of her life."

The Duke could see the guests were all intensely watching him during every single comment.

"I hereby posthumously Award Aida the Legion of Empire Merit with a "V" for valor with the emperor's stamp." Duke Tinktar reached in his pocket and pulled out a nice size gold medal attached to a ribbon and hung it from one of the corners on the framed picture of Aida.

Duke Tinktar then said, "There is someone here now who was with Aida in her final moment. Chester would you please join me here by her picture and give us a few comments about your journey and experience with Aida."

Chester stood up doing his best to hold back his emotions. He knew down deep in his heart he had affection for Aida. They had experienced much together including glorious lovemaking. He knew he could not give details of the mission and carefully chose his words.

"Aida and I were good friends. She volunteered to go with me and assist so that I would not fail. Without her presence, I can tell you the mission would have failed, and everyone involved would not be living today. So, we owe a lot to her."

"During the mission, Aida and I were somewhat trapped and would soon both die without an extraordinary evacuation that was not feasible due to the situation we were in. Aida was hit by a lucky bullet and was severely wounded and would likely bleed to death because of her wounds. She told me she was not going to make and didn't have much time left and would cover for me. She wanted me to attempt to break out of where we were trapped, and thus laid down aggressive field of cover fire so that I could make it to an area with good cover and bug out. Thanks to her continuous firing until she ran out of ammunition, I was able to escape. I also was able to see her die and take her last breath before she was consumed in death."

Chester now had tears going down both cheeks. He felt utterly terrible watching Aida die in that fiery inferno that consumed her. "Thank you, Chester," Duke Tinktar said.

Linap put her arm over Chester's shoulder as he sat down and tried his best to hold back his sadness. She now knew there was a hell of a lot more to the story which Chester would never reveal.

The two dogs were observing in total silence as Princess Tiffany was copying every one of Brooklyn's movements.

Duke Tinktar then walked over to Brooklyn and continued addressing the crowd.

"What I'm now going to reveal is something that I do not want anyone present to reveal or discuss with anyone outside this party. Our illustrious Brooklyn here was also part of the mission. He assisted Chester and Aida to penetrate their target area. Without Brooklyn's assistance they would not have been able to complete their mission. During this event there were several times Brooklyn placed himself in severe risk to assist his Papa Chester. The mission was thus a success only because of Brooklyn's participation. For that reason, Brooklyn will also receive a Legion of Empire Merit with a "V" for valor with the emperor's stamp."

Duke Tinktar then put the ribbon around Brooklyn's neck then clipped the medal portion to his Royal fabric covering his dog collar and service saddle jacket.

There was an applause as everyone at the table clapped.

Daniell knew what was going to happen next as she and Duke Tinktar had privately discussed it and she had tears going down her cheeks as well.

Duke Tinktar walked up to Chester and said, "Now I have one more award to give. When the mission began, they quickly discovered they were facing overwhelming odds with a key piece of missing intelligence that doomed it from the start. Chester evaluated the situation an came up with a new plan on the spot."

"Chester presented the new plan to the ship's captain and the military commander sent along to provide military support if required and they concurred the change in plan had to be incorporated which led to Chester and Aida working together in a manner that added greatly to force protection and allowed the mission to succeed."

"It was also Chester's idea to take Brooklyn along to use his abilities he thought would provide additional help in infiltrating the hardened target. For Chester's unique service and dedication on this mission he is also awarded Legion of Empire Merit with a "V" for valor with the emperor's stamp. His Legion of Empire Merit also receives the Oak leave cluster with my personal stamp for multiple acts of bravery in direct service to me and the emperor. Thank you, Chester."

Duke Tinktar held out his hand and shook Chester's hand. Then he put the ribbon with the double wide medal around Chester's neck. He then did something that astonished the emperor an everyone there and reached down and hugged Chester who was having an emotional spike.

All the women present had tears and some of the men. They knew Chester had been through a lot and to watch this woman die saving his life must have put a terrible scar on his psyche.

The orchestra that had been playing pleasant dinner music then stroked up a chord. Duke Tinktar who had numerous recordings of Earth music had them start the classical music Chester no doubt was familiar with, Saint-Saëns - Symphony No 3 in C minor, Op 78. That music seemed to have calming effect on Chester. Duke Tinktar then walked down to the end of the table and stood by Chernega, and he nodded at the music conductor who then lowered the volume of the orchestra as this was all planned in advance.

"I have one more award to give out. The Battle of Martos has not been well publicized mainly because the emperor hoped the anger could die down and we could build a lasting peace in that part of the empire. One of the most important elements of that Battle was when I had Regimental Commander Chernega perform a faint to force the enemy to split their forces to give us a better disposition of more equal footing with the enemy.

Chernega's forces were positioned on and escarpment where they could readily defend from half of their position and only take the brunt of the punishment from one side. I led the overall task force, so I got to see first-hand everything that took place on battle management holographs. I emphasized to Commander Chernega he had to hold this position for at least four days which threatened the enemies' flanks, so they had no alternative but to attack his positions. He ultimately was forced to hold that position for eight days taking almost 50% casualties until the battle was decided and Commander Chernega needed to be emergency evacuated because he sustained terrible wounds during the battle and came close to dying as it was."

"So, you can see I'm already in great debt to Commander Chernega for his loyal service. During the recent mission when Aida perished, Chernega was the overall military commander and had significant involvement in the operation. His accomplishments were more than we could have hoped. Because of Commander Chernega's excellent execution and force protection, we sustained no serious casualties during the mission aside from Aida's death that could not be avoided in such a hard target."

"For Chernega's unique service and dedication on this mission he is also awarded Legion of Empire Merit with a "V" for valor with the emperor's stamp. His Legion of Empire Merit also receives my Oak leave cluster with my personal stamp for multiple acts of bravery in direct service to me and the emperor."

Since Chernega was not from earth or used to handshakes, Duke Tinktar gave him a long bow and put the ribbon attached to the medal around his neck. "Thank you, Commander Chernega."

Chernega then stood up and bowed at Duke Tinktar, then he turned and bowed at the emperor followed by turning and bowing at the Valet Swìnlàgār who also had a major involvement in a lot of events with Chernega the public was unaware of. He then sat down with the prestigious medal hanging from his neck.

Chester then understood a lot more now. The 'Librarian' was another one of those innocuous persons like the 'Valet' who really ran the show behind the scenes.

Margrét and Gandolph Hansen sat utterly stunned the man whose dog visited "Princess Tiffany" and his dog Brooklyn were now official *Heroes of the Drolupric Empire.*

Margrét had another satisfying feeling of having received Chester's Scorpio Stinger and its Scorpio Venom and she will cherish the moment and should there ever be another opportunity, she would request the satisfaction of the Scorpio Stinger again. And if he ever stung her again and deposited the Scorpio Venom, she would send word to Linap how great it felt as she looked over at the woman with a jaundiced eye.

In due time the emperor excused himself and Valet Swìnlàgār went with him.

Gandolph Hansen didn't like the way Margrét was focused on Chester, and he decided it was time for them to leave dragging Princess Tiffany along who didn't want to leave Brooklyn. The other two couples were right behind them after saying goodbye to Duke Tinktar and Daniell and performed respectful bows towards Chernega and Chester.

With everyone else gone, Linap said, "Chester, I would like to invite you and Brooklyn to my home to visit for a while."

"I think we would like to go." Chester responded.

They stood up and walked to Duke Tinktar and Daniell who were greatly moved by Chester. They said goodbye and left.

Chernega, already standing walked up to Duke Tinktar and said, "This was a great event. I'm glad you honored Aida because she earned it."

"Yes, she did and I'm very sorry it cost her life."

"She would much rather go this way if she had her choice. I think saving Chester's life as well as Brooklyn, gave her great satisfaction she could help them survive and flourish."

"She will be missed."

"By many of us," Chernega said and bowed and walked out to the front in time to see Linap's Sky Limo take off and the Royal Sky Limo pull in to take Chernega back to Duke Tinktar's estate where he would no longer be living. In due time it would be Chester's estate.

It did not take time to reach Linap's home where they were soon enjoying Zvèzdnàyà Rōzā while Brianna was with Brooklyn watching his favorite holographic video, 'Other Worlds Animal Review'.

As they were cuddling on the sofa Linap said, "Do you realize there are very few men in the empire with any award from the emperor?"

"I suppose so."

"There is so much about you I wish to explore."

"It might be best if we leave history behind."

"Are there things you wish to forget?"

"All but one."

"And what is that?"

"One day when I feel comfortable to discuss it with you, I'll tell you all about it."

"I have an idea Chester, why don't you unify with me then what ever you plan on telling me will not matter because we will be unified, and I will always stay with you no matter what it is."

"I'll consider doing that but there is something I must do before."

"Is this another one of those missions?"

"That is a question you know I could never answer."

"Your Omission answers it for me. I don't need the grizzly details."

"You are a businesswoman, you make deals all the time, right?"

"That's correct."

"If you promise to love Brooklyn as much as I do and always protect him as much as you would me, then we could possibly get unified."

"That's easy to do."

Linap was now calculating her future. Chester was the real deal and all he wanted from her was to be considerate of Brooklyn, the lovely dog. Never had a dog captivated her. She loved birds and plants. And she also understood the significance of a dog being an empire hero. Such a feat had never happened before. A talking dog that's an empire hero. That combination automatically makes the dog a superstar.

Chester was now in for a huge surprise as Linap initiated their lovemaking which quickly moved to the bedroom. By the end of the evening, it was a repeat from a while back with Brooklyn sleeping on the sofa in Linap's bedroom with her and Chester cuddling to sleep together.

Shortly after Chester woke in the morning and took care of business, the home's artificial intelligence said softly in the background, "Chester, Brianna wishes to enter the bedroom to give you workout clothes sent to you to wear this morning. Do you wish to let her enter?"

"Yes, please invite her in."

Brianna walked into the room and handed Chester the clothes to change into from his sleeping attire, then left the room.

Chester was soon dressed and Linap asked, is there something you would like to eat before you leave?

"No, I will get my morning energy drink during the workout."

"Why do you have to be working out so soon after a mission?"

"I never know when the next mission will begin so I have to stay in shape."

Are you a spook?"

"What do you mean by spook?"
"A spy?"

"No, I'm a problem solver."

"Must be a big problem if people like Aida get killed. I know her and have seen her around. I know she used to be Duke Tinktar's lover."

"Sometimes big problems require big results."

"If Duke Tinktar allows his former lover to get killed, I would say so."

"He didn't know she would get killed and be caught in a trap with me during the mission."

"May I ask a question?"

"Sure."

"Was that Aida who tried to shoot Duke Tinktar?"

"I can't answer that question."

"You and Brooklyn were sitting right next to the woman and Brooklyn received some injuries, don't tell me you don't know."

"I have a better answer."

"What's that?"

"I'm not going to answer your question, and I need to leave now."

Chester walked out of the bedroom with Brooklyn right beside him and walked directly to the front entrance and out the door where a Skycar was waiting. They got in the Skycar that had only Chernega as a passenger.

"Have a good night?" Chernega asked.

"I did until a few minutes ago."

"What happened a few minutes ago."

I realized Linap was not my cup of tea."

"She's not going to like hearing that."

"That's okay, if I'm going to spend the rest of my life here, I think there is only one woman that I can have a relationship with."

"And who's that?"

"You will laugh, I'm sure."

"Not necessarily, but in curious."

"Chūn Fāng, she works for Madam Pang on Zeta Bantor."

"Interesting," Chernega said.

In a short while they arrived at the training camp, and just like many times before, they fed the birds and had their morning meal of energy drinks for Chester and Chernega and dogfood for Brooklyn. The birds were now completely friendly with Brooklyn. Then something very weird happened. Brooklyn somehow figured out the bird's language and made replica bird sounds out of his speaker box.

There were replies and soon a cacophony of bird sounds as they all chimed in demonstrating and incredible acceptance of Brooklyn who was now irrevocably now part of their flock. The secret surveillance video made it to Doctor Akssiar who was now in awe of these Earth transplants. He knew the scientific community would soon be busting at the scenes to learn what the birds and Brooklyn were communicating to each other.

Duke Tinktar was nowhere to be seen. But true to his form Chester took off and was running with Chernega and they hustled as much as they ever did and put in 5 miles in 24 minutes and were drenched in sweat ready for a little break then stretching before exercises. At precisely this minute a Royal Sky Limo arrived and landed near them, and Duke Tinktar wearing Royal Formal Attire, exited the Limo and approached Chester and Chernega.

"Looks like you guys are getting a good workout, all covered in sweat as expected."

"That's why we are here and you should be with us," Chernega said.

"I'm sorry but the emperor tasked me early this morning."

"That's understandable," Chernega said.

"Let's go for a walk around the track so we can talk," Duke Tinktar said,

After they were about 50 yards away from anyone else, Duke Tinktar said, "The emperor is very interested in the Blue Beam Weapon situation and in case you don't know Raul Bebca the computer security manager who worked with you guys yesterday, works exclusively for the emperor. He is instructed to inform the emperor of any findings of significance. As you know he can unlock any files."

"I know why you guys wanted me to come here to inform me of something that is of the deepest and darkest concern since the traitor is very close to the emperor."

Chester and Chernega were both quite amused at what Duke Tinktar said, but it did not surprise Chernega in the least bit since intrigue seemed to follow the emperor around like a dark cloud.

"As soon as you released Raul Bebca, he went back to his office and opened up and studied the 1500 files you copied to your private folder."

"He informed the emperor what you discovered, and we know Norman von Sweringen is a traitor. Since he reports directly to Swìnlàgār and was designated to replace him as the emperor's personal Valet when Swìnlàgār retires in a few years."
"We had no choice to have a private meeting with Swìnlàgār because the emperor thought it was crucial to let Swìnlàgār know Norman von Sweringen is a traitor."

"Chester and I thought it would be a good idea to run Norman von Sweringen as a double spy for a while."

"I'm sorry but the decision has already been made."

"What is that?"

"I'm going to take Chester back to his suite so he can bathe and change clothes. He and I are going to take the prisoner somewhere. One of the reasons why I was late this morning is I was involved in the arrest of Norman von Sweringen who has been detained and ready to be transported to where Chester and I will be taking him."

"Why does Chester need to be involved in this?"

"I think he wants to be because Norman von Sweringen is responsible for Aida's death. Had Norman von Sweringen not filtered out quite a few files we could have planned on taking out those blue beam weapons by other means and Aida didn't have to die."

"She was going to die anyway," Chester said.

"Chester, Aida wasn't going to die. I know you would have delayed the execution until return from the mission which would have given me time to commute the sentence and give her clemency based on the numerous missions she did in the past."

"You are probably right."

"Us get you back and cleaned up."

"I want to take Brooklyn with me."

"Why?"

"He saw Aida who he liked die. I think if you explain all this to Brooklyn, he would want to see Norman von Sweringen suffer the way Aida died."

"Alright. I agree, let's go get Brooklyn and go back to the estate."

"Your excellency, would you like me to go with you?"

"Chernega, after you finish your workout, go back get cleaned up, then go over the emperor's mansion and meet with Raul Bebca and Swìnlàgār so they can enlighten you on what they found in those 1500 files you would have discovered today."

"Understand all, Your excellency."

~~~~~~
~~~~~~

Chapter Twenty

ZETA BANTOR, GIVE ME ONE MORE TIME

Chester was dressed in casual clothes that would not identify Royal association. Brooklyn seemed to be excited going on another adventure. Brooklyn was wagging his tail in the control room being with Chester, Duke Tinktar, and the captain he got to know during the previous mission taking the same Frigate to Zeta Bantor.

This would be a high-speed transit to Zeta Bantor. There would be little secrecy or a safe house.

It took less than a day for the Frigate to high-speed transit to Zeta Bantor and enter orbit.

In the spacecraft control room Duke Tinktar handed Chester his stiletto knife and said, "This is the official changing of the guard. You are now the keeper of the knife in case you need to use it in the future."

"I will guard it like a special treasure."

"I know I can count on you. You've never let me down."

Several shuttles left the Frigate with Duke Tinktar, Chester, Brooklyn, and a half dozen security men and the prisoner who was bound in edible rope the Sabretooth Hogs would love. The shuttles landed right down on the middle of the hog farm in a grassy area. Everyone exited the two shuttles. The Sabretooth Hogs feared the machines and the numerous people and stayed back watching.

Duke Tinktar said to Chester, "You are the director of ceremonies. This is your project."

"Thank you."

Chester looked at the senior agent and said, "Put him down on the ground face up and take the tape off his mouth and face."

With four big boys holding Norman von Sweringen, Chester stood over the top of him and said, "Aida is dead now because of what you did. You almost got me killed as well and quite a number of others. Traitors like you are despicable. Got anything to say to save your life or bargain for?"

"Fuck you," Norman von Sweringen in his native language which Chester understood.

"That was the wrong thing to say to the man who could have saved your life."

Chester bent down and cut the man on his arms and legs and with the four big bruisers he couldn't stop it. The white garments Norman von Sweringen was wearing quickly turned red with blood. The Sabretooth Hogs could smell the blood and were starting to get wild making noise.

"Alright everyone, get back in the shuttles, we are leaving."

As soon as they were all loaded up Brooklyn said, "Wait a minute Papa I have something to say to the Sabretooth Hogs."

"Alright, hold the door open for a moment," Chester directed the pilot.

Brooklyn walked over to the side of the Shuttle and screeched out a very long series of sounds. Suddenly the Sabretooth Hogs started running towards Norman von Sweringen in a stamped.

Brooklyn said, "You can close the door and take off."

The shuttles took off and Chester directed the pilot, "Hover for a few minutes I want to watch this for a few minutes in honor of Aida."

The pilot looked at Duke Tinker with an astonished look on his face suggesting he wanted to say "WTF." Duke Tinktar gave the pilot and a nod indicating *just do it*.

The two shuttles hovered, and Chester saw the man's body start jerking as the Sabretooth Hogs sliced his flesh open and licked the blood almost in an orgy of activity. For about five minutes Norman von Sweringen jerked around and suddenly he stopped moving. Chester knew he was now dead. "Alright let's leave,"

"Would it be okay if we make a stop along the way?" Chester asked which kind of surprised Duke Tinktar since these men knew Chester was the boss for this mission with Duke Tinktar along for the ride wanting to watch the traitor get what he deserved.

Duke Tinktar told the pilot, "Fly us to Madam Pang's."
The Pilot, one of the special force's guys knew Madam Pang's all too well and had no need for directions and flew directly there.

It was just around sundown when the shuttles landed in the open street long past rush hour.

Duke Tinktar said, "Bodyguards come with Chester, Brooklyn, and me. The rest of you fly over to the airport and refuel so we have a full tank going back up to the Frigate. Inform the Captain he will have to stay in Orbit for a few hours. We have some administrative functions to do here before we return."

Madam Pang was not expecting Duke Tinktar and was sad when she found out he now had an empress. She had been in a sour mood all day long.

Chūn Fāng wasn't in any better shape feeling sad she had met Chester then he seemed to disappear forever. The two women were behind the bar with a couple bartenders going over future events and planning when suddenly a couple well dressed strangers came into the building and took seats at the bar. Right behind them a moment later Duke Tinktar, Chester and Brooklyn walked in. One of the bartenders yelled, "Get that dog out of here."

Duke Tinktar suddenly said, "That dog is with me."

Madam Pang suddenly said that's okay bring the dog in us take him back to my special room. Duke Tinktar smiled at the mouthy bartender. About that time Chester made eye contact with Chūn Fāng who came out the side of the bar with Madam Pang following her back to her special room.

The room was spic and span clean for a future event. The three Amigos and a couple body guards went in with them.

Duke Tinktar, Chester, and Brooklyn all sat down at one table and the bodyguards at another.

Chūn Fāng was all smiles now, so was Madam Pang.

"I'm surprised to see you," Madam Pang said.

"You should know by now, we'll never stop seeing each other," Duke Tinktar said.

Suddenly Madam Pang had tears falling down the side of her face. It was a tender moment because one thing she learned over the years, Duke Tinktar always lived up to his promises.

Chūn Fāng pulled a chair up close to Chester. She knew by now Chester was well connected to Duke Tinktar the next emperor, which made him super special. She felt so joyous to be near him. Her day was now turned upside down from sadness to happiness.

Duke Tinktar knew he owed Chester and Brooklyn more than he could every repay so he astutely took this moment to give Chūn Fāng a special gift which would help pay back some of what he owed Chester.

"Chūn Fāng, the reason why we stopped by here tonight is Chester has something he wants to tell you."

Chūn Fāng looked into Chester's eyes with full expectation and wonder.

"Chūn Fāng, I love you."

Chūn Fāng grabbed Chester and suddenly started weeping. It was a tremendous emotional spike. Madam Pang had a few more tears.

These men were full of surprises tonight!

After all the emotion died down, Madam Pang said, "I'm going to go get some drinks and tell the Chef to make you all something special to eat."

"Thank you," Duke Tinktar said.

"I'll help you," Chūn Fāng said.

Soon the women were gone. Duke Tinktar looked over at Brooklyn and asked, "Brooklyn, when we were at the Hog Farm you squealed something to the Sabretooth Hogs, and they came running. What did you yell at them?"

"Your Excellency, I yelled, *Dinner is ready come get it.*"

"How did you know what to say to the hogs?"

"I learned that by watching *'Other Worlds Animal Review'* holographic videos."

Paul D Escudero
保羅・道格拉斯・埃斯庫德羅
Feb 17, 2023

Dramatis Personae
Elixirs and Essentials

Drolupric Empire where Chester and Brooklyn are taken after the abduction at Ski Beach.

Norman von Sweringen, traitor

Raul Bebca computer security

'Other Worlds Animal Review' A holographic video on the Alien planet Brooklyn the talking dog enjoyed watching and learning from. Chester's lover at Madam Pang's: Chūn Fāng   pronounced Twin Fong

Chūn (春) Chūn is a very popular Chinese name that simply means "spring."

Fāng (芳) Fāng is a cute Chinese name that means "fragrance."

Dmitkron, Duke Tinktar's Alias

Casaniagra, Chester's Alias

Daniell, Duke Tinktar's receptionist and future empress

Daniell's mother, Madam Dominika.

Planet Barcejena, part of Drolupric Empire where General Crontyke was located.

General Crontyke was one of the coup chief conspirators against Emperor Tinktar-II

General Crontyke received collateral help and funding from the Drolupric Empire's enemies, the Wubars.

Panot Tsimor - informer

Doctor Boonkar psychiatrist helped Chester deal with post mission stress.

Jazmin, The masseuse.

Sandstrom construction superintendent that gave Chester a tour of the new dome city New Velaqratantor

Linap, had multicolored leopard skin color and was one of the richest persons in the Drolupric Empire. Linap becomes Chester's lover and is also and a friend of Duke Tinktar.

Brianna, Linap's maid

pink liquor referred to as Zvèzdnàyà Rōzā

Trang, female waitress

Fŏcìn de Oín, champagne

Baked Placstra, tastes like pheasant.

Swìnlàgār, the Valet, also provided emperor personal security.

Chernega, Librarian is a retired Army Regimental Commander.

Battle of Martos, Key battle Chernega and Duke Tinktar fought.

Margrét Hansen the wife of an intergalactic banker. Gandolph Hansen

Princess Tiffany, Margrét Hansen's poodle

the hog farm on Zeta Bantor where traitors are executed.

Madam Pang owner of bar/brothel

毒蛇 *Dúshé* (viper) *Dúshé Dragons*

龙头马 *Lóngtóumǎ* Dragon head horse.

Drolupric Aliens have pink skin

Tasha, researcher on spacecraft that abducts Chester and Brooklyn

Tymasoara the capital city of the Drolupric Empire.

Neurological Sonifications, electronic brain washing.

Rayalna, Dog groomer

Aizere Chester's maid

Aida: Duke Tinktar's concubine.

Grand Zumbido, purple elixir laced with psychoactive drugs

Doctor Akssiar secretary: Aiaru   maid: Selina   butler Nolak   Chef Brently

Doctor Akssiar Favorite elixir Chamboreé de Lián

Doctor Akssiar's assistant Tasha

Brooklyn the talking dog

Abagail wife of Chester Toland

Chester Toland, the talking dog Brooklyn's owner.

Dr. Nigel Foster working designed and implanted chip into Brooklyn's brain.

Microneural Therapeutics Research Inc. Dr. Nigel Foster's company.

Authors Note

This Novel is a work that is entirely fiction. There are no real living people, places, or things depicted in this book. If there are, it's a coincidence.

Just when I thought I was done with this book I made the blunder of calling my buddy Kevin Keeney to ask him if he thought I should skip the Author's Note which I normally put in my books because I have a preface that I thought covered most of the things I wanted to talk about and didn't think I needed an Authors note. Then Kevin schooled me. Kevin's a brilliant person I've known for 50 years with incredible professional experience. During his professional career there were times when I interfaced with his agency and he dealt with some highly technical issues in several of his roles, so his comments are a valid data point to make me think about things I should further research or think about. He also is a human pointer to pointers to data and worthy subjects.

As I discussed with Kevin things I should write in this Author's note, he did not beat around the bush and came out with some comments about Artificial Intelligence, which I have a lot of in this book as well as in many of my other Novels. And as Kevin elucidated some issues about artificial intelligence, it's safe to say I had a Red Flag moment.

Some words Kevin mentioned that I've read or studied in the past included, algorithms, machine learning, cashless society, facial recognition, and implementation of payment methods for mass transit, especially in China. China has a lot of brilliant people and people that know me and read my novels know I've published two substantial Novels in the Chinese Language. Two weeks ago I published a book in Japanese. I've published books in Russian, French, German, Spanish, and Italian now. I'm very interested in those languages and others. I have a Arabic translator who works for an international translation services who will edit my Novel I will one day publish in Arabic. I will do the translations and reading, and she will do the corrections. Why am I mentioning all that? Those foreign language books are the result of artificial intelligence.

Other publishers are now looking at me because I'm the first author really to initially publish books in multiple languages in the manner I did. What made that possible in such short time frames was artificial intelligence.

When I first started translating and building books in Chinese and Japanese I had at least 5 paper dictionaries. I studied Chinese by translating books written by Hemingway and Asimov to Chinese, read them and color coded them in the process. Back in the days when I was using paper dictionaries, it took me 9 months to translate some books which included U.S. Army History such as the Battle of Guadalcanal, Battle of Midway, Papuan Campaign, and U.S. Special Forces in WW2. That U.S. Special Forces in WW2 book was 80% in the Philippines mainly because General Douglas MacArthur was one of the very few senior officers to really endorse the use of Special Forces, and those Forces worked out extremely well in the Philippines who also had their own cadres of special forces. I had all those experiences thanks to artificial intelligence.

Then I made my second blunder of the day and called my son Tetsuro who just graduated from UC Berkeley with a degree in Data Science. I could spend the next 10 years studying all the elements of that conversation. That son is a product of UC Berkeley, and I can tell you he got his money's worth because he has extensive knowledge of Data Science and thus gave me numerous things to think about.

If you do a word count you will discover, I use the term Artificial Intelligence 88 times in the drama of this Novel. Everything from home security, driverless SKYCARS, artificial intelligence in the homes of wealthy people to virtually operate and communicate for everything exists in this Novel.

My impression of Artificial Intelligence which I wrote about in previous novels scared people because they recognized I was predicting the future. And then my son awakened me to all kinds of issues.

In my Novel *Sanctuary City*, which is a spy novel, there are numerous facial recognition activities as well as biological 3D printing face lifts so that spies can quickly change their identity. Do you think that's going to happen? I have a friend of Facebook who's a doctor that does face lifts here in San Diego. Next time I'm going to talk to her, I'm going to ask her opinion on 3D printing of faces for spies. I want to hear her take on it.

Algorithm bias in facial recognition is actually a huge problem. Some of those processes could be racist or cause problems for specific ethnic groups of people.

Then he opened my eyes to Generalizability *can my algorithm work well?* What is the error rate empirical risk? Then we got into a dicey discussion on Model complexity and Bias vs Variance in Machine learning. There are some catch 22's in all this. Do we fine tune the algorithm so much its no longer actually doing its job and how would we know?

And then we get into a very serious problem SECURITY for ANYTHING that takes in DATA. What are the risks?

In this talking dog Novel, there are spies. An entire mission was almost undermined because a mole in the organization near the top was TAMPERING WITH DATA. Reports that should have been sent to higher authorities was purposely omitted which set up a scenario they would be flying their spaceship into an area during a mission and they would have been killed. What saved their lives was one person on that ship traveling along not for that mission, was there for another reason warned them she had sent up the report, and one of the mission planners was on board and didn't know that critical information that had been purposely held back that would lead to a lot of death and destruction.

That traitor was identified because all they had to do was track the woman's information feed to discover at what level it had been omitted.

The Pentagon is not going to like this book if some General and Admiral reads it and reads this next paragraph relating to computer security. And it's a very evasive problem.

What are the Adversarial Database Leaks Implications and what data will be leaked? And here is the source of the problem they had better quickly recognize:

Embedded security differential privacy statistics. And what's a huge example of that? Infer single data point GEO LOCATION GPS. They track you wherever you go.

There are aspects of all this that deal with morality, machine consciousness, and correlation to causation. Another huge question is PROFITS. What will they drive? Then of course we have the issue of very large systems and how larger companies can crush the smaller ones. The larger companies can afford to spend far more on Data Analytics.

Google's Eric Schmidt claimed that every TWO DAYS we now create as much information as we did from the dawn of civilization until 2003. In the future that will speed up and in a few more years instead of taking two days it will be TWO HOURS.

The current surveys this is approximately how much time is applied to handling data:

Building complex Formulas 40%
Consumer Psychology 25%
Business Acumen 25%
Programming languages 10%

That last number will shrink. Why? Artificial Intelligence and Machine Learning.

I think complex formulas and Business Acumen will also decline, but Consumer Psychology will grow and end up at 40%. That's my speculation. All because ROBOTS and ARTIFICIAL Intelligence will be doing it.

Computer security is going to become a huge problem as we become a cashless society. EBT cards, Credit Cards, ALL OF IT will be susceptible to nefarious activity because of MACHINE LEARNING.

Finally, as you read this Novel you might think the notion of a talking dog is ridiculous, but thanks to machine learning and artificial intelligence its going to happen and in 10 years Talking Dogs will be a fad for the rich people who think drones and robots are cool now.

I have a friend I meet at Ski Beach often. He has two dogs and when he gets tired of throwing balls for them, he gets out his drone and flies it about 8 feet in the air and those two dogs chase it like crazy. I did have a scene in my recently published Novel *Drones Robots Trains & Aliens* where a dog almost got to the drone, but the Robot beat him to it then used high frequency transmissions to cause the dog to get disorientated and run away. The owners went chasing after it. Too bad it didn't have a dog leash!

Here you go, research on Talking Dogs:

Talking Dogs, Really? - Neuroscience News

The research, published in the journal Proceedings of the Royal Society B, showed that talking to puppies using dog-directed speech makes them react and attend more to their human instructor than regular speech. To test this, the researchers use so-called "play back" experiments.

How to talk to your dog – according to science (theconversation.com)

What is going to accelerate all this talking dog business short of installing a chip in the brain as this Novel suggests?

Two words:

Artificial Intelligence.

One last remark, in the Novel there is a process used to speed up learning languages. Not only was the Earth human training that way so was the talking dog who learned the Alien language very promptly. In the drama the character says he was having some type of nightmare seeing the Alien words flow above him like a cloud formation. Back 7 or 8 years ago when I was spending countless hours learning Chinese, when I laid my head down to sleep at night, I had clouds of Mandarin Characters floating above me. It was slightly rattling to me and I wondered if I went nuts! Well if you read my novels you will think I went nuts. But just remember as Einstein said there is a fine line between genius and insanity.

If you go to Barnes and Noble and look at the free pages of Jeeapa II and the color coding I did to make it easier to read, you might ask yourself the question: Why is it our school systems do not use this process?

Why did I do this to begin with? I felt that foreign language teaching in schools dishes it out too slowly. I wanted to learn Chinese a lot quicker. My motive was I wanted to be able to read a Chinese book on Acupuncture.

If you take a look at this book in Chinese some of you that are interested in educating your children, just might have an oh WOW moment. I developed a process to help you learn foreign languages much FASTER.

The speedup factor is enormous to me, especially if its color coded the way I did it to help you follow along in multiple languages a lot easier.

NOOK Tablets | Apps | Accessories | Books at NOOK® UK (barnesandnoble.com)

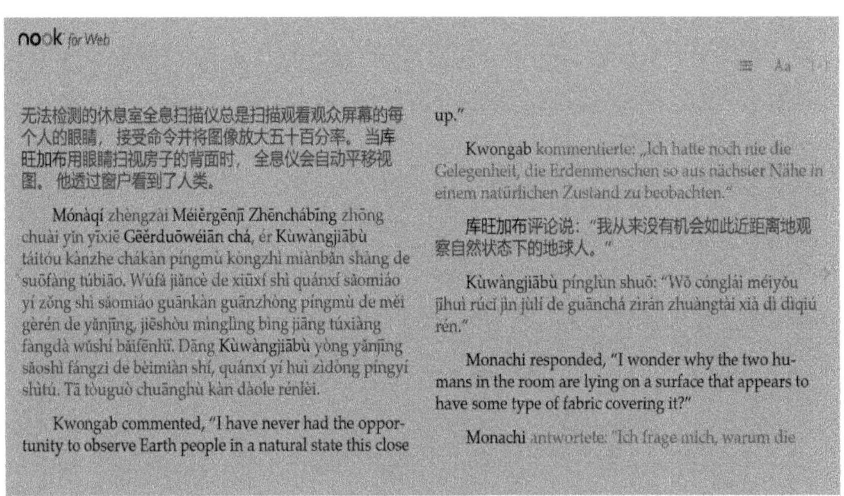

nook *for Web*

无法检测的休息室全息扫描仪总是扫描观看观众屏幕的每个人的眼睛，接受命令并将图像放大五十百分率。当库旺加布用眼睛扫视房子的背面时，全息仪会自动平移视图。他透过窗户看到了人类。

Mónàqí zhèngzài Měiěrgēnjī Zhēnchábīng zhōng chuāi yǐn yīxiē Gēěrduōwéiān chá, ér Kuwàngjiābù táitóu kànzhe chákàn píngmù kòngzhì miànbǎn shàng de suōfàng túbiāo. Wúfǎ jiǎncè de xiūxí shì quánxī sǎomiáo yī zǒng shì sǎomiáo guānkàn guānzhòng píngmù de měi gèrén de yǎnjīng, jiēshòu mìnglìng bìng jiāng túxiàng fàngdà wǔshí bǎifēnlǜ. Dāng Kùwàngjiābù yòng yǎnjīng sǎoshì fángzi de bèimiàn shí, quánxī yí huì zìdòng píngyí shìtú. Tā tòuguò chuānghù kàn dàole rénlèi.

Kwongab commented, "I have never had the opportunity to observe Earth people in a natural state this close up."

Kwongab kommentierte: „Ich hatte noch nie die Gelegenheit, die Erdenmenschen so aus nächster Nähe in einem natürlichen Zustand zu beobachten."

库旺加布评论说："我从来没有机会如此近距离地观察自然状态下的地球人。"

Kùwàngjiābù pínglùn shuō: "Wǒ cónglái méiyǒu jīhuì rúcǐ jìn jùlí de guānchá zìrán zhuàngtài xià dì dìqiú rén."

Monachi responded, "I wonder why the two humans in the room are lying on a surface that appears to have some type of fabric covering it?"

Monachi antwortete: „Ich frage mich, warum die

Paul D Escudero
July 2023

www.ingramcontent.com/pod-product-compliance
Lightning Source LLC
Chambersburg PA
CBHW051129300726
48978CB00011B/210